'How fast does a man run when the Devil is after him?'
Andre St Jean is about to find out, as a young man collapses at his feet and presses into his hand a strange scarab ring, containing the secret of life . . .

Jehanine: demon or saint?
Her days she spent at the Nunnery of the Angel; her nights in the vicious backstreets of Paradys, wreaking revenge on men for the wrongs she had suffered at their hands.

The stranger pushed a note across the table:

'In a week or less I shall be dead.'

In a week, he was, and most unnaturally. She found herself drawn to the house where he died, to unravel the web of mystery and horror that had been spun about him . . .

THE BOOK OF
THE DAMNED

THE SECRET BOOKS OF PARADYS

I

THE BOOK OF
THE DAMNED

Tanith Lee

UNWIN
PAPERBACKS

LONDON SYDNEY WELLINGTON

First published in Great Britain by Unwin Paperbacks, an imprint of
Unwin Hyman Limited, 1988.
This edition 1989

UNWIN HYMAN LIMITED
15–17 Broadwick Street, London W1V 1FP

Allen & Unwin Australia Pty Ltd
8 Napier Street, North Sydney, NSW 2060, Australia

Unwin Paperbacks with Port Nicholson Press
60 Cambridge Terrace, Wellington, New Zealand

British Library Cataloguing in Publication Data

Lee, Tanish, *1947–*
     The book of the damned.
     I. Title
     823′.914[F]
     ISBN 0–04–440322–4

Set in 10 on 11 point Baskerville by Grove Graphics, Tring
Printed in Great Britain by
Cox & Wyman Ltd, Reading

STAINED WITH CRIMSON

Le Livre Cramoisi

We were young, we were merry, we were very very wise,
And the door stood open at our feast,
When there passed us a woman with the West in her eyes,
And a man with his back to the East.

Mary Elizabeth Coleridge

Stained with Crimson

How fast does a man run, when the Devil is after him?

I was seeing it, but unknowingly, as he came towards me up the cobbled hill, his breath cawing with the effort, his eyes colourless and bright. The afternoon had grown late and the sky rolled with storm clouds. Slanting light, driven down between the cliff-like walls of the Temple-Church of the Sacrifice, gave only greyness to the alleys. I had come from Philippe's séance dulled, and with immeasurable foreboding, dissatisfaction. And into all this, the storm-light, the stony channel, my vision, the runner ran. His arms were outstretched and his long rags streamed behind him. He seemed to have been clawed by great thorns; hair and clothes. I stepped to one side to let him by. I thought him a madman. Instead, he fell at my feet. 'Ah,' he moaned, as if, thirsting, he discovered water, '*aah*.'

I drew back again. His hand clawed after me and gripped my ankle.

'Take your hand off,' I said, 'or must I make you.'

'Lean closer,' he answered, 'Lean down.'

His voice was cultured, and sounded young, though my impression had been of an old man. The hand was elegantly kept, the nails clean and trimmed. Rings adorned it. Suddenly I imagined him some helpless noble creature set on by scoundrels. I knelt beside him.

'Who attacked you, monsieur?'

He laughed. It was an awful noise, as if his throat had been cut. He turned, and I was gazing into his face. It was the countenance of a man in early middle life, no more. How had the other idea got hold of me? And he was handsome.

'Listen,' he said, 'I have only a moment.'

'But –'

'Ssh,' he said, soothing me. Then he laughed again, softly. 'Young man,' he said 'I am *so* glad to have found you. Ah yes. Now I will give you the secret of life. Do you want it?'

'Who does not?' I took his words for a joke, though he lay on the cobbles before me.

'You are right. Who does not. Do you?'

'Perhaps.'

'Oh, perhaps. Here is my other hand. Open it.' He offered me a closed fist. 'I can't unclench the fingers,' he said. 'You must do it.'

I was bemused by now. I took his fist in both hands and prised it open, which was not easy. There in the palm was another ring, that burned in the half-light a deep smooth red, like a drop of syrup. Yet the boss, highly polished, had also been engraved. Something insectile it would seem to be.

'There now,' he said to me. 'Take it.'

'This?'

'What else. Yes. Take it.' I took it, to calm him, for he was becoming very agitated. 'Your name,' he said, 'give me your name.'

'St Jean.'

'What more?'

'Nothing more. Andre St Jean. That is all. Let me help you up. Where did you mean to go?'

'Away,' he said. And abruptly he was scrambling to his knees; next to get upright. I assisted him as best I could. Then he sprang forward, away from me. I called after him, but he only turned back to me the profile of his madman's face and gave a raw snarl that might have been amused hatred or simply terror. He was old again, an ancient lunatic escaped from some hospital, with bits of wire wound on his knotted hands. He rushed flapping and flailing up Sacrifice Hill, and was gone into the dark stone ditches under the church.

An urge came on me to hurl after him the thing he had given me. What could it be but a gaud of glass, or something much worse. But I stole a look at it again, and it had remained immutable. A huge polished ruby, incised with a snub-headed insect of folded wings. I closed my hand on it in a sort of spasm.

The encounter had unnerved me. I leaned on one of the blind walls by me, my head full of gentle buzzings. What was he fleeing from? Oh, pursuit, of course. His keepers must be after him. Or he had robbed someone of the jewel, and the City police were on his track.

The rain began a moment later, a thousand stilettos flung into the street, over and over. The rain would revive me, probably.

When I heard the shadow, I raised my head. I had expected the pursuit, but not the shape it took.

Two black dogs, lean and long, with jackals' pointing heads, came loping up the cobbles through the rain, slick and wet, altogether like

2

basalt. They barely glanced at me. They went swiftly by, and it seemed to me I felt their heat dinning through the chilly air. After them rode a man on a black horse. He was cloaked in black and cowled against the rain, like a priest. But he, as he drew level with me, paused. Through the water, against the black of the hood, I saw his pale face, and the black eyes that fixed on me and seemed to impel the heart out of my body.

'Did he go this way?'

His voice was quiet, but it reached me easily. It was the voice of music, and its colour too was black.

'Who is that?' I said.

'Don't play,' he said. 'Answer me.'

'Yes,' I said. I lifted my hand to point, or to show him the ring, which must be his, but in that instant he turned his face from me, and lightly touching his horse with the spur, set it racing over the stones.

He was gone. The air seemed cold as iron. I wondered if I would follow, to see what happened, if he would catch up to the other. I had a notion now the lunatic fled to the Temple-Church for sanctuary, but that it would do him no good. The desire to go after the rider, to make him speak again, perhaps to insult him or somehow draw him out, was very strong. But I had not liked the look of the dogs he did his hunting with in the lanes of Paradys. No, it would be better to go home.

I was turning down into the old market, when I thought I heard a thin high terrible screaming, far off, back up the hill.

Since ten in the morning I had been in the house of crazy Philippe, where the séance had been held with such pomp. It led to all types of manifestation, attractive rotten things, like death-bed lilies. The furniture had moved, a decanter smashed; a naked ghost-child appeared to prophesy – stupidities that were certainly faked, or induced by the energy of suggestion. But it had left me sensitive, left me wanting, in need of a supernatural completion as in need of food or sex or sleep.

What then had I been a witness to? A running man, a riding man, two striding dogs. And had I even heard those dreadful cries behind me?

I stood in the rain below the steps, wondering if he would come back, Satan, Prince of Darkness, on the night-black mare, the broken body of his victim flung casually across the saddle. But no one came except a woman of the alleys, who wished me good-day, looking slyly to see if I would go after her to her lodging.

Stumbling, shivering, I turned for my own.

Philippe, Le Marc, Russe, and some others, stood in the street shouting up at my window.

I opened it, and looked down.

The bell was ringing midnight from Our Lady of Ashes across the river. A howling dark, with intervals of deaf stillness. The candlelight touched their faces oddly, making them look mad or damned, the very things they strove to be.

'Regard him!' Le Marc cried in turn, of me, 'death's-head with a book. Come down, corpse, and be happy. Despair is so sensuous, so delicious, it will wear you out.'

'He is sulking,' said Philippe, 'because the little ghost-maiden didn't sit on his lap.'

'Go with your legions to hell,' said I.

'Later, later.'

They clamoured at the outer door until my landlady trudged up the house and admonished me at the inner one. To keep the peace, I descended. And because, of course, I had nothing better or worse to do.

We went to the *Iron Bowl*, and later to the *Cockatrice*, drinking, drinking. The red wine that opens the eyes, and the black brandy that blinds you.

'He's still wearing that ring. Look. Three whole weeks. It must be some token.'

'You are a fool,' said Russe, going back by the wine to the sombre forests of his blood. 'Some cut-throat will have your finger off for that one night, when you're sprawled in some alley.'

'The left hand,' said Philippe. 'He doesn't care what happens to that. As long as the right hand can write.'

I gazed at the red ring, the ruby, with the beetle engraved on it.

'Who gave it you?' said Philippe. He smiled. 'I know who would like it.'

'Philippe, you know everything, why do you bother with us?' said Le Marc.

'*Who* would like it?' said Russe. 'The Devil?'

'What Devil?' I said, feeling my blood on its path turn and rise and move another way.

'It is the Devil's ring,' said Russe. 'I never saw anything so clearly. Let a thief steal it. It will bring you sorrow, and horror.'

'What's new?' I said. I put my head on my arms on the table. Philippe stroked my hair, long as the fashion now was in the City of Paradys, and hennaed ''Martian'' red, since the fashion too was for such colourings. Blond Philippe, a Narcissus, a snow-

4

chrysanthemum from birth, laughed in my ear. 'Don't you want to know whose ring it really is?'

'Tell me, you liar.'

'A most beautiful woman.'

'Liar, liar,' I murmured.

'Not tonight, you are too drunk tonight, and it is too late tonight. Tomorrow we will go to her. And you shall return her the ring. The most beautiful woman in Paradys.'

'Who is that?' said Le Marc.

'The old banker's wife,' said Philippe.

'Oh, I heard of her. Yes. He lets her hold her salon, like the other empresses of the City. But they are foreigners.'

Nearly asleep, I swam through my skull, and sometimes listened. Philippe and Le Marc half carried me home.

Philippe guided me up the stair and shut the door of my room. He moved about, fingering books, caressing the sheets of paper, some with a single line of prose upon them. 'The light drains from the great window,' he read, 'like blood from a fainting face.' He overturned the ink-well, shaped like a gryphon, and with a candle dragged from its socket drew in the ink a crucified Christ, screaming in ecstasy.

'Burn that in the morning,' he said. 'It will be unlucky.'

He sat down on the bed by me, pulled off my shirt and tugged down my breeches. Bored finally by the long caresses, similar to those lavished on my papers, which evoked no sustained response, he concluded his act with a violent introduction and sudden achievement, wracking the house with his groans and cries. He fell asleep lying on top of me, on my back, his white hair getting in my mouth, so I constantly awoke to remove it. Once he whispered again. 'Tomorrow, I will take you to her.'

A man in a black cowl galloped over and over through my dreams and I was slung across the saddle before him. Near dawn, barely conscious, I too climaxed with a slight shuddering that woke Philippe and caused him to curse and punch me in the ribs.

Before he roused himself I got up, dressed, and left the stinking room.

I went down into the City valley, to the river, coiled like a sliding serpent in the mists of earliest day. The buildings rose like crags from the mist, like hills weathered into oblongs. Birds flew for miles, back and forth.

I thought of casting the ring into the river, but might not some fish swallow it? And then I, cutting into the prize sturgeon of some dinner

5

at Philippe's house, find the ring again, glowing up at me from the fish's backbone?

I had searched the journals, I had asked everyone, but there had been no mention of a particular body found in the yards of The Sacrifice, or of a phantom hunter accompanied by black dogs.

I turned from the river and wandered up towards the tall libraries of the Scholars' Quarter. Philippe would lie in wait for me at my lodging a while, and, as usual, I felt myself done with him for ever, until the next occasion of our meeting.

Two days later, he called on me, at his smartest and most exquisitely dressed. It was mid-afternoon.

'Come to my house.'

'As you see, I am working.'

'Let me look.'

'No.'

'Oh you,' he said, 'like some country girl with her lower parts. Very well. Give me a copy when printed. One more slender volume . . . Till then, come to my house.'

'Go away, Philippe.'

'It is tonight,' he said.

He had odd eyes, one much lighter than the other. It enhanced his looks, though as a child, he had been disturbed by it. The nurse his dead mamma had got for him had said it was a mark of evil. She urged him on. At thirteen he raped her.

'*What* is tonight?'

'She opens her salon, like a rose.'

'Who?'

'That lovely woman I spoke of. The wonder of the City.'

It was hot today and hard to work now concentration had been shattered. I laid my pen aside and put my head in my hands. Philippe trailed a flower across my hands, my neck. Presently I got up and followed him out.

Philippe's house stood up against the old City Wall, near the Obelisk, where they had burned the dead in millions during a plague named 'the Death'. Now a variety of trees rooted out of the stones, casting a wet feverish shade. The elderly house was shuttered, an old thing itself, despising the human lizards who flickered through its lofty rooms: they lasted only a moment, better let them do as they wished.

'How I hate this house,' Philippe had said, a hundred times, cheerfully. Now his father was dead, he did everything he wanted there. It was the scandal of the district, but he was rich.

In one of the marble baths I lay soaking, like a piece of statuary dug up from the muck and taken to be cleaned, while one of Philippe's domestics stropped the shaving razor behind the screen. When I vacated the bath-chamber, drugged and stupefied by hot water and balsams, a valet put me into a suit of Philippe's clothes. We were almost of the same fitting, and everything of his might be worn with loose ease by me.

'Oh what a beauty,' he said, flitting round me, most malign of the lizards – one better caged.

The light was growing heavier, more solid, slabs of it in the pillared windows and fallen across the road outside.

'Do you want to dine?' he said.

'I want nothing. I want to go to sleep.'

'Bloody slug. Come on. Where is that ring – you do have it?'

I had stopped wearing it. It had been in my pocket, *his* pocket now, and I took it out and offered it to him. He skipped away. 'No, no, Andre. But you must show it to her.'

'Her. This woman. She had better be worth all your trouble.'

We went out, and along the street together, two young princes in a democratic Paradys that no longer recognised such beings. But who would know me, anyway. A scribbler. A few had seen my plays, and read my essays and miniature novels in their closets. But I was not in the mode, unlike my hair, and now my clothes. I said things that cut too near, or not near enough their candy bones. (Or maybe only I was no good at my trade.) Three pamphlets of mine had even criticised the City Senate, but they took it in good part. *There* was shame. Probably I would rather have been hauled off to jail, unless I had been.

'Philippe,' I muttered, 'if I die –'

'Here it is again,' he said.

'If I die, see to it – make that wretch of a printer take it all and print it all. Every word. Anything unfinished even, and all the pieces he has refused.'

'This ego,' he said. 'Who will care? If you're dead. Do you think you will?'

'No. But I care now, I care this moment. Promise me.'

'Very well. As before. I promise you.'

'You. I can't trust you. You never read a line I ever wrote.'

'Many lines. Now, how does it go – "Light leaving a window like blood in a faint" – what was that?'

'Something I can't remember. A dream I think I had.'

'Like that other dream. I could make you once. You used to yell louder than I did. I used to listen in amazement.'

'You see,' I said, 'but you don't listen to the *words*.'

'When you die,' he said, he swung towards me and took me by the neck, by the snowy linen of his own wardrobe, 'when I *kill* you, Andre, I will make sure every line of your fretful *oeuvre* is published. Shall I bite through a wrist vein and swear it in blood?'

I pushed him and he drew off.

'This woman,' I said, 'who is she?'

'I have told you.'

'Her name.' (Give me your name, the running man had said.)

'Wait, and see.'

We walked on, through the thick, tree-interrupted light, as the bells of the City sounded seven o'clock. We were moving west towards the Quarter of the Clockmakers.

'Where does she live?'

'On Clock-Tower Hill.'

'Tell me about her.'

He said, 'Bloodless skin, ebony hair. A pale mouth that seems drawn on to her face, but is not. Eyes like all-blackness.'

He had been an artist at one time. It informed his speech, if no longer anything else.

'No eye is ever black. You go close and look into it, the eye is some other shade.'

'Not hers, Andre. Ah, such a blow in store: you won't be disappointed.'

'And the husband?'

'If he is. Monsieur Baron von Aaron.'

'A name after all.'

'A foreign name. He's antique. A marriage of convenience.'

'Oh,' I said. 'You have had her, then.'

'Not yet. Never, I should think. She isn't to be *had*.'

Fashionable strollers patrolled the lower walks of the Wall Quarter, from the Obelisk Gardens to the Observatory. Some greeted Philippe, with flippancy or caution, and whispered when he had gone by. On the Observatory Terrace the tables were out, the gossips, gamblers and drinkers, cards fluttering like red and black pigeons, and the resinous clink of glasses of black coffee and liqueurs. From here, by means of an architectural gorge running through the City of Paradys, you saw the masonry precipices drop down, through coins of roofs and flutes of steps like folded paper, into shadow depths

8

veiled in parks, with little bright sugar churches appliquéd on to a mellow sunset, which shed a glamour now like the lambency of some old priceless painting.

We crossed the Terrace, and went up Clock-Tower Hill, where, thirty metres in the air, the gilded white face stares four ways at time.

The house which the Baron von Aaron was renting was one of the stuccoed piles along the inner shoulder of the hill. A lamp hung over the wrought-iron gate, alight. The gate itself stood wide. We went through, up some steps to the porch, and rang the bell. The house was mildly pulsating with its occupancy, and in the dimming atmosphere, the windows of the second floor were quietly burning up.

A domestic opened the door. Philippe handed him at once a card. That was all. The man, an absolute blank, moved back to allow us to come in, and next, having shut the door, solemnly walked ahead of us. We carried our gloves, and would have carried our hats too, had we been wearing any, straight up the curving stair and to the salon.

The card was given over to another blank at the entrance, and borne away across the room. There was nothing unusual in the salon, but for the strange soft candlelight at odds with the softer deepening radiance of the sunset windows, an exciting, expectant light, that would, as ever, lead you fiercely on to nothing. The house itself all around seemed blind, and echoed. Though fresh flowers had peered from the vases by the stair, the building was not exactly alive. The salon, painted and upholstered in the way of such rich men's rentables, was a pastel, and already filled by smoke. There were groups of men, and a handful of women. Some of either gender I knew, others by sight. No one to be interested in; rather, to be avoided. The cadence of talk was low but ceaseless. Now and then a breaker burst, laughter or an exclamation. Somewhere someone was playing a guitar.

'Be patient, wait,' Philippe said to me.

He began to move through the groves of men, the trailing willows of women, accepting as he went a quip, a cigar, muttering, 'Oh God, is *she* here?' over some woman he was not pleased to see. White shoulders flashed and white pipes puffed up at a ceiling of plaster acanthus.

Near the long windows was a piano, and leaning on it, the guitar-player himself, strumming away. An oil-lamp of dense crystal rested on a low glass table, and cast its bloom upward. It caught her hand as she took Philippe's card from the attendant, and her face as she bent her eyes on it to glance. Then, it caught her little, little smile, as she set the card down by the lamp, into a petal-fall of other similar cards.

'Madame,' said Philippe. He bowed over her and took her hand up again and pressed his lips to it. 'I am so glad you allowed me to return.'

'It is my husband you must thank.'

'Then, I thank him, with all my heart. Madame, may I present my friend.'

'Of course,' she said. Her lips stretched once more in the little, little smile.

'The writer, Andre St Jean,' said Philippe.

'Of whom you won't have heard,' I said.

She raised her eyes and looked at me directly, for one entire and timeless second.

'I am afraid that is true.'

'Don't be afraid, madame. If it is to frighten you, most of the City would have to share your terror.'

But her eyes were already gone. They seemed to gaze down into the lamp, so I might go on looking at them, but not into them. They were perfectly black, as Philippe had assured me. So black the charcoal shadow of the lashes, cast upward by the glow across the heavy lids, was ghostly in comparison, and the black brows also seemed pale. These brows were long, and unplucked, and the lashes long and very thick. In the bloodless face, the mouth was a pale ivory pink, the line of the lips' parting or joining accentuated by the lamp, as if carefully drawn with pencil . . . Black hyacinth hair, the kind that thickly and loosely curls; the sheerest shoulders, slender and boneless, above a dark dress. Not a jewel, except the marriage rings which I would diligently search out when her hands came up again.

'You see, Madame von Aaron,' I said, 'I don't hanker for fame at all. But it is at moments like these I wish I had it. If I were known, then you might look at me with some attention. As it is, what in the world can I hope for?'

I felt Philippe's whole body shoot into lines of overjoyed and spiteful satisfaction. She raised her face and gave me one more look, a cold look of surprised indifference. She did now know what to do about me, or my arrogant sally, and so would do nothing at all.

And I? Having bowed to her, I walked away to a table where the valets were pouring out white wine. As I drank it, I imagined her say to Philippe, 'Really, my friend, might I ask you, in future, to spare me such acquaintances?'

But she would not say that. He was no friend of hers.

It was the truth, what I had said, so naturally I confronted her with it. The others would fawn and keep their place. She did not care for anything original, it seemed.

I thought of the sort of women who liked me, some of them even aristocratic. But she was not of their type. She would be tall when she stood, almost my own height, perhaps equal to it. Neither did I care for her, she was so cold. Her hands, (beautiful probably, it had seemed so), would be cold as ice to touch. Splendid hair, and eyes. Otherwise, nothing much. She might give the illusion of great beauty but in fact was not beautiful. Though a voice like the music of the night.

I remembered that ring, then, the gem of hot syrup in the pocket of Philippe's brocaded waistcoat, and slipped in two fingers to find it. At that moment someone else entered the salon, and there were loud, acclaiming calls.

Who was this? Who could it be but the husband, the ostensible lord of her court. The groves were parting to let him by, the men were shaking his hand, or clapping his shoulder. He was tall himself, but stooped and grey – his artificially-curled hair, his expensive coat. He paused to sample someone's tobacco, then shook his old head sadly. The foreign look was exotic in her, and not quite palpable, but he surely had it, in all of his massive face hanging forward off its skull. A cunning, just, ineloquent face.

He passed me, not seeing me, of course, for who was I?, and went on to the window and the piano and the lamp. The guitar-player instantly rose to greet him, and Philippe, who had stayed at her side with four or five others, hung about there, looking glad and expectant, awaiting the man's notice. Stalest of all tricks; it was the husband he had come to see, the woman only a pleasurable diversion encountered on the path.

Philippe now bowed, and shook the old banker's old bankering hand. Was I to be recalled and introduced again? It seemed not. I had disgraced myself. I stole a look at her. She was actually plain. Just the eyes, the hair, the grace. Yes, clever. Women with more made less of it than she. Now her hands rose to greet her husband too. Lovely hands, and there, the big silver rings, one with a pale jewel catching the lamp. When should I give her this one, the red ring with the Egyptian beetle cut in it? Was it hers, this drop of crimson blood? It was all hers. Everything.

Now the old baron raised his hands and the metallic lace on his cuffs glinted. He addressed us. Poor old fool, buying *that* for himself – was she a virgin still? She looked untouched. But knowing, also.

11

Cold all through, or passion somewhere? (Their wine was potent, a good clear wine like water, dazzling the lights). Her skin was fresh and pure as a young girl's, but she was not a girl. Somewhere in her eyes, a hundred years had looked back at me. No wonder she hid them so quickly from my discernment. I thought of lying on her, and what would her skin be like then, and all her textures? Of reaching through her, deep and deeper, and making her cry, if she ever did, her eyes sightless and her pale sculpted mouth wide on its gasp for life –

But I did not want her. She repelled me. She was not for me.

' – And I know you will all help me to persuade my modest wife. Now, Antonina, my dear. The piano, if you please!' He finished in mock severity, and, in mock docility, she rose and curtseyed to him, and glanced one glance across the whole now breathless silent room. Then she went to the piano, opened ready for her. Someone held the stool, seated her, another offered a sheaf of music. A slight shake of her head, so burdened with its mantle of hair. Then, her eyes unfixed, looking miles off, a hundred years away, and her hands straying to the keys of the piano –

The day had turned to dusk in the windows of the room. We might be anywhere, on a mountain that gazed out to other mountains, spires of granite and quartz in a sea of air –

The first note drew me forward. I was glad, glad to have the excuse of the music. I went to her, moving forward, forward. They had all come, all pressed near, yet no one touched me, or impeded me. I reached the piano, and the vibration of the music purred against my side from her fingers. My glass was empty; it too seemed to reverberate. She could not see me now. I could look at, and all through her.

The wine, or the music, had made me drunk, in a wild disembodied way. I wanted the sounds of it never to stop. I believe she did play for a long while, entire stanzas of melody and convolutions of development. It was sombre, the music, scattered by hard white arpeggios, and tumbling white streams of glissandi, and under these the ever-moving river of Death.

When it finished, it had sucked all the strength from me. I leant on the piano and wanted it only to resume, or not to have ended. It was like deepest sleep, in which you dream of making love, always on the verge of ecstasy, to waken fumbling, exhausted and unable.

She rose from the piano, the banker's wife, and the salon frantically applauded her. I clapped her, desultorily, the empty wine glass hindering the gesture. My head ran. I felt nausea. As if, all through

the music, I had been having her, and was suddenly dragged away
by my hair, and slung out on a cold street before sunrise.

Only I remained by the piano. Everyone else had gone away. In
a tiny oval of clarity, I seemed to make her out, standing near the
fireplace, where a summer fire was being kindled, holding now a slim
white dog, rather like a small greyhound.

Philippe was beside me.

'Well, I had never heard her play before. She's a virtuosa.'

I went to the wine table, and took another full sparkling glass, and
poured its bright blood into my own.

'What do you think?' said Philippe.

'A cold bitch', I said. 'Look how she's frost-bitten him.'

'Yes,' he said, gloatingly. 'Come to a crossroads with me. Let us
spill something's blood and invoke the Devil. Make him send us cold
her.'

'Give her the ring,' I said. I managed to find it again and extract
it. 'That may tempt her to you. If you want her so much.'

He looked at the ring. He said, 'Is that a scarab, that beetle?'

'The symbol of renewing life,' I said. I held it out to him, and
abruptly he snatched it, and strode off. I watched as he encountered
her. What could he say? The husband was not particularly close, but
others were about her. I saw the ruby flame out, as he extended it.
It reminded me of something – a spurt of blood in a duel.

Yes, she looked at the ring, but did not take it. How was he ex-
plaining his action? There was too much noise in the room to hear.
Then, she had turned to me. I stared back at her. I wished I had not
drunk so much of the bright wine. She moved, and then she was in
front of me, with Philippe, and the rest of her court at her hem.

'Monsieur,' she said, 'am I to understand you are offering me
this?' She laughed, the way women generally do, falsely. It had a
special quality when she did it, most unpleasant. 'That is surely
rather improper?'

'You're mistaken, Madame von Aaron,' I said. 'I am not a
jeweller. My friend brought you the ring to show you. He seemed to
think you would find it unusual. However, if you would care for it,
I should be delighted.'

'He gave me to believe,' she said, 'you wished me to have the
ring.' Another slight laugh. 'And before witnesses.'

'Is it not,' I said, 'already yours?'

'Not at all. I never collect red jewels. I dislike them.'

'Then you had better give it back to me.'

Her eyes were never once meeting mine. She avoided my eyes. It

13

was not reticence. There was always something more vital in the room that needed her attention. Yet every time her eyes glided by mine, my pulses jumped. She was less than an inch below my own height. To avoid me took dexterity. Now she looked at the ring.

'Where did you obtain this stone, monsieur?'

'Oh, nowhere of interest, madame.'

'I think it is very rare and exceedingly old, monsieur. Have you never had it valued?'

'Perhaps,' I said, 'your husband could advise me?'

'Oh,' she said. 'I don't think so. I am sorry.'

She held out the ring. I took it back. Her hand was like ice, and the ring was icy cold from her.

'Grant me five minutes alone with you,' I said quietly, 'and I can tell you how I came by the ring.'

'Oh, really, monsieur.' Arch now, truly horrible.

'I won't tell you,' I said, 'when another can overhear.'

'Ridiculous,' she said.

'Or do you already know the story?'

Then her eyes did meet mine. It was like some sort of shock of burning searing cold. Black mirrors, black water frozen to iron, trapped under the surface to freeze or drown.

'I think,' she said, 'your sense of drama is running away with you, monsieur. Of course, did Philippe not say, you are a writer of some sort?'

And turning, she went back to the fireplace and the dog and the husband.

Left alone, I put down my glass and sought the door. I was on the staircase when Philippe came running after me.

He said nothing, till the domestic had let us out into the street. Then he said, 'That was her name, before she married.'

'What are you talking about?'

'Antonina Scarabin. The scarab. Do you still say it isn't her ring? Someone stole it from her. She'll send you a letter privately, tonight. I'd bet on that. What mysteries. Promise to tell me every item!'

My blood had leapt, sunk.

'She didn't want the ring. I doubt if it was ever hers. And she has nothing to say to me or of me, I'm sure, but the very worst.'

'No red jewels, those were her words. No red flowers or fruit, either, in the house, did you see? No red wine. *No* red-haired *men*. No *red*.'

'Once a month she must betray herself,' I said.

Philippe laughed and sprang in the air, like a cat after a moth.

14

We went down to the *Cockatrice*, then to the *Surprise*. We drank. While Philippe engaged himself with two of the girls, I held another in my arms, kissing and caressing her until she moaned and shivered and fainted into sleep.

I dreamed of the great window again, perhaps more clearly. The long dark wall that had risen out of slumber two weeks before, and the dagger-thrust of casement wounding it. It was in the height of some tower, one sensed an abyss around, and almost primal open spaces, as in the cranium of the sky. The window was petalled by glass, red glass that shaded through maroon and blood and scarlet into crimson and into rose, and finally into the palest rose of all, nearly colourless, and through these panes I seemed to trace mountains far away, but I was never sure. And as the light went, so the colour went, and all form. And so, too, the dream.

She did not write to me, and I did not suppose she would write. I could think of nothing but her. Snatches of the tidal wave of music would return and sweep me under, and in the same way the memory of her eyes and her shoulders, her hair, the sinuousness of her body as she moved across the salon. If I saw a white dog on the street, my heart turned over. I did not dream of her, but waked with the feeling she had been in the bed beside me, (that sagging bed with its torn and sallow sheets), her hair spread everywhere and her fingers and lips printed all over me, but I, the fool, not opening my eyes until she was gone. I thought of her, and across the single leaves of parchment, her description was set down again and again, always a little differently.

In a few days I wrote her a letter, and disdaining the bureau of mail, gave it to a runner to deliver. What did the letter say? Not what the prose, the poetry had said, certainly. I had bludgeoned and possessed her body a hundred times, eaten her alive, licked up the juices of her flesh, gnawed her bones, and hanged myself in her hair. But, though she would guess, I could not commit the truth to paper.

'Esteemed madame,' said my letter, 'Allow me, if you will be so good, a minute of your time in which to tender my apologies. I fear I was discourteous to you. I would be glad to make recompense, and also to discuss with you that ring you saw. I am woefully ignorant on the subject of stones, and should value your advice. I remain your servant, madame, with every respectful wish for your continued health and pleasure in life. A. St Jean.'

15

This, after I had bound her and time after time crucified her with my lust. Well.

She returned no answer.

In a few days more, I walked over to Philippe's house. He would tell me when again the salon was to be opened.

He was lying on a sofa in the inner courtyard, under the plane tree, eating cherries from a china bowl. He looked wan, a wreck. What had he been doing that he had not attempted to force on me?

'Oh, sit, sit,' he said, 'you wear me out, standing there.'

He began to talk about books, knowing quite well, from his sidelong grimaces, what I really wanted to discuss. I watched him eat the cherries and call out scruffy Hans to go and fetch some more for him from the market. Grumbling, Hans set off.

'And what have you been writing, eh, my dearest Andre?'

'Very little.'

'Not a single poem? I see you have taken to wearing that ring again.'

'And I see you have been sliced again by that senile fool of a barber,' I retorted, for his neck linen, on the left side, was stained right through by a blotch of blood.

'How wise you are,' he said, 'never to let any of them shave you, here. Just strop the razor and get out. And you are always so closely shaved, it's quite a miracle.'

'Be quiet. Tell me when she holds the salon again.'

'Oh, who?'

'Your banker's bitch.'

'Not for some time, I should think,' he said. He lowered his eyes, and allowed himself, faintly, to blush.

In the hot afternoon, a surge of heat went through me like the most scalding cold.

'Oh then,' I said, 'she truly is a fool.'

'Ah, Andre,' said he, taking my hand, 'such amazements – she – oh, she. Do you want me to tell you everything?'

I flung off his hand and he laughed.

'Actually,' he said, 'for a while, she and I. Even when I took you there. I wanted to see what you thought. You know how I revere your opinion. But she has been in Paradys society less than a month. I met her one day in the Gardens. She was in her carriage, do you see, and the little dog was wanting to get out. So I bowed low and I said, Madame, allow me to take care of your little dog.'

My heart lurched and roared. I said, 'And what of him? The foreigner. He's complacent, I take it.'

'Most complacent. He likes her to have lovers. Decorously, naturally. Like a new dress, or a new string of pearls.'

'When do you expect to be replaced?'

He leaned forward. 'Kiss me,' he said. 'Perhaps you may still detect a trace of her. Try for it.'

I struck him in the face; it was not enough and I had to hit him again. He sprawled backwards off the sofa, and staggering up, came for me. We struggled in the lacy shade of the plane, and now and then rolled together over its roots. We had fought before, always viciously; continuous bouts of fighting in childhood and adolescence had eventually ended in haphazard orgasm, and so the similarly struggling, thrusting, desperate union of sex. But this time I seemed to want to kill him, and it was only my realisation of it that at last reined me back. I left him lying under the tree, went to the china bowl and scooped out the last of the cherries. I kneeled over him and crushed them into his fair bruised face, his snow-blond hair, and into the muslin of his cravat to stain it and his shirt more thoroughly than the blood. That done, I abandoned him, spitting and weeping with his fury and hurts.

My first impulse, next, was to leave the house. Then I thought better of that. Let the ancestral mound overlook a few more of the antics of this lizard.

I used the third of the bathrooms – cold water in the heat was not amiss – and dressed myself, as before, in one of the more breathtaking of his suits of clothes. His brushes through my red hair then, and his mirrors to show me he had not left a mark on me, but for a contusion along my knuckles. The scarab ring, however, had done him some damage, blacked his eyes and split his lip for him. He was vain. Would he go to her like that, with his prettiness spoiled? Or maybe he would seek her mothering solace in his pain.

Lastly I visited his library and took off his shelves a novel of my own, given him a year ago, the latest finished work I had written. He had never read it, I thought. No, here was a page turned down one quarter of the way in, that had a look of midnight yawning. I'd made him no dedication, I had only inscribed it *Andre St Jean*. ('If I die, it may be worth something, for if I die they will know I was a genius. They will be safe then to do it.').

With that under my arm, and his fine garments all over me, I left the house. I had heard nothing further of Philippe, but I met Hans by the basement step. 'Be careful,' I said, 'how you take him those cherries.'

What would she be doing? The single Bell of Prayer was sounding from Our Lady of the Wounded Rose, the shadows lengthening under walls, trees and gate-pillars. At this hour, lying on a sofa as he had done, probably, but indoors, out of the sun. Reading, the little white hound on her lap. Too hot still to play the piano. And no one of any sophistication dined for three hours yet, if at all, since it had become the rage for suppers at midnight, or one or two in the morning.

I reached the von Aaron house, announced my arrival, was let in, and waited. I had thought of assuming another name, but did she even remember the real one?

The domestic came back and said. 'Excuse me, monsieur, but Madame is resting, and not to be disturbed.'

'Please tell Madame, without disturbing her more than is essential, that I shall remain here, in her hallway, until I have seen Madame.'

Off he went again, and back he came again, and conducted me into a downstairs side-parlour. 'You may remain if you desire,' he said, 'but Madame regrets she may have to keep you waiting a long while.'

'Tell Madame I will wait as long as is necessary. I imagine,' I added, 'that eventually your employers will think of moving house, and will then discover me, a skeleton, still propped in one of the chairs. Pray ask Madame which, as I should hate to ruin a favourite by expiring in it.'

When he was gone, I poured myself a brandy from the decanter, then another, for I was misgiving and in a cold sweat. God knew, *he* might come down or in, and then I should have to talk to him, the cuckold whose horns apparently I wanted so badly to refurbish.

An hour passed. A small porcelain clock told me the news, chiming sweetly. Did she then remember me, if only as unwelcome? If so, this was a politic ploy, for if she left me to kick my heels a sufficient time, I must get bored, or only hungry, and skulk away. I looked about for something I could disfigure with a secret message, something she must discover with time. If I were able, any more, to write anything, I would have written of her, flayed her with her own self and my delirious fascination with it, and published. Sent her a copy. Let her read at length and in detail, what she had been to me, I the magician who drew every night her soul out of her body, remade it into flesh, and over and over possessed it.

I expected she would never appear, but after five more minutes, I turned, and found her in the doorway. It was an afternoon gown she wore, a robe for reclining, dark, as previously. Her face was expressionless and flat. Was this she? Was she only this, nothing else or more? Her eyes, after a second's black burning, she lowered.

'Thank you,' I said, 'for coming down.'

'I am afraid you have had to wait some while.'

'I'm afraid I have.'

'It is not the hour for visiting.'

Her eyes lifted, looked a mile beyond me. She searched the horizon for something, or someone. But she had come alive for me, by speaking, or only by existing. Yes, she was more, much more.

'You received my letter,' I said.

'Oh yes, indeed I did receive it.'

'But did not think to reply.' Nor did she think to now. I said, 'Naturally, I'm no one you would have to reply to. But it would have soothed my remorse.'

'You really should not suffer remorse, monsieur, on such slight occasion.'

'I offended you. That was enough. So. Here I am again to offend you again, merely by my presence.'

'My husband,' she said, 'is a banker not a jeweller. For myself, I know nothing about jewels, except in a very ordinary way.'

'You told me, madame, the ruby was rare and old.'

'Which was all I could possibly know of it.'

'I added that, given five minutes alone with you, I would tell you how I had come by the stone. Here we are.'

'No,' she said, very quickly. 'I'm not at all interested, Monsieur St Jean. Please excuse my frankness.'

I felt myself go very white.

Walking straight across the room to her, before she could drift away or disappear through the partly open door, I held out my book. It was precious to me, as were all the things I had written; even where I despised their inadequacy there was not one I would disown. Each tore its way from my entrails. Each had shortened my life, killed me with its own especial little death, regardless of any other thing I had ever done with or to myself.

'Please take this, madame. I'm aware you can't want it, a book by an unknown writer, doubly of no consequence to you. But nevertheless.'

'Why should you wish me to have this book?' Her eyes floated over its surface like black water.

'One day you might read it, madame. In, say, a fit of aberration. And if you had forgotten me sufficiently, you might even enjoy a passage, a sentence, a phrase, here or there.'

'Oh my dear Monsieur St Jean. This constant spectacle with which you present us all, of your bleeding body, mutilated by a thousand wounds, pegged out for the vultures and our chariot-wheels always to be at you.'

I turned and threw the book, the precious book, on to the table by the decanter.

'I can say nothing to that,' I said.

'Indeed,' she said. 'Do you think I want something that was hurled at me?'

'Give it then,' I said, 'to your beloved Philippe. I must confess,' I said, 'that I have rather marred his looks for you, if only temporarily. I hope that will not distress you too greatly.'

She stared at me, with all her eyes, then walked by me, crossing the room to one of its windows.

'Are you now resorting to blackmail, Monsieur St Jean?' she asked the street outside.

I was angry with a child's anger, and could only choke it down, which left nothing to be said, for sure.

I thought, in a blinding, sickening horror, You will not escape me. You will not get away. The pin of the pen, if not the lance of lust, will go through you because of me. Redress – I must have something!

She said, 'My husband, of course – '

'Of course knows everything you do, and condones it. Ask Philippe, he may tell you some of the things *I* have done. I'd never want to cast stones, madame.'

That uttered, somehow, I walked out, into a place of despair, into an endless down-pouring of hell, not knowing where I went.

All the cafés and the bars of my world would see me that night, and none would be any good to me.

As I stepped paralysed down the hill, someone came flying after me. I started round, and there was the man from the door, bowing, and trying to give me something – a book. Mine.

'Forgotten in my hurry to leave,' I yelled at him, 'did she say so? *Wait.*'

And drawing out my matches, I struck one, and wrenching the book from him, set fire to it. I burnt it, my book, so precious to me, there before the startled domestic, and a multitude of faces appearing like pale turnips in several windows of the thoroughfare, attracted by my scream of anguish.

It did not burn all through, but most of it was gone, when I gathered up the ashes and the brittled leather, and thrust them on the servant, who was still waiting there patiently, as required.

'Take her that,' I said. 'Take her *that*.'

He did not argue with me. He clumped stolidly off up Clock-Tower Hill, with ashes in his arms for Antonina von Aaron.

"Antonina, I love you – I cannot say: as I have never loved another thing, for there are other things I have loved so well – the night, the sun, music, beauty itself, *life* itself. Yet all these things I have loved are now valueless to me. You have put out the light. Priestess of darkness, you.

"Antonina, even your name, even the misery you have afforded me, are worth more than anything I ever owned. I would give it all away in exchange for you, even those scraps of a blazing talent, all in fragments, that you would never recognise, but which are all I have and am, and for which, solely, if ever remembered, remembered I should be.

"What can I do? I would murder you, I would cherish you. I would torture you and take you by force, I would lie across your door and die for you. But you want nothing of mine, or of me. Who is he, you say, if you think to say anything: ah, a little second of annoyance. And to me you are everything that exists. The soul of my soul. Black light, by which I see.

"Oh, let me go down and find the waters of forgetful night, and drinking them underground, unremember you. All memory take, your face, your voice, your eyes, all of you, till nothing remain – but still I would be in agony, all of you forgotten, yet all of you unforgettable and with me still, my sin of omission – Lethe leaves me to grieve, though I no longer know why."

This I wrote to her, and much, much besides. But did not trouble her with it.

A month, it seemed to be a month, went by. Days and darknesses. Nightingales sang in the parks, and one night fireworks burst over the city, it was the democratic decade of the Senate, Year Ten of Freedom, a celebration. All Paradys stood in its trees, on its roofs and balconies to watch. I watched. If my heart would burst like one of those gunpowder lights, into stars, falling. Ah, it was not to be.

During the days, I lay on the bed, I slept when I could. At night I roamed the avenues, the squares, the boulevards. I resisted the temptation to climb Clock-Tower Hill, or to scutter lizard-like to Philippe's domicile and hammer on its doors and shutters.

I avoided the women in the places where I drank. Some came mewing to me. I gave them money to go away.

21

Alone, in my room near dawn, I once or twice tried to summon up a demon, or something dead, to instruct me. Numbed by wine and brandy, burning with spirits, I requested spirits of another kind to come to me. The candlestick, the gryphon ink-well moved, and papers flew about like birds. Heat filled the room, then clinging cold, but all these happenings ultimately failed and went away, leaving nothing behind them but a common mess. The climax of manifestation had not been achieved.

Why should it be so difficult to die, so impossible to live?

My landlady trudged to my door, and asked me if she should summon a doctor.

'Why, madame, are you ill?'

She explained that she was not, but that I would seem to be, I had been screaming in the night again with bad dreams.

'There is a window,' I said, 'it drips blood, it runs with tears.'

I heard them say on the narrow stairs that I was in the process of going mad and should be evicted.

Russe, who had found me at the *Imago*, attended on me from a discreet distance as I spewed into a gutter. When I was done with that, or it with me, he lifted me off my knees, and took me to his own lodging. Here I was placed in a clean bed, between sheets that had the fragrance of new bread and lavender. His mistress kept house for him very nicely. I slept far into the new day in this unaccustomed comfort. Then the two of them came to perch by me, while she fed me milk and fruit.

When he sent her away again, he said to me, 'Why do this to yourself?'

I lay in the marvel of the bed, watching the shadows of birds fan over the ceiling. There was a bird in a cage, too, very thrilled with itself and tweeting, not aware of something missed.

'We are each given a life,' I said, 'do with it as we may or must.'

'There are other roads to the sewers and death,' he said, 'more profitable and more gallant than this.'

'Take them, my dear Russe. You are so solemn. Take them.'

'Over some woman,' he said. 'You bloody idiot. You're behaving like some stupid girl yourself.'

I laughed, drearily, not without appreciation of his wit.

'This is not being kind, my friend,' I said. 'Nurture me if you must, or put me out on to the street. But let me do what I am inclined to.'

His girl began to sing, charmingly, downstairs in the house. I had never wanted that, the nesting proximity of a shared life. Never.

22

What then had I intended with her, my lady of shadows? Not to leave her with her husband, surely, enjoying her at random? No matter. No question could arise of it.

To make a little conversation with grim Russe, lurking in his ancestral forests, responsible for his fellow men, I said, 'And where is my beloved erstwhile companion, Philippe?'

'My God,' said Russe. 'You haven't heard. Well, you have been hearing nothing, have you, but the sound of corks got out of bottles.'

'Heard what?' I thought, He has run off with her. That will be it. It seemed at a great distance. It did not matter.

'Philippe has vanished. Fifteen days now, and sixteen nights. Even the City police are alerted.'

I said, 'Well, you won't see him again.'

'What? Why do you say that?'

'He will be out of the City, over the borders, with her.'

'With whom? What do you know of this, Andre?'

'If he purloined her, how could he stay? The old banker might have wanted satisfaction after all. Old bankers are notoriously unpredictable.'

'If you are speaking,' said Russe stiffly, 'of the von Aaron woman, she has nothing to do with this. She is in her house. She holds her salon twice a week now. Most fashionable. Everybody goes there.'

The bed seemed to slip away under me, a boat casting off to sea.

'He told me he was her lover.'

'Probably he lied to you. She is supposed to be virtuous. Oh come, Andre. Philippe – is *that* what began this –'

I wanted to get up, I was not certain why. I had some notion I should go over to Philippe's house, and that he would be there. Then, since nothing else could then conceivably have happened, I might refind myself also. If I wished to. She no longer seemed a part of me. I had drunk Lethe, all the brandy-black glasses of it, and after all, did not recall her quite. Nearly faceless now, just the cowl of hair, the coals of the eyes – Her voice, murmuring something foul to me.

Russe would not let me get up. His girl ran in and joined his lament. I lay back down again.

In the middle of the night, when they were making love below, and the tweety-bird slept, I got out of the bed of bliss and dressed and crept down the house with my boots in my hand. Someone had polished them, these boots, as I saw by the glow of the moon and the street light outside the door. Polished the boots, laundered all my filthy linen, cleaned and brushed my coat. It was Philippe's coat too, in fact. I had kept it, to go drinking in, to write and weep and vomit while wearing, to die in along some alley gutter. Well, better return it now.

From Our Lady of Ashes came the four o'clock bell.

I shambled towards the Wall Quarter, the old City barricade that once fenced Paradys above the river. Sometimes I laughed at the moon, she looked so like a nun, a priestess, with her bloodless face cowled by night.

The shuttered house too was gaunt in the moonlight. Was it not somewhat like a tall thin skull, eye-sockets, nostrils, cave of mouth with its teeth knocked out. And what about that phalanx of round attic windows above? Of course, the scars of the bullets which had gone through the brain and killed it long ago.

(In a skull then, the lizards played, darting, fighting, resting. And they had stored clothing, swords and books, and a rocking-horse, behind the bullet-holes.)

The bell jangled mournfully. It seemed to echo away over the chasms of the City. Would anyone come, at this hour, to let me in? So frequently Philippe, with the door key, much later than this, would go in to find one of them, Hans or Poire, dozing on the wooden seat in the hallway.

A lamp fluttered up behind the glass. A face pressed itself there, like a prisoner's, staring out at me.

The door was opened.

'Good morning, Hans.'

'Yes, monsieur.'

'Is he awake?'

'Not here, monsieur. No. Haven't you heard?'

'Oh that. He is here. Hiding from us all. Don't you remember he used to do that, as a revolting child. He hid constantly from his hysterical mother, and the nurse. But I recollect every hiding place.'

I came into the house, and Hans allowed it. He looked bovine, and anxious, he looked wilful, too, for I was not the master here. I was the impecunious writer, Philippe's guest, and other things.

But then again, I had accustomed them to obeying me, or to tolerating my commands.

He stood there stolidly now, feet planted, relaxed.

'Come on,' I said. 'We will search him out.'

'Yes monsieur,' said Hans.

He plodded after me. Very likely he thought I was drunk, and was humouring me. For Philippe might abruptly return and chastise him otherwise; Philippe might even be behind it all.

We searched the lower floor first, the two parlours and the dining room. (We would leave the basement area, I told him, the servants' cells, until the last.) Philippe was not there, so upstairs we went. Still he was not found. In the library he did not conceal himself in the curtains or among the volumes. Beneath the massive desk there seemed some chance of locating him, but neither was he there. We ascended to the bedrooms. Hans was tired now, and had begun to remonstrate with me, for the game was gross and silly.

'He's here,' I said. 'Can't you tell?'

'No, monsieur.'

'He is.'

Beyond the last bedroom – its canopy investigated, and even the chamber-pot dragged from under the ruching – the gallery led across to the bathrooms at the rear.

The lamp faltered in this corridor, trying to give up its ghost, as disillusioned now as Hans.

'Trim the wick. I mean to find the bastard.'

Unhappily, Hans trimmed away, and the light steadied as I squinted into the stone-panelled privy.

A kind of coldness seemed to flow along this upper floor, disuse perhaps, for he had apparently been gone all the while, those sixteen nights. Or some essence of demons had been trapped between the walls, left over from his séance, and from the ghost-girl. But it was like absence rather than presence.

Hans began sneezing nervously.

'For God's sake quiet,' I said, as if afraid to disturb something. Why? Surely Philippe must know we were upon him?

The largest of the bathrooms, the remnant of the bath-house which had formerly stood separate from the rest of the building, raised its marble façade into the lamp-smear. Philippe had favoured this one's round tub most often. I kicked the door wide open, and the watery light fell in.

The sinking moon was there before it, coming sideways through from the vanes of glass in the roof. And there, below, Philippe lay, in the bath.

Hans gave a high, pig's squeal. He did not drop the lamp; habit, presumably, not to break his master's things.

After a long time, I said, 'Did you never think to come up here?'

'Oh monsieur,' he bleated, 'only yesterday – and the maids, to clean – it was always done, every day –'

'Then it seems he came home this evening.'

'No, no,' he said, panting now and sobbing. 'No, not possible –'

'Not through the front door then,' I said. I looked from Philippe's uptilted unlistening face, towards the glass vanes. One stayed open. 'Climbing on to the roof over the attics,' I said, 'they let him down through the skylight. How curious. How agile.'

He was clothed in shirt and breeches, his coat and linen were gone, he was barefoot. He was white with a solid thick whiteness, like plaster. The density of his pallor, though not its colour, clogged the room, which was like a winter vault.

'Go down,' I said. 'Get Poire and the others. Send someone for the police.' He stuttered, and shook. 'Don't take the lamp,' I cried out in a ritual fear. He implored me. 'Take it then. Christ, there's the moon.'

In the cold moonshine then, and alone, I went and looked into Philippe's waxwork mask of plaster. His eyes were shut, and his lips parted. His hair now was darker than his skin. He did not resemble anyone I knew, and seemed dead a year, though it could not have been more than a day.

The bruises and cuts of the beating I had given him were all healed. Only the barber's gash had not gone from his throat, or it was a fresh one. From the puffy dark mottling on his neck, one long dried trickle of blood had flowed out black, running down under his shirt, down to where the nipple had checked it. There was a similar abrasion on the inside of his left wrist, and the sleeve there was stained, plummy, under the moon.

Then I saw – he had not been quite dead, when returned. No, not quite, for on the bottom of the bath, in his blood, the artist had been drawing, as he had once drawn in the spilled ink . . . I looked closely. I thought I could make out the indication of a horse, slender and running, with a slender hooded thing leant forward on its back – and before that, two slender running hounds –

'Philippe,' I said, urgently, as if he would hear me.

What must I feel? I had spent it all, all emotion, all sickness, for her. I was bled out and had nothing over to offer him. Drained like the window of its light, like Philippe of his blood.

I sat down on the floor by the bath, in the coldness of his death, to wait a while, to see if he could catch me up.

Called to a painted hall in the Senate Building, I, with several others, was asked various questions. Russe, my surety, described to the officials, while clerks busily scribbled, how I had been taken sick, and spent a night and day in his home, overseen continuously by himself and Mademoiselle Y –, whom he did not wish to bring into the affair unless it were unavoidable. Philippe could not have been dead more than an hour or so, when found in the bath-house, this the doctors had quickly verified. Besides, the operation across the roof, the lowering through the vanes, these postulated several persons labouring in unison.

One by one, forming into irked and vocal groups, Philippe's friends, amours, money-lenders, debtors, and scavengers extraordinary were summoned, quizzed, and dismissed to pace the antechambers.

One sensed that, with all the muck that came swiftly to the surface, the murder of Philippe seemed not only inevitable but perhaps aesthetically fitting, to the members of this Senate Investigatory Committee.

At no time did I think I would be apprehended for anything, despite having arrived at an unsocial hour and plainly knowing the exact whereabouts of the body. Such behaviour was too pat for an assassin, or if I were one, they could not be bothered with me. At length, they turned us all out on the street, as innocent. The Committee had got hold of the idea that some enemy from Philippe's past had done the heinous deed, then fled over the northern borders. This was deemed a proper programme. They liked it, and did not like any of us. If a single murderer had been proved in our midst, I think it would have disgusted them, for evidently the itinerary of Philippe's life had not pleased. They desired the whole thing filed rapidly and put in a cabinet.

The death of Philippe was discussed generally after that. Many theories, including that of an ingenious suicide, were aired. At the *Iron Bowl* a fight broke out, and at the *Cockatrice* two more, though the *Surprise* and the *Imago* remained quiet. Indeed, under the black beams of the *Imago's* medieval roof, they concocted weird scenarios of witchcraft. It was the Devil who rode over Philippe's attics and dropped the corpse into the tub. Had there not been a drawing, in blood, to that effect, all over the walls, ceiling and floor? Better ask Andre, who had found the remains.

When any of them came to badger me, they found me out, asleep, or drunk.

'Well, and are you to grace the funeral?' said Le Marc, who had cornered me at last, partially sober, in a library of the Scholar's Quarter. 'You had better go. You may want to write about it later on.'

This was quite true. Besides, I had known him almost all his life. I would have to put him to rest somehow, and to see the lid of the coffin's ponderous cigar-box closed on him might be the only way.

What a funeral this was. What a brave quantity of followers. Ancient fragile aunts had come from their towered and chimneyed crannies in the pastoral suburbs of Paradys, supported by equally elderly retainers. They doddered on each others' arms in black lace mittens, stove-pipe hats, and veils. Had Philippe ever met any of them, or remembered them? Relics outliving his disastrous sprint of youth, did they hope to be his heirs? (It transpired that in a way I was, he had left me a quantity of largely unspecified, useless and bizarre treasures from the attics, to be collected by myself at my own inconvenience. A patronising, perfectly suitable bequest. Odd he had made a will. We stood amazed.)

His friends, if such we were to be called, also arrived at the graveyard gate. And, apart from this gathering of vultures, the morbidly curious of the neighbourhood strolled up to take a stare.

The memorial was to be conducted in the Martyr Chapel of the Sacrifice; he was then to be ladled into the ancestral vault behind the Temple-Church.

'Hallowed ground,' said Russe, to whom Philippe had bequeathed three huge clocks and a dresser too big for any of his rooms. 'But he died godless, of course.'

The most savage of the vultures had found dark clothes to wear. I wore the coat I had stolen from him the last time, when I crushed the cherries into his mouth and hair.

The absurdities of his will, as I had heard them out, kept recurring in my mind. The jokes were too contemporary. They would not have worked when we had all grown old. He must have known he would die young.

Trap after trap drew up with its black horses and black ribbons, disgorging more and more derelict aunts. Then at last came the coal-black coach, whose black horses, like the steeds of Pluto, had each a black flame of plume upon its head. The overcast was also turning black. It was a hot and airless afternoon, with a sudden rough, similarly airless wind, that tore between the trees of the burial garden, while the immovable massive hills of the Temple-Church pushed up at the monumental sky. We, whipped and blown about below, were of no importance, but anxious not to face the facts, we went on playing at our rôles. Out came the coffin, nails already firmly hammered home. Supposing he had changed his mind? That would be like him, crashing forth in the midst of the service, cursing and shouting for his valet, in ineffable bad taste.

28

But the professional porters of death had the coffin up on their shoulders now, and bore it away along the gravel path. The aunts were permitted to go next, then the rest of us. Somehow I walked the very last, an afterthought.

I was not paying much attention to any of it, the stony fields of asphodel, the shaggy bear-like cypresses. The Chapel, with pale windows, lay ahead, and we would all get there.

Then came a noise behind me, another carriage, arriving late, pulled up, horses snorting, passengers dismounting, the gawpers at the gate, with a murmur, giving way. I halted, and turned. Along the path towards me walked the illustrious banker-baron, von Aaron, in darkest, greyest mourning, and on his arm, her feet scarcely touching the gravel, she. I took two long steps back, out of their path, standing as if at attention beside an angel on a pedestal of basalt.

As they went by, von Aaron nodded to me, not looking into my face, but quite courteously, as if out of consideration for my grief. She did not look anywhere, but straight ahead. Her habitual black was augmented by a strange dramatic black veil, like a mantilla, raised on a pearl comb, covering her hair and also most of her face.

When they were gone, when they and the rest of the funeral had quite vanished into the Chapel, I went after. The usher was shutting the door as I stayed him to get in.

A full house. I did not look for anyone, but stood at the back, alone.

The windows had closed with the afternoon's darkness. When the wind clawed at the building, the candles flounced. Quickly, quickly, let it be over with. I rested my head a moment on the stone of a pillar, wondering how many others, overcome by this insidious faintness, might have done so. I must think. But why, and of what?

For example, had that running man come up the very path we had taken, had he reached this place? I considered. Not the Church, certainly, with its sacred altar of sanctuary, not that, for then how could Satan have claimed him. Where, among the angels and gargoyles, the marble praying children and stone wreaths, had the black hounds pulled him down? I had trodden in the face of his ghost. Or imagined the whole episode. Did I find the red ring in a drain?

The Chapel was mumbling now with spoken responses, the words of the priest in a magpie gown of white and black stripe. Everything swung to and fro, like a ship in a sluggish storm. Rain pummelled the windows. The shut doors shook. Another latecomer was wanting to get in. What was out there? What rider on what long-maned mare of the daytime night? Of the endless night, inescapable night, washing round us, which would have us all. Antonina, save me from this dark, this precipice into which I, with all the world, must fall –

Thank God, it was finished. I drew aside again, and let the porters and the cigar-box go out, and the tide of flesh and crêpe, the aunts twittering and sniffling now. And caught in the tide, the cameo of a face under the water of its veil –

The graveyard had become a desert sailed by cloud.

It was an old mausoleum, and it leaned. Through the tilted doorway they took him, and left him behind there. Some of the aunts were now being assisted. The smell of aqua-vitae travelled up the slope to me. His friends broke and ran, waving their arms. They must hold a wake now, what else was to be done? Drink the man down.

As the crowd thinned, separated, dissolved, some of it toiling or hurrying past me, I realised the rain had begun.

I stood in the rain, indifferently trembling, and watched the banker talking quietly to the priest. The door to the vault stayed open. She was inside. Did no one think that strange?

Of course, none of them mattered. Props, strawboard things, not real at all.

I walked down the slope in great strides, and went past them and by them, as probably they gazed at me distractedly, and up to the narrow, lopsided door of the darkness, and through.

There was an array of stone boxes, the family of Philippe already foregathered, but the coffin, being brand new, was shining on its slab in the light of the white candles.

She was poised the slab's other side, her veil off her face, her naked hand lying on the coffin top, with a crimson rose between the fingers. As I entered, she let the flower go. She let it lie there, a drop of reckless colour on the dark. It might only have been her excuse for coming in, but was not even that – what had she said to me? – *rather improper*? To drop the bloody tear of a flower on the coffin of one's salon's mere occasional visitor. A cliché, too, madame, of the worst, and you waited, static as a doll, for me, or someone, to come in and see you do it.

I said, 'But you do not like red. Are you insulting him then, madame, his poor helpless body?'

She said, 'My husband is just outside.'

'Don't be afraid,' I said, 'the extensive branches of his horns would never let him through the doorway.'

'You are so very insolent. Arrogant and rude. You were from the very first. Do you suppose the earth turns around you, monsieur?'

'Around you,' I said. 'As I see it.'

The candles lit her eyes, still veiled always from mine.

'You observe,' she said, 'how I am placed. I have a husband, and a position in society.'

'And a lover, previously.'

'There is *nothing*,' she said, 'for you.'

I could not mention that they had murdered Philippe, one or other or both of them, for she would then resort to the former accusation of blackmail. Otherwise everything just said was irrelevant. Neither the slab nor the box was very wide. I leaned across them and slid my hands around her throat and brought my mouth against her pale cool skin. Beause she did not struggle, there was nothing turbulent or unwieldy, nothing to ruffle the deathly serenity of the tomb. It was also quite fitting that I should kiss her over his corpse.

She let me, did not stay me or cry to implore help, but her lack of resistance was itself a stay. Neither did she concede. She had no scent, no odour at all, only perhaps the faintest fragrance in her hair, like the clean fur of a cat that has been out on a chill moonlit night. Her eyes were shut, to exclude me, no concession either there. Then they opened, and I saw them stare beyond me, to the horizon. I had only pressed her lips gently. I set my mouth to her cheek, and temple, and the smooth bone of the jaw beneath the ear. The lobe of the ear held no jewel, but a tiny incision remained in it, for a jewel's piercing. With that, where I had not ventured to part her lips, I allowed my tongue an instant for its curiosity. Then I took her hands and kissed them in their turn, the palms, the strong and slender backs, where the two silver rings pressed against the knuckle-bones, the wrists; they were icy cold, dipped up from some lake within a piano of snow mountains, rinsed in liquid music, over and over, they burned ten freezing notes across my mouth, before I let her go.

'You say to me,' I told her, 'there is nothing for me, of you. Perhaps not, perhaps not.' I, now, did not look at her. It seemed to me that, this being the case, her eyes were fixed on me intently, terribly. 'But there's no use your telling me anything, or warning me in this conventional mode. I am beyond any such pale. What you say is meaningless. Do you think I have no spirit, Antonina, that I can be *told*, can be *instructed*, how I may or may not desire you? Do you believe my emotions are so volatile they will simply evaporate at one sensible soulless little word? What am I? Your servant? No. You are in my blood now. You've coloured everything, stained me, just the way blood stains. I'm marked by you indelibly. It will never come out, the bloody dye of what you are. Stained through and through.'

Each act, even unfinished, or unbegun, knows for itself its proper completion. I left her at once, and went out, into the air and daylight which seemed neither.

The wet heat almost struck me down, the darkness. Von Aaron was standing solicitously at my elbow.

'Monsieur St Jean, you do not look well.'

'How is it,' said I, 'that you know my name?'

'But you have been so good as to call on us, in company with your friend.'

'Yes. I hardly thought it was through my literary glories.'

'I must repeat, monsieur, you are not at all well. This shocking business of the gentleman who has died . . . Our carriage is below. May we have the pleasure of driving you to your home?'

'Why did you come here?' I said. The rain teemed round me, making everything unstable, shifting and falling down; my condition would not matter.

'To pay our respects, naturally.'

'Naturally. You should dissuade your wife from wasting flowers on the dead. A silly custom. They do better in the houses of the living, or growing in the ground.'

'Monsieur, monsieur, can't I entreat you to reason?' He smiled, encouraging me. A wave of deadly nausea passed through me. I fought it away. On my lips, the touch of her icy fingers still burned ten times over, on and on.

'You are too kind,' I said. 'Your wife would perhaps not like it, some wretched stranger in your carriage, at such a moment. Good day.'

As I crossed through the graveyard, I seemed to see an old man flitting about there, huddling down behind the stones, and two black dogs, slicked by wet, questing without hurry.

On the cobbled alley, I walked in my trance. The rain rushed by, as it had that other day. I felt I might die before I reached the bottom of the hill. There was some sickness on me, some plague, something. Gladly I welcomed it. Come thou sweet night, close mine eyes.

And all the books unwritten. Well, let them go.

And all the songs unsung.

And Philippe in his box, not hearing the rain.

'They're to close up the house.'

'Like the damnable coffin itself.'

'Boarded. The neighbours are complaining, there are noises in the night. Hoary old Father Mouse-whiskers, that priest, has been asked to perform an exorcism. But is afraid to. Must apply to his Holiness to see if he may.'

'The servants meanwhile hold drunken parties in the basement. They don't give a *that* for any phantoms.'

'But whatever else, Andre,' said Le Marc, 'if you don't go there and collect those bits he left you, you will never get them. The bailiff's men are also reportedly to go in. A debt or two unsettled, we are given to understand.'

The onset of the soft and tender illness, which for a week now had sustained me with its shadow, had enabled me to resume my life. I would not have to put up with living much longer. So, as with an unwanted love shortly due to depart for ever more, I could afford to be polite. It might take months, of course, but months were nothing. Even a year or two was possibly to be borne. Every lissom overture of the malaise pleased me. It was sensuous, fastidious. A weakness, a loss of appetite, even of the appetite for drink, the desire to sleep a great while. The vague aching of the limbs was like a lullaby. I needed only to surrender, to collapse, for it to sink into a delicious nothing ambient to all the physical senses. There was the invalid's concupiscence also, febrile, intense, and entirely easy to accommodate, uncaring of object. From the depths of slumber I returned with an awareness of wonderful dreams, glowing with enjoyment and colour. Free of me, I was whole. I had begun to write, an outburst that surprised and energised me. Working, I passed through the outposts of the dulcetly aching messenger of sleep or sexuality, passed through with bright banners of words starting from the pen almost faster than my thoughts could envisage them. Surely faster than the ink could set them down. Until undeniable exhaustion at length put paid to me, snuffed me out and let me free again for that other world inside, beside, beneath, above, wherever it was, the heaven of my invention, liberty.

In this condition I was amenable too. I would heed, and sometimes be kind. Now I would get up and hire a carter for a few coppers with his cart, and go to Philippe's house. I would climb, albeit slowly, up to the attics, and rummage, and take, and go away again.

Despair, the worst of all the deadly sins, since it is denial of the self, of the god-in-self, since it is so seductive, like the snow-death, so warm. Ah, who would tear himself to pieces when he might lie down in such arms, in comfort, and cease. Bless you, my despair, my dear and loving despair. So painlessly you take my pain away. Oh Father, by no means dash the cup from my lips –

The carter was solicitous. The wind was cold today, he said, blow-

ing from the north. He tucked my muffler about my throat and did
up the buttons of my greatcoat as if I were his child. It was entertain-
ing. On the road where I was going, scarves and coats were not
necessary. He had had a sad life, the carter, all about which he told
me as he pushed the cart, on our journey up to the Wall Quarter.
Dear friend, I nearly said, Why not abandon hope. Why not do as
I do, and escape. Perhaps he had already contracted the plague from
me, if it was contagious. Then again, the thought of him as a companion on a trip to the Underworld, constantly retelling episodes of his
misfortuned days, as now he did, decided me against his inclusion in
my party. One might ask Charon, of course, to push him off the boat
into the River Styx. But you could not be sure of Charon. I had seen
ferrymen like him, plying their slender vessels through the morning
mists along the City river, looking for fish, or that night's drowning
victims, who might offer a gem or a pocket-watch, or a fine head of
hair to hack off and sell the wig-makers. Charon would be of that
sort, maybe. Of some sort, anyway. For I did not suppose only
nothing lay beyond the great gate.

I fell asleep as I walked, and the carter woke me solicitously when
we reached the house. I reminded him he should wait for me. He did
not say, why else had he come?

'Take care,' he did say. 'You're not looking too well, young
gentleman.'

The domestics were now all out of Philippe's house, or else hiding
under the boards like mice. Not a light showed, though the street was
already cast for night. In the west, framed by the alligator scales of
the roofs, a red sunset. The dome of the Observatory would appear
to have a winged dragon seated upon it, but that was a cloud, or
some hallucination. I turned from it in puzzled pleasure, and used
the key with which Philippe's executors had presented me.

Inside, the dimming house would soon be black. I would not bother
to light a lamp, I should be able to find some candles upstairs. As I
ascended, here and there a carnation shaft struck through the shuttered windows from the sky. One such pierced through the ruby
scarab, that today I had put on again, red through red, such a colour
the eyes were besotted by it. I stopped a full minute, gazing, until
the sun had moved. Were her lips as red as that, her cheeks that red,
after she had drunk the blood of Philippe? The old stories said so, but
I did not credit it, any more than I trusted her hands could ever grow
warm.

The Devil, the Devil is in it. But where?

On each floor I paused to rest, supporting myself on the bannister, breathing with a wonderful awareness of air, the machinery of lungs and heart. I bypassed the floor of the bathrooms without a qualm or even a jibe. On the final landing, below the attic stair, something was different. I had begun to breathe in long gasps. My heart beat untidily. My head swam, but it was not from weakness but in a dreadful resurgence of strength.

My sinews, my very skeleton, seemed to toughen. Blood coursed. My eyes went black, then cleared to a sharp perception.

I stared upward, to shadows where the attics began. Then took the steps, opened the door, and went in.

There was the clutter of centuries, much of it older than the house. Every one of the brief lizards had left something, like a pebble laid on a cairn. *Remember* me!

What had Philippe left, then? What had he left for me? Some priceless volumes, some costume bodice of his mother's, crusted with pearls? No, I did not care at all. Already, instantly, across the stacks and mounds, the pillars and tomb-stones of things, I was searching. And there, a round window, shutterless, was burning with the last of the red sky. In its path balanced the wooden rocking-horse, black lacquer, with his fearful grin of teeth, his maenad eyes, and thin blood skimmed on his back from the sunset.

I walked on, stepping around and over things. As I passed him, I touched his rump, to make him go. He creaked and leisurely fell into the motion, sounding like an oar grunting in its lock. Such sins that black horse knew, such confessions. The first taste of lust from the thrust of his hard lacquer saddle between the thighs, the first taste of flight, of getting away, poetry, vision, death-wish, dreams –

Books all over the floors and I stepped on them. Where the Italian chest squared across the window, a movement, too. Then she stood on glass-paned red fire, black-cloaked, cowled like a priest – Yes, the Devil was in it.

I felt her eyes, before I saw them; they drew me forward. If I had been bound, unable, physically, to go to her, my spirit would have gone to her in spite of the flesh, and my heart leapt out of my body. No. There was no need of that. No chain could have held me, seeing her there, her eyes looking into mine.

'I have been waiting for you,' she said. Her voice was very low, very dark. It did not seem to come from her at all, but out of the light, the shadow. 'Since the funeral, I have come here each evening. Seven days, seven nights.'

There must have been a key he had given her. Or did she melt through walls, the way her kind might do – not her *kind*. There was only Antonina.

'Such protestations,' she said. 'Then to make me wait.'

'I was here with you,' I said. 'I must have been.'

'Yes, I think you were. Sometimes, a flicker of the edge of your sleeve, your hair catching a burnish. There, or there. Your ghost. But now, it is you.'

There were also books scattered round the chest. Standing on them, careless of them as I had been, had made her taller than me. She stood above me, in the halo of the dying window, like a madonna. I could only just make out the pallor of her face, which I had kissed, the pale mouth, but the eyes, like the voice, were in a separate dimension. They lived and blazed on their own.

I did not ask her why she had changed to me. It was superfluous; besides, only this made any sense. The denial was the lie.

'Your husband?' I inquired, with no conviction.

But she answered stilly, 'He will do as I tell him. He is only my servant. He serves me. Him I may tell and instruct what he may desire of me.'

'What now?'

'Whatever you wish,' she said.

'And you?' I said. 'You, oh, you.'

She put out her hand and touched me then, first my forehead between the eyes, next the base of my throat, then above the heart. Finally she took up my left hand and touched the ruby ring. I felt each touch, cold flame, like a kiss on my forehead, starting a race in my breast. Even through the stone of the ring, I felt her.

She said, 'I divine that you understand, Andre St Jean.'

Her eyes held me, close to her, held me far off. I could do nothing to her yet, she would tell me when, and very soon.

'Philippe's not watching,' I said.

'I thought that you imagined he might be.'

'No. He believed in nothing. No god. Nothing beyond himself as he was. Nothing after death. He's dead then.'

'But you believe differently. In God, do you believe in God, Andre?'

'Death is God,' I said. 'Life is Man. The day we are born begins our love affair with death.'

Now, said her eyes.

I stepped up on the books with her and she slipped down to a little height, her head against my shoulder, tilted back, her lips parting. Her hair was like a river flowing through my hands, and the hooded

36

cloak, and under it her skin, only some silken thing between us, and her small, her beautiful breasts –

We slid down beside the carved chest, on to the dust and the books, with the window turning wan and grey above us. We slid into the dark –

(Once, somewhere on the shores of those black spaces, the rocking-horse stirred, settling, as if someone had climbed up on to his back).

How slow the rhythm, now, the rhythm of Death's River – it was she who guided me, through the deep spirals of the river's course, its deepest pools. Stars filled the attics, splashed on the air.

Ecstasy was always near, it came and went, swelling, singing, widening, never finished, never begun. Her coldness was warm now, like the snow. Her lips which had come to my throat so quietly, had begun to burn. Her lips were fire. She drew me down and down, into the caverns of the night, where sometimes, far away, I heard myself groan, or her murmuring voice like a feather drifting – Her mouth was fire and her body was snow and the cradling night held both of us. The long endless resonant spasms came and went and came and went like the throb of strings, like the circling wake of the slender boat. She was the ferryman. It seemed to me I had not ceased to look at her. That never once, meeting mine, her burning eyes had closed.

It was almost morning, and all the stars had died . . . Whose face was this, peeking into mine so dolefully? And these damned hands, fiddling with me, worrying at me.

I struck him off. He recoiled.

'Oh monsieur. Christ knows, I thought you were a dead man.'

I was lying flung across the volumes and the old carpets of the attics. Above me towered a hill of carven chest, and over there the wooden horse with its mad and pitiless eye. Between, miles up above me, the carter with a candle, and the bloom of false dawn on him from the window.

'I waited for you, monsieur. And then, I confess, I went and got myself a drink or two. A cold study it was, waiting out there. But I thought, Well, he knows what he's about I suppose. But then, having come back, and nothing in the cart, the bell goes for midnight. I knock on the door. No answer. So then I curl up, in my cart, see, and I take a mite of sleep. No trouble. Once some woman passes. I think to myself, Did she come out of the house, now? Is *that* it? But then she vanishes away and I forget her. Then I'm blowing on my fingers for the cold, wishing I could do the service for my toes, and finally I hear five o'clock. Up to the door again, and now it's open.

So I think then you meant me to come up, and up I come. What a house, monsieur. Horrible, so dark, and empty. They said in that drinking-place, it's haunted by the young man that died here. Vicious murder. But you know that. Then I can hear a noise. I nearly perish of fear I don't mind admitting.'

Through all this I had lain on my back, smiling, my eyes taking in the beams in the pointing ceiling, watching the light begin to return from the dead, the sky deciding if it would put on pinkness or only paleness. What sound could he possibly have heard? Some moan from me, perhaps, sprawled here with my shirt open and my breeches unbuttoned, a ludicrous shambles of some dream I had been having of a woman I wanted to possess.

'It was that rocking-horse,' said the carter, 'creaking and bucking away. No one on it, unless it was you, monsieur, and you fell off. Well, then, here you are. I reckoned you'd been set on. Blood-stains on your shirt. But there's a bite there, on your neck. That will be a rat, no doubt of it. The house is full of them, all rustling away behind the walls. Now if you'll listen to me, you should go straight to a doctor with that bite. Nor you shouldn't have brought a lady here.'

Still on my back, I took out some money, and tossed it to him. He caught it, but looked at me reproachfully.

As he watched me, I sat up and put my clothes to rights. The blood that spotted my shirt had dried to the colour of rotten plums in the half-light. It was the way Philippe's blood had appeared to me. When I tried to rise, I fell.

The carter aided me down all the stairs.

It was true then. Not a dream. Not, not a dream. Antonina –

'And you have a fever, you're burning,' the lugubrious carter congratulated me.

I had not collected my bequest. The carter, not I, closed the door of Philippe's house with a senechal's attention. Then, strong-armed, he put me into his cart, where I lay semi-conscious, euphoric. In this manner I was trundled home, to my landlady's dismay.

I threw myself on my bed, clothed and stupid. Let them have the day, any who wanted it. Sleep, let me sleep. Tonight I would go back to her. And she would come to me.

Thinking of her, as she had been for me, all of it rushed up and overpowered me. Down I fell, through the abyss of the bed, past a grinning rocking-horse with the spectre of Philippe cavorting on its back, past Baron von Aaron in a waiter's uniform, past pages of my books, my childhood, past all the hours of my life, seen as when drowning.

Unfinished, the manuscript lay on the table before the window. There was no need to write any more of it. Let me live it now, quickly through, to the last sentence. And there end. Amen.

When I woke again, it was very late. I wakened with the knowledge of having made a grievous error – oh God, the midnight bell was sounding from Our Lady of Ashes over the river. What had I done?

I must get up, find myself clean linen, run across the City to the house –

I remember I reached the table where the manuscript lay. Nothing else.

I woke again, as in a nightmare, somehow on the bed and dawn was returning. Someone must help me now. Some demon or angel. My head seemed full of the galloping of hoofs as I hurried about. But I was stronger. I could wash myself, I could look into the pitted mirror and even pick up the razor with a steady hand.

How long before I could be ready, how long before I could essay the stairs, the streets? My plan was already made. I must go directly to the house on Clock-Tower Hill. She had said, he was her servant, nothing else. The only impediment had been Antonina herself, when she was afraid of me, before she surrendered herself to the truth.

There was straw on the roadway. This meant that someone on that wealthy avenue was seriously ill. They had put it down to muffle the wheels and hoofs of passing traffic, but there was also a liveried man sitting in the gate, to make sure of proper silence, and perhaps to turn away visitors before they jangled the door bell. It was her gateway he was seated in, and he wore the banker's livery.

I went up to him. 'What is the matter? Is the Baron unwell?'

'No, monsieur. It is Madame who is very sick.'

I gaped at him, and he, more circumspectly, at me. I was dishevelled enough. The day, growing hot, beat down on us both.

'You say – she – Madame von Aaron – is sick.'

'Yes, monsieur. Monsieur, please don't go up to the door.'

'But I – must – I will inquire of the Baron –'

'Very well, monsieur. I will see to it. Who shall I say?'

I swallowed, my throat seemed engorged and hurt me. I glared at the man haughtily. 'Say Andre St Jean.'

'Very well, monsieur. One moment.'

And leaving his post, he went in and around out of my sight,

39

presumably to a side door. I waited a few minutes, expecting to be turned away, to make some scene there on the pavement before the house, having a picture of running to a window and smashing through it.

Was it a plague, the ancient one called the Death? Had we both caught it, she and I, in the house near to the Obelisk where they had burned the corpses centuries ago? Only a hundred years ago, it had returned, that plague. Cloaked death had stalked the City. The crematory chimneys had turned the day sky black, the sky of night into blood, with their ceaseless smokes – so many of the writers of the day had left accounts of it in their journals.

'Please come with me, monsieur.'

The doorman was back. He took me up to the front door, which had now opened. Inside, another man led me over the polished floor, into the side-parlour where I had been shown previously, and there left me.

Would it happen again? She, coming in, telling me she was afraid I had had to wait. And then would I fall on her like a wolf, unable to control either lust or terror? Why did you shut up the house this way? Oh, to be free for you, only for you, she would answer me.

The blinds were down. The room sank in a dull parchment shade. Even the little clock had left off ticking. My hands shook, I paced about. Then the door opened. I turned to it with a stifled shout. The Baron entered.

He looked more frightened than I, that was the first, the only thing I really noticed.

'It is very good of you to call,' he said.

I stared at him. We had both gone mad. Dispense with these ramblings then.

'Tell me what has happened – ' I cried.

'I regret – an illness, an hereditary ailment. We had hoped – '

'Doctors,' I said, 'who is attending her?'

'The most capable physicians, of course, monsieur, I assure you. And among our own household, the use of herbal medicine is not unknown – but in any event – ' he broke off. He said, with sudden and sinister calm, 'You should not be optimistic, Monsieur St Jean.'

I clutched one of the chairs. I said, 'What do you mean? You'd let her die – '

'Oh monsieur, please. You do astound me.'

'Let me see her at once! Where is she? I'll search your house – throw me out and I'll return with the City police. You are not a citizen, Baron. An alien – they can deal with you – '

'Please, monsieur, these threats, these outcries, are uncalled for, and wasteful of your strength.'

'You say to me she's dying – '

'I tell you there is no hope at all.'

I stood there staring. I stared, but saw nothing, and when he poured the cognac for me and put it in my hand, I drank it down, though it might well have been poison. What did I care for that?

'I will tell you, Monsieur St Jean, what it would be best for you to do. Go away now, and come back, perhaps in the early evening.'

'I must see her,' I said. I took his arm, his hand, imploring him. 'Please, for God's sake – '

'Tonight then, if you wish,' he said. 'It's not possible now.'

'You expect me to go, and leave you to get on with killing her – '

He was so serene now before my ranting. He said to me, 'But she has told you my place, has she not?' He withdrew his hand from my grasp, gently. He put his own hand upon my shoulder. 'Now do as I say, monsieur. It is beyond any of us, but I'll assist you as best I can, for as long as I can. You have my sympathies.'

I laughed. This was what I should have said to him.

'I love her,' I said. How vapid, such words. 'If you must kill someone, then here I am.'

'I know you love her. I have nothing to do with any killing.'

Without knowing what I did, I walked towards the door. I could dash up the stair, and fling open all the doors – the commotion of that might finish her, if what he said was a fact. But it was all a surreality. She could not die.

Out in the hallway, I gazed up at the curving stair, and for a moment I seemed to hear the piano being played, above in the salon, but the music only rang through my head.

'There, monsieur,' said the kindly placid cuckold. 'Now do as I say. Return this evening, or I'll send for you if there is any improvement. But that is of course unlikely. It is improbable.'

As he finished speaking, an awful, unearthly, etheric cry tore through the house. The shock of it threw me round on him again, almost taking him by the throat – 'What in God's name –'

'That is her dog, monsieur. Howling. The dog knows, monsieur.'

It was not until I had left the house, not until I was on the hill again, that I comprehended what I had all this while known. It was I who was the murderer. In the blissful whirlpool of adoring, death-wishing delirium, I had never thought *I* might be the poison. Or had she foreseen – was it that which made her hold me off? That fear which finally brought her to me?

I had no strength now. None. But I would return in the evening, duly as he said. Come back and die with her.

The dim piano continued to play within my skull, and now and then the dog howled there, or voices spoke to me, as if into my ears. The borders between unconsciousness and waking, between dream and reality, had long since given way.

Above the door of the *Cockatrice*, the sign of the scaled, snake-headed cockerel turned its look on you and blasted you to a stump. Then you went inside to the damp and greasy cave, where sometimes only the spits turned, or coloured lanterns were lit in the ceiling, so it became hell. Today it was gloomy.

They had all avoided me, the intellectual riff-raff of the tavern. I was a plague-carrier, I was accursed, and they knew it by instinct. No one I had ever known well was present. I guarded my corner like a wounded dog, and nobody drew near. A meal was served me I did not eat, and wine. Sometimes I wrote a line or two on pieces of paper I had found in my coat pockets. Generally I slept. Time had stopped. The day would not move, it sat there on the sills of the slit-eyed windows. The bells, the clocks, they continually kept striking the same hour, three o'clock, over and over. When would I be done with it?

Then I woke and there was a new shadow running with the spilled wine from the bottle. The windows had pulled closer and day been shoved out. I poured the last glass and took a mouthful. The room was unusually silent, and two men in black were before me by the table. How long had they been there? Were they there now, or did I conjure them?

'Are you real then?' I said, with a flippancy that oddly stirred me.

'You are to come with us,' one said to me.

In the cock-snake's cave, eyes glittered out on us. We were an event.

'Sergeant Death, are you arresting me?' I said. 'Who sent you, and why must I go with you?' My heart had stopped, I could not feel it beat. 'From von Aaron? Is she dead?'

'We do not belong to the Baron. But that is the house. Get up, monsieur.'

'Or will you make me?' I said.

'If necessary.'

'It will not be.' I put down the glass. My heart flickered, it had only been sleeping. I did not feel as I had done. I was alert, I was expectant. What had happened? Oh she was alive. That must be so. She was alive. She had sent them for me. Yes, they were hers, these creatures white-faced in their black. 'We'll go then,' I said. 'as quickly as you like.'

I went out jauntily with the death's-heads, one on either side. Plainly, I was a prisoner on my way to execution. Yes, the silken rope about my neck, the dagger of pleasure driven through and through.

People turned to look at us on the streets. The infernal escort, the happy condemned. They did not prevent me when I whistled a popular song of the City, or when I plucked a spray of flowers off a bush growing in a wall, and insanely twirled it. Sometimes I spoke to my guards. I asked them if they had had difficulty in finding me. Not much, they said, my haunts were known. Now one spoke, now the other, but each seemed to have use of the same voice.

From a height, I glanced behind me once, and saw the river, a scimitar of pure metal, white-hot, as the City lapsed in the shallows of the dying afternoon. A boat or two moved on the water, the brotherhood of Charon was out early.

Then they took to the alleys, avoiding the Observatory Terrace, and going around at the back of the tall four-faced clock on the hill, not wanting me to be seen by the influential or the fashionable of the district.

My excitement increased. Sex and anguish were mingled in it, doubt and nervous delight. Most of the straw was swept from the street. No man sat to bar the gateway of the house. I hurried up the steps and rang the bell, and they came on behind me, the two black dogs who had hunted me and brought me soft across the City in their mouths.

The door was opened. I burst in, then stood looking about as if I owned the property.

'If you will go up to the salon, monsieur,' said the domestic.

I ran up the stair. I had not felt the paving stones under my feet throughout our walk here. Twirling the flower-spray, I thought, None of them either conducts me or follows me. I am to go there alone. Something pristine in that. Only the purified accolyte may enter the presence of the high priest.

The salon was full of the last flare of sunlight, its blinds raised. All the dazzling brilliance centred in one flaming entity, before the fireplace.

Antonina stood there.

It was not Antonina.

A man in a white satin coat, all in white but for the long black loosely-curling hair that was the Freedom mode of Paradys for both male and female. Her black brows, perhaps a little more thickly accented, her heavy-lidded eyes, heavily and blackly fringed, blackly burning in the pale triangle of the face that was larger and cut with a bolder hand, and as hard now as white granite.

He looked at me, out of a different distance, for he was some inches taller than I. He said nothing, did nothing, only the left arm, leaning on the mantle, the left hand with a pair of white kid gloves in the long fingers – her hand exactly, grown a size or two, a man's hand, elegant, ringless – that gave a little flick, a little omen of gesture.

I cannot say how long this moment lasted, while he looked at me, and I at him, seeing her, losing her.

Gradually I became aware that von Aaron stood to one side, and two other men with him, advisers or lawyers, or merely witnesses. But even then, I could not look away, look at them. My arms had fallen to my sides. They weighed on me like lead. The boom of my heart shook me. And the black eyes went on burning into my skull. That was all there was.

Then the Baron spoke softly, maybe even timidly, from the wings.

'Monsieur St Jean. I can't prepare you. The news is bad. My wife – we lost her a few hours ago. I see that you already knew it. Well. This gentleman – ' He did not go on, I sensed him slip away again, only his mute gaze on us.

Then the man in white spoke to me.

'I am her brother. Perhaps that is obvious to you?'

'Yes, quite obvious.'

He nodded, as if I had done something clever, a clever trick.

'And you,' he said, 'what are you? In my eyes, what are you? It chances,' he said, in his exact and musical voice, 'that I arrive here and find this. Her husband,' he did not glance aside, 'will do nothing, but, Andre St Jean, I am not insensible to my sister's honour, or to the cause of her death.'

She could not die. I could not proclaim as much.

The light and the dark came with the crashings of my heart, ocean on to rocks.

Well, let him get on with it.

'What do you say now?' he said.

I shrugged, and let the spray of flowers fall to the floor as I did so.

'I will give you my name,' he said. 'It is Scarabin. Anthony Scarabin. You got hold of a certain ring, I believe. A ruby scarab. Yes, well you will give it back, I will take it back tomorrow, after I've finished with you.'

'You mean to kill me,' I found I said. 'Will it be so easy?'

'Nothing,' he said, 'easier.'

He moved from the hearth. He walked across to me, and with his gloves slapped my cheek, so lightly, it might have been an idle caress. He smiled. Her mouth, changed. And the skin, fine and fresh as hers, but more dry, and roughened by shaving.

'What will you have?' he said.

'Whatever suits you.'

'Pistols, then. That is the vogue in your city, I think. Pistols at dawn. Can you come by a gun? How splendid. Will six in the morning be convenient?'

'Most inconvenient. I'm not by choice an early riser.'

He raised one of the black brows at me. Cold, as once she had been.

'Don't play,' he said. 'Answer me.'

'I will accommodate you,' I said.

He said, 'The choice place, I hear, is the wood below the Observatory. Bring your seconds,' he said, 'I shall have mine.'

No one else spoke a word. There was not a noise in the house. Only the sunlight seemed to scrape faintly, as it crept down the windows.

What next? I need only turn and leave the room. It had all been arranged, and now there were things to do besides. How mundane this was. I had not predicted the deadly ordinariness of death.

I would not request that they let me see her body. There was no body. All that remained of her was here, was *him*, this other.

I felt neither exhilaration nor fear. As I walked from the salon, I heard him give a contemptuous little wordless sound, like a note or a chord of music, low down in the register.

Don't play, answer me, he had said that before to me, on Sacrifice Hill. He would know that I remembered him. But then, on that former occasion, when I would have held out the ring, he turned and was gone to his hunting. All this had had to come between. Besides, then, he had only been a demon.

Satanus est.

I walked away into the city, and found a notary. By his reluctant candlelight I set my affairs in as much order as I could, and allocated such possessions as might be of any worth. I had never thought I should do such a thing, or that there would be any margin to do it. For I would be assassinated on the street, or perish in some stupor. Nor was there left me a Philippe, unreliable, impassioned, to take the residue of my writing to the printers, if he ever would have taken it. Would it concern me, in hell or in the grave, to recollect my unpublished works? Who would remember me in a year or two? But in two centuries, who would remember anyone, and in a hundred hundred years, all the paper would have transposed to paste, and dust. All the words, all the concertos, all the shrieking and the shouts, lost in the void of life. Oh, let it go.

The business with the gunsmith did not take long. The barber's took longer.

It did occur to me that perhaps I might also seek a priest, and make to him my confession. But in the end, I had visualised it so thoroughly I seemed to have done it. And I did not want to go over all my sins again. Instead, I composed an ambiguous letter to Russe. I did not call on him. I wanted no one with me when I died but Death himself. He should surely be sufficient.

Having paid my landlady, and told her only that I was going away, I went to bed.

At first I woke several times, choking and panic-stricken. Then I slept deeply. I knew I would wake at the four o'clock bell, and so I did, with a mild surge, as if cast up by a wave upon a beach.

Because I was to die in public, last night my vanity had determined it had better be as beautifully as possible. And so, last night, the barber's shop, with its hirable bath, and then my hair washed and curled and freshly laved in 'Martian' henna. From the launderers' came the shirt with all its ruffles starched, the linen and muslin immaculate, (Philippe's coat), and so on. Even to the boots my vanity went, and had them polished up again with a rubric molasses to bring out their red.

I had put on the ring. He would have to take it from my hand himself.

The gunsmith's man had been told he must make his own way over to the duelling place, with the case of pistols. But he knew where to go. As Scarabin had said, it was the preferred venue for those who wished to kill each other. The Senate winked at such illegal fights. Who could say what went on, at sunrise, in the thick woods below the planet-searching dome of the Observatory, which saw only space and stars?

The sky looked nowhere near the light when I went down the stairs and out into the City. All Paradys seemed to lie dumbfounded under a high black lid. Not a window awake. The street lamps glimmered, drunk to their dregs; many were out. There was a tingle of frost on the air.

Two or three times I paused to drink from a small brandy-flask, a worthless metal thing from which, for a while once, I had never been parted. I was glad of it now. All natural feeling was gone, yet the world seemed far too real, and so insistent. It rubbed its bony sides against me. To die had no glamour left, because the practicalities of its arrangement had revolted me. Yet I wanted it more than ever, with a kind of hunger, and a desperate dread of its complications.

It appeared to me I wandered more than walked, but I had left plenty of time to get there. I even went along a little way by the river, but no slender ominous boat came drifting from the mist.

Then, as I began to climb up into that gorge of masonry, up towards the Observatory hill with the woods lying dark upon its lap, a kind of quickening came again, just as on the stairway of Philippe's house. A terrifying brilliancy, a sumptuous fear. Not the reality I had just stumbled through, but the true reality, dramatically plunging its beak and talons in my vitals, and bearing me up on its wings.

The vault of the night had swung higher, and eastward some rogues had set fire to the sky. I came to the railings and got over them, and walked up the mound of frosty turf, and into the trees.

In the hollow, where it is done, they were waiting. A group of three men there, and there another group of two, where the folding table had been set up and the cases of guns put out. The surgeon sat nearby on a camp-stool, recognisable from his bag beside him, his arms crossed, indifferent. Up on the other slope of the hollow, a couple of carriages stood under the trees. They would have come in by the lane that ran past the Observatory, and would go out again by the same route. I wondered if I should be packed into one of them, or simply left lying, as sometimes happened.

Seeing me arrive, the gunsmith's man was now checking Scarabin's pistols, as one of Scarabin's seconds investigated mine. His pistols had not been hired for the occasion. They looked very white, disembodied, in the twilight. He, too, in the white coat, seemed to float between earth and open sky.

I had forgotten I would urgently *want* to see him, to look at him. I was drawn, pulled over the grass towards him. But suddenly the gunsmith's man got in my way. I tried to put the obstacle aside.

'No, monsieur, wait a moment. There's some irregularity here.' I halted.

'Oh,' I said, 'What?' I thought he was going to say I must have

47

a friend with me, one at least, but I would rejoin it was a formality and dismiss it.

'The bullet in this fellow's gun – there is only the one, and in the one pistol only.'

I looked at him. 'Well?'

'Well, it is – '

I said, 'Silver?' he nodded.

I put my head down, shuddering, as if I had received a blow, and the gunsmith's man caught at my arm. 'Monsieur, you have every right to object – '

'Yes, yes.' I dislodged him. I moved on, towards the being in its white coat. If he was an icon, yet the black boots were planted on the ground. Framed in the priest's cowl of black hair, *her* face, unfamiliar and the same, its cruel changed lips compressed. And the eyes, waiting for me.

Overhead, above the trees, the sky had bled out to nacre.

'Are you ready to begin?' he said.

'Why is there silver in your gun?'

'An eccentricity. Humour me.'

'I can object to it, the man says.'

'But you will not,' Scarabin said. 'Or are you going to dare to prolong this?'

'Where did you get it, the silver? Since you mean it for me, I have an interest.'

'Don't concern yourself,' he said. 'You will be penetrated only by the very best.'

One of the men chuckled, slimily.

'Some heirloom,' I said. 'Holy silver from some priestly cross.'

He stood and gazed back at me, arrogantly, disdainfully.

I said, 'There was another before me. What about that one? Or do you think he will be no trouble?' Did you always do this service for her?'

The men, his seconds (although I guessed he did not know them particularly, more of the Baron's tribe, perhaps), were faint outlines at his back. Did they realise what we spoke of, and think we were mad?

I said to Scarabin, 'I'm sorry now I acquiesced to pistols. That's too removed. I'm sure you were trained to the use of a sword, but I never was, or I would clamour now for two honed blades. I should like to cut that look off your bloody face.'

'Such a pity,' he said.

I stepped up to him and slapped him hard across the left cheek.

His skin was so fair, the blood at once came up like thunder beneath it.

'There,' I said. I nearly laughed aloud. The contact with his flesh – had energised me. 'I am ready to begin, when you are.'

'Oh, come then,' he said, mockingly.

We walked to the table. His hand settled on the nearer of the white pistols.

'I shall require only this,' he said. 'You may take both your weapons, if you wish.'

'One will suffice.'

A man came between us and spoke the litany.

'Gentlemen, your witnesses have been given to understand this meeting is by mutual agreement, and that both of you have made your arrangements suitably. It is understood that the affair can be settled only by a death. Then, gentlemen.'

I tasted frost in my mouth, but already the wind of dawning was combing over the sky. Birds sang. A rook's rasping bleat trailed like a flag as it passaged down into the City. – I saw only the eyes of the man who must kill me.

' . . . Paces to the count of ten. And on the count of ten, to turn and fire at will.'

The speaker stepped away.

We stood, Scarabin and I, under heaven. Then turned, as instructed, to begin our walk.

'One,' said the man who counted, 'two . . . three . . .'

The cord that bound us drew tighter as we moved further from each other. It tautened, ready to recoil, and plunge us home, breast to breast, eye to eye.

' . . . Six. . . seven . . .'

But here is the day, and soon it will be gone. Here am I, but where, tomorrow?

He is making sure, with his silver. Antonina is the quarrel between us, lying at ease in her white coffin now, a white dead hound coiled at her feet. He would take the ring off my finger, but the electric coldness of his touch I should not feel.

'Ten.'

I turned again, in a noiseless spinning roar of lights, and brought up the pistol, sighting along it, not seeing. Just the shining blur of him against the maze of dusk and morning. I moved my arm, letting the pistol tilt, to miss him, and fired directly. In the same second, he also fired at me.

I heard the shot. I heard a tearing sound.

There was an impact. It threw me over and the earth slammed against my shoulders.

This then, was this death? No, he had not hit me. No.

Into the white shield of sky, the elongated dark silhouettes of men came stooping. I lay under water and looked up at them. They wavered and were folded away.

The pain was a spike driven into my arm. There was a rawness in my chest. Ah then, he had hit me. The left arm. I should be able to continue to write. Someone held me, as I lay along the ground, my head was supported. Russe? No, Russe was not with me –

I opened my eyes and the surgeon leaned forward. He peered at me. How insignificant and human were his eyes. 'There is nothing I can do,' he said to me. 'You are a dead man. You comprehend me?' Then, he raised his glance a short way and said to someone, 'You have your satisfaction, monsieur. You will forgive my haste. Good day.'

He rose up once more into the sky and was gone. They were all gone. There, across the grass, a solitary figure stood, in dark livery, and on a leash, a black dog rippled in and out of existence, a phantom thing, and beside it, another. Their black eyes stared at me. They scented blood.

Who was it held me, then, my head on his thigh, the blood staining his white coat?

'Is it you?'

Not a word came out of me, I thought, but he seemed to hear.

'I'm above your City laws,' he said, 'and so not afraid to stay.'

'To be sure of me. Where – am I hit?'

'In the heart. An astonishment you still live.'

I lay above the agony. I could not see him, only the red hair and the red blood, soaking across the skirt of his coat.

'Take the ring,' I said.

'Not yet.'

'When?'

'Presently.'

The tears ran out of my eyes and I did not feel them, or the grief. All my days reduced to *Presently*.

'Go now,' he said to me. His beautiful voice, it gleamed, like darkness. 'You can hardly remain.'

'I haven't any last words,' I said. 'They must invent them for me. Someone must. Dying is like the final moments of the carnal act, I suspected so. The intimation, the galvanic tremor that foreshadows it, then the unavoidable giving way, the surge, the sinking. Yes, I was right. Did I die before, to know it?'

But I had ceased speaking long ago. My lips were fractionally parted on the words I had not whispered. My eyes were wide. And then his cold hand came gently to my face, and closed my eyelids down, carefully, as a mother might brush a leaf from the face of a sleeping child. And I was dead.

The bird was tapping on the inside of the shell. I heard the sharp beak, its noise grated on me. Tap, tap, tap.

Be quiet. Let me think.

I was moving now, it was not unpleasant, there in the dark, to be moving. It was the boat, surely, for it was a wooden thing. Hush then, you need only lie still, and let the rocking lull you back asleep.

Tap, tap, tap.

The bird kept tapping at the shell. It sensed daylight. It wanted to get out.

But I did not want the light, only the peaceful dark.

Then the boat jolted, Charon making an error with his oar, or the Styx was choppy today. Well, I might open my eyes, might look to see what this country was like, after all. My eyes would not open yet. Well, there was no hurry. They were shadowy, the river banks of Hades, not much to gaze at.

My thoughts, unable to lift my eyelids or operate any part of my body, swam up and down within me. Some sensation had returned, for I felt the wooden planks, and the touch of my own linen against my skin, and my own hair.

Then abruptly the boat fell down. It fell and hit the bottom with a smack, rolling me about, making me move my hands and feet and head as I could not myself.

Thereafter, cessation. And then a reverberating thud against the black air above me.

It was the sound of a spadeful of soil flung in on to my coffin. I had not reached the shadowlands: I was still alive; and alive they were burying me.

I tried to shout. I had no voice. I was not afraid. I lay in the dark, and listened to the earth thudding in to cover me up.

This was a foolish thing. I had only to depart. He had told me, someone I had known, he had said to me, *Go now*. It was so close, the Shadow, the River, so near in all its vastnesses. Anything was possible, there. How had I lost my way.

Tap, tap, went the bird. More earth slammed down. Tap, tap.

When the burial was complete, and the last vague shakings and thumpings of my world had ceased, the vagrant thought in me composed itself. Though the bird continued to irritate me by random

51

flinty pecks, the sheer comfort of this state allowed awareness to be reabsorbed. I abandoned the sensations of my outer skin, and sinking inward again, I glimpsed the threshold I had lost, quite suddenly, so accessible and near – and in that instant the bird's beak ripped through the shell like a knife.

I screamed aloud and my eyes flew open. My hands flew up, and took hold of the flimsy botched coffin, and broke it. It shattered around me and the earth poured in, and like a fish leaping from some depth of water, I drove myself upward. I exploded from the pit in a fountain of blackness, soil and stones and splintered wood. Almost asphyxiated, I kneeled in the broken grave, retching and coughing and choking for air: all the horrors of birth.

The moon rose later, as I was lying there. Next I heard bells telling the hour. Where was I? Some ruinous cemetery, with a little church. A coffin of plywood, and the diggers anxious to be off and drink the money from the job. A pauper's makeshift grave; the only reason I had got out of it.

What city was this? Was it Paradys, or some other place? Did Paradys exist? It had been a dream, maybe.

The moon was so cold, staring in my face. It made something glitter, too, lying near me. It had come up with me from the earth, a silver nugget of some sort. I took it in my hand. It was blunted and tarnished, but surely it had been pure?

To leave the vicinity I had to claw my way through brambles, clamber over fallen tomb-stones – a deserted corner. When I came to the church, the door was firmly locked.

As I stood there, I thought I saw a white greyhound rush across the cemetery. What was it chasing? I turned to see.

Then I heard ordinary voices, and some light began to come, weaving through the thorn trees. Two men appeared, gallants going home from some feast, by way of death's garden. They were drunk. They saw me, and exclaimed. The one with the lantern came up to me, leaned over me by the church wall, holding the light high.

'Now what has been happening to you, eh?'

My voice would trouble me. I spoke very low.

'As you see, something unpleasant.'

'Well if your sort will frequent such spots. Why are you dressed like that? Some brute made you, did he? The rotten scoundrel. What else did he do?

He put his hand on my neck, his fingers into my hair. He leaned hard on me. Did I remember these things? Oh yes, long ago.

'What's your price?'

They put the lantern on the ground among the weeds. The first one had me the first, urgently. Then his companion took his turn, and time. When they were done, they left me a handsome sum of money, and as they were buttoning their breeches, the first said to me, 'You were lucky, in meeting us. But another night, better be more careful, sweetheart. Go on home now, and put your dress on.' The other said, 'If she wants to dress herself as a man, I've no objection to it.' And he grinned at me before they careered away through the briars under the moon.

I met an old rag-picker, an old bent woman, as I was leaving the cemetery. She stared at me, as the moon had done. 'Oh, lady,' she said, 'oh lady you are in a fix.'

'I shall be better soon.'

'I thought it was a man,' she said, 'a boy. But there's grave-dirt in your hair.'

'Do you know,' I said, 'is there a monument near here – a monument of plague?'

'Oh, not far. Don't you know where you are, girlie? Been looking for someone, I suppose, trying to dig him out again. Well, it's a sad world.'

'Where is this place?'

'How should I know? Some place without a name. What's my name? What's yours?'

'I – forget – my name – '

'There now. And so it is with that place. All those nameless bones. The headstones weather and wear, if there are any headstones put for them.'

'Young men killed in duels are buried there.'

'Yes,' she snapped, 'and old ones, too, that ought to know better.'

She raised her threadbare body an inch or so, and held my hand as she pointed away towards the Obelisk Gardens. There were no rings on my fingers. She could only be jealous of my youth.

I crept down the ancient avenue, there was such an ache in my side, under my breast. I pressed my palm over it. My boots were too big for me.

Grass grew between the stones, which were pied here and there from the sheep that had been herded through the day before, to the markets – but to which markets, now? And the Obelisk? Yes, the Plague Monument, I had been asking after. I recalled it. Nearby was the house. The house would help me, perhaps, if I met no one on its stairs . . .

Further bells rang in the City. I did not note the hour they struck. The night seemed in suspension, between dark and dawn affording me as much time as I should need to reach my sanctuary.

And truly, like a temple's high altar it was, the house, the moon behind it, the aisle of the street blotted all through by shadow.

Up the steps, and oh, the ache in my heart, I went so slowly, and leaned my forehead on the door. Not boarded up. But locked, as the church had been, and yet I had a key – perhaps? I rifled the pockets of my curious clothes, and found a key which seemed the one I sought. It entered the lock of the door, and mastered it with the formal goodwill of a handshake.

A black chimney, the house, with the spine of the stair ascending. Familiar scents were dying. New smells of vacancy. With the turning of the seasons, damp would come, beetles would eat the wood and mice gnaw through the walls. The house would collapse at last like a dead tree.

I climbed, sometimes stopping to rest against the bannister. My debility was luxurious. If I wished, I could fall down and lie there. Who would ever come to disturb me? Yet I must reach the top of the skull, the attic. Why was that? Someone had left me something – it must be collected, for it was mine.

The attics, when I did reach them, had a familiarity I had missed in the remainder of the house. For instance, I remembered reading the books lying about the floors, and hiding in various parts of the hoard. I had often ridden the rocking-horse. It was on one of these rides, it seemed to me, a child of perhaps nine or ten, that I made the decision I did not want to live as a girl or woman. There had been a contrary example constantly before me, a snow-blond male child of my own age. He had taunted me and provoked me. Always copying him, I was never quite successful, while I remained female. Eventually I took the logical step. I altered. I became what he was: a boy. And later I remained masculine as I grew up. Here I was still in both their clothes, the garments of the blond Philippe, and of the young man who, until very recently (but how recently?) had been myself.

Presently I opened the press where Philippe had stored articles of his mother's wardrobe. She had been a tall, slender woman; we were of a size. The clothes would seem strange to me at first, as my voice had done. But that would not linger. (The fortunate mode of Paradys had outlawed any but the lightest corsetry). My body itself was a garment only partly recognised. There was a deep stain on the breast of the shirt, but nothing on my skin over the heart. The grime of the burial, too, had been shaken from me; it was mysteriously and satisfyingly gone, which was as well, for there would be no water left in the cisterns of the baths, no soaps in the jars. But here were ivory-backed brushes for my hair, and the pearl-handled nail-clippers. How did I seem now?

My night-sight, sharpened by immersion in the ground perhaps, had been good enough for my wanderings and seekings so far, but, as I bound my waist with a sash, I had an urge to *regard*. There was a candle in the stand I located and lit with matches from a discarded male pocket. Holding my light, then, I went towards the one round unboarded window at the attics' end. There was no other mirror.

And in the black panes I saw my dim reflection, a young woman with a cloud of long and curling hair reddened by 'Martian' henna. Nothing amiss with her, just a faint mark to the left side of the throat. I returned immediately to the press and took a woman's lace stock, and wrapped my neck and breast in it.

I had just filled one of the mesh purses with all the left-over items of my male pockets, when I heard, four storeys below me, the house door grate, hesitate, then thunder open.

All the house clanged like a bell, roof to cellars. A fine trembling like a fine dust was left in the air.

Then came footsteps, jumping, stamping, running and stumbling up the house, just the route I had come, but headlong and precipitate.

I took my purse, and the discarded apparel of Andre St Jean, and walked across the attic softly, as the other footsteps blundered nearer, shaking the building to its roots. I left the candle burning on a stack of volumes close to the rocking-horse – as I passed the beast, too, I put a hand on its hindquarters and set it going vigorously. There was a large Italian chest by the window. Lifting its lid, I threw in the clothes, the purse, and got in after them. Here I was again, in my coffin. I lowered the lid of the chest, and the door of the attics burst wide with a crash.

There were two arrivals. They paused as one. Then, through my wooden crate, I heard:

'Look at the candle! And the horse prancing – my God, someone *has* been in this room.'

'But no one is here now.'

'They say it's haunted, this bloody place. How not, the things that were done here? Oh, perhaps.'

I knew both voices. What were their names? One deeper than the other, heavy as if leaden.

'The front door had been unlocked. Can a ghost not pass through a door? Does it need keys, and candlelight? Well, who knows. That fool. Why couldn't he explain himself in his letter.'

'Andre is – Andre was mad. He and Philippe.'

'It was in my mind, he must do something unwise. The insanity over the woman. Then her death.'

'I told you, Russe, I heard them saying at the *Iron Bowl*, there was another duellist's body found in the Observatory woods.'

'That's not unusual.'

'They buried it, as always – no identity, and no questions. That was before dawn yesterday. But when did he send the letter to you?'

I listened, marvelling. When he said, this second man, whose name was surely LeMar – when he said 'dawn yesterday' he meant a morning gone, one day and night. Could it be that I had lain all that great while, deliberating, between ending and resuming, before I moved and flung up from the prison? It had seemed to me to be only minutes.

'It may be Andre has only gone away. They think so at his lodging. This is what his letter implies. But I am perturbed by the reference to a debt to this man, this Anthony Scarabin.'

'*Her* brother – Russe, Russe. Don't you see? Scarabin shot him. Andre is dead, and in a grave. We've searched the City. Where else could he be but under the ground.'

'Here in this house.'

'Yes, *in this house*. We come searching, we see the flicker of a light and rush in – but where is Andre, tell me that. Oh, he is here. He is here, Russe, but not in the flesh. Ah *God*!'

The cry was sudden and full of a kind of gratified terror.

Russe only cursed, in his heavy way.

It came to me the candle had been blown out abruptly, by an invisible agency.

I heard the noises of the flight of that one, that LeMar – Le Marc – all down the stairs again, howling, and out into the street.'

But Russe remained, and he said, 'Andre? Andre, are you truly dead and truly here?' (I had the desire to answer, sepulchral, from the chest. But he would not know my voice now.) 'Ah, Andre, if you are. I warned you. Horror and sorrow, unholy things. You were a fool to meddle with it, Andre. Well, I'll go to the house of the Baron. I will ask him outright. It must be settled.'

I crouched amid the chest and heard Russe in his turn go down the stairs. Then I rose up. I started – for the first tide of daybreak was in the window. I could see by it the candle, smoking.

Perhaps Philippe and I had played another game upon our friends.

Of whom had Russe been speaking? This Baron. I must follow the two men, and learn.

The lid of the chest fell, shutting in, conceivably for ever, perhaps, the shed bloodied skin of dead shot Andre. I had the bullet, however. It must have worked its way out like a splinter.

I took up one of the woman's veiled hats, the mesh purse, and a pair of respectable gloves, and went quickly down the house, ignoring the soft cracks and hissings it made at me. I locked the front door, then tossed the key high, at the crowns of the trees growing from the old City Wall.

Andre had known the way to the Baron's house, but I was not so certain. The peculiar light before sunrise showed me the agitated figures of the two men, about a hundred metres up the street. If they should chance to look back, they would think me only some lady of darkness hurrying to her lair, or lady of virtue hastening out to church.

I felt much stronger now. I felt the edge of laughter, but scarcely any pain, under my breast.

And how quaint the lady's shoes sounded on the pavement.

We went downhill, and crossed a terrace, and heard, far below, the City stirring.

They climbed another hill, my guides, with a clock-tower on it. I climbed after.

We came to a street along the hill's inner shoulder, and here memory sharply returned. The stuccoed houses were still asleep and blank as mausoleums, all but one. There was already some activity there. A pair of carriages stood outside the wrought-iron gate, reminding me of another pair of carriages, or the same, under the trees above the duelling hollow. Grooms had been holding the heads of the horses; now a coachman came and got up on the box of the foremost vehicle. Russe was on the pavement, arguing with a domestic from the house. Both spoke intensely, quietly, not to wake the street, LeMarc sometimes joining in, flapping at the house, the carriages, the sky.

Across the road I spied on them, concealed in another gateway.

LeMarc had turned towards the iron gate, now ajar, and the steps. The domestic tried to restrain him. The voice of Russe rose suddenly.

At that moment, the house door opened. Something was coming out. In the twilight, so pale it seemed to float of its own volition, a faceless glimmering shape – but two servants bore it between them. It was a milk-white coffin. Down the steps, the gate opened out for it. A groom pulled wide the carriage door. They eased the coffin into the interior.

It had had its effect, this manoeuvre. LeMarc was immobile, nonplussed. Russe had foolishly removed his hat.

And now the Baron, the banker, von Aaron – I recalled him very well – was coming down the steps. I listened with great concentration, and heard him say, to Russe, 'This is not the time, not the place. What is it you can want?'

'We are concerned,' said Russe, holding his hat, 'for the safety of our friend. Monsieur St Jean. I believe you, or your guest, may be able to help us in the matter,'

'I? How can I do that? Her brother, to whom I take it you are referring, has insisted that the body of my wife return with him to – to a previous residence. I am to follow. As you see, that second carriage is already loaded with my trunk and boxes. There is no time now, to discuss any of this. If you must, you may call on me upon my return.'

'When will that be?' said Russe.

'I'm not certain, monsieur. You must excuse me, you really must. I'm surprised, monsieur, at your lack of taste. To accost me at such a moment, almost across the corpse of my wife.'

Russe stood, frowning and out of sorts at this reproach.

LeMarc cried, 'And the duel? There was one – you admit as much?'

Von Aaron said nothing. From the porch above, a clear voice cut sinuously and crystallinely down, like a fencer's sword.

'If that is your problem, you must address yourselves to me.'

There, in his white, white as the coffin, my enemy, gazing at them from his battlements of flawless arrogance and contempt. My heart leapt. The pain of death's memory wracked through it: my heart recollected. And in the purse of mesh the silver bullet, blunted on my muscle, flesh and bone, seemed to jump and scrabble.

'Then,' said Russe doggedly, 'we do so address ourselves.'

The man Anthony Scarabin, descending to the street, said in passing, 'I can tell you only this. Your friend caused harm. I therefore shot him, two mornings ago. You will find his grave, I believe, in the derelict cemetery that is generally used for such purposes. And now, if you would move aside.'

As if they could not refuse, they obeyed him. Then as he stepped into the first carriage (which contained the coffin), LeMarc bawled: 'You murderer!' But Russe took hold of LeMarc's arm. From Scarabin there was no reply. (And from the flat windows all about, not a face squinted out.) The groom closed the carriage door. The coachman unfurled his whip. The horses came to life and sprang forward. With a grumbling jangle, the carriage was off. It bowled along the street, and up on to the crest of it. Watching, each of us beheld it run away, looking weightless as a shadow-ball, around the tower with the clock, and then, taking the downward path, it was gone.

'This is not over with,' said Russe.

LeMarc broke out shouting, and just as quickly broke down in silence.

'I shall present the business to lawyers,' said Russe.

Von Aaron nodded.

'On my return, I will be at your disposal. But now you must let me get on'. He nodded to them, and turned abruptly, marching back into the house. The door was shut by the domestic, who had followed him. The one remaining carriage, humped with its luggage, without a coachman still, and with only the groom beside the horses, waited like a thing of stone, in the stony light.

For a few instants, LeMarc continued to complain and flail. Then Russe had him in hand. Russe declared there was no point in their loitering there any longer. They would go straight down to the Justiciary, and be ready when the doors opened at eight o'clock.

Once they had dwindled from the street, the groom took out of his pocket some pieces of bread and dark chocolate, and began to eat them hungrily.

When I emerged from my gateway, crossed the road and approached the carriage, the groom did not look at me with any special interest. When I opened the carriage door and got into it, he said merely, 'Now – ' but nothing else. Obliged to keep the horses in check, he did not pursue me, nor call again.

I placed myself on the upholstered seat, adjusted the veil of my hat so that my face was lightly filmed, put my gloved hands on my purse, and waited for von Aaron to come back.

He was not very long. Probably he had only gone in again to evade Russe and LeMarc. Now the coachman also came, and going round, got up on the box. I heard the groom say in an undertone, 'Some girl has got into the carriage.' The coachman grunted with no amazement.

But von Aaron, when the groom had opened the door for him, froze in the middle of his ascent into the vehicle.

'Who the devil are you?'

'Your fellow traveller.'

59

'This is,' he said, still bowed over in mid-entrance, 'a private coach.'

'Quite so.'

'Then please get out, mademoiselle.'

'I will not,' I said. 'You had better get in, instead.'

His engraved face loomed before me, at a loss. Then he pulled himself up and sat down across from me. The groom hovered at the door and von Aaron indicated this fact with his hand.

'Must I have you ejected, mademoiselle?'

'Don't consider such a thing.' I stared at him through the veil. 'I am going where you are going.'

'And where is that?'

'After the other. The man in white, and that white coffin. It's perfectly simple. Why delay us both.'

His hand went into his cuff of metallic lace and drew out a lace handkerchief. He put it to his brow and lips. His eyes never left me. Finally, he said, 'It occurs to me that I know you, mademoiselle.'

'Not at all.'

'Yes. I've seen you before. I – ' quite suddenly his face grew very white and still. Only the lips separated from each other, and the eyes darted up and down me, up and down. There could be no doubt; I was a woman. He was thinking to himself, was he, that I was some relation of Andre St Jean? A cousin, perhaps, or a sister. At length he glanced away, at the hovering groom, and told him to withdraw and to shut the door of the carriage. The groom did so. He went back into the gateway and stood there looking at us, not much intrigued, surreptitiously slipping slivers of chocolate into his mouth. Von Aaron said, 'You will render me your name, mademoiselle, at once.'

I lowered my eyes. I replied deliberately, 'My name is Anna Sanjeanne.'

There was a pause. The difference in the 'Sanjeanne' was very slight from the one he had been expecting. It caught and held him, trying it over, licking his lips. The handkerchief fluttered again. I closed my eyes, my hands folded upon the purse in my lap.

'And you – he said, 'you will not get out?'

'No I will not get out.'

'God in Hell,' he said. He swore. He compressed the handkerchief and thrust it away. Then, he leaned from the window and shouted at the coachman. As von Aaron lurched again into his place, the whip cracked outside and the vehicle juddered. We began to move, rolling forward, the wheels grinding over the stones, as I had seen happen with the first carriage.

Sleep, or faintness, stole over me. I leant my cheek against the seat's cushioned support, my head turned from the Baron towards the other window. The world swam and streamed, all Paradys streaming away. My lids fell again.

Von Aaron said to me from far off, 'I shall not, mademoiselle, exchange another single word with you. You must understand this.'

'Do as you please,' I murmured.

He laughed bitterly, just once.

The jolting of the carriage as it gained speed joined with the furious knocking of my heart. The roar of wheels and hoofs flowed in my brain. Awareness, Paradys, they poured off me together. The City was going, being left behind, as if we lifted into the morning sky. Somewhere, thin and hard and pure as steel, a thread led away out of the labyrinth, at the other end of which there ran before us a blazing gem of white.

The carriage travelled through the day, almost as the sun did. There was only one brief stop.

In the first hours, I saw very little from the window, after the fragmentary passing of the City. Once, after we had clattered across the great bridge that spanned the last northern loop of the river, a vagary of the curving road laid out before me one ultimate vista of Paradys. It rested behind us in a valley of light, glittering there like water, for the day was already growing hot. The towers and domes had melted down into the molten whole. It was a landscape solely, only possibly inhabited. And thereafter, the only bells we heard, the speechless, sweating Baron, and I, were the sheep-bells from the orchards and pastures at the roadside.

Later, the dust came and furred the windows, already shut by glass and sun. We rushed then through a pollinated world, lost in bright mist. When there were woods, the carriage darkened. Here and there a fountain jetted from a rock, or a stream-bed widened, flashing like diamonds.

I slept, or swooned, rising in and out of deep silences to the clash of wheels and the groans of the vehicle. I was not alarmed he would set on me, my companion, that I should be taken up unconscious and thrown out on to the road. He had acceded. He had given in to destiny which had assumed my form.

At noon, the sun was overhead, striking the carriage roof with its spears. I rose from my stupor and lay in another one of unbearable heat and savage excitement. I was proceeding where I must. I was a creature that was itself beyond all transgressions, all impediments.

61

I could revel in that, half-dead in the heat and deathless, as the Baron mopped his face and drank water from a travelling bottle.

Afternoon came, and all things slept but we. Black sheep lay in the shade of colossal oaks. Crows on a parched field stood as if petrified. Blond wheat parted at the wind of our passage, and closed again together like the tines of a fan. Black as agates, the grapes on the vinestocks, among the grey and dusty leaves –

About three in the afternoon, came the halt. There was an inn above the road, and the horses were to be changed. As it was seen to, a man materialised at the Baron's window, and handed in a hamper.

The Baron unfolded for himself a wooden tray, and spread a napkin over his knees. He ate shiftily, then took a goblet from the hamper and a bottle, uncorking and pouring the red wine. Now the glass bulb glowed like a huge garnet. He gulped the glass, spoiling it.

Just before we started up again, von Aaron, discarding the remains of his meal, the tray and napkin, leaned diagonally across the carriage and offered me a glass of the garnet wine.

'The day is very hot.' He apologised for showing kindness or pity, breaking his vow not to speak. But I respected the vow. I raised the veil of the hat, and drank a little wine. A very little – I had no intention that nature should force me to quit the carriage. Though he superstitiously dared not put me out, an independent withdrawal would obviate destiny in an instant.

When I set down the glass, he was staring at me in distressed fear. He shook his head, retrieved the goblet and himself swallowed all its contents. Then, he spoke again. 'Mademoiselle St Jean, if you would reconsider. Do you see that inn? It's very pleasant. I have money here – and I must come back this way, and can then . . . Surely –'

'No.'

'Why this stubbornness?' he pleaded. 'What can you hope for?'

What indeed? The hope, ghostly, unclaimed, flooded me like fire at his question.

'We were not to converse, I thought,' said I. 'And you have misremembered my name.'

The man appeared at the window for the hamper, and von Aaron pushed it out to him. He dropped a coin in the man's hand. Hamper, wine and waiter moved away.

Perhaps a quarter of an hour had elapsed. The coachman called a query from his box. The Baron shouted out to him to go on. Nor did the Baron evince any want or need to vacate the carriage.

The new horses started forward with all the rush of the old.

Towards sunset, when a pink-geranium glare filled the vehicle, the Baron spoke again.

'I think, Mademoiselle St Jean, that we should talk.'

'Formerly, you thought otherwise. You were then correct.'

'Mademoiselle – Mademoiselle St Jean –'

'Sanjeanne, if you must.'

'This is very ill-advised on your part.'

'You believe so.'

'This venture. Let me tell you what I conclude. That you have some strange irrational dream of vengeance on your mind.'

'Vengeance for what, pray?'

'The death of your brother.'

'I have no brothers, Baron.'

'The – gentleman whom you saw leaving my house in the City – he is not to be trifled with. You should not – I'm telling you, mademoiselle, you are embarked on a dangerous course.'

I laughed. A girl's laughter, it came to me unexpectedly and delighted me a moment.

We plunged on through the radiant pink light, and pines began to come along the road, which rose upward, upward. Then we entered a great vault of geranium sky, with, hanging in it, cliffs and spires of rock, the dark forests boiling over them, and the sun, a transparent burning-glass, only the colour of the air.

As I gazed at it, he said quite crisply, 'You will have to cross the northern border, mademoiselle, if you mean to go on with this. Do you have papers?'

But it was the beauty of the sunset which was real. The Baron apparently did not understand about the being of reality, its translucence, its elasticity.

When the sun sank, the forests closed on us. Now it grew chilly. Timelessly time advanced.

It was near midnight, and I was numbed and stiff with cold. I had slept further it seemed, or at any rate, been absent from the carriage where my body journeyed. Now, the carriage had stopped again.

This, and the stealthy movements of the Baron, had alerted me, but I gave no sign. I lay motionless, scarcely breathing, my eyes shut. Soon I heard the carriage door softly opened. Something eased itself out, and then the door was tenderly closed. A footstep on earth. One of the horses blew and stamped, and the carriage rolled and steadied. Nothing more.

I opened my eyes. Beyond the windows the pine trees pressed on the carriage. Between hung the lucid avernal daylight of full moon.

Von Aaron was gone. Not prompted by any natural urge –

Sufficient space allowed, I lowered the window and looked out with care.

The road had become little better than a track, packed earth littered with small shards, through the edges of which the roots of the trees had sometimes clawed. And there indeed was the coachman, box deserted, plodding in between the pine stems to relieve himself.

Ahead, a second carriage stood across the road, blocking the way. It was like a phantom thing; it had no horses in the shafts, and no driver.

I opened my door and got out, the far side of the vehicle from von Aaron's coachman. I walked along the track in the moonday-night, past each pair of black horses, and then across the interval of track between the carriages.

The vehicle which blocked the road had, within its body, a white coffin, whiter than the moon. It rested on the floor where one of the long seats had been removed to facilitate its presence. On the opposite seat lay a pair of pale kid gloves.

I went beyond the carriage, walking now off the track, among the pines. The road dipped up and down, and just over the brow two men stood. I heard the voice of one of them, I hesitated, then stole on until I was some nine or ten metres away.

'Well, you must send her back again. Take her yourself, since I tell you you will be going.'

'I think,' von Aaron said, 'she lacks documents. She could not cross the border.'

'Well then.'

'This is your last word.'

'As you are aware.'

Scarabin, tall and slender, a pillar of ice, black midnight of hair poured down his back. The other fawning, placating, angry and helpless. Before them both, the lands of night. The moon rode high, stopping for no one.

'She was sleeping,' said the Baron.

'Perhaps.'

Von Aaron looked back apprehensively, directly at me, staring into my face, and did not see me at all.

'Do you suppose? But where could she go?' Back again he looked at Scarabin. 'I will put her out, if you tell me to do so, Anthony. She would be lost in this place. Let me come on with you, as it was arranged.'

64

'Who arranged it? You. Your constant expositions. Return to that City where you let her out, where you let her do as she wanted.'

'I? How could I prevent it – how can I answer you – what terms will you accept? It is *you* – '

They were no longer speaking of me, but of another. Of Antonina.

And Scarabin turned in that moment too, and thrust von Aaron from him.

'I'm tired of listening to this. You have no say in any of it. You'll do as I tell you, nothing more. Now get away, get out of my sight.'

But, 'There are the horses coming,' said von Aaron importunately, pointing down the track ahead. Black movement from the black pines there. A fresh team of drays being brought for the foremost carriage, to replace others already taken. Some village hereabouts, or some other servitor of Scarabin's.

'Anthony,' said von Aaron now, 'you may yet need me – '

There was no strategy in overhearing any more. I turned and retraced my way through the skirts of the pine shadow, to Scarabin's carriage. I opened its door and entered it, and shut myself in. There was a vibrancy in the air of it, scentless, tuned and pitched. I put my hands on the lid of the white coffin. How secure? But I had broken one such box already.

I drew up the lid with ease, it had not been secured at all.

Within, in the dark bed of silk, a woman's outline was deeply imprinted. I had known there would be nothing else. I had known that Antonina was not here, not *here*. Instead, I stepped into the silk, and lay down in this shape of her, which fitted me. Then I drew the lid up and resettled it. This time, some jigsaw groove connected with another. It sealed itself above me.

I placed the mesh purse under the folds of my skirt, and crossed my hands over my breast. I had not lain so eloquently or so neatly before.

How peaceful the dark was, out of the strident moon.

In a short while I heard the horses come up, and that they were being backed into the shafts. A man vaulted to the box. Then, the door opened. He came into the carriage, he, Scarabin. I knew him, by his step, the susurrous of the coat he wore, the faint intake and expiry of his breathing. Now he sat, now took up the gloves and threw them down again. Now the beautiful voice called out its order to the driver.

Hoofs trampled and wheels revolved. The carriage was angled and positioned and set northward on the road, and with only this prelude, exploded into a great and nearly maniacal speed. The floor bounced under me. I was stunned by it, by the intimacy of its noise and motion. Then a light gentle impact came above, the click of a boot-heel. Anthony Scarabin had put his feet up on the coffin.

We came to the border.

I was by now hypnotised in my shell. I heard, or felt, the carriage draw up. At the window, muffled voices courteously insisted that the passenger must descend. He did so. Out on the roadway, I heard a man say to him, 'And the coffin. Regretfully, we must inspect it.' In response I could ascertain only the notes of his voice, no words. But then the door was opened, and rough nervous hands came down on the lid of my shelter.

I ceased at once to breathe; I had learnt this knack in the grave. As the lid sheared off, moonlight and shadow sprinkled me like cool water. A man drew in his own breath harshly, then let it go in a long sigh. I sensed, but did not see, that he crossed himself. Then the lid was awkwardly replaced, grating about until the grooves again engaged, and the dark, my coverlet, covered me.

'Your papers are correct. My condolences. Your sister's death is a great misfortune. Ah, a sad loss, so young. She seems only sleeping.'

Scarabin re-entered the carriage. Orders were spoken on the road. The horses broke into their run. We raced across the northern border.

He had carried the box from Paradys for show. He had therefore required papers which noted it. Finding such luggage empty the border's watchdogs might have torn the receptacle apart, but a vacant coffin was no crime, an eccentricity, like a silver bullet . . . But full, such a sad loss, the young sister, looking only as if she slept. He knew now he had company.

Would he speak? Would he himself lift off the lid, and should I see that face look in at me, and those eyes?

He might do anything.

He had had melted down the silver of Antonina's wedding rings, that had made the ammunition for his duel with me before. He was inventive, and capable, and quite as fey as I.

Nothing happened for a little while.

Then he called again to the driver, and the carriage halted, the driver dropped down and was at the window.

Scarabin said: 'You see this?'

Together they raised it from the floor of the carriage, and I was borne a short distance, as it seemed, from the road.

Cautiously, as I was swung with the coffin in their grasp, I raised both hands and pressed against the lid. I could not in any way shift it. Some trick of the grooved mechanism made the box accessible only from without.

'Here. This will do,' said Scarabin, above me.

The coffin was lowered, and let go. A slight fall, yet it jolted every bone of my body. I repressed the urge to laugh at his malice.

I made out their footsteps, retreating.

Then, in another minute, from some way off, I heard the carriage start up and tear away. After that, came a great stillness.

Having spontaneously evicted myself from the earth of a grave, the insoluble problem of the coffin bored me. I lay and did nothing, did not even think of it. I thought only of the carriage bounding along the tracks and roads between the pines. How should I find it? How catch up?

My mind flew after, never lost him. But I never could. Wherever he might go, my dearly beloved enemy, into whatever dim, invisible reach, I must come on him again at last, by design, or by accident. We could not be parted.

I relaxed, I composed myself.

What now?

There was a scratching on the lid of slumber. As I wakened I knew better than to call encouragement. Perhaps some hopeful thief had found me. He would be frightened off if the corpse merrily greeted him. Or perhaps it was some bird at work, or a large insect taking its constitutional along the lacquer.

Then the coffin-lid moved. Brightest daylight entered like a dagger. As I lifted my hands to assist, the lid was abruptly shovelled off and fell away. Against a blinding lace-work of leaves and sky, I saw the pagan beast-face of Satan himself, gazing in at me. A handsome black goat with a long Roman nose, and whorled medallions of horns.

I sat up with a cry of elation, and he frisked away.

I came from the coffin and stood in a young meadow. The spot was fringed by pines, but a wild orchard bloomed between, and here the goats were feeding. The tindery sweet scents of morning sun on clover, the wholesome stink of the herd, were here and there touched by the fermentation of fallen red apples lying in the grass. There was no sign or symptom of any road or track.

I cast off the veiled hat into the coffin, and took up the mesh purse and spilled it over the silk. Like the field-lily, it seemed to me I had no need of items such as money, paper, or matches. So I buried the latter, for fear they might combust and set the land on fire, and left the rest. What a sight it made, the opened coffin on the grass, and the papers and the coins, and the hat. The silver bullet alone I placed in the bodice of my costume.

Then I strayed away over the meadow, among the feeding goats, and picking up an apple, ate the red skin and the white flesh of it.

Possibly I might come on a goatherd. I would say, Where is the road? And he or she, meeting the eyes of Anna or of Andre respectively, would blush and hoarsely inform me there were no roads at all: this was Elysium.

But I met no goatherd.

Light and shade rained down and spangled everything. Then, on a slope beyond the orchard, I found a path after all, not wide enough for any carriage, yet I followed it. What did it matter if I lost my way? I should find it again. Help was always available. And he, like the moon in the sky of night, could not hide himself for very long.

The day was an idyll. I think I never spent such a day. Perhaps I had, as Andre; some picnic or excursion into the hills above the City.

I was all alone in a country that had no human things, only sunshine, trees and wild flowers, only the strands of streams and huge boulders clung with moss. Birds flashed and fluted. And though I saw animals playing and eating, never once did I discern a cot or hut, let alone a village, let alone the mirage of any distant metropolis.

How quickly it came and went.

Noon passed over like a wave, and afternoon, three waves, or more. The sun westered, the world slipped back towards the shadow.

High among the pines, I came on a stone that might have been an altar. Beyond, the forest lessened. Far away, miles away, in a cup of distance, I saw an architectural structure, which I knew from some dream.

Going down the escarpment I lost the view, but found a broad stream, not at all shallow. It wound away northwards, under the trees. Not quite a river, but by the stones, a small narrow boat with one long pole, lay tethered and waiting.

Though not underground, the Hadean stream coiled through the trees, and night began to fill the hollows and put out the afterglow. Then a mist did rise, out of secret places in the banks; cold and fragrant. I stood in the boat and poled my way along. Often a fierce current drifted us downward with no labour on my side at all.

Blackness came, and black willows swept to the stream. I poled my way through mourning-veils. The pines seemed more animal than floral. Did they move about when I had passed, with huge soft steps? The mist encircled my thighs, my waist, but rose no higher. And now I myself was Charon.

Suppose this is not the way? Then I will find it at another hour. Is there time? All time and none.

How wonderful it was, the sense of abandonment. All things gone but one focused goal. And that pristine and sure, whatever was or would be between. Liberty. Truth. To have two names, and neither, to be one being now, and there another, and perhaps no one, perhaps all. Here is the dark, and here am I, *of* the dark.

I followed the graceful stream.

It came at me suddenly, with an awesome shriek. I could not see what it was, but I raised the pole and swung the length of it between us. The merest collision resulted, but the pole shuddered and the boat pitched. Not quite letting go the pole, I fell to my knees.

From the blackness, two albino eyes, a beak of burning wire. Wings. It flung itself at me again.

Some nocturnal bird I had dismayed, or some guardian of transit.

The feathers of its black wings guttered and ignited as it threw itself at me again and again. Now an eye seared. Now the beak stabbed for my throat or sight. A talon scored my hand. It dashed itself against me, to take the blood, and I let go the pole and seized its neck like a snake's, and broke it.

I hurled the corpse into the stream, the night.

Horror and hell were all around. I had no strength. I had fallen down into the boat and lost the guiding pole, also my only weapon.

Fool, to abandon the reality and laws of the sensible world, to set out on this perilous course.

Now I lay in the boat as in the coffin, less optimistic than then, and only the current drew me on.

I cannot go to you armed then, in armour. When I approach with pride, with a book, a loaded pistol, these are of no avail.

The stream ran fast now, and straight. We plunged out under the open sky. The moon had not risen, yet there it was, down among the trees. The boat sidled to the shore, and rocked there, refusing to continue.

I was following the moon. A land moon, crossing the surface of the earth. She glimmered between the trees. I reasoned to begin with that this must be some man or woman, at last, and carrying a lantern.

The village, to which the moon led me, was deserted. It lay outside a palisade of trees, all up an incline, like fallen stones. As I came out into its grass-grown lanes, among the toppled chimneys, I saw for the first that what flitted along before me was the figure of a girl. She passed through the houses in a way that gave me to suppose she was not solid, not flesh.

Where the derelict village ended, the land opened to a sheet of black mirror, a tarn of water. The girl, a quarter of a mile away from me now, seemed to glide out on to it, bobbing there like a candle-flame, but when I too reached the brink, there was a massive causeway, with huge paving-blocks, well able to accommodate a carriage.

After the causeway and the tarn, appeared the structure I had seen at sunset.

It was a ruin, of course. In the darkness the impression was of solitary standing walls, perforated by round glassless spoke-framed windows, like colossal wheels, similar to those found in ancient churches. Higher than the highest, a tower broke the sky. It was out of all proportion to the landscape, or so it seemed, too tall, like a funnel spun of black night, yet it also was cleft at the top, blasted wide as if by the hand of God.

The glimmer of the ghost-girl went up the shore and in among the ruin like a moth attracted to warmth or light. There was light. I made it out as I drew closer.

In a wall against the tower, a featureless door had been cut, and the ground rose up to it in a flight of steps. Above this door a window like a spiderweb held a sonorous living glow.

The ghost, if she was, had disappeared. No carriage, and no horses, were in evidence. Only the lit window. The tower leaned and the wind of night sighed through its great axed cranium, the alleys of shattered corridors, the window-wheels, as through the fingers of the pines.

I climbed the sunken, uneven steps, and touched the door, which opened.

It was a priest's chamber, perhaps the ruin was indeed that of some religious building. The light came from a pale and leaping fire, and from candles in silver stanchions. There were a few pillars, with a soft, grey-velvet texture, a long table of darkest mahogany, pulled close to the fire, with some objects on it of glass that caught the flames and reflected them down into the wood. Three silver crucifixes of various heights stood on the sculpted mantelpiece above the hearth, and above these, hung a sword in black chains. This was all the room seemed to contain.

I shut the outer door, and advanced across bare flagstones. As I passed the table, a crystal apple on it turned to red amber, then to insubstantial pearl, as the flames brimmed and drained it.

In the farther wall there was an inner doorway, with a dark curtain thrust to one side. Beyond, through the echo-chamber of the great barrel-vault of tower, a sound was tenuously beginning. Was it music I heard, or only some deception, a whining in the coals of the fire, my own blood singing, silence itself?

No, the eerie sound came full upon me now, sweeping down the arteries of stone into the small mouth of the doorway.

High in the tower, Antonina played her piano, as in the rented house at Paradys. She played the carriage-ride, the savage headlong race across the plains of darkness, the rough track, and the race of the pines overhead – she played the slowness of the Hades stream, the languor of relentless willnessness, obsession and dim night . . .

Close by, the ghost-girl clung to a pillar. The firelight came and went in her, as in the apple of glass. Did I recall her from some occult tampering in the house of Philippe, some séance? *Was* she a girl, or a crone? She looked familiar, and not so. She throbbed, the whole length of her, to the pulses of the piano. I said to her: 'What are you doing here? Your time is over.' And she faded to nothing. She was gone.

The piano crashed like thunder. It ascended and rushed down the scale, searching new peaks and abysses of cold brilliance, power and menace. It was not Antonina who played.

Presently the torrent stopped. I turned from the door and retreated to the far side of the hearth. It was a retreat, but not unstrategic. I had remembered a stance Philippe's mother had been wont to take, her back straight, her head slightly raised, her hands clasped together at her waist above the fall of her gown. I assumed it, and when I heard his step, on the stairway, on the flags of the room, did not turn to face him.

He came to the table, but it was between us. From the tail of my eye I saw him now. He was no longer dressed in white. The fire sprang, he dazzled and sank.

'An unexpected displeasure,' he remarked. I heard the gentle clink of glass. From a decanter on the table he poured wine into a goblet – red wine, or white? 'I would have thought,' he said, 'under such trying circumstances, you would have had a wish to go home.'

'Your domicile is haunted,' I said. 'Perhaps I'm another ghost.'

'There are no such things,' he said. He raised the glass and drank.

I turned, and looked at him. He wore black, like a priest. As she had done. The wine was itself blacker than ink, a black brandy or some unknown distillation. Some while since we had been so close.

Not since the duel, the day he killed me – but we had been closer then. His eyes bore upon mine like a weight I could not bear. I lowered my gaze. And he said, 'But you lack papers, I believe, mademoiselle, and cannot cross back over the border.'

'Who am I,' I said, 'do you think?'

'I don't think about it. Your identity is your own business.'

'Your dog, von Aaron, will have given me a name.'

'Von Aaron's deductions are usually faulty.'

'And so you sloughed him. You would find that easy.'

'But you have proved more difficult,' he said. 'What is it that you want?'

'My revenge on you,' I said, 'of course. Because you have made me suffer.'

'That was your choice.'

I raised my eyes and stared at him. I stared into his eyes which were her eyes, as, all along, her eyes had been his.

'You are abusing me as she did,' I said. 'You're telling me that if nothing is given me I must try to *take* nothing. That I must starve.'

'Then take some drink by all means,' he said. 'You've a long journey before you.'

He moved from the table to the hearth, as I moved from the hearth to the table. I reached out to the wine and discovered it was after all a blackish red, it had been reflecting his clothing and his mood merely. It had the taste of wormwood, however, when I drank it.

I smiled, and said, looking into the wine, 'You have no husband to hide behind on this occasion. Or do you have some convenient *wife* stashed in an upper room? Is each assault to be different, or are all of them the same? A snake eating its own tail.'

'Mademoiselle,' he said, 'I give you the freedom of all the night. I request only that you leave me this small part of it, my privacy.'

'What will you do,' I asked, 'in your corner of the night? Lovingly dwell on the darkness?'

I put down my glass. Fire filled it, and sank from it. Blood filled and sank from my heart.

I moved around the table and stood quite near to him, though not quite near enough to touch. The flames burned, throwing their flimsy architectures to the roof, and dismantling them again.

'Let me,' I said, 'enrage and unnerve and trouble you. Let me speak the truth to you, Anthony, to your face for once. No, don't look away. If I have the courage to meet your eyes, at least salute my courage, however little you value or desire it. Are we not, all of us, on a field of battle? I betray myself, I am my own enemy. She gives me to you, in chains, like the sword. You see, I offer you nothing at all any more, not a book, not a line of prose. You may think I have written this, but if I had or if I ever do, these are words drawn from air, magic, or a dream. Only think how strange it is, that I have formed a whole cathedral out of nothing, where for you the chance is only a pebble, a moment's acute annoyance. All the passionate song stemming from the same fount as your little indifference and dislike. It is you who have made the monster, where I invented beings with wings. Well, I love you. Nothing is changed. I have no more fame than ever I did, or I could offer you the bribe of making you immortal. You'd spurn it anyway, until it was too late to take. Then, perhaps. But who will remember me? And who will remember you?'

At the end of this recital, each of us lowered our eyes. The fire too lowered itself. The night was very still.

'Well,' he said at last, 'you have had your say.'

'And you have kept your silence.'

'Go home, mademoiselle,' he said. 'We are at variance.'

'Put me out,' I said. 'I'll lie across the doorway.'

'Oh, please,' he said, 'must we now have this?'

'You may step over me as you choose, or on me. I would prefer not the latter, but can't quarrel with it if you do.'

'There are other measures I might take against you. You're very troublesome.'

'That is the nature of life. Risk and trouble. You may do as you want. And so shall I. To go away from you is, for me, to be annihilated. I've said before, command your own actions. You may not command mine.'

He lifted his glass, as I thought for a second to drink, but instead he cast it across the room with tremendous force. It struck some obstacle, perhaps a pillar, and shattered into a glittering spray.

'This then is your notion of a revenge,' he said.

'Yours was, perhaps, more conventional.'

His hand flew upwards, as if to strike me, but he checked it. In turn, I caught his hand. It was so cold, what could I do but warm it a moment, before it should be snatched away.

'Where is the ring?' I said.

'You will never find that.'

'I shall find it. A drop of blood on all this palette of pallors and shadows, in a tower of shadows. Perhaps in the wine?'

'Certainly, look.'

'Not there, then.'

I let go the cold hand, which withdrew itself.

His eyes, since we had drawn so much nearer, seemed lost in the fiery dark.

I said, 'Have I made you hate me yet? That's better than uninterest. I'll give you something in exchange for the ruby scarab, shall I?' I put my hand to my breast and drew out that snub-nosed silver thing. He stared down at it. He did not ask me what it was, avoid or take it, and I did not say, See, even this failed. More lightly than he had thrown the glass, I cast the bullet into the dying hearth.

The fire was hurt, there. It turned a curious red. As I gazed at it, he walked away from me, towards the inner door with the curtain. His footsteps echoed up from the stones. The clash of the rings, when he drew the curtain over after him, repeated itself in the air, the way ripples do in water.

I listened to this noise for centuries.

After the fire had died, I continued to sit on the stones of the hearth. I felt a deathly peace, only that. When the sun rose I must go away. I must choose unreality, for reality, going by the name of the Unreal, would no longer harbour me. But I was lost at last. Therefore, sit, and await the dawn.

But the night stayed a great time, it was fond of this place.

Having discarded my paper, I wrote with a piece of charcoal from the fire along the stone. All single lines. What I had said to him, and other things.

Also, once I wept. If there was any alteration in Anna's weeping from the raging grief of Andre, I did not notice it. I wondered if the stones of that priestly hall would hold my pain long after I had gone.

Then, dawn came. The spiderweb window changed to silver. Even down the chimney of the hearth the anaemic resin seeped. Suddenly, beneath the curtain of the inner door, there ran out a pool of blood.

I came to my feet. I stared at the revelation. Slowly as if afraid, I went towards the bloody light, stepped into it and stood half a minute, wading. Next, I put my hand on the curtain and drew it aside.

What had been a black funnel, the tower, was now the cavity of a burning rose.

High, high above, just before the top of the tower had broken, hung the wound of a mighty sword, a window petalled by glass . . . magenta and maroon, crimson and carmine, blood, scarlet, madder and pomegranate – it *bled*, this glass, every petal, and as it fell down towards the east, the sunrise, it paled through every flushed nuance of roses. Tears of blood – I knew its name, had named it in the City when it formed inside my dreams. Beyond, a horizon of mountains, dim and fine as if drawn with a brush. The very land about was a mountain, which I had climbed unknowingly, within its mantle of pines and water. One only sees such things as mountains for what they are when they are far off.

My foot found the first step. I must approach the window. Through a gauze of crimson light, ascending – such a shaft it was, it too seemed made, the light, of glass. Birds of thin alabaster might have been set in it, or carven fish leaping. I moved upwards through the hollow core. It had a perfume, this colour, like the gardenia incense of some temple. And a sound, a low and sombre drone.

Trembling, the air, the light – I had reached a stone landing, and a gallery. The window seemed suspended, and it was possible, turning here, to touch the glass. Huge drops, they rained, some transparent, some opaque, some translucent – they passed me and went on below. I was dizzy now, the tears seemed to fall in actuality – I put my hand against the panes. But they were not wet. They were cool and dry. And under my very fingers, a creamy stone, not glass at all. I had found the gem from Antonina's marriage rings. Yes, it was true. Still in its oval setting of silver, lacking the band, pushed now into the glass, a single pane. Then I looked up, up the window. And saw there a ruby tear with, incised in it, a beetle with folded wings.

You could look a year and not see it. Or, staring only a second, see in a second. As with any mystery.

I stretched myself, all my height and more. If I had had Andre's stature, it would not have been so difficult. At my back the uncertain railing of the gallery, the drop below. Before me the blood-jewel of the scarab. My fingers sought it and my nails prised at the rim. Let it come out. It was mine. It shifted. It twisted, paused, and fell into my hand. Still in its metal band, it remained a ring. It burned my hand, so cold it was. I slipped it on my finger, which, though more slender than that same finger of Andre's, it seemed to have shrunk itself to encircle.

I turned and went along the gallery and in at a doorway.

The first room was very bare. The piano stood in it. The lamps had burned out, and one tall candle frilled with wax. There was a table with large old books spread over it, a rack of pens, a chessboard with only two or three figures standing or lying on its spaces. The red light of the mighty window had come in. It lit the lettering on the page of a single book: *Benedictus qui venit in nomine Domini*.

The second room, opening from the first, had light of its

own, a round eastern window of plain glass. Here, morning was white.

As white effigies lay on the marble of their tombs, so he lay, on the bed. The pillows of it, the covers, were heaped about him like sands, or foam from the sea. He was stranded in the wake of these things, hair spilled, lifeless. His sleep resembled death, was that so curious?

I moved closer. It would be impossible to wake him. I need not be afraid of it. He might never wake again.

The sheet would seem to have been dragged off him by some external agent, leaving the left shoulder and the left arm bare, outflung. The left hand rested, palm uppermost, and open, as if it awaited some gift or some caress. A vulnerable hand. He slept without his shirt.

I stood above him now, and my shadow fell across his face. Without the open eyes, the face was like a mask. I leaned down and touched my lips to his cheekbone and his jaw – with some surprise I felt the rasp of new beard starting against my mouth. The orbs of the eyes moved under their white lids. These were smooth, as the lips were . . . The reserved kiss did not wake him. No, nothing could. Nothing, nothing.

Like Psyche, who had searched for her love in hell, I leaned to his flesh. But the onus of the myth had been to dash aside unconsciousness. I was not Psyche, though he might be said to be Love.

He was Love, and he was Antonina. He and Antonina were one thing, as Anna was Anfre. Vampires, shape-changers, incubus-succuba – such vacant names.

I drew all the sheet away, and gazed at him as he lay there. He slept on. What might I not do?

I put from me any clothing that impeded me, and slipped into the white bed with him as if into a bank of snow. My skin touched his skin. I fastened my lips to his. His mouth parted under mine. I drew the soul out of his mouth, and in his sleep, unwaking, he moved against me, as if we lay beneath the sea.

Refuse me now. No? You will not do it. This you will do, and this.

I lay over him, curved to his body. In sleep, his excitement had answered mine. We swam together now. So beautiful, my love, you are so beautiful. The strength of you, and all the pain and glamour of your body, your bones, your silver spine arching – now, now –

The white light was cloven, stayed, *Not yet*. As with the first kiss, my lips sought, closed, against his flesh.

Yet, I am she and she is you and you are myself. I hold you and am held. You are my slave, and I am yours. You destroy me, and are destroyed. I give myself and receive myself. We are one thing and all things. And nothing. We are nothing.

I felt and heard him catch his breath. I need not wait any more. I raised my head and cried aloud under the sword of death.

And the cloven light burned, but only like a fire.

As the interior of the coffin had borne her imprint, so the mattress had retained the shape of him. There was no other trace, save for two or three long and curling jet-black hairs.

The interim might not have been sleep. Some blank omission from awareness following the summit and the fall. What had occurred? Ah, was it only that? I left the bed, and hesitantly went about the room.

In the round casement, the landscape was framed, under a high sun. It was midday, perhaps.

There had been some failure. Something amiss, or mistakenly done. Did I remember what it was? I wound the black hairs about my finger, around the scarab ring. I was depressed and weary. I left the bedroom, crossed the chamber with the piano – quiescent in the noon dusk. The great window beyond was a symphony of crimson by day, nothing else or more – I descended the tower with a strange sense of permanence, or memory – not my own, but others. The ghosts lay thick as the shadowy sunlight on everything. In the hall, a woman was busy at the dead hearth. She was scrubbing with her rag, erasing the words I had written there during the night.

I stood and looked at her. What was she? Was she a creature of normal reality, or a phantasm, or had she crawled from some aperture between these states? Her rag made a husky noise. How dared she obliterate the ramblings of my heart's soul? An illiterate, she could not read them, she thought them only the marks of the soot.

'What are you doing?' I said. 'Leave that at once.'

To my gratification, she did stop immediately. She got up and observed me. She had a quiet, vegetable face.

'Where is he?' I said. 'Do you belong to him?' For some reason, I found it hard to speak his name, any part of it. But she nodded now. She was some villager, from some village, a servant. 'Well,' I said, 'where has he gone?'

She stared. He came and went as he pleased. How would she know.

I sighed. What did I want?

A dreadful lassitude, almost a revulsion, threatened me. I had possessed him and it was done. It was no more than a convention.

There had been so much poignant drama, did it only end in this unoriginal deed of lust? The storm of orgasm was so soon over. What could one say after it but, Farewell, or, Again and *then* farewell. Or, for ever and ever, Amen, and God preserve all from that Amen. Passion is not self-begetting. It must burn up brighter and consume. It must always be in doubt, and in anguish, and perhaps even in agony – to this, carnal love was nothing. It would be better to die in the act. Such fireworks, and then to go out in the habitual dark behind the sordid roof-tops?

The woman, relieving herself of any duty to make conversation with me, had turned and was going out of the door. I followed her, naturally. She went down the steps, which looked peeled in daylight, and walked along the shore. How was the rest of the scenery by day? I could not have said. It was a place I passed through. The huge tarn of water gleamed, hard as a gem. My eyes were hurt by so much truth-discovering light. I shielded them, and was glad when she went in at another entry in one of the standing walls.

I found us then to be in a sort of kitchen, with long ovens and a wide hearth, fireless now. By the hearth sat a girl with a snow-blonde chrysanthemum of hair. She did not glance at me, she was taking from a wicker bag a baby, only a few days old, and next a leather bottle with a teat. She fed the child from this as he sat naked on her lap. His fine floss of hair was paler even than hers, and one of his eyes was lighter than the other. They had a look of someone I had known, both the girl and the infant. I realised it was a decided resemblance to Philippe.

The older woman now busied herself with lighting the hearth fire. That achieved, she took a broom, of the pastoral sort, a bunch of twigs tied together, and began to sweep the floor, up and down, back and forth, with an aimless determination.

I sat down facing the girl, and pushed back the red hair from my face and shoulders. Hers, cotton-white, straggled all about her.

'Is this child yours? When was he born?'

She glanced at the woman who swept, but that one only went on sweeping. The girl pursed her lips, readied herself, and spoke to me.

'Not mine. Another girl's. But he makes things happen, so I bring him away.'

'Makes things happen – what do you mean by that?'

Her skin was lucent. Now she blushed.

'Well, he does.'

The child turned then and stared at me. He could not be more than ten days old, less maybe, or a little more. But his odd eyes seemed to look upon me with knowledge and some sly amusement. I had known Philippe when not much older.

'Do you mean,' I said softly, clandestinely, leaning forward to the girl and endeavouring to catch her eye, 'that things move about when he's in the room – that, say, a candle will blow itself out, or some hanging thing will be swung to and fro?'

She nodded. 'And the shuttle goes on the loom.' She lowered her lashes. 'The priest, he says it will stop as the child grows. It's not a demon, but the spirit is restless.'

Behind us, the woman swept the floor, up and down, and round and round.

'But you've come here quite often,' I said. 'When *he* is here. The master of this ruin.'

She smiled. She would not look at me now.

I got to my feet. 'You must heat water and fetch it up to me,' I said, 'for the bath in the upper room. You understand me?'

The child pushed the leather bottle away. He crowed. Ah! Philippe cried, reborn between a peasant's thighs, you see, here I am again to mock and torment you.

But I turned and left the room quickly. I went back along the shore. Light pierced open-work windows like flights of arrows. Walls leaned as if about to come down. Birds were rising from trees on the farther bank; perhaps Scarabin rode there, on one of the black horses. Or were all the horses metamorphosed now to white?

I wondered if the girl would obey me, but when I had climbed up again through the tower, she presently came with two buckets and filled the porcelain bath with scalding water and with warm.

I made her remain in the chamber as I bathed. She was shy, and would not look at me, but she wandered about the room, more surely than I had done, now and then picking up some item, a brush, the razor from its bowl, an ivory pencil-case that lay under the window.

'You're familiar with these things,' I said. She did not answer. 'And with that bed, also. He's had you. Is that not so?' She darted one glance at me. It was true. Was it jealousy that burned through me? No, it was a pang of horror at the vulgarity of it, that I had only been that, too. A woman had by him, and he, a man I had had.

I dried myself, and put on again the costume of Paradys. There was not a stain on it, not a rent in its soft fabric. And I, stained like the church-glass of the unholy window, immutably, and rent by silver – I was damned because I had failed, had failed.

'Come here,' I said to the girl. 'Brush my hair now.'

She brushed my hair, with long smooth strokes, more nicely than her fellow had swept the floor.

'There,' I said. 'We're friends.'

I stood over her, some inches taller than she. I took her face in my hands and kissed her fresh mouth. He had kissed her, I kissed, deeply, and she leaned against me, letting me caress her, her flower-like skin, her warm breasts. As there had been Anna within me for Philippe, so Andre now sampled this girl on my behalf, for my sake, since Anthony had made love to her. She was like Philippe herself, as the child was. She and I, had by the same one, were, briefly, the same one. And I remembered the exaltation of my abandonment in the sexual climax of desire. Of course, it was nothing of any value at all.

When I let her go, I asked her name. Shivering, her lambent eyes on mine, she said she was called Oula. I wondered then why I had asked. What did her name matter to me?

There came a sharp clangour from below.

'The child!' she cried. And turning from me ran away, out of the rooms and down the tower again. I hurried at her heels. And going by the window of the tears of blood, thought, Passed and repassed and so past. So it becomes a thing of no consequence. I am used to it, now.

In the hall below, the woman had come back to work, with her broom, and had brought the child in the bag. His cobweb mane and anemone arms protruded from the wicker. Meanwhile, one of the three heavy silver crucifixes had been crashed from the mantel. Now another was rising, and wafted through the air, as if weightless. The woman watched it, stopped in her tracks but with no appearance of alarm. The girl Oula called out something in the dialect of the north, another language, which I did not know. The child gurgled and laughed.

Oula ran across the floor and whirled him up. She lifted him high and shook him a little. The miniscule face was vivid with evil glee. The second crucifix too clanged on to the stone floor.

I looked at the broom-woman and shouted: 'Take him. Take him out. Do as you're told, you bitch.'

She made a vague move towards the girl and the fiendish baby. Just then, the decanter rose from the table. It flung itself at me and instinctively I threw my hands before my face. With a stinging drizzle of lights, the glass smashed at my feet. The liquor spurted up, and I was splattered, all over the fine old gown, as if with blood.

I ran across and pushed my hand against the baby's laughing sneering face. 'Yes, I remember the fight, and the cherries. Yes. Enough.

80

Go away and forget. This isn't for you.' And the face fell, enviously. Toothless gums tried to bite. 'Give him to her,' I indicated the woman to Oula as if they had never met. 'He must be taken out.'

But the child had abruptly lapsed into a sullen exhaustion. It was borne away and put back into its bag. The older woman, having propped her broom on one of the pillars, taking the bag, and without a word, plodded to the door and down the steps.

Would she walk into the tarn and sink there, becoming some aquatic animal? No, she simply trod her route along the shore to the causeway. Oula and I, standing in homely fashion in the door, watched her out of sight.

Oula timidly put her hand on my waist. I removed it.

Together we replaced the crucifixes. If they were an iota from their stations it would be sure to be noticed. 'Sweep up the glass.' She swept it up and took the fragments away.

Drearily I stood before the hearth. What a barren place this was, when he was not in it.

I did not properly believe that Oula's habitat, village or otherwise, existed. She, or any other, evolved and retreated to some secondary plane, inaccessible to me. There was therefore nowhere I might escape to. When he returned, whatever should we do, he and I? With Antonina, when it had been Antonina and Andre, the progression was unavoidable, rushing away downhill, tumbling forward into the pit of delicious darkness. But this. Dear God, suppose it should become domestic?

But suppose too he did not return.

Terror fastened on me. I lay against the hearth in fear and misery. And was aware, through these monstrous concussions, that I was glad of them.

Just after sunset, I heard Oula laughing along the shore. I had been standing under the tower window, watching the light go out of it, to see if this happened in the way I had formerly described. Her laugh came like a flying thing, and flitted round me. Hearing it, I knew Anthony had come back, and was with her somewhere in the ruin.

My eager foreboding drew me across the pillared hall, to the doorway. Here I looked out and saw smoke still tapering from the chimney of the kitchen room.

The tarn was a bath of wine, the whole sky had become a red window, and made all the broken open wheel-windows red, the tower a black fire-iron against incorrigible space.

On the threshold of the kitchen, some colourless flowers lay scattered. Inside, it was an oil on canvas, though not from Philippe's quirky brush. Pale Oula was kindling two hanging lamps, with alabaster arms highlighted, while dark Scarabin stood by the hearth.

As I shut out the afterglow in the doorway, both looked at me and then away. They had formed a liaison against me. I was to be excluded.

There was a table of wooden planks near one wall, and two wooden benches. Here I sat, as if at the *Cockatrice* or the *Imago*. After a moment he took a place at the table across from me, without a word or further look. Oula brought an earthenware jug and set it down, with a glass for him.

'Bring a glass for me,' I said.

She went at once to a cupboard and extracted another glass and gave it me.

He took up the jug and to my surprise, poured the drink firstly into my glass. Tonight the liquor was cloudily pale, an absinth that seared the mouth.

During, and after this, we sat in silence, and the girl prepared a meal, moving to and from the fire and the ovens and here and there. Scarabin drank steadily. His expression was lazy, but his face held tensely in against the bones. His eyes were fixed far off. They looked sightless, so densely black, giving no access, having no floor. The mouth was sulky and cruel. In the muddy lamplight, sometimes it seemed to me the face of a handsome man, sometimes of a beautiful woman.

When the food was ready Oula brought it to the table. White meat and bread, and a dish of cheese and apples.

'Sit down,' he said to her then. The room quivered at his voice, as if a coin had been thrown into a well. When she only stood by him, he got hold of her and gently pulled her down at his side.

Then, as if she were some clever clockwork doll, he began to feed her. It seemed she ate nothing, only drank the absinth, but her he fed, with infinite persuasion, persistence, and care. The attention, or the food, brought the blood into her cheeks. Even her hair pinkened, appearing to blush a little.

Beyond the door, the dusk had drawn its curtain.

'Why do we eat, Oula?' he said, 'Why drink? Could we not do without sustenance, don't you suppose so?' But she had now ceased herself to eat, or he to feed her. She lay against him, her head on his shoulder, sometimes playing with the buttons of his coat. Her hands were gracious for a servant girl's, and the nails clean and trimmed. 'What is reality after all,' he said. 'Did we not invent all this, are we not God, any and all of us?' He spread his own elegant hand on the table. 'I could pass my hand through the wood as if through water. Any man, any woman, could do it. No chains, no bindings. It's a world of chaos restrained solely by the human mind, which then, afraid of itself, steps back and says, see this colossal machine over which I have no power at all.'

I said, 'She won't understand you. And I already know it.' But he ignored me.

Soon after, he stood and drew the girl up with him. He said to her tenderly. 'Where now?' And she murmured her laughter. They went away.

The room, in which the fire still crackled, turned cold, solid, and deathly still.

Stars were in the sky above the tarn, I could see them through the doorway, huge stars that blazed too brightly.

I closed my eyes, and saw instead Philippe, a maddened child of eleven years, on the rocking-horse, riding faster and faster, with his head thrown back.

I had nothing to write with. The hag with the broom and rags had finished cleaning off the stones of the hall when I left her unsupervised. Write with my voice then, on air, or with my nails in the plank table. Or with fire, scour the kitchen out with arson.

Plucking three of my own long, curling hairs, I wove them together with the black hair I had found in the bed. (What colour had my hair been, before the 'Martian' red of Paradys?) Then I burned the hair together.

Water was sadness, air a vision, earth was thought. But fire, fire was the will.

Since reality and the physical world were only chaos, illusorily subdued, I did not perhaps pass through night along the ground, or through ruined halls of stone. Ascending, what did I climb but the heights of meaning? Certainly the tower had grown taller. High up in it, I was on some rarefied and open summit, where the air was thin and chimed with ice. There were no dimensions, or they were different ones . . . No, they were the usual ones. A bedchamber lit by a few candles, a man and a woman embracing.

I walked about them, round them, once, twice. They did not (did they?) know I was there. Hungrily they annexed each other with their mouths.

I put my arms over hers, around him, and my hands on hers – and drew them down from his body. Standing at her back, I wrested her quietly from his grasp, and when I had her, putting my mouth to her ear, I whispered, 'That is over. What are you doing here?'

She opened her eyes, and looked at me with a somnambulist's smile. Then, in the way of a peasant girl released from some temporary office, she bobbed me a silly little curtsey, and drifted at once across the room. The candlelight made lace, a bridal veil, over her hair. She vanished through the doorway, or only altogether.

He stood and looked at me, already in his shirt, a libertine's face of arousal, the eyes of dreaming death.

'It *is*,' he said, 'all one. You, or she, will do. Come here, then.'

I went to him and said, as he took hold of me, 'Not for this. Only I, or you, will do for this,' and took hold of him as he had taken me.

The bed received my body like a cloud. How low the candles burned, the room seemed full of a darker sunset . . . In the sunset of the cloud, his weight lay on me with the heat of fire. In the hell of ecstasy, the caverns below were flame, and the river molten. Down and down, fall down with me into the underworld of red forgetful night. I am the ferryman. Lethe is all lava. My mouth is at your throat as you press your face against the pillows and your hands clench upon me –

And rising and sinking in the billows of shadow, the light was cleaved to crimson, crimson through and through, a dye never to be washed out, through the wounds of a redeemer might wash away all sins and stains. Crimson, crimson, the caves, the river, flowers and fruit and crystal and blood. Crimson the benediction; the waves, crimson, that never ended and were never begun, and were never begun or ended.

And in the morning, he lay beside me still. He was not asleep; when I kissed his skin it was only faintly cold, all the coldness fading from it. There was no pulse in the wrists, no heartbeat in the architrave under the breast. The texture of his jaw was unaltered, today it would not require a razor – The long lids of the eyes, fast shut, harboured darknesses.

A few drops of blood had spilled on the sheet. Under the left wrist, the blood had left an odd mark, but try as I would, I could not make it seem to resemble or suggest anything.

I had not failed. Things were as they must be. Antonina with Andre. Anna with Anthony. First one, now the other, was lost. To say she or he was dead was a great simplification. The exquisite taste of his blood – did I even remember it? Had she remembered the taste of mine?

I stretched myself along his body, and held him a brief while, reluctant to leave go.

But the room itself, by barely perceptible little shifts of the light, by distilled mutterings of the wood and the bed-curtains, did not permit too long an indulgence. I might grieve if I wished – surely grief was in the order of these new emotions, euphoria and dread, a bacchanal needing no wine – but not here. I must run from here, as from any place in the future where this should elect to happen. Forests, hillsides, city avenues, such a wealth of them should see me in flight from this. What aisles of woods and masonry groves of rooms would shelter me.

As I descended the tower, I recalled my agitation in Paradys, not knowing what I must feel or be or do. I had changed in more than gender. Eventually, perhaps, all these huge sensations would be worn down, or cauterised, and then must come a final act –

But not yet.

I ran along the shore. My pain tore from me like a birth. It pinned me to the earth and crushed me against the sky.

Towards evening I went over the causeway, and down into the derelict deserted village. Which had come alive.

I was not amazed to see it, the grass-grown lanes where now people walked, and the broken windows coined with lights. A shepherd drove his little flock of sheep across the slope under the trees. In the square, where only leaves had blown before, tables were set out, barrels and bottles and platters of food. Women were bringing oil lamps. Three wiry old men crouched near an open fire, one tuning a slender fiddle, one warming a drum-skin just clear of where the spits were roasting rabbits. The third worried a cloth through the notches of his pipes. It was to be a village feast. And there, a stout man in a good coat, with Oula on his arm, and a young man with bulging arm-muscles, and some gossiping wives. A handfasting, was it? Oula and her rustic swain.

I paused on the edge of the ripening lamplight. There would always be helpers. Always to hand, slaves, victims, other characters in the play. One called them up like spirits, and, more reliably than spirits, they came at a need. This – well, it was straight from the etchings and aquatints of the City, the bucolic world as seen through the eyes of Paradys.

When I moved forward, the villagers looked askance at me, but not in an unreceptive way. The stout man, Oula's sire or uncle, came up to me, handing me a russet rose.

'For your hair, mademoiselle. Here you are, for the celebration. You're most welcome.'

So I put the flower in my sash and sat at Oula's table.

The beer and the sour potent wine gushed into the beakers. They crammed their mouths with food, and danced madly when the fiddle, pipe and drum struck up a wild and scrambling tune.

All around, the sheer glare of fire on faces, and in the shadows young lovers running off to the fields beyond the lanes.

A tallow moon rose.

Oula danced with her beau, who, presumably, did not care she had been deflowered by the local landowner. The beefy arms swung her round and round. Beyond them, I saw a woman suckling a baby. She looked like no one that I knew, but the child was the child who moved things, and was perhaps possessed by Philippe. Oula dashed by in a dance of skirts.

'Will you honour me?' said the stout father.

I came to my feet. He took my hand and waist, and we danced. It was a paraphrase of the intimate dances of liberty, and rough.

'The one who touched you last,' he said. 'What has become of him?'

I looked up into the massive face, at its jowls which were hanging forward so earnestly, its uneasy eyes. Was it the face of the banker-baron, was it von Aaron in flighty disguise? He looked younger. He had no metallic lace at his cuffs, he smelled of garlic and tobacco.

'Become of whom?' I asked, as he bore me round in the prancing dance.

'Of *him*. Is it done? Has it taken place?'

'Possibly. If I take your meaning.'

'Dear God,' he said. He panted from the speed of the dance, and called a jolly greeting to Oula as she sped by. 'We are all,' he said, between his gasps, 'in the mill-race of destiny.'

'I don't – believe in destiny.'

We plunged so fast now, both of us panted for breath.

'Believe in it. You will perceive it, for all the facts are now before you, or almost all the facts. He hates what he becomes, that is his pleasure, the hate. And to punish the cause, and to avenge it. With her, the same.'

'Are you speaking of your daughter? Of a wayward son, perhaps.'

'Dance, dance,' he cried.

A sustained and ghastly sound shot like a spear over the dancing-floor.

Everything ended. The curvetting dancers turned to stones, and the tiny band stood with its instruments aloft and voiceless, eyes twinkling with terror in the firelight where the skeletons of rabbits lingered on the spits. The drops of the lamps blinked in the scores of stares like tears.

The stout young baron had let me go.

Fear came to me, with an electrifying tingle.

'What noise was that?' I said.

'A dog,' he said, 'a dog howling.'

As I walked away from him, across the burnished square, they watched me go with curious pity, and relief, with distaste, in silence.

And beyond the village? There lay the mirror tarn, and there the causeway, gaping like a bridge of bones under the moon.

I glanced over my shoulder. There were no lights among the trees, where the feast had been, and the dancing.

As my feet met the earth, a strange vitality seemed to course up into me. The dew was down. I was afraid. Oh let me feel and caress the fear. Close as a lover it clutched me.

The night pulsed with fear, all the land was in terror, but where was fear's source?

Up among the forest trees, a pale glimmering. Had Oula run after me to be comforted? Or the ghost, that ghost of some predecessor of my own? How ethereal it was, that whiteness, yet it was neither quite human nor quite ghostly. There, and there, threading in and out between the poles of the pine trees, there and there –

At once something leapt out, and another thing, two white bolts that flew down the incline, the distance and the dark, towards me.

Two white dogs.

I took my skirts up in my hand, and I ran. I ran towards the causeway, I screamed aloud as I did so. I had seen fear's source. It was two white hounds, lean and long, with jackals' pointing heads. And after them rode a figure on a white horse, clothed in white and cowled against the moon like a priestess –

Sanctuary – where was it? The ruin, the high altar of the crimson window and the white bed stained with crimson. Run, run, never look behind you.

I felt the heat of their desire upon me. I felt the teeth of the hounds rip the hem of my dress and their talons comb my flying hair.

The causeway slammed against my feet. On either side, the water like a precipice. And now, shining there, three white stretching ribbons of fire.

How fast do I run, now the Devil is after me? I am learning, but unknowingly, I have no time to tell. And she is a woman, the Devil,

Princess of Darkness, clad in white. She is Antonina, hunting me –
I have sold them both my soul.

I can make no noise, have no breath for it, but now I have reached
the further bank. I fall against the stair to the tower door, then stumble up and rush on. I do not shut the door at my back. What good
would that do?

Through the hall, the silver crucifixes staring down. I am on the
inner stair. My heart is divided and beats twice at every blow. I cannot see the window, only a vertical pool of ink.

I am in the bedchamber. The bed, of course, is empty.

I hear my own breathing, like that of some dying thing. Which is
apt enough.

And now I stand waiting, facing the doorway. The moon shines
through the eastern window, striping the night, showing me all I will
have to see. She is on the stair. She is coming towards me. She is
Death.

(One day, or dark, I will slide the ruby scarab from my finger. In
some graveyard, on some hill, I will find some other like myself, one
who comprehends the real nature of reality. Shape-changer. Only
then, and if, can I discard this horror and this appalling joy. A finish
then. But not now. I am on the wheel with her. I am on the wheel
with both of them and both of my selves. The snake devours its own
tail. There is nothing domestic in this).

The doorway slowly changed its shape. It glowed, and whiteness
entered the chamber. In the room beyond, a dog shone like zinc, and
beside it, another.

In the white cowl, the pale face, and the black eyes fixed on me.
Then she spoke.

'I am his sister. Perhaps that is obvious to you?'

In my terror I smiled. I dropped to my knees.

'I will give you my name,' she said. 'Before my marriage, it was
Antonina Scarabin.'

I kneeled at her feet. She came towards me, floating on her own
whiteness. Andre struggled in turn towards her, deep within my
flesh. She saw him in my gaze and bowed her head. She kissed my
mouth, slowly and sweetly, and sank the steel of a dagger, warmer
by far than her lips, into my raging heart.

She held me in her arms until I was dead, then gently closed my
eyes.

MALICE IN SAFFRON

Le Livre Safran

Every Night and every Morn
Some to Misery are Born.
Every Morn and every Night
Some are Born to sweet delight.
Some are Born to sweet delight.
Some are Born to Endless Night.

William Blake

Malice in Saffron

A young girl with pale yellow hair was walking between the wheat fields, her hands at her sides and her eyes cast down. It was very early in the morning, the sun had only just risen, discovering in the sky tall northern hills black with pines, and lower down some black goats in a field busily feeding.

As the girl walked, a man's voice shouted loudly to her. 'Jehanine!' Jehanine hesitated, then halted. She looked over her shoulder and saw her step-father, Belnard, riding down the track on his shaggy donkey. At once she sensed not merely trouble, but danger. A brutal, coarse man, strong as a bear, he had beaten her frequently and often abused her in small ways. He was an important person in the area. He had received his own farm and lands for past service had pleased his lord, and Belnard had even ridden with this master, twenty years ago, crossading to the Holy land, and returned not only with scars, but with certain riches. Having a fancy for Jehanine's mother, Belnard had wed her, though she already had a baby, (Jehanine), at her breast. Thereafter the woman gave birth to several sons and daughters who were Belnard's own. Of these, the favourite was Pierre. Lucently handsome (and as it transpired gifted by God) Pierre had been the joy of them all. Over the years, Jehanine's mother grew sickly. Belnard's proper daughters were sluts, and his other sons swaggering drunken louts like their sire. Beautiful Pierre, in whom even the lord had taken some interest, was now seventeen and gone three months to the dream-like city in the south, to be apprenticed at the studio of a great artisan. He was to become a famous painter, and a prince would be his patron. Meanwhile:

'What are you at, eh, mooning along there?' said Belnard, riding up on his step-child.

'The goats are in the wheat,' she said.

'Chase 'em out then,' said he.

So Jehanine ran forward into the field, clapping her hands and calling, and scattering the goats away into the pasture beyond. Once there she had a mind not to go back to the path, but Belnard, anticipating this perhaps, had ridden through the wheat after her, and now approached her again under the pear trees.

'Do you miss your brother?' said Belnard, riding along beside Jehanine.

'Yes,' said Jehanine.

'Yes. It seemed to me, you and he were always close. Too close maybe for brother and sister. Teach you some tricks, I expect, did he? And you him a thing or two.'

Jehanine lowered her eyes and clenched her fists. She was now beginning to be afraid.

Belnard reached up and plucked a pear. But it was unripe and after a bite he spat and threw the rest away. This waste was part of his flaunt of ownership. He could do what he liked here.

'Now, on the other hand,' said Belnard, 'you and I are no proper kin at all. I'm not your dad. Christ knows what son-of-a-sow got you on her.'

Jehanine picked up her skirts and began to run.

With a hearty laugh, not put out, Belnard kicked the donkey into a gallop. Presently he rode the animal straight into the fleeing girl and tumbled her under a tree. Swinging from the donkey's back, Belnard dropped down on her. She tried at first to fight him, but he said smiling, 'Don't you raise your hand to me, my girl. Or I'll break your nose. Do you think I can? So, then. Lie still.' And so Jehanine lay like a piece of wood. He pulled up her dress and forced her. 'By bleeding Christ, a virgin still,' he said. In another minute this was no longer the case. 'Move,' he grunted then, 'move, you bitch.' So Jehanine obediently moved. He soon finished, collapsing upon her. When he recovered he rose and left her in her blood on the ground. He glanced only once into her tawny eyes that looked now almost as white as her face. 'Well not much to that,' he said. 'Perhaps you'll improve with use. Don't take all day there. There's milking to be done. And don't let any of my men catch you like that. Pull your skirts down, you trull.'

Jehanine pulled the cloth down over her thighs and lay under the pear tree watching Belnard ride away. When he was out of sight beyond the orchard, she kneeled and vomited. Then she wept, but not for very long.

That evening, when Jehanine, with her younger sisters and the farm girls, served the men their supper, Belnard seemed to have forgotten what he had done in the orchard. Though it was of slight consequence to him, nevertheless now he had accomplished it, he might wish to repeat the venture. Virgins were somewhat scarce. Of course, too, the act had been a sin. Belnard might feel bound to make a confession and give the lord's priest some money. Jehanine, since all women were besmirched by the fall of the first woman, Eve, would be held largely to blame.

Jehanine's mother whined and complained during supper. Afterwards two of the brothers fought in the yard and returned with wounds. Much later, when the moon rose outside, the farm was full of snoring and sighs as the family and the house-slaves slept. Somewhere off over the hills, a dog, or perhaps a wolf, bayed at the moon. Jehanine lay awake on the edge of the mattress she shared with her sisters, and listened. She thought of Pierre, who had always been kind to her and who, on leaving, had made her a promise. 'When I'm rich, I'll send for you. You shall keep my house for me. I'd trust none of the others. But you're clean, and clever. We'll have servants, and you can order them all. When I come home from decorating angels on to the walls of some church, or goddesses in a private supper-room for a prince, I'll lie down with my head in your lap and you can comb my hair and sing to me. I'll give you three silk dresses, Eastern silk from the Spice Lands.' 'You'll marry,' Jehanine had murmured. 'Marry? Not I. A girl or two, maybe. But you're the only one I'd want in my house.' There had been nothing between them that was sexually familiar, but Jehanine had always been in love with her golden-haired brother. He was the only beautiful thing she had ever known, beyond the natural things, the weather, the country and its beasts, whose beauty harsh everyday use had inevitably spoiled for her.

When she had finished thinking of Pierre, Jehanine thought of her step-father's rape, and of the fact that he might like to repeat it. Then she listened to the wolf, howling in its ecstasy of lonely freedom.

In the middle of the night, Jehanine got up and put on her clothes in silence. In equal silence, opening the clothes-chest, she took one of her sisters' mantles, for they were of good quality and so more durable than her own. Although she had never really considered the thing she now began to do, in some part of her mind she must have made a plan. She went about it quickly and quietly. She first spoke softly to the big house dogs that lay by the hearth. Then going into the stone larder, she took a slab of bread and another of cheese and wrapped them in a piece of linen. Then she took a jar of milk and drank it dry.

As she left the farm and stole across the dirty yard, by the well and the hen-house and the duck-pond, Jehanine felt neither regret nor anxiety.

She skirted the huts of the labourers with care, because their dogs did not altogether know her and might give an alarm. When she reached the track between the fields, the moon was going down. There was another long hour to sunrise, and no Belnard would be stirring much before.

The track ended and Jehanine came out upon a road, old as the hills and kept in repair by the lord. This was the way Pierre had come, though he had had a donkey to ride, and one of the farm men to accompany him.

Jehanine, however, did not feel a lack. She had known only the farm and the surrounding landscape all her eighteen years. Now she was heedlessly eager to be off, to discover the rest of the world which lay waiting. She turned south, for the road conveniently ran that way. She walked briskly, holding her small bundle of provisions, looking ahead.

By the time the dawn began, Jehanine was well down the valley, and above her, eastward, she saw the humped tower of the village church. The bell was not ringing, for the priest was a sluggard. Inside the church stood a golden crucifix with jewels on it, which the lord had had made with some of the wealth brought back from the Holy Land. In a niche a pale and melancholy Madonna exhorted women to do their duty. She wore a golden crown, also the lord's gift, because she had obviously done hers.

Belnard, too, had relics of the Crossade on show. A great Saracen spear was hung up in his bedchamber, its tasselled sling still dark with blood. Besides, there were some jewels, or so he and the brothers said. Belnard had once announced he would give each of his daughters a jewel on her wedding day. He had been drunk at the time. But he had also vowed to give Pierre something at his leavetaking. This might have been true.

Brighter than all jewels, the sun pierced through the sky.

Though men and women were out in the fields few saw Jehanine, or if they did, apparently reckoned her on some errand. Once past the cultivated lands of the lord, the road went down among the pine forests. An unfriendly place in winter, full of hungry wolves and starveling robbers – or so they said. Bears even sometimes loitered in the pines, not to mention creatures of the Devil. But winter was a way off, and surely the City nearer?

Among some fallow fields, Jehanine heard hoof-beats on the road behind her. She withdrew hastily to the side of the road, but there was nowhere to conceal herself. She was suddenly afraid her stepfather might be after her, for it sounded like his donkey – only the lord's sons had horses. She crouched down.

Sure enough, the donkey came clumsily pelting along the road. On its back sat a heavy, hairy boy, not Belnard in fact, but one of the younger sons. He blundered past and reined up, hauling the animal round. He had seen his sister in the shallow ditch. The hood had slipped from her hair and the sun fired it like a pale torch.

'There you are, you cat,' said Belnard's son, Jehanine's half-brother. 'He said you'd be sure to go this way. When the sluts woke up and found you gone, he said to me, You take the ass and go and bring her back. She's got work to do. He told me something else, too,' said Jehanine's half-brother, riding up to her. His shadow came between her and the sun. He slid down from the donkey abruptly, dropping, falling against her and rolling her over in the ditch. 'If you did it with him, now you can do it with me.'

Jehanine did not struggle. Her eyes went wide and blank. She said, 'If you want. But not here.'

'Here, here and now,' he said, fumbling at her.

'No. The priest may come along.'

Her half-brother considered. If the priest did come this way, or the lord's steward, which was also a possibility, Belnard's son would be fined, or pilloried, for they were bloodkin, he and she.

'Get up then, quick,' he said. 'Come there, where the trees are.'

He dragged her over the fallow ground, but not so fast she could not stumble and pick up as she did so a spiky, hand-sized rock from the soil.

As soon as they reached the trees, he pushed her against one, and Jehanine struck him in the face, on the forehead, as hard as she was able. She only stunned him, but he poured with blood, and staggering aside, he fell. Then she ran round him, kicking and beating at him with the stone, now from one side, now another, until his howls and groans ceased and he lay still. The rough vengeance gave her satisfaction, but she was also frightened. Looking back down to the road, she saw no one was there. The donkey had wandered away into a patch of clover. Left to itself it would gladly feed all day, and perhaps be lost. Belnard would think his son had not found the runaway, but continued on to an inn to get drunk.

She was not sure she had not killed her half-brother, though he was breathing. Strangely, it seemed the other inner part of her mind had again been formulating plans, even as she beat him unconscious.

Though he was bigger than she, his clothes in their turn were rather too small for him, being cast-offs of the slender Pierre. She stuffed the loutish boots with leaves and pieces of her own shift, to make them fit, and with a strip of her shift she bound her breasts before she drew on his tunic and sleeveless surcoat. With the innocence of thoughtless knowledge, she also tucked a roll of the material inside his hose – now hers – at the appropriate juncture.

She left him naked under the trees and ran back down to the road. She could not ride, and besides did not dare to steal her step-father's donkey.

The boots, so much too large, would hurt her before the day was done. But the clothes gave an extra freedom of movement, and though she did not care for their odour, this too would help in disguising her.

She had now gone so far on her career she felt the rightness of it. She strode out, her heart was light.

An hour later she left the lord's estate's behind, and came down to the brink of the pines. She had never been so far before. This in itself would be her talisman.

The journey absorbed several days, and Jehanine kept no count of their number. Everything was so unusual to her, the area, her aloneness, the act of her flight itself. By the second day she was convinced that Belnard would not attempt to have her followed further, or that if he did so, she was now immune to his search. The weather was consistently fine, and even the nights, when she slept on the earth, were fraught only with owls.

She walked south, which was quite easy, though the first road vanished on the first day. Later on, there were other tracks, and other better roads. Sometimes she passed through a village, where she would beg for food. Generally they gave her something; the summer had been plentiful. They thought her a boy off to make his fortune. Though her clothes were travel-stained and not new, they were those of a wealthy peasant, and her chiselled features led women to believe she was the by-blow of some duke. Now and then too, Jehanine passed the estate of some other lord, and once a fortress craned above the woods. But she had no difficulties. The land changed again, rolling and swooping, clad in wild flowers and ruined towers, then vineyards.

Finally, she had the luck to fall in with a sort of caravan, the wagons of a tanner and an apothecary, and certain others, making for the City, which was now only one day away.

The apothecary seemed keen to take the boy, (who gave his name when pressed as Jehan), into apprenticeship. It was conceivable too that the apothecary fancied Jehan. Nevertheless, the man's advances were mild, and he was inclined to feed his travelling companion, while allowing him to ride in the wagon among the vials and antique bottles, spilled powders and dried scorpions.

'The City is a wonderful place,' said the apothecary, boastfully. 'You've never been there before? Stick by me, I'll see you don't go wrong. Have another sausage.'

In the middle of the afternoon, Jehanine put her head out of the wagon and saw a hilly plain below, awash as if in a sea-flood in the amber light. A river cut the plain in long burning loops.

'There is Paradys,' said the apothecary even more boastfully, as if he had built it, pointing into the plain. Jehanine could see nothing but the landscape, then, gradually, she began to make something out. It was like a heavenly city, all hollow arches and disembodied towers, floating on a ring of walls half-way up the sky.

Then the apothecary began to fondle her leg, and Jehanine was forced to round on him with a gruff 'Leave off.'

'Now, young lad. This is the City. It has got great markets and avenues. We are building enormous churches to the glory of God. We're sophisticated here. Slough your peasant morals.'

Jehanine considered her blistered feet. She said, lowering her eyes, 'Well, maybe tonight, then.'

Having said which, she remained silent as the apothecary's servant drove the wagon across the river, and along a winding road full of traffic, and up hill, and at last through the ring of City walls. Soon they were caught in a jam of carts and mules. Jehan-Jehanine absented herself from the wagon on the excuse of nature, and thus gave the apothecary the slip.

She was now in famed Paradys, without a coin or a scrap of food, clad in her brother's clothes and her sister's cloak, and the shape of a boy, knowing only the name of an artisan to whom Pierre had been assigned. But armed with this, and the meal the apothecary had given her, Jehanine looked about her boldly.

She knew nothing of Paradys, scarcely its title, which was almost as much as Paradys knew of itself.

She wandered a while, carelessly aware of everything, for everything was different from all she had ever known, and consequently she observed it through the lens of familiar concepts, and could by this means discount it. The people pushed and shoved at her like herds. The bulging, craning and leaning buildings, which frequently met overhead in the narrower thoroughfares, reminded her of defiles among the rocks, or overgrown woods. The air, rank or sweet with smells of cooking, perfume, humanity and filth, was only an outdoor variety of the air of farmhouse or hut. Since she had nothing worth stealing, no one attempted to rob her, or if they did, it was performed – and disappointed – without her knowledge. Climbing up the hills of the city, even as the sun began to slide down them, she started to catch glimpses high above her of a massive form, in fact a building that was in the process of birth. Brown walls and skeletal scaffolding towered into the sky. This was unlike anything from experience, and must be one of the churches the apothecary had mentioned when inducing her to sin. At length, remembering a conversation between Belnard and Pierre, Jehanine detained a pedlar, at this moment the only creature in sight.

'Is that the great Temple-Church they're making there?'

'Is so,' said the pedlar, a tall dwarf she now noticed, the crown of whose head reached to her ribs. 'The Temple of the Sacrifice of the Redeemer.'

'Then,' said Jehanine, 'does Master Motius – ' the name of the artisan – 'live hereabouts?'

'Oh, are you going to be apprenticed to him, or to model for the class? You might buy a ribbon for your sweetheart. Here, look – '

Jehanine pushed the tray aside. She frowned.

'Tell me,' she said, in a tone Belnard used with his slaves. 'Or I'll tip your tray in the muck and black your eye for you.'

'Vicious thing,' said the dwarf, skipping back. He grinned. 'It's one of the young men you're after. Who is it? I tell you, you won't find him here. He'll be in his lodging. Or in the tavern. I can guide you there, where all the students of Master Motius go drinking. Buy a ribbon for your sister.'

'I haven't any money,' said Jehanine. 'Sod your ribbons.'

The dwarf spat neatly on the cobbles between them.

'See that alley? They call that Satan's Way.'

'Take it then and go to Hell,' said Jehanine. Her male attire, freeing her tongue, pleased her. She went by the dwarf and continued up towards the gaping caverns of the part-built Church. However, to her annoyance, she realised the dwarf was creeping after her. There was nothing lying about suitable to throw. He must be ignored for the present.

Above the alley, circling the Church, a street of decent houses followed an old walled garden. A trough and an impressive well stood in the midst of the street, with steps, and carved figures holding up the well's cowled roof. Something again fluttered in Jehanine's memory. This was the very street where the artisan lived and had his studio.

Jehanine ran to the first house and spontaneously struck the door. A small panel was opened. A pudgy face looked out.

'What do you mean by it?' a voice demanded. 'Be off.'

'Wait!' cried Jehanine, her own voice rising to a wail. 'Is this the house of Master Motius?'

'It is not. Be off.'

And the panel slapped shut.

From the tail of her eye, Jehanine was aware of the irksome dwarf still watching her. She walked across to the well, released the bucket and let it down into the water. As she was hauling it up, another house opened itself, this time by means of a small side-door, and out came a fat woman with an apron and keys at her belt, attended by a boy with a cudgel.

'Hey! What are you doing there?' bawled the woman.

Jehanine leant to the bucket and drank from it. The woman flumped over, the boy at her heels.

'As you see,' said Jehanine. 'Isn't God's water for all?'

'Indeed not. We pay taxes for it,' said the woman. She eyed Jehanine, Jehan to her, with a round eye. 'But the damage is done. Pray Heaven you've not let loose some disease in the water.' The round eye was now a lascivious eye. Jehanine played her part. She smiled at the woman, and leaned on one of the carved figures of the well. 'Lady,' said Jehan, 'I'm looking for my brother, one Pierre Belnard – '

'Ah!' cried the woman, and threw up her hands. 'What a beauty he is. And a proper resemblance. You'll be one of those younger brothers. Not trouble at home?'

'I must find him at once.'

'Not here,' said the woman. 'Master Motius has the "Autumn Cough", there was no work today. Though why he can't cure his cough, with all he knows – stop in a moment at the house. My old master's off on his business – always off on something. I'll feed you up, skinny boy. He'll never know.'

But, 'A drinking-shop . . .' suggested Jehanine impatiently.

'Well, your Pierre, the naughty one, that's true. Down across the river. The *Cockatrice* is where they drink, bad fellows, and get up to all sorts. You ought to be careful of yourself. Now why don't you come in – '

But Jehan-Jehanine was running on blistered fire-hot feet. Affronted, the woman turned to scold her cudgel-boy.

The dwarf had already vanished from the scene.

Darkness closed on Paradys. But the night City was no worse, no more impenetrable, than a night in the country. This too had its own strange sounds, its own pitfalls, and generally the City gave more light than the forests, hills and fields, which were lit only by fire-flies, fungus, stars and moon. The City moon was made of dull plate, but lower down other luminosities shone out. High round windows in various towers of a college where the students pored late over huge books and parchments, dim bars of light behind iron grills and panes of sheepskin. Sometimes, at the gates of a fine house, or along the river and its bridges, torches flashed on poles. But on the lower bank the hovels crowded to each other in sympathy, darkling, though here and there an occasional fire bloomed on stones in the street.

It had taken Jehanine a long while to find the *Cockatrice*. She had chosen wrong turnings, directions had not always been helpful. Twice, thrice, ladies of the alleys had spoken very ill of her, when the young man she was garmented as refused their services.

Above the inn door hung the sign of a cock with the head of a serpent. Superstitiously, Jehanine would not look straight at it. In the lord's village, only twenty years ago, a man, coming home drunk one night, had disturbed a real cockatrice in the wintry pastures. One glance, and he had petrified to stone. The place was still pointed out, and the stone which stood there, hunched over in terror, ivy growing thick on him.

Having gone under the sign into the doorway, Jehanine was prompted to cover herself, head to toe, with the cloak. Pierre had of course never seen or would ever have dreamed of her in male clothing. She sensed he might in some way be offended.

Just then, men emerged from the inn, arguing. They blustered past Jehanine, partly throwing her against the timbers. Their features and expressions had the inimical alien look which the girl was accustomed to seeing on the faces of fellow human beings. While, at the edge of the night, lit by the opened door, she beheld the tall dwarf lurking in an alley. It seemed he had stuck to her tenaciously through all her wanderings. Jehanine hastened into the *Cockatrice*.

It was a place whose light seemed only to contribute to its darkness. Beams crossed close overhead, below, a fire jerked and spits revolved. Opaque shadows had massed at tables, on benches, or passed her through the ochre gloom. The air too was thick with noise and smells. In such a place, where was her brother?

She began to wade slowly forward, looking cautiously aside into meaningless faces. Beakers clinked or were spilled. Men shouted. Serving-girls screeched. Then she heard his laugh, so known, clear and musical and all-embracing, across the formless din. On instinct, she swung towards it, almost collided with one of the servers – who cursed her flightily, thinking her after all a male – and got between the tables into an alcove.

Five or six young men sat there, indeterminate in the unlit light, oddly amalgamated by it to an entity. But in their midst, a holy face, sculpted and painted by sun-tan on ivory, and hair gilded by a master craftsman with costly gold-leaf mixed in honey.

'Pierre,' said Jehanine.

It was not by way of an address to him, but a magic word, spoken as an amulet.

But hearing it from an unexpected quarter, her handsome brother turned, and stared at her blankly.

'What's this, eh, dear prince?' one of his companions, whose arm lay across Pierre's shoulders, inquired of him. 'Fallen foul again of the sorority of the streets?'

Pierre smiled, and shook his head.

'I don't know her,' he said.

Struck in the heart, Jehanine stood in silence. For the first time since her escape, she was at a loss. She could see it was true. He did not know her.

'Well, what does she want?' said another of the men. Nearest to her, he caught at her suddenly, squeezing her flank. 'We're not ready for your single talent yet. Try us later.'

All of them burst out laughing, and Pierre's beautiful laugh rose up again with the rest.

Jehanine shook off her hood in terror. She clutched her hands together at her throat. 'Pierre – Pierre – '

'Oh, she's glue, this one.'

'Go on, you hussy. Clear yourself off.'

'Wait,' said Pierre. Now his voice was low and shaken. He reached suddenly across all of them and caught down one of her hands. '*Is it you*?'

'Yes – '

'What in Christ's name – what are you doing here? Am I drunk and dreaming you?' Then, breaking through his guffawing and shoving friends, Pierre came out to her. Ignoring the fresh outcry, he began to drag her away with him, into some darker than dark corner. Vaguely she saw skeins of onions hanging from the roof about them, vaguely she heard all the clamour recede like a rumbling in the earth. 'Why are you here, Jehanine? What's happened?'

All of her seemed to give way at once. She wanted only to weep, and that he would take her instantly to some private gentle spot, and comfort her. But something in him, something new and novel, something old and well-known, warned her not to lean on him or shed her tears.

'I couldn't stay,' she said. 'He raped me.'

Pierre only gazed at her. His eyes were wide. What girl was he seeing here before him?

'Who?' he eventually said, without interest, only bewildered.

'Belnard.'

'Do you say our father – '

'Your father. Yes. He raped me. And later another of them would have – but I – ' something stopped the phrases of how she had used a sharp stone. 'What could I do but – '

'Oh, Jehanine,' Pierre interrupted her. 'What are you saying? As if he'd do such a thing.'

And now it was her turn to gaze in astonishment.

'Oh very well,' said Pierre. He lowered his eyes, put out that such matters must be verbalised between them. 'Perhaps you were unwise with some man. I won't judge you. But to say our father did that to you. That's disgusting.'

She closed her eyes. *It is true*, she cried out at him, soundlessly, hitting and clawing at him with her heart as she stood there motionless, defeated once and for all. Ah Pierre. Fair hero, but a man. How could it have been otherwise?

'Well,' he sighed. 'I must get you back to the farm.'

A word, despite everything, sprang from her mouth, like the frogs of witch-cursings in tales. '*No.*'

'Don't be tiresome, girl. I'll have to spend time on this. I'm not best pleased, I can tell you. I have other things to do.'

'No – no – let me stay with you. I'll care for you and – '

'*Christ's teeth.* You fool, Jehanine. I lodge in a sty. You can't come there. You must go home.'

And as they stood there, among the grove of onions in the dark, the smothered light burned in his eyes, on his hair, and suddenly touched also a spark under his throat. Having glimpsed it, she could not look away from it, though she had no understanding of what it might be – a fleck of mysterious fire, or the eye of some creature clinging inside his tunic.

'No,' she murmured again, but her purpose was gone. She spoke now on a dying reflex. But he answered in anger: 'Yes, by God. Home you'll go, you damned and stupid sow. Coming here and shaming me like this. Do I want you? Stupid fool, I'd rather hang myself than say you were my sister, flouncing here like some trollop.'

And then she saw what the spark of fire, the eye, really was. It was a jewel, a perfect topaz set square into a small crucifix of gold. It was the fabled gem Belnard had promised his son at his leave-taking. A gift for the boy, an abuse for the girl. As with the rape, these harsh words, this betrayal, oh, what else?

Jehanine whispered, 'Forgive me, Pierre. What shall I do?'

Her heart had now died, and she felt nothing at all as he brusquely told her. Nor did she listen. The dead have no necessity to heed or to obey.

'What's up with you? There now, ssh. Tell? I'll listen.'

Jehanine struck out feebly, but the bending shadow dodged her blow. The shadow moved a space, and leaned philosophically on a wall. It sang: 'Fero, fero, fero.' Then: 'I could have told you. Whatever you are, girl or boy, that sort – they use you up then cast you off. No use begging in this blighted world. Stones for bread, poison for milk, kicks and cuts and cuffs and curses for a kiss.'

It was the dwarf, still following her. She supposed he would know about stones and curses. But that did not make her fond of him.

Directed by her brother to sit in a recess in the inn doorway, she had done so, the way a dog follows a command, meaningless in itself, by tone. She could not recall the direction. Other than herself, and a sleeping, toothless crone, the recess was vacant. Beyond, the drinkers came and drank and stayed or went. Pierre had also said he would return and fetch Jehanine, when he was done. Though she had not heard the words, she had assimilated the fury of his irritation.

After a short while, seeing it was ridiculous to remain, she got up again, left the crone and the *Cockatrice*, and wandered away into the City.

Somewhere – unlit houses, perhaps an open square under an arch – she sank by a wall and began to weep.

She did not know why, and assumed the sobbing would quickly cease, as in the past it always had. It did not. Then the dwarf approached.

'You see,' said the dwarf now, 'the world isn't God's, it's the Devil's. Satan is Lord. You make a grave mistake, calling out to the other one. Think how it hurts him, Prince Lucefiel, the Morning Star, to be passed over.'

This blasphemy was gibberish. Jehanine wept. Rising, weeping, she pushed by the dwarf, and wandered into the open arch, and through, and on, and away.

The rain began much later. The moon had set, hardly a lamp burned anywhere. Only bells sounded across the lakes of the night. Then into these pastures and caves of the City, the rushing water crashed.

A curious thing happened. Though she had almost forgotten it, someone still followed the girl, and now she became aware that by following, he *led* – he *drove* her, as the shepherd and the goatherd drive their flocks and herds. She did not understand how this was, yet it had happened. Mindless in her grieving nullity, he had somehow sent her up and down the City, and now she had come through a labyrinth of alleys, in the rain, and so to a long high wall of stone. And then there was a gateway, and thick black doors studded by iron were shut fast in it.

Jehanine entered the gate for shelter and slipped down against the doors.

'Knock,' said the dwarf, 'and be answered.'

'Why have you brought me here?' she said.

'I? Brought you?' He smiled. He had rain for teeth and eyes. 'Fero, fero. *Knock.*'

She raised her fist and saw it dimly, like a wet white bone. She knocked on the door.

Presently a grill rustled above. Jehanine did not bother to raise her head or face. She bowed there in the rain. A woman's voice whispered to her. 'Demoiselle, what do you want? Do you wish to come in?

Jehanine thought: It will be a brothel.

The voice spoke so softly.

'You are at the gate of the Nunnery of the Angel. I will open the door at once. Don't be afraid.'

Jehanine had an urge to drag herself away. She looked about now to try to see the dwarf and to say, He knocked, not I. But the dwarf had disappeared again. Then the door was unlocked and one leaf of it swung inwards. A robed female shape, holding a pale lantern in a staring-pale gorget. A nun.

Jehanine got up slowly, the Bride of Christ helping her, and the lantern enfolded them both and drew them in. Another robed, veiled nun locked shut the gate. Beyond the light was darkness, and the faint adrift dagger of a bell-tower. The rain stopped suddenly.

'Come now,' said the lantern-nun. 'You're safe at last. Our Lord has brought you here.'

Jehanine laughed. God was male, Jesus a man.

Black by night, the structure of the nunnery turned white by day.

Jehanine woke to such whiteness, and the scent of lemons, and the distant female notes of a chant. Such things haunted this place.

In a small wood oblong to the north of the gate, lay the six cells available to guests and itinerants, and Jehanine in one of them. Her chamber gave on to a cloistered yard with a well, and two lemon trees. Through an arch in the cloistering was visible a paved inner court, dominated by the church door and the implication of the tower. From the height of this, the bell tongued out mutedly over and over, at its three-hourly intervals night and day, and the nun-bees droned, punctual as the bell, their ghostly songs to God.

As Jehanine had travelled to Paradys, she travelled through a light fever, through sleep and time, to an empty amazed awakening. As previously, she had not counted the days. But the same birds fluted, the same bells moaned, and there rose the same eerie singing.

A young nun stood at the foot of the pallet. Her face was flatly suspended in her gorget. Below, subserviently waited her body in the robe of the order, which was fulvous, the autumn-leaf colour of a yellow fox.

The nun asked Jehanine no pertinent questions. She merely said, 'You are here. Do you remember where you are?'

Jehanine gazed in silence.

'The Nunnery of the Angel. You may stay or go, as you want.'

'I've nowhere to go.'

The nun said, 'This is sometimes the case. We ask nothing from you, but you're strong and healthy, perhaps you will perform some small domestic services for the order, in return for sanctuary. Get up now. I'll take you to the refectory. You may wish to pray. I'll show you the chapel. Later the Mother may send for you.'

Jehanine, ignorant and uneasy, said, 'If I remain, must I be a nun?'

'That is your choice. The order never asks it.'

While Jehanine garbed herself in the bounty of the nuns – a shift, linen stockings and garters, a plain gown and worn cloth shoes without heels, the nun stood by like an icon, with averted eyes. (The male clothes had vanished, no comment had been made on them.)

The nun conducted Jehanine from the yard and across the court, past the vault of the church door, into the refectory. The morning meal, served at seven o'clock after the office of Prima Hora, was done. But behind an angled wooden screen at one end of the long

105

room, cup, spoon and platter had been laid on the table. Jehanine felt only an unspecified shame, then, seated, only a ravenous hunger, and devoured the warm porridge and black bread fiercely. While she ate, again the nun stood by, hands folded in her sleeves, her eyes concealed. Her forehead was smooth and her little chin firm and rounded. She could not be more than nineteen or twenty years. Yet she seemed old, set in her ways, perhaps wise.

The jug contained water. Jehanine was disappointed, for the priest at home had drunk beer and milk and wine.

'Are you concluded?' said the young-old nun. 'You didn't thank God for the food.' Jehanine, whose tragedies far overbore such a minor omission, still coloured and bit her lip. But the nun said, 'It isn't needful. But come to the church now. I will show you where you may pray.'

The food had made Jehanine drowsy again. She thought that in the church she might conceal herself and sleep once more. Or she might find some crevice in the garden that ran by the refectory and away into an orchard of plums.

Beyond the garden, on the south side of the church, there was a massive cloister, where a fountain was standing dry on the sere sunny grass, but they went quickly through a small door into shadows. Within, the occluded windows of the church were high and narrow, perhaps for purposes of defence. Yet eastwards lay the altar, with metal things burning on it, and above a strange unearthly mirror hung in the dark air. Jehanine had not seen coloured glass before, and it bemused her. She had the impression of movement and force where there was none, only hues glamoured by light – with a wild shaft hammered down out of them, for the sun was now directly behind.

The shaft fell unbroken into the quire, and caught in the slanted pillar of it, a white-robed figure seemed to levitate just above the floor.

Jehanine halted. The figure filled her with awe – she turned instinctively to the nun for guidance. But the nun did not pause, only went gliding on into the nave. Turning back then, Jehanine saw that as the shaft of sunlight shifted and faded, the white image was no longer there.

Nevertheless, on entering the quire, Jehanine stopped.

'What are you looking at?' said the nun. 'That is the Great Light.'

'What picture is that?' said Jehanine.

'It is the Angel,' said the nun, and as she spoke, she made a genuflection towards the altar, bowing knee and head, but also touching her hands to her forehead and breast.

The Angel in the window flamed out of a sunburst of molten brass. His sunflower hair was rimmed by a halo like a coin of new gold, and in his white wings every feather was veined with fire. His gaze fixed downwards, and one foot rested on a shining globe. A sword of fire was in his hand. He was beautiful. It made her think of another . . . of Pierre. Jehanine's eyes scorched with water. She turned from the Angel in anger and pain.

A small chapel stood north of the altar. Here the non-initiates might essay their orisons.

Jehanine knelt on the stone floor dutifully. She did not notice anything else.

For a long time she made pretence at humble prayer, then she glanced about and the guardian nun had left her.

Jehanine rose. She had forgotten the idea of sleep. Her skin held tight to her bones. She thought of what she had done and what had been done to her, and that here she was in a kind of prison or trap which she could never leave. She found as she thought of these things, that she looked back towards the High Altar, to see if the shaft of light would fall again out of the window, but the moments of the light were past.

Eyelets of saffron glass, merely, dappled the candlesticks and the cloth. Jehanine, seeing them, thought of the topaz crucifix Pierre had been given by Belnard her step-father.

Then, in a sudden flaming thoughtless and inexpressible trance, she fell to her knees again. She offered up, unconsidered and patternless, her agony. It was neither plea nor prayer, it was not an acceptance. She was no saint, certainly no pure virgin, crowned with the snow roses of martyrdom.

The bell, balanced far overhead, and sounding for the office of Tiers, startled her to her feet. She ran from the church like a guilty thing.

Days passed, leaves that fell, birds that took flight.

Jehanine served the Nunnery of the Angel. She swept its yards and scrubbed its flagstones alongside the girls, some younger than she, of the novitiate. The novices did not aspire to a habit but only wore plain gowns like her own, their hair bound up as hers was each in a bleached scarf. Sometimes they innocently giggled, told stories, or sang gentle sad songs as they worked. One was very pious. Her name was Osanne. She kept herself from the others, sweeping and scrubbing alone, muttering prayers, toiling until her knees were raw and her back stiff, for the glory of God.

Sometimes they would work in the garden among the late-blooming bushes, pruning and weeding, picking plums, berrying, and gathering herbs for drying and flower-heads for pressing. They rinsed linen and tawny robes and hung them to sweeten in the sun. They hauled water from the two garden wells, one of which was ancient and brackish, fit only to wash floors or sluice the privies.

Sometimes the novices went away into the House of the Novitiate, to learn from painted books, and left Jehanine alone. They spoke, even in daydreams, of their bridal, and the white Bride's robe embroidered with gold tears, the marriage once and for ever to their Lord, the Son of God. They were like any girls before their wedding. Half afraid, half lost in love-desire.

Jehanine could not adventure with them. She was not to be a nun. Besides, they were of good birth, these girls, surplus daughters sent away. Jehanine was a peasant, from the north outlands. She could not read, and knew no songs. They allowed her their company, for she was couth enough, and in her tall slender blondness there glittered some truth they sensed but would not know.

Jehanine feared and despised, admired and liked them. Osanne's fanatic hauteur seemed more natural, however, and if anything Jehanine was more comfortable in its presence.

Beyond the thick walls of the nunnery, the City lived and had its being, too. Occasionally some noise came from it, and often the huge stenches of the falling year. Within and without the wall, the weather was the same. Should she wish to re-enter the City, the world, Jehanine had only to say so. But, having done that, self-exiled, she could not return.

Had Pierre ever searched for her? At first it had seemed he might have done, and that he was afraid for her. But swiftly these hopes of love and renewal died. They were simply the pangs of healing. She knew quite soon that she was whole, though now scarred and crippled out of shape.

She was not unhappy. The chores of the nunnery were nothing to the labour of the Belnard farm. The food, though less various and not always so fresh, was sure. And in the house of women, the threat of male wickedness and strength could not intrude.

Now and then, playing their innocent ball or catcher's games in the south garden or the deserted hostel cloister, the novices elected Jehanine as the Boy. She must give judgement, she must threaten. Once or twice they kissed her. In much the same way one found an infrequent garland on the brow of the stone child, perhaps a boy, who held the bowl of the dry fountain.

The Mother had never, after all, sent for Jehanine. Perhaps such orphans were beneath her notice. Jehanine had briefly believed it was the white figure of this Mother, this queen of the hive, that she had glimpsed light-pierced under the window. But on certain days, the Mother would enter the refectory and herself read passages of scripture as the nuns silently ate. Around the edge of the screen, Jehanine saw her, another fox-robe, a proud full face, and plump hands. The vision of light, therefore, unsolved, remained Jehanine's property: all she had.

The garden and the trees turned brown.

Here I have been, then, thought Jehanine, by which she meant she had lived there thirty days or more, though she could not reckon them. A season was nearly gone.

She knew now by ear the call to all the offices, from Matines to the office of the evening star, Hesper, and to Complies which closed the day. She knew three ball games, and certain secular songs of the novices, though she did not sing them. She learned the uses of the herbs from the garden, and, by rote, paragraphs of herbal lore and myth, read from a book by an elderly lay-sister.

Who had she been once?

One twilight, she saw a white-robed woman walking before her down the roofed passage that ran between the church and the House of the Novitiate. At the opening of the passage the white robe blended out and was gone. Nobody was in the hostel cloister beyond. It was then, a ghost. Jehanine knew fear, and disappointment.

In the hostel-cell where she still slept her few hours each night, she looked about. At a dying spray of vivid leaves in a cracked jar, a cross of wood on the wall and a pallet on the floor, a low straight chest which contained her cloak, and oddments of linen, and had on its top a comb and a small crock of water, in the shallows of which a fly had drowned. Such were her possessions, and two of them dead. She had never had anything much. A doll of her mother's when she was a child that the half-sisters broke, carved sticks and pebbles a boy called Pierre had given her, then retrieved.

The ghost was common to all who could see it. It might harm her but was not hers.

The bell rang for the office of Hesperus.

That night the Mother entered the refectory. She opened the Bible on its stand and read these words: 'God so hated His Son, that He gave him to the world that the world might have him.'

In a dream, Jehanine was seeing the City by night, and it was like a wasteland of rocks. Nothing moved, no lights showed. The moon hung low. Then in the east there seemed to be a bright star rising, which sent its rays across the roofs, and lit their edges. Brighter and brighter the star became, and then it opened like the petals of a flower, and things rushed out of it.

At first she thought they were insects, then birds, then men and women riding over the rooftops of Paradys. But on the church at home had been some rough-hewn gargoyles, and now she identified the galloping throng – they were demons, with the bodies of men, even sometimes with the breasts of women, but the horned heads of goats and snouts of lizards snapped and grimaced from their long wild hair. Their bodies were the colour of the tired low moon, and glimmered in the same way. The mounts they rode were of all manners: huge black dogs, winged baskets and poles, or other creatures like themselves –

They were horrible, yet they laughed and called to each other, and filled the air with a robust foulness.

Jehanine, dreaming, had a terror they would see and catch her up, but it was another they took, who had been standing waiting not far off. He leaped to join them, and in a moment he went by Jehanine, mounted on a monstrous beast part pig part bat. He was Pierre, but he did not see her and he rode away with the jolly host of Hell.

'*Jhane!*' cried the dark. 'Jhane!'

'Jhane. Wake, Jhane.'

Jehanine opened her eyes and rose from sleep to fill them and her body.

Before her, dark on dark, a figure leaned. Jehanine was terrified, then stupefied. No monster, but haughty Osanne, who of all the novices had never before abbreviated Jehanine's name in this way.

'What do you want, dem'selle?'

'Don't call me that. I'm to be a holy sister. Say that. Say, *sister.*'

'Sister.'

'You trouble me,' said Osanne. She sat back now, beside the pallet. She wore a cloak over her shift, but her hair was unbound and coiled all about her restlessly. 'Were you dreaming? Stop it. Attend. I want you to tell me why it is you won't come into the shelter of this order? Stubbornness. Your low birth, your unlearning – such things don't matter. Do you love God?'

Jehanine was silent. Osanne breathed more quickly.

'Answer me, girl – *Do you love God?*'

'If I must,' said Jehanine. How soft the night. Hell did not ride the roofs. The dream was dying.

'Sinner! Evil sinner. How can God live except by love? Every such word hammers in the nails afresh.'

'Demoiselle – Sister Osanne – leave me alone.'

'No. I must save your soul. I know it now. God has revealed it to me. Get up at once. Kneel by me here.'

'Go away,' said Jehanine.

'I'll make you if I must. Stupid girl. Do you want to burn in the Pit for all eternity?'

'What pit is that?'

'Fool. The Pit of raging Hell. The cauldron of live fire where Lucifer is king. The torture never-ending. Didn't you hear the lesson tonight that the Mother read at supper? God loved the world so well he sent his only Son, Jesus, the Christ, to be our saviour.'

'But she said – ' began Jehanine. She stopped saying it.

Osanne, unheeding, curved forward like a snake, and gripped her, pulling her up from under the cover. Suddenly Osanne had seized her prey. She wound her arms about Jehanine and buried her mouth, hot as the fire of which she warbled, in Jehanine's neck.

'Jhane, Jhane, pray with me now. I'll save you. Dear sister in Christ. You have the marks of goodness on you. So fair, child-like, yet rough like a boy – put your arms about me, Jhane.'

Jehanine did so. Osanne fell upon her, and as they floundered on the pallet, enormous waves began to pour upon Jehanine, of alarm and physical pleasure and horror. The darkness of the room, half hiding everything, seemed to make all things foreign, removed and possible. Osanne squirmed and writhed. She lay beneath Jehanine now. She wrapped Jehanine with all her limbs, (a demon, mounted), and abruptly let out a hoarse mad cry, a moan, a grunt, and fell back.

What have you done?' she gasped. She pushed Jehanine away. 'You're evil. Dirty and foul. Possessed. A monster – one of the Devil's minions – oh let me go – '

She crawled towards the open air, sobbing and gulping. The room seemed icy cold. How comfortless it would be in winter.

When Osanne, her sounds enfeebled and muted by dread of discovery, had gone, Jehanine dressed herself. She trembled violently as she had not done at the rape of her step-father.

Leaving the cell barefoot, she crossed through the yards into the south garden, and passed over it in the moonless nothing of the night. A small bakehouse, now seldom used, stood against the outer wall, and here a tree spread up, already leafless. Jehanine climbed it without effort, pulled herself atop the wall, and looked out not in dream, for the first time in those years of days, on Paradys.

Where the nunnery was situated she had never properly known. Now she saw the locationless gullies of alleys, hills of masonry, no lights, and the stars' cooled clinker. Then she sprang from the wall, into an abyss two-and-a-half times her own height.

She fell into harsh and lumpy softness – a pile of sacks, filled perhaps some by meal, and some by goose-feathers, for elements of such dust and fluff puffed out at her impact.

'Well, you've made me wait,' said a voice. 'That's the only sly way, you see, that tree, then down. But I'd thought you would be sooner tired of them. Here. See what your friend has brought you.'

Jehanine, lying on the sacks, looked up through muffled lantern light, to a grinning face and two hands dangling a tunic, hose, a boot of sheer leather. It was a dream, like the other, and since dreams make their own laws, Jehanine got to her feet and grabbed the dwarf.

'Hey, hey. You can even go back. We'll see to it, we will. But somewhere else first. Put these on. You can't travel as a maiden. I'll look the other way.'

Jehanine hit the dwarf across the face. This time, the blow met flesh and spun him. He dropped the samples of male attire, nearly the lantern. Jehanine bent to the clothes, found the complete set, and picked them up.

They were not her half-brother's rubbish. These seemed unworn, garments of a lord of the alleys, gaudy, elegant – what a man might thieve who was clever at thieving.

It was a dream.

'Go over there,' said Jehanine. She started to pull up the drawers and hose under her skirt even as the dwarf turned away. She thrust and hauled on the robber's clothes; they were a panoply. She made a bundle of her own, like a discarded skin, and left it rolled into the sacks. In a dream, who would discover it?

'Good! Come then, this way,' said the dwarf, skipping ahead.

His lantern suddenly blared out. There was no longer any need of caution.

Jehanine had forgotten the freedom of such clothing, how she had been a boy, a young man, but now her body itself remembered. She laughed suddenly, and the dwarf said, 'This way, Jehan. Praise the Prince it's a fine night.' They slipped between the alleys, down the long worm-burrows. They passed by loops of the river seen beyond black and rotting walls. Fires burned uncannily between some of the hovels, and now and then a weird-lit face peered at them. Up a cobbled lane two torches volleyed before a house with noisy windows. It was an inn with a swinging sign that showed a ghostly figure with wings – an apparition. The dwarf went through a side-entry and up a spine-broken stair, Jehanine following him. In the corridor, where her head, if not his, nearly brushed the sagging beams, he rapped on a door. It was opened from inside. They stepped into the hollow of a room, ringed by faces. Fat candles were blinking on jugs and blades.

'Here's Fero.'

'Welcome to the *Imago*,' said the dwarf. Then, to the room at large, 'You see, my mates, I brought you him, as I said I'd do. What do you think?'

Jehanine stood stock still. Was this another betrayal? Even in dreams, such might occur. She said, speaking low but loudly, 'Who cares what they think. Who does the choosing here?'

There were men in the room and boys. Each was a thief, you could tell at a glance. In every belt at least one knife, in every mask the eyes of wolverines; they wore the dress and ornaments of men who clawed and snatched above their station.

The dream-dwarf, perverse and mad, had brought her to join them. Why should he? Well, he must have sniffed her criminal air.

'*We* choose,' said a man from the ring. 'But you look agile and leery enough. The dwarf's generally right. He found me, didn't he?'

'Then,' said another, 'we want the gift, the buying-in.'

'Do you know what he means, new lad?'

'I'll tell him what I mean. I mean something precious from him to us. A Judas kiss. A game. Proof. So what's he going to offer up?'

'His own self's enough,' replied one.

The dwarf, Fero, idled, sidled from Jehanine's side. Jehanine, Jehan, she-he stood alone, the door at her back, the rowdy inner inn and the black tunnels of night City beyond. She said, 'You can have a gift.' She felt herself whiten to a skull, they saw it and attended. (But it was a dream). 'I've kindred in the City, one who wronged me. I'll give you him.'

'What use is that? Is he wealthy?'

'Not much.'

One or two swore. A man came close and put his hand directly on her groin. She moved aside before he could tell he had touched only a cunning bulge of cloth – and bringing up her fist she mashed her knuckles into the base of his nose. As he left her, blinded by tears and roaring, the roomful laughed, commending her. She had seen her half-brothers and her step-father fight. She had learned their tricks, it seemed.

As the blinded robber crouched on the floor, the tangle of his body reminded her of Osanne. Jehanine kicked him in the back, and he fell down.

She said, 'What I offer is my brother. I hate him. I can manage things so you'll have him alone. He drinks late at the *Cockatrice*, and perhaps he's there now. His clothes are good, strip him and leave him naked. He's handsome. Do what you like. From his neck hangs a gold crucifix. There's a gem in it.'

Her head whirled. She closed her eyes.

Someone caught her by the shoulders, and a cup bumped against her lip. She drank bitter wine.

'What is it, you boy, this vengeance?'

It was the man who had spoken first, and who was also the dwarf's protegé. He apparently liked the look of Jehan and might protect him, so her. She pushed his arm off.

'My vengeance is your buying-in wanted gift. What more?'

Because it was a dream, she knew that her brother, beautiful Pierre, would be at the other inn. She knew that if she led them there, they would find him.

The dwarf sat on a table, drinking; he showed no inclination to make up the party, barely any interest, but six or seven of the fellowship were nudging at her now. Together they went down the twisted stair, with a clatter, and out. Jehanine did not know the way back to the *Cockatrice*, they did. They walked in a bunch, bravos, swaggering, not afraid. This was their holding, this trample of middens and slips along the river bank, these rat-holes. Sometimes they were challenged, from a wall-top or hovel's depths, passwords were exchanged, whistles or dog-barks, and once, two of the men made water in a well, to pay out an old score. Then some invisible border was crossed. The formation of the band altered. They were more wary, and walked two by two or three, knives to hand.

'No knife of your own?' Jehan's champion put his free hand on her shoulder. 'This brother – did he sour you for your birthright, maybe?' he asked, continuing the earlier dialogue. 'My whoresons brothers did that on me.'

Abruptly the inn of the *Cockatrice* appeared, surprising Jehanine with recognition.

'Wait here. I'll go to see.'

'No jokes,' said one, but that was all. She might have known them all for years, grown with them from desperate infancy like flowers on the dunghills of Paradys.

She went towards the serpent-cock, boy-walking as her brother's ungainly boots had taught her to. She spat, under the inn-sign. The inn was hardly awake, flickering with dying candles. All the drinkers seemed gone but for a sleeper at the hearth, and a man at his work with one of the wenches on a table.

But it was a dream, and so Pierre must remain. Where had he sat before, that night she came to entreat him? She could not be certain of the place.

Two men came down a stair. Brushing through the strings of onions, they yawned and grumbled. They had been with a girl, but she had turned them out before cockcrow. Old Motius would be aggrieved at their condition this morning. But old Motius was an intellectual dolt who conducted esoteric rituals, but thought mice ate the unground paint his pupils had stolen and sold. Motius was in love with Pierre. Oh, yes he was. One look from the lucent eyes, and the old fellow would probably pay for their harlots out of his own purse.

As Pierre came by her, Jehanine took his sleeve between her fingers.

He turned, gazed at her. His handsomeness, not spoiled by the debauch, turned her heart over. Seeing her, he seemed to see a spectre.

He said nothing. His companion said, in wonder, 'Your living *shade*, Pierre.'

Jehanine said to Pierre, 'You must come with me.'

The other student said, '*Oh* no. Come on, Pierre. This is some rogue.'

Jehanine stepped in their path. She shoved the student away from her brother. Being tipsy and fatigued, nor having either the strength of her hard life, he stumbled back and fell into the hearth, banging his head, landing among the bones and ashes. He lay there stunned, and presently threw up there, which caused discontent in several dark quarters of the inn.

While that went on, Jehanine drew her brother after her, staring in his eyes, beckoning to him but no longer touching. He followed, he did not seem to know why.

As they went out through the door, he said. 'Who are you?'

'Your sister,' said Jehanine. But not aloud.

She led him almost listlessly to the alley where the *Imago* thieves waited. She pulled him by a leash of air. Then, in the alley, she took her brother's hand and drew him forward.

'See,' she said to the thieves. A light flared and went out. Three of them leapt at him and flung a sack over his head, shoulders and arms. Pierre struggled. They beat him and he fell and was scrambled away with. They dived and tore a route into a copse of gutted hovels, where ratlets swarmed from their advance.

She stood by, she watched, lamped in the glow of a far-off light-cast – some brothel's beacon – as they removed the garments from Pierre's body, the dyed leather belt and fashionable shoes. At his throat, the topaz glared. They were leaving it till last. Pierre lay moaning, his head still furled in the sack.

'Now what?' said one.

They crowded grinning, and slowly unravelled the cloth from their captive's face.

'Your kin, decidedly.' They lifted him over on to his belly. 'Do you want him?'

'Incest,' said Jehan. Jehan smiled. Then walked off and leaned on a post, not watching finally what was done to Pierre Belnard, turn by turn, by the gang.

But Jehanine heard Pierre scream more than once, a hoarse masculine shriek. She had not cried out at her own rape. Nor had she been so appreciated, for his abusers spoke love-words to her brother.

At length, there was silence, but for the heartbeat of the City, a strange noise Jehanine had begun to hear, compounded of every beating heart that inhabited Paradys. Uncovering her eyes, she noticed that the beacon light had grown in magnitude. Next a cockerel crew deep in the alleyways. Then one by one the bells sounded across the river, closer at hand, the tongue of Prima Hora, dawn.

Jehan's protector, whose name she had picked out as Conrad, shook her shoulder now. He sweated, and his odour was ripe. She moved away from him. 'You're proved,' he said. 'You're one of us. Sin for damnable sin.' The others mumbled. 'Now do it to him, too.'

'No,' said Jehanine.

She walked towards the heap of flesh that was her brother. He lay on his side now, senseless perhaps, breathing through his open mouth. He was naked, covered by blood and filth. She leaned down and drew up his head a little by the soaked silk of hair. The dawn was spilling on the world. His eyes spasmed open. He looked full at her, knowing her, if not who she was. It was a look so terrible, so agonised and ruined, so utterly devoid of any hope for help or pity, that it reminded her of the face of the crucified Christ, and she shuddered at it.

'It never happened,' she said to Pierre softly. 'Such a disgusting thing.' Then she said to the others, 'I don't want him. I'll have

116

something else.' She ripped the crucifix from his throat, and let his face fall back into the dirt.

The gang of robbers eyed her in the revelation of the light.

One indicated Pierre. 'Better kill him. Then scatter.' To Jehanine he added, 'You give that here.'

'It's mine,' said Jehan.

Turning, Jehan bounded out and up from the wreckage. A running male figure, sprinting westward from the sunrise, towards the note of a bell earlier identified as that of the Angel.

Some of them dashed after Jehanine.

It was a dream: she lost them easily.

It was a dream, but in her hand she held the topaz cross.

Well then, waken now. But waking was not to be had.

She saw the nunnery ahead of her, rising from a tide of flotsam streets. The dwellings were of better quality here, and the river, a road of crystal cut by a ship's mast, was not far away – none of these things had she known before.

She came below the wall where the old bakery was, and saw the tops of the tree she had climbed, two and a half times her height above her. The sacks were gone, but tucked against the stone her clothes lay in a bundle almost as she left them. And down the wall itself, from a bough of the trees, hung a hempen rope. The dwarf had returned again to aid her. For, after all, it was not a dream.

She tied her female clothes to her body, and seizing the rope, climbed up the wall. In the tree, she undid and coiled the rope and took it down with her.

She changed her garments amid the bushes under the tree, in the wetness of the dew, for the nuns would be coming from the church to breakfast, and in the refectory some of the aged lay-sisters would be making the porridge.

As she went however to her cell, accessories bunched in her skirts and excuses ready, Jehanine met no one.

Into the chest she laid all her new possessions. The rope, the male attire, a knife Conrad had awarded her during their trek to the *Cockatrice*. Lastly, she laid the topaz cross upon her pallet. The thong had been broken and lost. She would search out another cord, then she might wear it, under her dress.

Paler than the dawn, the Eastern topaz shone for her. From desert lands by a sea of salt, under the mountains where God had walked, and from whose stones He had carved his devastating laws, from the tombs of prophets and messiahs, from the dazzling shrines of the Infidel, this jewel had come.

The Book of the Damned

She saw again her brother's appalling face.
She put the crucifix away into the chest.

Sister Marie-Lis paused in an arch of the south cloister, as Jehanine
watched her. Presently, her hands folded in her sleeves, the young
nun floated out on to the plot of grass. The dry fountain with the
wild-haired stone child holding its bowl, had been garlanded again.
The child had a kind of crown of thorns of twisted leafless creeper.
Sister Marie-Lis seemed not to pay attention to these things. She
came to the opposite arm of the cloister, where the northern girl and
three of the novices were sweeping.

'Come here, Jhane.'

Jehanine approached. Jehanine's hair was confined in its scarf
from which tendrils escaped like rays of winter sun. Otherwise she
was decorous, always excepting her looks.

The young nun eyed her, then called the novices.

'Where is the novice Osanne?'

The girls looked about.

'But she's here – '

'She came out with us. She had no breakfast. She sets herself
penances.'

'The Mother says Osanne is arrogant in her humility – '

'Hush,' said Sister Marie-Lis. 'It was the duty of Osanne this morning to attend the infirmary.'

'Well, she'd be pleased to do it.' The infirmary contained sick,
senile nuns and vats for boiling soiled linen.

Sister Marie-Lis said, 'Our Lord himself had compassion on the
sick. On all who call to him.'

Jehanine raised her eyes. She listened, and heard Sister Marie-Lis
saying:

'Did he not make the world against the will of his mighty father?
Did he not risk all and forfeit all that mankind might live? And as
he fell, his torch kindled the moon and stars, and the roots of
mountains.'

Then one of the novices exclaimed, 'Why, there is Osanne. She's
on the flags on her knees, scrubbing and *suffering*.'

Along the length of the cloister, over the parti-stripes of shadow
and sun, the mystic figure of Osanne rocked with its rags like a sway-
ing serpent.

'Osanne,' cried the young nun sternly, 'leave that work and go at
once to the infirmary.'

Osanne seemed not to hear. Sister Marie-Lis took a step, smooth

118

as if walking on water, towards the kneeling shape. And in that moment Osanne rose. Without a look or word, she went away, passing through the elbow of the cloister, and out of it into the garden. Her dress flashed very white as she vanished.

'That wasn't Osanne, sister!' said one of the novices. 'And see – the flags aren't even wet – '

'Hush,' said the young nun once again. She found a hand in her sleeves and touched it to her forehead and breast.

Jehanine felt a desire to follow Osanne as Jehan. Or she might bring in one of the thieves, Conrad possibly, and give Osanne to him as she had given – that other –

A dreadful pain tore through Jehanine, unseaming her. She sank suddenly to the ground and lay still. When the novices squeaked and came running, peering into her face, Jehanine covered her eyes with her hands. The young nun had gone away. Then the bell rang: Tiers. The novices fluttered. They must go to church at Tiers, and what of Jhane?

Jehanine got up slowly. What had happened to her was nothing, she was at her monthly bleeding, it was only that.

As the novices ran away, she realised she would not be able to return among the robbers for a few days, for at these times they might scent her, like a bitch, and so learn her true sex.

As for Pierre, they would have killed him, by what they had done, or afterwards with their knives.

She must think of him as dead, and of herself as his murderer. That was all it amounted to.

Going over to Osanne's discarded pail and rags, Jehanine detected a curious but delicious fragrance. It fled in a moment. Kneeling down, she began to wash the stones carefully.

In the succeeding days, Osanne was spied at her duties and devotions continuously, but not consistently. It appeared she must be sick, or that the passion of her faith drove her often to lonely prayer – for in the church they saw her most of all. But on their hurrying in she went away, was gone. She spoke to no one. They said the Mother had sent for Osanne, but it seemed Osanne did not attend the Mother.

'See, *look*. There she goes, she,' said one of the novices to Jehanine, as they passed together along the roofed passage between the church's north wall and the House of the Novitiate. The weather was turning chilly, but they carried between them a cask of candle stubs, due to be melted down for new, and this was heavy, heating work. The figure of Osanne flitting before them gave an excuse to hesitate and lower the cask. 'Look how white her skirt is, and her scarf. She must bleach them over and over – ' the process of bleaching, which intimately involved mules' urine, was disliked; doubtless Osanne would revel in it.

'Osanne!' cried the novice. 'Let's run and catch her.'

They ran, but did not catch. Beyond the passageway, the hostel court was empty, and the churchyard beyond empty also.

They returned for the cask of candles, and the novice started to talk of her marriage to Christ.

Soon after the bell of Matines, Jehanine dreamed the dwarf came into her cell. He carried a stone bowl on his shoulder, the contents of which – fire – he tipped on to the floor.

'Fero, fero,' said he. 'Why do you make me wait about under the damned wall?' said he. 'Get up and come to the Inn of the Apparition. You know the way. Or you can find it.'

Jehanine opened her eyes and the fire and the dwarf were gone. Her female bleeding had ended, and getting up she opened the chest and looked in at the items there, the male clothes and the rope, and the topaz cross.

Soon a long-haired boy came out of the cell and took his quiet stealth across the courts. The nuns were at their disembodied chanting in the church, but in the garden a nightingale, disturbed, whirred mournfully that the summer had died. Here and there, the garden had begun to smell oddly. The stink of the midden had grown less, but the moulder of fallen leaves, where visiting cats had relieved themselves, seemed sharpened by the cold night. The elder well smelled bad, and might require cleansing. The stealthy boy went on, found his tree, climbed it and roped it, and spent himself into the dark City. The cares of a nunnery were for a while no longer his.

The *Imago*, which owed its Latin name to some obscure story entailing the Roman troops once quartered on this bank of the river, (when Paradys was but a hedge of huts the other), had not changed: roared and thumped, and scaling the stair to the upper room, Jehan had slight need of caution.

She did not knock. She flung the door wide. There they were, staring astonished at her. The dwarf she could not see, but Conrad was the first to his feet cursing her. Others lunged forward, but halted. She they thought a he had come back to them. What plot was in it?

'Thief,' said the fat man.

'Bloody tricky swine,' said the man with the scar down his long nose.

Jehan shrugged elaborately, in the way of young men.

'Did you bring it?' cracked out Conrad.

'What?'

'The jewel – '

'It's mine. I didn't come to act a contrition.'

'Get him,' said Scar-Nose. There was a surge again, which now faltered on Jehan's high, maybe unbroken, voice.

'I'll find you better.'

They cascaded against her, but the vicious rush had become a pawing query. She kicked and pushed them off.

'Who leads this herd?' she said.

'No man. We're one. A brotherhood. An equal share, an equal voice for all.'

She supposed then it was actually the dwarf who ruled the gang. She had suspected it. But they were embarrassed to admit the fact, pretended otherwise, and resorted to high-flown phrases of fraternity.

'Tonight *I'll* lead you,' said Jehan. 'Again.'

She was mocked. She took no notice. Where, in her apron and skirts she had no say, now, her breasts bound, and weaponed with cloth in her hose, she had a say, and would say so.

'Be quiet, you pigs. Listen. Didn't I give you nice sport before?'

'And then cheated us.'

'What's a paltry bit of coloured glass? It had value for me, not for you.' For a second she was prompted to demand if they had knifed their victim, Pierre, her brother. Something stuck her tongue against the roof of her mouth, and when she could speak again she said, 'The upper bank of the City, near that great big church they're fussing up. I know a woman there. It's a wealthy house. You'll see how we'll find out its secrets.'

The idea of the fat woman, the housekeeper with the keys, who had accosted her in the street by the statue-fountain that first day, had come to Jehan this very morning, as she sorted herbs in the infirmary annexe. That the house was a rich one had been evident. That the woman had charge was probable. The master was "old" and "always off on business". Come in, she had urged Jehan.

For a while they debated and said No, but, standing silent in the door, watching them with clear eyes, she brought them round. Conrad declared this boy was a fiend, and another that fiends were lucky to the wicked, and they all laughed and spoke of hair the hue of sulphur, and after that ten of them went with her down the stair, and only three stayed sullenly behind.

Under the wall of the overgrown park, in the sky-sailing shadow of the embryo of the Temple-Church, the thieves stared across at a house Jehan had indicated. And the City bells rang for Laude.

'Stay here then, I'll go rouse the fat dame,' said Jehan. 'When I'm in the house, Conrad – you come across and wait by the door. No other, till he gives the signal to you.'

Jehan ran lightly, dark to dark, to the side door of the house, and shook it. As she had supposed, the boy she had seen was porter there, and in a moment he whined at her through the panels. 'Is your master at home?' said Jehan.

'No. Master's off,' came the high voice, stupid with sleep and resentment.

'The housekeeper then. Your mistress.'

'She's in her bed.'

'Wake her,' said Jehan in a low and terrible tone.

Through the door, with an uncanny night-hearing, Jehan heard the boy stumble away.

(From the wall across the street rose a mutinous shuffling, and she cursed it down, making no sound or sign.)

Then, above, in a toadstool bulge of the house, the pane of a window lighted. Again, Jehan heard the noises of human things aggrieved.

(Conrad was out, standing by the cowled well. Jehan flung an arm out at him in a gesture of rage, and he lurched down behind the trough, hidden.)

The woman's flat fat tread was descending through the house now. What luck, they were alone there. No other servant even, it would seem, and the old man "off".

'Who's that? Who's there? You rogue – '

The woman's voice was breathy but not alarmed, not even entirely prepared for anger. She might be prone to night callers. Jehan put her mouth to the door and moaned, 'Kind lady, let me in for the love of God. I'm known to you – that brother of Master Motius' student, Pierre – ' her voice quavered on the name, which was fortunate. 'I've been set on, mistress. Robbers. Help me – '

Then great billows of righteous outrage and passion the far side of the door, and bolts and bars being sprung.

Wrapped in her bedclothes, the woman flooded the door alcove. She thrust her candle out, and Pierre's handsome brother, Jehan, stood wilted and swooning in the radiance, one hand to his side, gasping.

'God's vitals. Poor boy. Come in at once. There. Lean on me, as hard as you like. I'm well-cushioned.'

'I knew no one else – ' said Jehan.

'And what of your fine brother? For shame. And the Master Artisan's pet, too.'

'He won't know me. Turned me off. It will break our mother's heart.'

'Where is he then, the disgrace?'

Jehan said: 'I know no more than you.' And staggered.

'Where are you hurt?'

'Only a little.'

'Yes, you seem unmarred.'

'In my heart the worst.'

In the kitchen, Jehan sprawled out in a chair. Her swimming vision told her that the pans were of quality, and the big hearth and its apparatus evidenced many lavish roasts. Instantly the woman had lit another three candles – extravagance, too. Then she used one of her keys, and brought wine. In her own right, the lady was also a thief.

'Drink that now. That'll bring you back. And I'll keep you company in a drop. He's got so much, he never misses the sip or two I take. A mean fellow. Pays me in pennies, works me off my feet. I must live. His poor relation you understand. Kept me from a husband, too, I've had my chances – all lost – '

Jehan tried the wine, thick as velvet, and began to revive.

Jehan asked nothing about the old man and his valuables. No need, for the woman spread the night with tidings, while sometimes patting Jehan's knee. Gold plate sat above, and candlesticks, a chamber-pot with gold handles, a box of money – the one key he stinted her of (no trouble when a dagger-hilt might be used on it) another of rings and chains, which he hid, as if she would touch it, God pardon him. There was a Bible too, and a book got from the artisan, who was a magician, both with covers warted by gems. And a robe trimmed with bullion, and gloves stitched with pearls – what a treasure trove! – and her without a decent gown for holy days.

Jehan, much recovered, aided the woman to more wine. As it was done, Jehan gave her too a kiss on the cheek, and dropped in her cup a powder of herbs from the infirmary.

'Well now, you saucy boy,' said the housekeeper, very much

delighted. 'I'll begin to think no one set on you at all, you only came here for a naughty reason.'

Jehan lowered eyes that, in the smoky light, were gold as any rich man's plate. Boylike, smiling, Jehan reached out, and gave the fat woman's vast bosom a gentle tweak.

Such shrieks. The neighbours would think her murdered, unless they often heard the sounds, which seemed probable. Then, such a gratifyingly big drink.

'And you only a youthful lad.'

'Willing though to learn.'

'Well, well. One can't even trust opening the door these nights.'

She drank again, in a huge swallow, not noticing the wine, eyes sparkling, breasts heaving. All the potion was gone, inside her. She reached and caught Jehan and pulled him down, massaging at buttocks and thighs. Jehan panted, fondled various mounds, imparted kisses and tasted in the wine-sweetened mouth the bitter tint of herbs, the powerful bringers of sleep –

Before the insistent hands could find out their mistake, they suddenly went sliding off. The fat woman rolled back, her eyes startled and still gaping as the first snore shook her bulk. Then her eyes shut on her. Protesting, snoring, kidnapped by unconsciousness, she cascaded from the chair on to the floor and lay beside a mouse-trap baited with cheese.

Outside in the street, a thief barked. They were growing anxious. As Jehan opened the door, Conrad shouldered through it. He glared at her, then stepped out again. He whistled, the twittering note of a bird, and one by one the others darted noiselessly bat-like over the gap between the shadows.

Conrad and another man caught the door-boy asleep at the stair-foot, hammered him on the head for fair measure and left him sprawled there. At the fat woman lying by the mouse-trap with her legs wide, some of them were tempted. They thought her only dead drunk. Her keys were taken. One mounted her. She quaked under him, gurgling, oblivious, and so was reckoned secure.

Upstairs the gang ransacked the house, Jehan having informed them of what might be found. Everything was found, even the chamber-pot, and the casket of jewellery, which last had only been inserted in the mattress, a common recourse.

Thereafter, Conrad and others slung their arms about the neck of Jehan, and crowned him with a gold chain from the casket, and poured a cup of white wine over his head to christen him in their fellowship, when once the wine-barrels had been got at. They remained, throughout the acts of carnage and celebration, quiet.

The house, so staid and safe without, was now inside a shambles. Only the kitchen had remained lit, and here at length they repaired, draped in the bed-curtains, toting their spoils, to drink about the laundry heap of the drugged woman.

There was time enough. The City gates would not part until the dawn, still an hour or so away. Even if the old fellow returned, he could not get in the City till after sunrise, and by then they would be gone. What a surprise they had left him.

'How Dwarf will cuss, how Fero will bite himself, when he learns what he missed!'

On the floor the fat woman breathed only in jerks and gutterings. Her face was grey and her lips slaty. The herbs had been generous in amount.

But the wine was good, and, not able to port it, they did not see why they should leave so much of it behind. The drinking went on, and in the middle Jehan sat on the table, looking under her or his lids, not speaking, scarcely-tasted cup set down.

Then the dark that came in at the alcove chink turned to a deep grey light. They roused to be going. They did not want to be seen.

As they stuffed the handy pouches in cloaks, surcoats, loincloths, with loot, there came sounds out of the speechless night. They were the hoofs of a mule that clucked along the cobbles, indeed, of two mules going in tandem.

'Not here,' said Conrad, 'God's tail, not here.'

But the mules picked delicately on, coming closer, coming to the door, and were there reined in. And now voices spoke outside the front of the house. A respectful mutter, an old man's pedantic drone.

'He's rich,' said Scar-Nose. 'He'll have paid the gate crew to open the postern. Back early, rot him.'

'When he's in he'll start a do. The world will come running.'

'Then when he's in,' said Jehan, 'we must stop his mouth.'

'I hear two of them, the old rat, and a young.'

'Both mouths stopped,' said Jehan. She moved from the kitchen towards the front of the house and its large door. 'This has a lock. Be ready.'

When the large key turned in the large door, the inner space was waiting, lined by flesh.

The old man came through, calling irritably to the porter-boy by name, his grizzled skull and fur-lined garment, his old body, creaking by a few inches from Jehan beside the door. Then, in the gloom,

125

someone whacked him. The blow seemed to split his head across, blackish liquid spurted, and he fell into the vortex of finished deeds without a cry.

Outside, in the twilight, the servant was giving his mule water from the trough by the well.

Jehan called to him softly. 'Sieur, sieur.' He turned, hearing a girl's voice addressing him so politely. Puzzled, not dismayed, he came towards the door and found it empty and unlit. He was a young man, strong and comely. He stood framed against the dusk, as all their eyes, unseen, fastened on him. Then he moved inside.

Two of the thieves took him at once. But he was not such easy meat as the old one. For some reason he did not shout as he evaded them, but his fists lashed out, his feet. The gang closed with him, and the walls seemed to totter, grunts were audible, now something went over with a thud, and there were oaths. As the battle swung, Jehan moved through it. She lifted her arm, with the knife Conrad had given her, she stabbed the servant in the belly. It was a death blow, but not quick enough. Dazed, amazed, he was sucking in his breath to scream and wake the dead. But Scar-Nose, an able hand, reaching over the young man's shoulder, cut his throat before his voice could sound.

Clambering across bodies, the thieves filed into the street and shut the door neatly. Conrad locked it tight with the key. Glancing at the mules, they rejected them, for they were over-ridden and besides conspicuous. The gang then broke in twos and threes or ones, and fled with bold strides away across Paradys and down, to the river, and over into the warrens beyond, losing all of itself as intended, Jehan with the rest.

The young nun stood in the yard, and coming from her sleeping cell, Jehanine discovered her. The face of Marie-Lis was grave and pure, but had none of the smug melancholy of a true Madonna.

'You weren't in your bed at sunrise, Jhane.'

(Jehan smiled under Jehanine's skin. Why, did you come seeking me there?)

'I was about early, sister.'

'Yes.'

'I was in the garden.'

'You came from there. With a bundle of clothes.'

'A piece of washing I'd forgotten, sister.'

(Careless on this occasion, she had returned late. She had seen the ghostly shapes of two lay-sisters bending over the refectory well, and the phantom nuns wafting in a dawn mist from the church. Now, under her gown, a golden chain, and on the chain a little golden cross set with a topaz.)

'But you roam at night, Jhane,' said Sister Marie-Lis.

'Some nights, when I can't sleep. How do you know, sister?'

'Where do you go to, Jhane?'

(Over the wall, into the blackness, into the night. You spy on me, but not enough.)

'To the chapel. Or sometimes I sit in the garden.'

'The nights are cold.'

'My cell also is cold.'

'We must endure, Jhane. We are not worldly, here.'

'No, sister.'

(And I washed off a dark stain in the dew. I thought of creeping to the other well, but it stinks, there must be a dead cat in it. And at the hostel's well under the lemon trees you might find me. Why are you drawing so much water, Jhane? Dew best.)

'We know almost nothing about you, Jhane. The Mother has never interviewed you. It's customary, after a time, to inquire if you have come to feel any yearning for the life of a Bride.'

Jehanine lowered her eyes.

'I haven't, sister.'

'Gaze on the window, Jhane, the Great Light, its petals of saffron and snow. Our Lord fell in his beauty, a shooting star. He brought light into the world. He asks only love.'

Jehanine frowned. She said. 'You told me, it's never demanded. I won't be a nun.'

The air filled with shrieks. In a fashion, Jehanine had become accustomed to outcry. She did not respond, as did Sister Marie-Lis, who whirled about and spun away. Through the arch she went, into the churchyard. The noises came from the garden. Slowly, cautious now, Jehanine followed. She had a vision of the fat woman erupting in at the nunnery gate, rushing through, to stand screeching of villainy under the bare fruit trees. But Jehanine suspected the fat woman might be dead, that all of those at that house, like Pierre, might be dead. She felt neither satisfaction nor distress. She was mostly indifferent, except to a certain tidiness that all the deaths together seemed to present, like duties performed.

The shrieks had ceased. Tawny fox-robes milled about the garden, clotted near the stinking ancient well. Across the turf the Mother was stalking. The nuns parted before her. She towered beside the well, imperious, ever a Queen Bee.

'What is it? Why does this well stink so? Pah! What's in the bucket?'

A murmur. The Mother drew back. She crossed herself and touched her fingers to brow and heart. She did not look in certain health.

Jehanine wandered close, and saw into the inner circle.

'I drew up the bucket, Mother, to look . . . I thought some animal might have died in the well.'

Jehanine had now approached near enough that she was able to look inside the bucket herself. She saw that it contained some murky water, and in the water a long pale fish with five fingers.

'Merciful Lord,' said the Mother. 'One of you run and kindle a lantern. It must be lowered. We must be sure.'

Two of the nuns fainted, one setting off the other. Yet another hastened away to a withered bush, into which she vomited. The Mother stood like a statue.

The lantern came, and they lowered it on a rope. And then there was a terrible wailing of lament and disgust.

The Mother drew aside quickly from her scrutiny. She said, 'I've seen the drowned before, from the river. This is not drowning. It is not a suicide. I must think. She must be raised.'

When the Mother departed, and the nuns fell away into groups, Jehanine went to the well and looked down where the lantern still hung. Beyond the fearful stench and beyond the light, a girl's body was wedged far down in the shaft. The water, and time, had acted on it, but also it seemed to have been subjected to fire, and to some cutting weapon: blasted and partly disembowelled it stuck there, mindlessly looking up with the remains of the face of Osanne.

The body was not to be raised. It fell to bits and its entrails poured out.

The Mother, kerchief pressed to her nose and mouth, instructed that logs be thrown in, then oil, and the whole set on fire. She was of course obeyed. At first, dampness seemed likely to wreck the scheme, but then the wood caught. A merry blaze leapt for a while from the chimney of the well, and a ghastly smoke gouted from it.

'I have written to the Father of the order,' said the Mother. 'Everything is explained. No suicide. I believe our daughter Osanne was struck by lightning. She bore the marks of it. God has gathered her home. We shall make a marker for her, and place it with the tombs of others who had died here in faith.'

When the blaze sank, earth was shovelled into the well, and finally stones.

'Thanks be to Christ,' said the Mother. She muttered some other brief prayer. She said, 'We will pray for the novice Osanne.'

All went to the church and prayed for Osanne.

Late in the afternoon it rained, water after fire. The smoke still hung low in the garden, and the evil of the stench remained in pockets.

Supper was a loathsome meal, for which very few had an appetite. The Mother did not appear. The young nun Marie-Lis lifted the cover of a book, not the Bible, but a theosophical work. She began to read to the silent and mostly motionless assembly.

Behind the screen, Jehanine, hungrily eating her black bread and soup, heard the beauty of the voice of the young nun.

'Why then did God so punish His formerly peerlessly beloved Son, made by Him an angel, a winged being of such power and beauty they are to men as men are to the little worms?

'It was in a rage that God did so, as when a favourite child has gone against the parental edict. What will you do? God had asked him. I will create a universe, I will make men in the image of the angels, replied the errant Son. For this, his Father flings him from the sky.

'For in his enormous wisdom, God knows that a world of men created must suffer, firstly the choice of good and ill, and the guilts and torments that attend upon both, and nextly must learn grief and disease, despair and death. God sought, in His compassion, to spare mankind, to deliver it from its very self. But our Lord said, Let them choose. And so he made the earth and peopled it. Then God said, If that is your wish, you I will exile. Go you into the very pit of that which you have made. And for the rest, let there be darkness on the face of the earth for ever, that they may not be afraid, through seeing what they are, and what they are at. So God made darkness and it hung on the face of earth. But the Lord, our Saviour, said again, Let there be light. He stole then one flame of the seven divine fires of Heaven. And with this he fell, burning, like the morning star. The sun was lit from his flambeau, and all the stars, and the moon, and all the lights of the firmament. And when he had cleaved through the earth and fallen to the deepest depth of it, that pit too became fire, a furnace that warms the earth's heart – a cleansing flame, the light of knowledge – until the world shall end.

'And for this gift of fire, men loved him. And when he saw their love, the love of those he had created, Lucefiel in turn loved them.

'Later, others of his brethren rallied to the banner of this Prince. They too exiled themselves from Paradise, and fell to earth and under it. From these he chose his captains, and on them his aegis lay as sternly as on his own self, and besides that, the furious censure of God. But to men the Lord gave only one commandment: Know what you are. But they forgot.'

When the reading was done, and the chores of the evening were done, Jehanine slept until the bell of Matines. Then she was Jehan, and she ran over the plains of the nunnery, got over the wall, and was gone into the rain and darkness.

Day by day the rain nailed heaven to earth. In the wintry night, the rain sighed and rushed and stamped. It was a curtain of disguise and a deflection of all other noises. It cleaned the spillings from the stones of Paradys, whatever they were.

At the *Imago* now, the dwarf sat sometimes on his table in the upper room. He sorted through the sumptuous trinkets and the coins, and petted the clever thieves, though never Jehan, the cleverest, their leader in his default.

'Jehan is a demon sent to guide us by Prince Lucifer,' said Conrad. 'Jehan is one of Lucifer's fair knights, a fallen angel. Sulphur hair and cat's eyes. Pretty as a girl, sweet voiced as a girl. And charms the girls, too.'

They gave the dwarf all their news, while Jehan sat by, yellow cat-eyes cast down. The dwarf gave them their news back again.

'Three wicked murders at a house near the building Church. An old rich man and his servant in their blood, and the housekeeper poisoned, and every bit of wealth plucked from the place. The little boy can't remember a thing, but he says he thinks a handsome youth knocked on the door and the woman let him in. But the boy's wits are addled since the blow the murderers gave him.' Restrained, tense as dogs who have done a cunning trick and wait for bones, the thieves listened and said how bad a matter this was, a shocking state the City must be in when a rich man could be killed for his riches. 'And another tale has it, a girl was honey-talked into letting in a young man at her window, but he brings his friends too, and while some have her down, others open the father's coffers. Many drunkards have been waylaid coming from the Snake-Cock or the Blacksmith's Inn, or on the South Bridge. Beaten senseless and their purses, their very boots taken.' Oh, a shocking state of affairs, yes, yes.

The nights had been busy. Jehan was full of Mercury and went before them. (Remember how he stabbed the servant in the rich man's house, not faltering?) Oh, they had known him for years, their Jehan. He was one of their own, and theirs, but polished brighter.

Conrad twitched. He had a powerful lust for Jehan. One night Jehan might kill him for it. You may eat the apple but not twine the serpent with the maiden's face.

'Well, Dwarf, you like our antics?'

But the dwarf said, 'I'm thinking. Fero, fero. It will be a hard winter. The snow will fall. The river may freeze. Then Yule. And the year's turning. The Janus festival, the Feast of the Ass.'

The dwarf stared at Jehan. He had never, plainly, told Jehan's secret. That Jehan had breasts and carried no dagger but the one in her belt, that Jehan lived by day in a nunnery, scrubbing the flags and sweeping the yards. Sometimes she slipped herbs into the drinks of their victims, opium, mandragoras. The thieves did not suspect Jehan of that, only of witchcraft. Jehan was fey, lucky, a shining thing of Hell. They did not ask him where he went away from them, or where he came back from – he put on animal shape, or wings and flew behind the stars as they went out. He sprang from the ground at the sun's setting. Winter, the time of dark day and long night, that was Jehan's country. They expected great events.

There was no more Jehanine in any case. There was only Jehan by night and Jhane by day, which two names were one, only a letter differently set, if he-she had been able to read or write and had known it.

Yet, as Jhane went about her work, always dutiful to the nunnery, modest and hard-working, again and again the young nun might be noted, standing observing her, or coming near she might say, 'Search your heart, Jhane.'

'For what must I search there, sister?' asked Jhane meekly. Jehan smiled and waited. In the interim, absconding, Jhane took care to leave during the offices, when Marie-Lis was in the church.

'Come over the river,' said Jehan to the thieves. But of this they were wary.

'The watch is fly-thick there now. Since our first visit.'

'Follow me then,' said Jehan.

The rain clattered like tin pans.

Some glanced at Fero the dwarf to see what he would do. But the dwarf did nothing save finger the columns of coins, an earring of canary beryl. One voice, an equal share – a fraternity, honour among thieves. While, beyond that cross he had taken and not thrown into the communal pile, and the chain Conrad had hung on him for a garland, Jehan took nothing.

All the robber band followed Jehan into Noah's night.

'We must build an ark, quick,' said the fat man.

'Agreed. Let's us wicked be saved this time.'

Near the South Bridge they beheld a party of tipsy gallants with torches in the rain.

'What now?' said Conrad.

Jehan singled out a young man, blond as the old man's servant had been. Alone, she approached him, and drew him aside from his friends who, in wine and rain not properly aware of his loss, went on over the bridge.

He seemed to believe, when the gang surrounded him, that he had been in conversation with an importunate girl. They took his money and stripped him to his tunic and drawers, like a Roman, and the rain had stopped. The resin torch still burned on his cringing, their jovial circle – his purse had been full, and the coins beamed too.

'He can dance for us,' said Jehan. 'Can't you?' She raised the torch and looked intently in the robbed man's face. 'Let me bring you light. Aren't you glad to obey Christ's command? Look, you've given all you have to the poor.' How the thieves giggled. Then Jehan put the torch down to the young man's garment, and up again into his hair. He was wet enough that there was a great smoulder, but also enough flame to send him hopping and screaming over the bridge, and Jehan pranced after him, clapping her hands and singing in a quire boy's voice, to an Eastern rhythm of the Spice Lands. Conrad and one or two more abetted the macabre fun, picking up the song, which had been born of some hot night's Crossade. The rest of the gang paused uneasily, the lower side of the water, not chancing the bridge. Half-way along it, Jehan pushed the youth into the river. Swollen with rain, it would not be happy swimming. Jehan seemed content, and at once returned along the bridge, with Conrad and the others at his heels.

'What shall I do?' said Conrad. 'You want me to go over there? Hang the watch, I will, if you want it. Up the hills. I'll go to Hell with you.'

'That door-boy at the rich man's house,' said Jehan.

'He's a half-wit now. No need to slaughter every one of them.'

But Jehan seemed to wish only deaths stacked methodically in the chest of deeds. Glancing in the river, one noticed the blond young man was not swimming at all, had gone down.

'Let me have you,' said Conrad.

'No. Don't try.'

'One time you'll let me.'

'I'll kill you first.'

Conrad laughed into the face of night. Much bigger and heavier than this boy, he could pin him now to the stone over the tumult of water. But did not dare.

'You love another,' jested Conrad.

'A lovely nun,' said Jehan.

'A nun? Where could you see such a thing?'

'I have seen. One night you'll get her for me. Skin like cream and eyes like deep thoughts. A young nun. You can take her, I'll let you.'

Conrad licked his lips. He was superstitious. Satan protected his own, and so did the other One.

It thundered overhead, and Conrad winced. The rain resumed. It was cold, it was winter.

They went back to the *Imago* to drink and Jehan to sit watching the dwarf count coins.

Seven o'clock in the frosty morning, not yet light nor yet still dark. The office of Prima Hora was done and Jhane stood at the church door as the nuns stole drifting out, to allow Marie-Lis to witness her there. But Marie-Lis passed by with the sisterhood, not seeming to see her, her countenance remote as ivory.

When the nuns were gone, Jhane went into the church.

A cold iron heaviness hung there. Smudges of light faltered on meagre candles, but nothing was given from the great window, which had become a whorl of leaden quarter-tones. The form of the Angel – Lucefiel – was mostly indistinguishable.

Was it that they worshipped the Devil here, or that Jhane had seen through a mask even they were unaware of?

As she moved along the nave, she saw the pale figure in the quire. It was not Osanne, for the spectral figment – or decoy – that had seemed to be Osanne, had ended its manifestations with the discovery in the well. This apparition was the original, a nun in a pale robe, tall and gracious, her face unseen since lifted in reverence to the blinded window. Jhane walked on, making no sound. The figure did not alter, only the hood or veil slipped back from its head. This nun did not effect either scarf or coif. A lion-like mane of gold hair burst out against the dimness, raying over the shoulders and down the spine.

Was this hair like the hair of Marie-Lis? Was this she? Had she turned into the side passage or the cloister, and re-entered via one of the smaller doors . . .

Perhaps not. The young nun was not so tall, and much slighter, surely –

Jhane halted. Something made her unable to approach any closer to the vision. Now the glowing quality of the figure seemed to be flowing upwards into the window – it warmed and waxed lambent. Suddenly colour shot into the glass and it came alive. The sun was rising and had pierced abruptly through the cloud. As the window quickened, Jhane saw that the image of white robe and lion hair was gone.

Kneeling before the Great Light, Jhane bowed her head and slowly touched her hands to brow and breast. A peculiar sensation went over her as she did this, an exquisite intimation, both carnal and spiritual. But getting to her feet, she soon turned her back on radiant Lucifer and all his works.

In the black icicle of the night, some young men coming out of the *Cockatrice* met with a sauntering blond youth. There were exclamations. And a pause.

'Stop! You – '

'What have I done?' said the youth, turning on them two beautiful lynx's eyes.

'No – but you're like – '

'It *is*, I tell you.'

'No, not the height or muscle. But a double, certainly.'

'Oh,' said the youth, not unnaturally curious, 'whose?'

The young men from the studio of Motius looked at one another. One of them said, 'Well, he's in the sewers – ' and was commanded to silence.

'Then I'm like someone,' said the youth. 'Where are you bound?'

'Come with us, where we're bound,' they said, and went off into the icicle with him, to a lower tavern behind a stable.

'Look at his hands, so delicate, and his face. What a model he'll make, our Jehan – you did say to us that was your name?'

'Come to the studio tomorrow. Present yourself to the Master. He'll take a fit, seeing how like – well. Do it anyway.'

They petted him, far gone in ale.

'Where is his house then?' *he* said, lolling there sober.

They explained with care the location of the house, and its appearance, and drew maps of the way upon the table in spilled drink.

> *O winter is, the poor birds sing*
> *And hide each head beneath a wing.*
> *So cruel to me my lady is*
> *Like winter snow that gives no ease,*

Malice in Saffron

My heart its head beneath its wing,
And winter is, my heart must sing.

Winter rode through Paradys on a grey horse, a lord in mail and armour, with a vizored helm, and his train behind him. The sky and the bare trees groaned and the honed winds blew. Branches, slates and birds fell down. The snow began to fall. The City blanched. The river froze for vast stretches, and all the wells. Love-songs listed cold hearts, but in the nunnery the nuns wrapped their feet and hands in cloth, the hearths were lit in the refectory and the infirmary, and braziers carried into the church, and quantities of blankets lugged to the sleeping cells. Two of the sick nuns perished, and were put underground. The matriarchal Mother took cold and kept to her chamber where a fire roared day and night. The novices slept two by two for warmth, which was not allowed. (On such freezing nights at the farm, even the unloving sisters of Jehanine had clasped her close.) But Jhane lay alone, cold as a stone, and deep within her body she coiled asleep. She did not fear the winter, it had no jurisdiction over her. And now and then Jehan went out across the wall and reviewed the City of Ice, its turrets and points sewing up an enamel moon, on the surface of which there now showed absolutely a Madonna's mournful face. Over the thick glass of the river by night, muffled shapes dragged secret wares on rough sleds. The ships lay dead at anchor.

And the lovely young nun read in the refectory, above the coughs and snuffles of winter. 'In the Book of Esrafel it says this: "Thus the man who was sent to the Angel asked him, 'Were it not better that we should not live at all, since we live in wickedness, and suffer, and know not why?' And I, the Angel, answered him; 'Weigh you the height of fire, and measure the tower of the wind, and call here to me yesterday.' But the man said, 'I cannot.' 'Believe then,' said the Angel Esrafel, 'in this manner also you cannot know the guiding intent of the Creator, cannot weigh or measure it, or call it here before you. Yet it is'." The young nun waited as two or three of her sisters sneezed and wiped their noses sadly. Then she read, ' "Hear, my beloved, says the Lord: be not afraid, nor let your sins weigh you down as the briars cover the field, that no man may travel it. Your sins are finished, tear up the thought of them by the roots. For the field choked by briars is put to the fire to be consumed." '

The thieves, wrapped fast, and sometimes snuffling like the nuns, came from their bolt-holes to the *Imago* to toast and steam. Once in, they did not incline to go out again. Gold burnt the fingers in such a temperature, the dwarf said so. There he sat, slit-eyed and brooding, saying not a syllable now. But Jehan prowled and some followed. Where there were no pickings to be had, Jehan would crack some costly window with a ball of packed snow, or scratch on doors with his dagger obscene symbols of the alleys learnt instead of letters. Jehan would inaugurate sliding games, which slides might break legs in the morning. And sometimes they would find a vacant house to get into.

On the far side of the river, a weird gleam went up by night, where the torches reflected back from the snow into the wild and chiming air. But it was forbidden, that upper bank. The great market, the great borning church, the house of murders, the enclosing arm of City Wall that held in it slabs the legions had laid there.

'I'll go with you. Up the hills. Who cares,' said Conrad. Scar-Nose added, 'For what?' The thin man said, 'It's cosier there.'

Jehan ran over the bridge, through the palings of ice-crystals, gliding where there was the horizontal ice, arms outflung graceful and demoniac.

'Come,' said Conrad.

Yet not one of them moved.

The well lit, climbing streets about the market were nearly bright as day, but black mud lay around the houses and torch-poles where the heat had melted the snow.

For Jehan, creature of darkness, it was early, not yet eleven o'clock. With the advent of winter when night began to come down in the afternoon, he sometimes took the risk of evolving during Complies, the completion of the nunnery's diurnal.

As she entered the street of the statue-well, Jehan gave her nothing to feel. She glanced at the house where the fat woman had died, the rich man, the servant. No watch was any longer kept on it. Meanwhile, across the way, stood the other more important house, the studio and dwelling of Motius the Artisan. Seven nights before, solitary outside the *Cockatrice*, Jehan had identified other students of the Master. She had fallen into chat with them. They had seemed stunned by Jehan's resemblance to someone they had known but would not coherently speak of. One had suggested Jehan might model for the studio as a young Patroklos or Dionysos. Jehan had not seemed averse, and so learned the house at which he should present himself.

Through the shutters light showed in the upper storey. Jehan knocked at the door. After a time, a shutter opened. A young man's face, unknown, peered down. 'Who's there?'

'Jehan.'

'Who is Jehan?'

Jehan shrugged, standing out in the pool of light to be seen. 'I was told to come. The Master might employ me as a model, they said. Perhaps not.'

Then the youth in the window gave a startled sound.

He withdrew. Voices came together.

(*It is one like Pierre Belnard. Oh me, oh my!*)

Feet bounded down a stair and hands unbarred the door.

A second youth drew Jehan in, shut the door to keep him there, stared at him unblinkingly in the flame of a flinching candle, then said something very fast, a sentence of Latin, unrecognised. 'So,' added the youth huskily, 'you don't vanish.'

'Shall I try?'

'Don't mock. Don't speak. Stay there, exactly where I have put you. Wait.' And the student rushed away, up the stair once more, the panic-splayed light borne with him.

Jehan stayed, unmocking, or speaking, and seemed to be waiting. Then he moved, went to the stair-foot, and looked up the dark funnel of it. In a moment more he began noiselessly to ascend.

There was now not a twitter, not a mumble, above.

Jehan entered a passage and came to a door, closed, with a keyhole of shouting light. Tickled by such aptness, he knelt to the hole at once, and looked through.

There before him was a morsel of fire-lit chamber, and in it a man stood, lean and old and bearded, stooping a fraction. One hand clutched at his breast, and the other held a chalice of wine, which he was pouring evenly into the flames on the hearth. The sizzling splishery intrigued Jehan, so much so that when it ended, and the man moved from the sphere of vision, Jehan did not react. Then came a motion across the light that indicated someone was returning to spring the door. Jehan was up in an instant, standing aside. As the second student burst out toward the stair, Jehan stepped directly in the doorway and said, 'Here I am.' Which brought the other back cursing foolishly.

The fine fiery chamber, opened out, was opulent. A hearty meal had been eaten in it at the white-clad table, not long before, and still positioned there were a gilt wine-jug and cups, a dish of yellow plums and apples – in winter Paradys – and two branches of candles that stintlessly burned. Through a part-closed curtain beyond lay the studio, darkened and asleep, but smelling yet of paint grindings, clay, oil and marble-dust. Here Pierre would have been wont to work late, and dine after-wards with the Master, a favourite pupil, as these, too, must be.

But Pierre had evaporated from their lives. Drinking and whoring had undone him in the alleys. Now on the threshold, his double, more exact after an interval, and so more miraculous.

Master Motius now sat in his carved chair by the hearth and stared as the young men did. He was, as keyhole-seen, old, bearded and wore besides a cap to warm his head and a fur-lined mantle in the hot room. And three rings on his fingers.

'You are the brother of Pierre,' he said.

Jehan smiled.

'Brother of who?'

The artisan sighed.

'Not,' said Master Motius.

'There was some gossip one of his brothers sought him out,' said the student who had looked from the window. 'That's why he went off without a word.'

The second student said, 'And this one was at the door, peeping through it, I'll bet. What did he see?'

Jehan looked down at his feet modestly.

'There was nothing to see,' said Master Motius.

'Except, you pour wine on your fire,' said Jehan.

The artisan said, 'That's a Roman custom. We keep the classic formula here. Otherwise, what do you say?'

'To what?'

'To our talk of Pierre Belnard.'

'Who is that?'

'You have never met such a young man.'

'I?'

'Do you know of whom we speak?'

'Is it possible?'

'He was my pupil and apprentice. He was well-liked everywhere, and well-known.'

'For what?'

'Uncivil, gutless, pig-souled dog – ' cried the second student.

Master Motius held up his hand. Leaning on the arms of his chair, he rose.

'I will show you,' said he. He took a candle-branch from the table.

The first student hurried to open the curtain into the studio, and the Master passed through.

'Go in,' said the second student to Jehan, threateningly.

Jehan smiled again. He went after the artisan leisurely and the students followed.

The studio was a big vault, where the candlelight collided with angles, drapes and shapes, was smashed and fell down. A peculiar being – a whole, if idealised, skeleton of wood – posed on a plinth, making a mad gesture. There were benches and cold braziers, long tables with parchment, canvas, jars and alembics. Things stood propped and lay prone; things sweated under wet cloth.

The artisan moved through this forest and stopped before the far wall. A small panel of wood had been fastened on it. He raised the candles, though his arm shook a little, from age or feeling.

'This he painted, in his third month with me. It is flawed, he had much to learn. But ah, so perfect also. What he would have been.'

Jehan looked at the painting.

Jehanine had never been shown anything the mature Pierre had fashioned, though he had performed some work for the lord of the estate. She could not properly understand the painting, however, for it was not real, not flesh and blood, and did not move. A girl sat under a flowering tree, her fair hair falling round her, and birds fed from her hands, and a faun, and a she-wolf with a cub . . . But Jehan was distracted somewhat by some strange scuffed marks along the lower wall and the floor. Did the students of Motius also draw on the ground?

'He called this painting *The Madonna of the Innocents*,' said Master Motius. He wept. 'Marie the Mother, but also the goddess Venus. Sacred and profane. But all beauty is sacred.' The tears ran down into his beard like flames, catching the light. 'Boy, if you know where he might be – no matter what depths he may have fallen into – whatever sink or vice – I beg you, you must tell me.'

'Who?' said Jehan.

One of the students said hoarsely, 'He *knows*, Master.' He moved towards Jehan. 'Shall we make him? I can do it.'

'No – no – no violence here. Perhaps he doesn't know. The likeness isn't so marked as I thought at first. We see what we wish to. I have studied men's faces.'

Jehan felt the topaz cross slide between his girl's breasts under the binding. He toed the chalky lines on the floor. He smiled and he smiled, and reached out to take the candles from the artisan.

Master Motius seemed surprised but not reluctant to let go of the light. Conceivably, he thought his guest wanted to gaze more closely at the painting, and that this might augur well.

Jehan, clasping the candle-branch, leaned forward carefully, and touched the fire to the wooden panel. A black line ran along the edge of it, and the paint bubbled. She seemed not inclined to burn, the Madonna –

'Oh God!' shrieked the artisan. His old voice splintered, he tottered against Jehan, striking at him, clutching now for the fire, now for the painted panel. Jehan turned and smote downward with the candle-branch. It cut the old man's temple and most of the candles showered upon him, catching webbed in his hair, beard and mantle. As he began to burn, so did the panel on the wall. Jehan stepped back, face composed and serious, the eyes very pale.

The students were running to their master, who writhed on the floor, stunned and crying and alight. As they came Jehan both avoided and met them, and dipping the last candles, with gentle strokes, torched each of them. They seemed highly inflammable, perhaps some constant contact of their garments with the paints and oils. It was very simply done.

Jehan flung the fire away against a hanging bolt of dry material, which flared at once.

The studio was illumined in saffron, and by hopping, dancing, screaming fire-creatures, that tried in turn to come at her, at each other, and which all the while beat at their own selves, until they went down and boiled along the floor.

Jehan dashed from the room. In the outer chamber he took fruit from the dish and snatched up the gilt jug of wine.

Escape was made by a lower window, into a side-slip between the houses.

In the open yard before the embryo of the Temple-Church, Jehan climbed a workman's ladder up a pile of stones, and seated there high in the air, watched all the street come alive in terror as fire exploded from the upper storey of Master Motius' house in one mighty blast. Some combustible in the studio had ignited, it would seem.

In fear for the wooden structures of their homes, men scurried in the street like frightened mice. Jehan, eating plums upon the stone pile, watched. It was like a scene in Hell, until the snow began to fall and, as the cumbersome buckets had not been able to, whisper by whisper, put out the burning house.

He had a fancy for the jug, and kept it by him. Springing down from the nunnery tree with the rope and the vessel in his hands, he found before him a young nun.

'There's soot in your hair, Jhane,' said Sister Marie-Lis.

'Then I have been in a fire, demoiselle.'

'And this is how you travel the City by night.'

'How else?' replied Jehan.

'But you return.'

'I found a rope hanging down to the street. I climbed it.'

'You are Jhane.'

'Presently,' said Jehan. He moved towards the young nun. He put his face to hers. She did not resist. He put his hand on her breast. She did not resist. 'I know a quiet cell, over there,' said Jehan. 'We shan't be disturbed. Or here, on the cold ground in the snow.'

'You are Jhane,' said the young nun again.

Jehan drew back. He lowered his eyes.

'Who will you tell?' said Jhane.

'No one. God sees.'

'You worship Satan,' said Jhane.

The young nun turned from her and moved away over the snow and vanished through an arch of white plum trees. The ground was too hard to have kept her footprints.

Jhane burned on her pallet. Garbed in fire she rose and ran into the south cloister to cool herself in the snow. She wished the fountain would play. It did so. It played fire. Fire like a golden tree splashed up into the black sky. By its light, she saw it was not a stone child who held the bowl, but the dwarf.

'Fero, fero, I am Ferofax,' said the dwarf. 'Fire-Bringer. I am a demon. But you're possessed by devils.'

'Lucifer, King of the World,' said Jhane as she burned.

'His first captains were Azazel and Esrafel,' said the dwarf. 'They hastened to him, and consoled him, after the fall.'

'I am burning,' Jhane cried bitterly.

She screamed: '*I am burning*!' And the nuns tied her to her bed in the infirmary where now she lay in the blazing fever.

'I'm burning! I'm burning! Fire! Fire'

'Lie still,' they said.

She hated them, but that was not new, to hate. There was a pain in her groin and her bowels. She saw an old man with a beard tied to a stake, and burning too.

'Pierre!' she screamed.

Ferofax sat cross-legged on the foot of her bed, crowned with stone flowers, eating a lump of paint. *The world will end in fire.*

'It is Yule Natalis,' said the nuns. 'It is the birth of the Angel as the Christ.'

141

Bells rang.

The Temple-Church rose and hung, unfinished in the sky, with great windows like flame for eyes.

When the pain and fever left Jhane, she was very weak for a long while and lay in the infirmary where the old sick nuns came to die.

'The world is a terrible place,' the old nuns said to each other. The City was the world in miniature, filled by lusts and malignities, killings and awful crimes. (Jhane wearily suspected they kept certain secrets and sorry events from her ears, out of regard for her illness.)

There were no novices left. Unfeelingly, they had wedded Christ, as Jhane burned. Christmas was past also. Soon the year would die. New Year would come, and two-faced Janus, an antique Roman deity, fling open the doors, at the Feast of the Ass.

On the estates of the lord in the north, as everywhere, the Ass Feast had been celebrated with riot. It was the contrary time, the letting of the bung from the cask, when everything must reverse itself, upside down, in order to come right for the remainder of the year. Carts of manure had been trundled through the village, and the unwary pelted. The priest would put on his gown inside out and the bell be rung, for once, but at the wrong hours. Processions roved the fields, beating drums and Eastern tambourines, and a garlanded donkey, though not Belnard's own, paraded about with an idiot or a young peasant girl made king, and riding on its back. You might do anything on the Day of the Ass: all things at their season. By that token, for the rest of the year you could be virtuous.

It had begun in classical times, the old dying nuns said now, disapproving, admiring. A beautiful god on an ass's back, drinking, and ritual, and other things.

Jhane, who had had hideous hallucinations and dreams during the fever, did not discuss the festival. The weather had changed. There had been a thaw, (Fire! Fire!), and there was an unseasonable warmth, so a few thin buds spurted from the trees and were chided. As soon as Jhane was able, she resumed her duties and chores. But, having spent so long with the senile nuns, she now moved slowly, ached, must lean often on her broom, sometimes fainted as she scrubbed the flagstones, could not remember easily anything.

Jehan woke, got up and dressed himself. Stowed behind the chest he found a wine-jug, gilded, which he had partly forgotten. He took it with him, along with the cross – which he had only once removed, when ill, for fear enemies might steal it as he raved – and his climbing rope.

He left sanctuary behind without a backward look, and made towards the inn, over the slush.

The torches burned as usual on the cobbles before the gate, but in the upper room, only three or four were gathered together.

They jumped up when Jehan entered.

'Where did you go?'

'We thought you were hanged.'

Jehan set down the jug. They gazed at it.

Then Conrad came and grasped Jehan, hugging him close. Jehan eventually pushed him off.

'Tomorrow is the Ass Feast,' said Scar-Nose. 'Tomorrow we'll rob the world and slit its gullet.'

They sat drinking most of the night. Jehan watched them. For the first time, he slept at the inn. When Conrad came slinking to his resting place, Jehan rolled over and laid the knife against Conrad's windpipe.

'When?' said Conrad.

'After the nun.'

'What nun?'

'The nun I told you of. There's a dainty nunnery not far off, near the river.'

'Never.'

'Ask the dwarf. He knows.'

'Did you burn the house?' said Conrad.

'A house?'

'In the street where the rich man lived, before we did for him.'

'We'll burn the Temple-Church next,' said Jehan.

'You're the Devil,' said Conrad.

'One of his captains,' said Jehan. He laughed softly. 'Azazel, Esrafel.'

'You laugh like a girl. Your voice never broke. Is that why you hate the whole earth?'

Jehan reached out and fondled Conrad. Conrad fell against him. He whined, struggling forward, labouring. Jehan ceased his attentions, spat in Conrad's face, and went away to another part of the inn to sleep.

At sunrise there was a colossal noise, the clashing of cymbals, pans and pots, the mooing and bray of horns. All the bells jangled. It was Donkey Day, All Fools Feast. The little madness that held off the greater, hopefully, while God, the Harrier and Destroyer, winked.

The gang of thieves came out on the street along with the rest of the City. Festivals were always fortunate. But sometimes, in the day's tradition, having gained purses and other oddments, a robber might infiltrate a coin into some poor man's satchel or pocket. A day of reversals.

On the bridges they were fishing with mousetraps, and throwing decaying fish back into the river. Huge chunks of ice still wallowed sluggishly by in the water. But the morning was clammy, and drops sweated on the stones and plaster, the foreheads of men.

Processions were going up and down, men with donkey masks, and donkey phalluses strapped to them, ran about shaking rattles, and fake priests in patchwork gave bawdy blessings, while pretend-doctors, carrying jars of leeches and enormous pincers for the pulling of teeth, lunged to and fro.

At Our Lady, over the river, the whores' penance would be enacted, and the thieves went, as if idly, across a bridge with Jehan. A country boy, he had never seen such a thing. 'Oh, it's worth your while!'

The City squealed and banged and sang and shouted.

Our Lady was a minor church near the quays, but on the open stretch before, slippery with fish-oil, a mass was being held, with an ass-bishop in a mitre with holes cut for his ears. At each snort and asinine trumpet, the crowd acclaimed the sagacity of the remark.

The whores came from the church presently, in chains, drawing metal balls behind them, but these things were of dented tin and skittered about as the whores screamed with mirth, flinging up their skirts, ribbons in their hair, bare-breasted, some of them.

A cavalcade was coming along the streets, going up towards the market and the Temple-Church.

Jehan pushed towards it, with Conrad and a few others who had not gone after the whores and the tin chains.

Men-devils, next to naked in the muggy day, horned and tailed, and armed with torturer's forks, pranced about a platform, dragging it up-hill. On a gaudily painted throne sat the festival's king. The crowds bayed and boomed about him, and he nodded at them his head in its diadem of gilded spokes, feathers and bells. His little feet were stuck in pointed shoes, a wooden sword hung at his side painted with the words: *Rex Urbi*. The wig of flaxen straw framed the handsome, unkind and deformed face of a child. It was Fero, the dwarf.

Jehan laughed with derision.

The dwarf heard him.

144

'Stop. Your king commands you. I have heard a beautiful sound. It must have been a lark singing.'

The platform waddled, tilted, subsided to a halt.

'Every woman turn to your king your face. I'm about to choose a consort.'

In the uproar, Jehan stood sneering, and the dwarf pointed at him. 'There. That one.'

'But, Sire, it's not a woman.'

'My command is law.'

As he was seized, Jehan did not fight. He hung, contemptuous of them, on the boisterous arms, and was lovingly hoisted aloft. The dwarf caught Jehan and smacked a kiss on to his mouth. 'Garments for my queen. You, you. Strip yourselves.'

Shrieking, various girls were made to give up various examples of apparel. They trooped in person on to the platform, twining the handsome youth, adorning him in cast-offs and embraces. When they were shooed away again, there was a sudden relevation. Draped in a mantle, a striped sash, and with a knot of ribbons caught through his yellow hair, Jehan was abruptly a girl.

'Sweetest Jesus,' said Conrad. He seemed stricken, white-faced, his desire bulging before him. But Jehan did not apparently care. He leaned on the dwarf's shoulder, looking arrogantly about. The glances were unmistakably male, in that young girl's face.

'Will my queen sit?'

'On your head, pig-dwarf.'

The crowd applauded with zeal.

'On my lap, dear queen.'

'And be got with another babe?' ranted the queen in his high melodious damsel's voice, playing the part now.

'I'll give you another!' offered a male in the crowd. Offers fell fast upon the boy-girl queen. She shook her hair, 'I came to Paradys to make my fortune. I came to be apprenticed to a trade.'

'Ohh-ho!' volunteered the crowd.

'I meant,' shouted Jehan. 'to paint pictures of the saints in the great new church. Not sit in a cart and be dighted by a dwarf.'

The dwarf caught Jehan and pulled him down across his knees. Jehan laughed, this time lightly and boyishly.

'On, slaves, you vermin. To the Temple. My queen shall paint it.'

They careered up the hill, the wineskins jumping through the crowd as if alive. Striving to get one, and to keep up, Conrad lost his brothers. He strove beside the dwarf, took hold of an edge of the platform to help it heave along. He stared at Jehan, who ignored or did not see him, with coals for eyes.

So they poured through the market-place, gathered converts, drove up a hump in the world and into a stone alley, crushed against the walls, the platform tumbling and righting itself in a storm of flesh and confusion.

The outer yards of the Temple-Church, when they got into them, were piled with stones, rubble, bales, ballasts, work-shops, sheds. Architects and menials alike were gone. It was to be their gift to God, the ornament of Paradys, what did it need of protection, the Temple-Church of the Sacrifice of the Redeemer?

Huge and hollow the walls arose: the window-places, finned with iron, gaped. The bones of the scaffolding stood waiting for embodiment, like the Word itself, once. But it had no life, no soul, only its sensed, unborn suspension. The cavalcade swirled about the ankles of future history, and asses defecated there.

'Come now,' said King Fero.

'Not I,' said Queen Jehan.

'It's a fact,' said the dwarf, 'my queen here has borne me thirty babes. We must be wed at last.'

The crowd brought censers filled with old shoes, and lit them, and the reeking smoke lifted to heaven. The donkey in the mitre was led up, and Jehan and the dwarf were married by it, the crowd itself suggesting the proper words.

'And so to bed,' said the dwarf.

'A favour,' said Jehan.

'More delay. What is it?'

'Give me the donkey.'

'I promise I'm better than the donkey.'

'Well, I'll take him anyway.'

Jehan, garbed in maiden's robes, intercepted the donkey, tore off its mitre – to yowls of sacrilege – and lifting his skirts, got up on the beast's back. Mildly clocking heels to its sides, Jehan persuaded the animal to a walk. They rode forward, past the king-dwarf, to where Conrad stood in ecstatic petrification. 'Wake up. Get up behind me' said Jehan.

'Rebellion,' crowed Fero. He drank from a wineskin and toppled over sideways from his seat.

Conrad flung himself aboard the donkey. He gripped Jehan by the waist. 'The Devil, the Devil, Satan, Lucifer, death, night,' he cursed and moaned, clinging.

They rode off with scant hindrance, the crowd separating to let them by, only cawing commiserations to the dwarf. At its edges, unattended, a pair of drunken men lay on the road.

The donkey trotted now, glad to be out of the press.

They went up a street with an artistic well and a burned house in it.

'Oh Christ, Jehan, Jehan.'

Beyond the walled park, some open land ascended. Presently one could see the wave-head of the City Wall above and to the east.

The donkey cantered. Conrad groaned and fumbled at Jehan, who shifted off the thief's hands from the area they sought. Conrad mouthed the smooth neck under the ribboned hair. He sobbed, and spasmed suddenly, giving the ass an unintentional kick that almost unseated both riders.

Having run its length, the donkey pulled up under some trees.

'You've had your pleasure,' said Jehan. 'Now where are the others?'

'No pleasure. You bastard son of Hell. They were at their own business.'

'Just you then, creep-thief. Spraying your lust on an ass's back.'

'Shut your damned mouth. I'll kill you.'

'No you won't. Now I want that nun.'

'I should slit your throat.'

Jehan swung from the back of the donkey and hesitated, finding himself sore and stiff. Had he never ridden before? The physical sensation seemed familiar, but he associated it with fear, trouble – putting the thought aside, he pulled off himself in a skein the girls' clothes and the ribbons. Conrad had also left the animal. He sat in the grass under the leafless, untimely-budding trees. He was crying.

'What a fine, brave, bold man,' said Jehan. 'The artisan cried. Don't burn my house! Don't burn my precious painting!'

Conrad seemed not to listen. 'That boy,' he said. 'I never should have. That boy, your brother. All my life. Sins, sins. I'll burn in Hell. The Devil sent you. We'll be punished, every one. God's wrath. God help me.'

'Do you have a home?' said Jehan casually, straightening his tunic.

Conrad wept.

Jehan left him there, and the ass feeding on a crocus. But as he went down across the rough land, towards the wall of the garden-park where once some palace had vaunted, Conrad stumbled after.

'A hut's my home,' he said, 'in Smith's Lane.'

'Good. Then we'll take her there.'

'Take who?'

'Christ's Bride. My young nun with the holy face.'

'I won't. Don't you fear yourself, Jehan? I won't do it.'

'Then take yourself off.'

Conrad strode at Jehan's side, head down, sweating.

'To Hell then,' said Conrad. '*Noli vade retro, Satanus*! What else did I expect?'

To travel back down through the City was slow going in the festival, particularly since Conrad's sullen gloomy face, and Jehan's purely intent one, urged others to assault them in many ways. The noon bell of the Sextus had rung itself out when they approached the nunnery. Conrad had forgotten it was unknown to him and therefore did not exist. He skirted the wall and the bell-tower, and went along with Jehan to the west side, and past the gate. By day, even while the alleys crouched and the houses stood with their backs to it, the clandestine nature of the place was gone. Anyone might appear, if only to deliver necessaries to the nunnery door. But the bakehouse made an angle in the wall, and beyond that the tree reached over. It had no premature buds, it had not been fooled. Only the rope still dangled from it, ever unseen, unfound – a sorcery of will-power or fate.

'Climb then,' said Jehan.

'What?' Into there?'

'Where else?'

Conrad baulked, so Jehan sprang first up the rope, and soon lay along a bough of the tree above, taunting him.

'Is it an apple tree, you serpent?' snarled Conrad. But he grabbed the rope and did climb, getting up into the branches as Jehan uncoiled from them and down into the shrubbery below.

This part of the garden was secluded, the bakehouse wall, the high bushes, screening it in. They crouched there.

Jehan said, 'You see that plot, with the plum trees? She'll walk into it in a minute and you'll see her.'

'How do you know she'll do just that?'

'She'll have missed me. She'll be coming looking, after every one of the offices, to catch me climbing in again.'

'What do you mean by that? Coming in again? Have you been having her here every night?'

'Living here,' said Jehan. 'They thought me a girl. You've seen what a fair girl I make, when I'm dressed for it.'

Disbelieving, believing, Conrad swore.

Then, between the plum trees, a slender nun walked out. She

moved towards the wall. When she was less than ten paces away, Jehan stood up.

'Here I am,' said Jehan.

The young nun did not speak, her pale face perfect in her gorget and her hands in her sleeves.

'Did you wonder where I was?' said Jehan. 'Look, here's a friend I've made in the City.' She kicked Conrad glancingly. 'Get up and show her.' But Conrad would not. Jehan leaned down and pulled on him. He rose then reluctantly, looking at the young nun from the corners of his eyes. She did not appear afraid or angered. Conrad said, stupidly, 'Excuse me, sister.'

'Yes, excuse him,' said Jehan. 'He's about to lay harsh hands on you.' To Conrad, Jehan said, 'Now do it.' But Conrad stayed rooted to the earth with the bushes, and now the young nun was turning away. As she went back into the plum trees, Jehan said, 'Get her for me now. If she screams, hit her. Cover her head with your cloak. Do it. Or you'll never see me again.'

Conrad lumbered out of the shrubs, his mouth forming a protest even as he rushed to obey. The young nun was among the trees and now Conrad was among them – vanishing. The rest of the nunnery seemed long-dead – obviously the Feast had not been observed here. Jehan stood and waited for Conrad to come back over the bare winter plot with Marie-Lis slung across his shoulder, and after a handful of minutes he did so. He loped heavily under his burden, breathing noisily, broken twigs in his hair. His cloak wrapped all of Marie-Lis, but the hem of his habit, which trailed out meaninglessly. Her head and upper body hung over his back, smothered. 'I hit her anyway. To be sure. And tied her hands with my belt. The blow wasn't hard. She didn't struggle. Maybe wanted to come.'

It was with difficulty and toil that Conrad, unassisted, got the package of nun up into the tree and down again into the street under the wall, but he managed the feat, for it was similar to thief's work, such removals. He was throughout industrious not to crack the skull of the prize, nor bruise its bones. Sometimes he inquired of it how it fared, chuckled when it did not answer. Conrad on the rope, put himself between it and the wall, Landed, he kissed it, adjusted it, remarked that it seemed weightier, perhaps the wench had taken on herself his sins. Remorse was plainly superfluous, now. He turned briskly and made towards the worst venues of the City, where lay Smith's Alley, he said.

Further along, they met crowds again, coming up from the river with a girl attired like a mermaid, and then in the long alleyways, which were stuffed with drinkers and fornicators. To the curious, Conrad presented his portable as a besotted comrade. So many strange articles went by in any case in the arms of others, what odds one more?

A blacksmith's forge dominated Conrad's domiciliary alley, close and boarded on this day. Behind, sheds and huts leaned on each other the length of the route, and into the last of these Conrad ducked.

It was a mere space, a sort of absence of anything good or comfortable, and it was foul. When the door was shut and tied with a cord, the only light came through a roof-hole. A stirring in one corner indicated a rat, but when Conrad had lit the single candle-stub, this ceased. Next he let down his bundle on the bed of rags and fleas. He bent over it solicitously, and began to fiddle with the folds of the cloak to come at its face.

'No,' said Jehan. 'Get out now.'

Conrad this time definitely remonstrated. The walls shuddered.

'When I'm finished,' said Jehan. He sauntered to Conrad and put in Conrad's hand a coin thieved earlier amongst the crowds. 'Go drinking.'

'No, you damned imp. This is my house.'

'Oh, your house. Your dung-heap, and stinks like it.'

'I could have you down. I could cut off your ears, and the rest.'

'Go away,' said Jehan. 'Come back later.'

Conrad ranted, and Jehan slapped him suddenly across the lips.

'Go out, or stay and *I* go out. Do you think I'd want her after you'd been chewing on her? Good then. Farewell.'

Conrad cursed the world as he left the hut.

The light in the alley was thick and grey, with all the day's yeasty heat panting in it. Jehan shut the door and re-tied it. Then he stood for a while, only looking down at the shape under Conrad's cloak. It seemed not to breathe. It seemed also larger one moment, then to shrink. The candle-end sputtered and would soon go out. If there was gazing to be done, better be quick.

Jehan found himself reluctant. He pictured himself beside the form of Marie-Lis, staring into her face, running his fingers over its sculpture, and then on into the loosened robe, along the statue of her body. And thinking of this, he felt himself swell erect, the weapon at his groin quite ready, having forgotten it was only a roll of cloth not even attached to him, as indeed at other instants of nature, it and he had forgotten.

He strolled to her now, and began to peel away the robber's cloak from the young body of the nun. Some earth fell out on to the floor, and then some broken branches. Then a white hand fell limp against his own and he saw it was not a hand but a piece of damp linen. Jehan stood back, then he fell to his knees and threw himself on the bundle, tearing it apart. Under Conrad's cloak lay a roll of washing, seemingly found drying in the garden beyond the trees. There was a shift filled with soil and muck, finally pushed into a convenient habit, and so brought away as the nun Marie-Lis. Ah, carried with such *care* down the wall. Conrad smiling, Conrad kissing, Conrad ranting he must be first at the rape to ensure dismissal.

A tumult of fury filled Jehan, so violent and tragic it was also true pain. He let out a cry, leapt upright, and was blinded by a rush of blood behind his eyes.

It blotted out everything, and caused him to stumble. As he fought to regain himself, he heard the rat rustling again, widened his eyes – and saw – it was not a rat.

No, it was not a rat at all. But it was between him and the rickety door. Conrad . . . come back to gloat? The door had been secured. *Not* Conrad – Jehan clenched his fingers on his knife, which might be useless.

The hut seemed to have dematerialised. It had gone to a vast, black openness. Then specks of light emerged out of the black.

The thing against the door was straightening up, and Jehan beheld it was the young nun, Marie-Lis. But she was much changed. Her gorget and veil were gone and her dark hair veiled her instead. An Eastern drapery covered most of her body, but it was thin as water and her breasts were bare, and between them was a golden sign, like a dagger pointing down. Her naked arms were outflung, her feet were set one over the other, and nails of steaming white-hot steel went through her palms, her feet. Her face was serene. In the fingers of her left hand, though it was nailed, tilted a chalice which she now somehow upended fully, and black fluid fell from it, bubbling and smoking. Then she howled. As she made the ghastly ululation, her teeth came visible, and they were like the teeth of a boar.

Jehan gibbered. He could not move, he could only watch.

And now the host were riding, streaming through the black, astride their Hell-mounts, which as they rode, they *used* in other ways, squealing and whinnying, winged and tailed and clawed. Jehan felt the leathery wings clash and scrape about his head in the stench of rutting – and he too howled, in fear.

There was a lightning. It tore everything. The beast-woman on her cross, the raucous riders, Jehan's scream – and fixed them. Every atom hung in black, in bright, in black again. Jehan's eyes died a second time – then he had a view of something – it was as fearful as the horror and ugliness which had gone before – yet it was beautiful, it was *beautiful* – and it was gone – oh what had it been? Some landscape, some palace, some gathering of a Heavenly populace with flesh of pearl and sun-drenched hair – Paradise, or Paradys itself no longer a parody of the parks of Heaven – translated.

Then sight merged back into his eyes. Jehan *saw*. The knife slipped out of his fingers. Intuitively he reached after it, but unable to look, to look away, and he thought, What does a knife count for? And gave it up.

That vast black openness was filled now only by one image.

The man who had entered there wore the garments of a lord, a prince of the City of Paradys-Paradise, and everything was white, so white, while a kind of glowingness shone through it from his skin under the Eastern silk. For his skin had gold in it, and his hair was a rage of gold, a furnace. And his eyes were like the wide golden eyes of tigers in one of the novice's books, which Jhane had once been shown.

Jhane had seen him before, of course. In the church of the nunnery, the white figure untrammelled between earth and air, sometimes static, sometimes moving before her with a woman's gait – or not – disguised as a woman – or perhaps not even that – in a white mantle. And he was a prince. Not a king. Not the world's King. Not Satan, not Lucifer. One of the captains of the fallen host.

Jhane stepped away, Jehan sloughed, everything gone like the knife.

It came to her that she underwent a vision, a religious experience of Hell, but no less holy for being profane.

Jhane's body would no longer allow her to her knees, she seemed to have altered to wood, unbending but capable of splintering. She shut her eyes, but the burning flame of the angel remained imprinted under her lids.

A wonderful aroma filled the void that had been the hut. Her head swam at it, in a moment she would lose consciousness and die, and fiends would bear her to the Pit –

'Esrafel,' she said.

'You have called me,' he said, 'I am here with you.'

And no sooner did the voice touch her ears, like no other voice in the world, like music never heard there, than his hands also touched her. (The palms of his hands were golden, as were the soles of his feet in the silken shoes.) The caress seemed to find her forehead, but her whole body was laved in it, even to the tips of her nails and hair.

'I never called you,' said Jhane.

'You called me. You did not see that I stood at your side. Which is common to mankind.'

'Who are you?' she said, not sure at all if she spoke to him.

'You have named me.'

'Esrafel,' she said again. 'the Angel of the Lord.'

'You recognise me as Esrafel,' he said. 'Then I am Esrafel.'

He was winged. She felt the wings enclose her as his voice and hands had done, and the perfume of eternity.

She began to cry quietly on the breast of the angel. Fires mounted through her. She clung to him and begged for release. Her whole flesh seemed sundered, and she too was winged, and as she rushed to the pinnacle of Heaven, she saw his heart blazing like a rose of gold beneath silk and skin, and on the heart of the angel was a scar of an old wound, wounded again, over and over. Then Heaven shattered. She fell. She fell and the stars were made and in the pit of the earth a light, to last until the last of the world, its ending, and beyond, for ever and for ever. So let it be. *Amen*.

Bells were tolling, and only half-aware she counted the strokes. It would be Nonus, the ninth office, three in the afternoon, for there was daylight, but on and on clanged the bells, near and far. It was not an hour or a summons, but the death-bell, sounded from all the quarters of the City.

Jhane sat up in the wretched hut. She had been lying on the flea-ridden bed of rags and itched to prove it. How much time had passed? There had been a wonderful dream . . .

A man owned the hut; he might return. Jhane rose, and on impulse, shook the soil and twigs from the cloak, and wrapped it about herself. It hid the masculine dress by means of which she had sought protection.

As she walked out into the sallow gloom of the alley, full memory returned to Jhane. It met her like a blow, so she dropped back against the wall, covering her face in shame and distress. But the enormity of what had happened, being insupportable, gushed as suddenly from her. She regarded, in the distance, her days and nights in Paradys, their culmination, and the ultimate and terrible advent of revealing light. She was calm, and under her breath whispered a prayer of her infancy. Through all this, the bells churned on. Who had died? (She thought of the priest in the northern village, and wooden coffins lowered with scant ceremony. Once a son of the lord's house died. That had been different, a hundred mourners on the skyline and the bell at its crying all day.)

At the end of the alley, by the forge – which had stayed silent – she saw a group of beggars sitting in the street, huddled together.

She thought, for no reason she could divine, *I slept too long*.

As she passed the beggars not one of them stirred, and looking at them she saw a single face, its mouth slack and black tongue protruding. The skin was mottled, and there was a smell of bad meat. They were dead.

Jhane went by, and came out into an open square of muddy earth where the houses crushed each other. Smoke went up from two or three chimneys, but otherwise there was no evidence of life. Under the bells a dog bayed ceaselessly. Premonition was total if unnamed. Moving over the square into another of the lanes, Jhane met an old woman and nearly started from her skin.

Jhane said, 'You're alive!' The old woman laughed. 'Is the City dead?'

'Pestilence,' said the old woman. 'After the Ass Feast. That's three days. Where have you been?'

'Asleep.'

'Done better, you, to have stayed asleep. God sleeps.' She craned away and pointed at Jhane. 'A man goes to his bed well and at daybreak they find him dead and black. At the festival some were falling down, spewing black blood.'

I lay in the arms of a demon.

'Don't come near,' said the old woman. 'You may have it on you. It comes from a touch, or a look.'

'Why?' said Jhane.

'The wells are poisoned,' said the old woman. 'Full of bodies and piss and curses. It's God's punishment. Perhaps I have it,' said the old woman. She licked her hand and smeared the spittle against Jhane's cheek. 'There.'

Jhane ran away through the alleys of Paradys.

As Jhane fled and wandered through the City, she found Death stalked ahead of her. She began to look out for him, too, personified, some hooded shape. One world had ended for her. Now she was in this other. She had left off dividing reality from dream.

It seemed, soon enough, that the City was on fire. The winter pall from the chimneys and the alleys had lessened, and the wider streets **were now full of smoke. Fires were burning on the cobbles, columns** of black going up in the still air. Sometimes people darted from the houses to renew the kindling or to throw in aromatics or sulphur. They were plague fires, set to burn the contagion out of the atmosphere. A breath could kill as well as a touch or a look.

Sometimes figures went by Jhane. Robed and cowled, their mouths and nostrils muffled and only the eyes visible, smudged around by smoke, they were like the Death she visualised. They might have been priests going to tend or bring comfort to the sick, or collectors of the dead, but they had a terrifying appearance, looming out suddenly from the smouldering vacuum, under the shadowy cliffs of higher buildings.

The chorus of bells rang continually. Now and then one might fall off, but later it would resume.

Jhane came to the river, which she had instinctively been seeking, though often in circles in the dark. The water had an aspect of stasis as complete as that of the sky. Not a ripple moved, and where any boat lay, it was lifeless as a fallen tree. The upper bank of the City too was lost in smoke, and a cloud rose from it, but without apparent movement.

As she stood there a black procession evolved nearby, a priest with a lantern, many coffins, a flock of carrion-crow mourners.

They passed away over a bridge, perhaps towards the burial ground of Our Lady.

From the houses Jhane began to hear sounds she had not heard before, cries and weeping, and sometimes screams. The dream world was becoming more real. Again she ran away. And having nowhere else, it was towards the Nunnery of the Angel that flight took her.

In her mind, Jhane had a knowledge that she must get in again over the wall, the way the boy had done, the young man who had possessed her, he who was the symbol of all the evil of the masculine species. She felt the horror of casting off the cloak, (the thief Conrad's), and being revealed for herself as a male once more.

On an open area between the houses, some carts were being loaded. This time, there were no mourners. All were dead except for the porters, who went about their task jeering and laughing, and sometimes drinking. Elected to such a duty, they did not reckon they could escape the pestilence. 'Drink and be merry!' They shouted to Jhane, then two of them gave chase, reaching after her with hands that had just slung the bodies across each other in the carts. But Jhane evaded the men, and they did not pursue her far.

The smoke was very thick beyond that spot, and at the end of an avenue of smoke, the gate of the nunnery suddenly appeared in front of her, and above, the ghost of the tower, the bell tongueless in it.

At that moment, the doors of the gate both began to open. Jhane stood still. The sight of the opening black doors frightened her, making her think of the first night she had come there, and also of the houses in the upper city, the fat woman opening one door, and then the student of Master Motius opening another.

But no one was to be let in this time. It was a group of nuns who were coming out. How strange they looked, their faces in the icon-like blankness with which they drifted into the church at every office. At their head moved the Mother. Her strong, fleshy countenance had altered, it was now gaunt and very pale, an icon like the rest. She glided out into the street, and the nuns of the Angel glided after her. A vague chanting, the note of bees, floated near but did not seem to emanate from them. They came on. They passed Jhane, not seeing her. And she looked at their Madonna faces in perplexity. When they were gone, had vanished into the vacuum of smoke, she realised she had not noticed among them the face and body of Marie-Lis.

Jhane approached the gate and went in through one leaf of the unlocked doors.

The smoke had barely got in here. Jhane could smell incense and herbs and tallow and women – familiar things. She sensed the bell should be ringing for an office – Nonus it would be truly now, perhaps. Her soul had memorised the times. But the tower was mute, and a great quiet lay everywhere – for all at once, all the bells in the City seemed to have stopped ringing.

She went through the outer court, and under the arch into the churchyard. She half turned towards the hostel then. She could go to her cell and hide herself there. Soon it would grow properly dark. Wrapped in her female clothing and the covers of her pallet, and the night, she might be safe. But no, all these layers would only close her more surely inside her own head, where fear was.

The nunnery was a desert. They had all gone out of it. Crossing over the south cloister, Jhane remembered sweeping there with the novices, and the phantom of Osanne with her rags and pail. What had it meant, the death of Osanne? Maybe the nuns had understood, for they had gone about disguising the death very swiftly. Jhane, before she knew what she did, sang aloud a snatch of song the novices had taught her: *Oh winter is, Oh winter is.* 'No, no,' said Jhane, and the cloister echoed. At its centre the stone child gripped the bowl of the dry fountain. Jhane hurried on. She entered the garden, and stopped immediately, for there was the young nun gathering up washing that had fallen to the ground.

Jhane flew forward. She would cast herself at the feet of the young nun. She must say: I have seen. Save me now, tell me what to do. But at the last instant, the nun turned a little, and Jhane saw that it was not Marie-Lis, but one of the senile sisters from the infirmary. Her wizened face was not an icon. It looked on Jhane, and parting the seams of its mouth, plaintively said to her, 'They left me here. Useless. Well, here you are then, too. I shan't die alone.' And the elderly nun sat down on the stone kerb of the poisoned well, (in which Osanne had been burned and buried), holding the two or three habits, and the linen things in her lap.

Jhane went to the old nun cautiously.

'What is it?' said the nun. 'Can you see me? I can see you.'

'Where have they gone?' said Jhane. 'The sisters, the Mother?'

'There's a plague,' said the old nun. 'Didn't anybody tell you? Poor girl. They've gone to nurse the sick and the dying, it's a part of the vows. Pay no heed to yourself, the Enemy strikes us down with his arrows by day and by night. But we must love one another. So the Mother prayed and took them all out, and most or all of them will catch the ailment and perish.' The nun was disapproving. 'They didn't think of me. I shall die, but it isn't plague, it doesn't matter. Come here, sit beside me. Did you know, this well can't be used any more? One of the novices drowned herself in it.'

Jhane went nearer. She said. 'Where is Marie-Lis?'

'Sister Marie? I must think. My old head . . . Three weeks since the plague came. The night of the Donkey Feast.'

Jhane crept close. She sat at the old nun's knee, trembling. Was it so? To sleep three days, or three weeks – she had seen an angel, he had put into her heart the searing light – a slumber of days, weeks, a hundred years, was nothing to that. She meant to say, I was granted a true vison: one of the Lord's winged knights came to me. But she said only, 'She was the youngest of the nuns.'

The old nun said, 'Alas, yes. Now it comes to me. It was like the other, the novice, Osanne. But Sister Marie hanged herself.'

Jhane now could say nothing.

'In her cell,' continued the old nun. 'Suicide, a mighty sin. But the Lord understands and forgives. It is a sin only against oneself. Now I know you. You were sick with a fever and they tied you down on the bed beside mine. Well it was that night she hanged herself, for I heard the talk that it must be kept from you, she had been kind to you, and you loved her.'

'Never,' said Jhane. She leaned her forehead on the old nun's knee and wept silently for some while. The old nun laid her hand gently on Jhane's hair. When Jhane's crying ended, the old nun said, 'We have a special dispensation, all the City. The priests are dying, or afraid and run off. Any man, or woman, may hear another's confession. Now you must hear mine.'

'If you knew what I had done – ' cried Jhane. She kneeled up and burst out: 'I saw the Angel of the Lord. How can I bear it?'

But the old nun only said. 'Be merciful to me, for I have sinned.' And then she recounted her confession softly, which amounted to some small jealousies and omissions. When she was done, she smiled at Jhane, then closed her eyes and began to sleep.

She will die in her sleep and leave me alone here, thought Jhane, and had the urge to wake the old nun up. But she looked so peaceful, Jhane did not do it.

Darkness stole over the garden. The fruit trees and the bare plots dissolved into the night. In a while there came up over the wall a straw-coloured moon.

Jhane imagined going back to the church and entering it and flinging herself before the altar and the window. Osanne's ghost might reappear and tell her: 'It was your strength that slew me. I got between you and the light. You thrust me aside. It was like the lightning bolt.' Or Marie-Lis might be there and say, 'I came between you and the light. I removed myself.' For Marie-Lis too had presented herself as a ghost, and to Conrad besides, for she had been dead by the Day of the Ass. (Or had Marie-Lis been the tempter, the evil one, the shadow mimicking the light –) But after all, maybe Osanne had only drowned herself in the well and some element in the water had marked her body like burning, and some creature had got down to her and gnawed her belly wide – and possibly Marie-Lis had endured a secret sorrow which she had ended for herself without a notion of Jhane, Jhane's power, or Jehan's crimes. And only Jehan's lust had summoned her back among the plum trees.

The Angel Lucefiel would not descend from the window to comfort Jhane. The Angel Esrafel would not console her ever again. Yet she had seen him.

Yes, she had seen a vision, and now her life must change. No, for it was changed already, she must only accept the change of it. Nor let your sins weigh you down – your sins are finished, tear up the thought of them by the roots. It seemed the other inner part of her mind had again been formulating plans.

There in the garden, by the sleeping, dying nun, Jhane pulled off

Conrad's cloak, and all Jehan's male attire. She unbound her breasts, and did not even notice when the penis of cloth was sloughed into the shadows. Jhane took from the old nun's lap one of the habits, and articles of linen. Jhane clothed herself. She covered her head and neck with gorget and veil, her body with the robe of the order, when everything was in place on her, she drew up the topaz crucifix and wore it there openly on her breast.

The old nun still slept.

Jhane took her hand.

Light as a husk, the old nun slipped forward and rested on her. Jhane lifted her in her strong arms and bore her back to the bed in the infirmary.

An hour later, at the office of Hesperus, which was not rung, the old nun died.

Jhane dug and buried her in a shallow grave, in the traditional area. She did not visit the church, before passing on into the City through the gate.

They had forbidden the ringing of funeral bells; they had forbidden processions of mourners. Who had done so? None but the unseen Lords of Paradys, her Duke or Prince, (and Jhane did not know which), the authorities of the City – most of whom had fled the pest, and sent their orders back with doomed messengers. Almost all the function of the City had stopped, however, and so to cancel funeral rites was nothing. There were scarcely any priests remaining to speak above the bodies. The graveyards were full. Now they dug up any spare land, and piled in the corpses on top of each other, twenty, thirty persons deep. There was no commerce this side of the river. Men lived by what they could get, stealing and hoarding. On the upper bank, some forms were kept, this far, but for how long? The plague seemed fit to withstand them all. The plague was healthy and vital. The Death, they called it now, as if there were no other kind of death in the world, and maybe there was not. Cadavers lay in the thoroughfares, uncollected a great while. They were blotched with black, black boils, and black blood. The dogs, scavenging, refused to eat them. Smoke still rose, the warding fires, and a few vehicles still trundled back and forth. Sometimes there might be a woman at a well, but since the wells were supposedly poisoned, these women were reckoned mad, or already infected – or witches and actually the poisoners, and were liable to be stoned.

It was difficult to traverse the river. The upper City had set the source of the plague on the other bank, fount of all villainy and misadventure, and sometimes extempore guards patrolled the south and west ends of the bridges. It was also pointless to attempt to escape the City, for the roads beyond the walls, rife with infection, fringed with rotting bodies, were also blocked by wagons and carts of which the drivers had perished, dead horses and sheep, while the fields and woods were said to be choked by wildmen who had lost their minds, and by desperate wolves which had come to a feast that, in the event, repelled them.

In the new world, Jhane took her way. Dressed as a nun, she was accorded respect. The female orders of the City had proved valiant and thorough, where the priests had frequently made off with their lives. Even the topaz cross on the girl's breast was not taken from her. What use were riches now? Could you bribe King Death? The plague was everywhere, (they said), civilisation was ending. And robbers who thieved food or apparel, let alone gold, they contracted plague from them.

It was simple and easy to tend the sick, when once all barriers were down in brain and heart. In just such a manner, she had found it simple and easy to do harm, to murder.

Not so much did Jhane expect death: she expected nothing. She walked among the victims of the pestilence, unafraid, and in itself this gave them a sort of courage. Jhane proposed no remedy for the symptoms of disease. She offered only her cool hands, into which they drove their nails in agony, which they clasped in dying, and only her quiet voice that murmured nothing important to them, and her nun's robe which symbolised divine respite and forgiveness. She heard ten hundred confessions. When hoarse whispers pleaded for God's grace, she nodded. Her eyes carried a wonderful conviction. She had done far worse than any of them, or so it seemed to her, and she herself had been consoled by an angel. That they called the world's Lord by the wrong name, this she overlooked. It was not, this hour of their death, any time to quibble.

Though sometimes she glimpsed other religious at similar work, she met no nuns of the order she had adopted. She met, however, with many forms of human fear and anger, acted out as if upon a stage. She saw pageants with banners, and orgies, when beer and naked limbs swilled down the street. She saw men who whipped themselves with thongs studded by nails, and women dancing in their skin to the pound of a drum. She saw a death-cowled priest who screamed that the Day of Wrath had come, and a young maiden embracing her lover's corpse, begging it to kill her with its infection, she would go with him. Jhane paid little heed. It was the new world. But then again, the earth, and all things in it, had never seemed familiar or sane to her.

The brown days of smoke, the blind nights, went by. Sometimes a Biblical, yellow-lit cloud stood over the higher City after sunset.

She saw and held children as they gave up the ghost, young men, maidens, crones. She learned all the degrees and stages of the illness, and all the guises of it. When they should begin for her, she would acknowledge them. They did not begin for her. Like a weightless feather she floated on the tide of misery.

'Oh, sister, devout lady, come to the bridge with us. You'll help us? They can't turn back *you*.'

It was in fact a funeral procession, though not clothed in mourning, which, in any case, most of it would never have afforded. Cartloads of the dead outnumbered the living. Everyone wept, which was now unusual, for apathy and despair, the greatest of the sins, had settled on Paradys.

A tall old man stood looking down into Jhane's face.

'We must get over,' he said. 'There are no places left here. Holy ground. They must be got into holy ground. Or when the last trumpet's blown, they won't hear it.'

Jhane did not say to the man, It will not make any odds. There is enough life for all. She did not say, He remembers even the fall of a sparrow. She bowed her veiled head in assent, as she had recently done whenever any request had been made to her that she was capable of granting. She led them towards the South Bridge.

There was a huge bonfire half-way across, uncared for and almost out. Even so, they must pick through the crackling rims of it, and a black fume rose.

Over on the other shore, some men in mail coats were standing about. They were soldiers, or a company from some lord's guard. One stepped forward, on to the bridge, as they came near, and drew his sword.

'No farther.'

The carts rumbled to a halt. Women began to cry and wail loudly. Jhane walked on. As she came closer and closer to the soldier or guard, his face engorged – firstly•with fear, and then with amazement.

'You can't,' he said, when she too halted, a pace or so from him.

'Yes.'

'*No*, sister. Take them back. There's no grave-ground here. *Christ's nails*. They're burning them, that's all. Look east, up there. Those aren't the pest fires. It's corpse fires now. Too many dead to bury.'

'Then,' she said, 'the fires.'

'No,' he said again. 'We're keeping the riff-raff away. We've checked the sickness this side. It's less here. But not if they all come over. They stink of death.'

Jhane stood motionless. She looked into his eyes and said, 'When I was hungry, you fed me. When I was thirsty, you gave me drink. I was sick and you tended me, in prison and you visited me. The Lord says, Even as you have done to the least of men, so you have done to me.'

The mailed man began to cry, just like the people around the carts, but perhaps only the smoke of all the thousand fires of Paradys was in his eyes. He stepped away, lowering his sword. The other men shifted. 'Let them by,' he said to these others. 'What does it matter.' They moved, and the carts began again to jolt forward. Another man in mail ran at Jhane and pushed the point of his sword against her breast. The first man came and eased the sword aside. As Jhane went on with the carts, she heard him say, 'Can't you see, you fool, she's the Virgin. It's a miracle. We'll be saved!'

As they proceeded off the bridge, the last cart toiled beside Jhane, and when she looked into it she saw the face of the thief, Conrad, but upside down. He was lying across several other bodies, which they had tried to arrange in a seemly way, although this was not possible. The tall old man trod by the cart. He said, 'That was my son. He was a wicked sinner. A cut-throat. He started doing evil as a child. I knew then he was lost. Whatever ground he goes in, or if he's burnt, it's the same – he'll be baking in Hell already.'

'You're wrong,' said Jhane. 'A woman saw an angel in Conrad's hut.'

The old man stared at her, but they were coming level with the outer yard of the church of Our Lady, and a fearful smell was in the air, worse than all the rest. Between the church and the quay boats had earlier been dragged ashore and set alight. This had laid the foundation of a pyre for multitudes, but was now mostly crumbling, a tower of glowing ashes. From thick smog a ragged priest or two was emerging. One ran forward and waved them away. 'Not here. No more. Go on to the east wall, the Roman wall. Up there.' Then he drew Jhane aside. Unconcerned with her now, the death procession moved by, and left her behind. 'Sister, I can see you've had the Death, and survived it.' Jhane said nothing. 'It's plain, you bear all the marks. I too. Look, you see? Like the mark on Cain's brow. There was one good doctor, he gave me myrrh and saffron, and bled me. On the fifth day the boil burst and I recovered. To show my thanks to God, I serve the City. When this is over, this terrible reckoning, I'll kill myself.' He paused, waiting to complete his catechism.

'Why?'

'Can you ask? There will be so few of us left alive. The whole world will have to begin again. Besides, God's punishment is so cruel. I'll thank, but I can't worship such a God. I defy him.'

'If someone must be the enemy of mankind,' said Jhane, 'and not Satan, then God, perhaps.'

'Blasphemy,' said the priest. He laughed. 'Stay here,' he said. 'If you go up there, you may get caught in some building. When the pest comes, the soldiers wall them up alive inside, the sick, the hale, the dead together.'

Jhane turned from the priest. He said again, 'Stay, pale rose. We have wine in the church.' But Jhane slid from him and was gone, climbing up the hills of Paradys, quickly lost to him in smoke.

Over Satan's Way, the ribcage of the unfinished Temple-Church had the look of a ruin, something which had been, but now decayed and fell to bits. A large fire had been built in the midst of the sheds, but it was out. No one was by.

Peculiar noises, often indecipherable, ascended and sank constantly in the City, generally isolated. One such now began in the street that circled beyond the Temple. Jhane came out on the street. It was not as she remembered. The decent houses, the ornate well and trough, the burned house, were in position as before, and yet everything seemed subtly to have misplaced itself. There were no fires here, as if once had been enough, and smoke coloured the air, but only that. Far along the wall of the old garden-park – which had not yet been utilised as a crematorium – mailed riders on thin horses sat under a battered, stained banner. They were directing the actions of some labourers in the process of boarding and plastering over the doors and lower windows of one house.

'Stay away, sister. *It's* here.' The man who rode towards her on the sorry horse did not meet her eyes. 'The only method to stop it, lady.'

Then he drew closer. He leaned towards her. On his face was a terrible invisible unmistakable shadow. He murmured, so the other men should not hear, 'I have it. I'm hot and cold, and a pain in my groin. Some live through. I might. I shan't. When this job's done, I'll go up on the waste land, where the fires are. It's like the Pit up there, the damned all crying in torment, and the flames. Confess me?

163

They say anyone can do it, but a holy nun's better if I can't have the priest.'

'Yes,' said Jhane.

Leaning from the horse then, as if he discussed ordinary things with her, he gabbled his confession, a sibling to so many others she had heard. And when it was over, he added, 'And they're on my conscience – the mason in the house there. He was at work on the Temple-Church. His wife and servant were taken out, dead, but then the order came, close the house. It's him and some lunatic son he's got, dying in there and hearing the plaster shutting round them. Better to go in the open. But I don't care. Rot the lot of them. Rot 'em.' Suddenly, no longer bothering with life, he rode headlong through the street, going eastward. His men did not pay much attention to him, the labourers none; they were at work on the final window.

'Let me go in,' said Jhane to the labourers, when she reached them. They looked at her, then at the mounted men under the banner.

'Trying to earn Heaven, sister?' one of them sneered. 'Go on then. It's up to you. If you can squeeze through the window, skinny nun.'

But two of the labourers assisted her politely through the narrow aperture, even fisting out some of the fresh plaster. When she was through, they asked her blessing. She rendered it as she had seen the Mother do. Then, she stood in the house and listened to the wood smacked back and the slap of the putty, and watched the light fade.

The house already reeked of the Death, but the odour was customary to Jhane. She climbed a stair and midway up she was confronted by a man – the dying mason. He raved at her, an intruder in his home. He asked her what she meant by it. But his breathing was hard. He coughed fluid into his sleeve.

'Forgive me,' said Jhane. 'Something made me come in here. I'll care for you. Recovery may happen.' She saw that this was unlikely. When he staggered, she supported him back to his bed. He had stopped reviling her. He smiled at her in a frightened and placatory manner, like a sick child.

Presently he said, 'Nothing, no chance for me. But the boy – '

'Your son.'

'Not my son. I wish I'd had – such a son – still-births were all she could manage, poor bitch. She's dead, poor bitch.' He coughed and choked and recovered, and said, 'Not long. The boy – might live. He's been sick a while – not this, before. That can – make them stronger to fight – I've seen it before. Before. He's lived through trouble before. Wits – gone – the worst of all – better any crippling – though not the hands –' The mason's speech wandered with his thoughts. He then said, 'Having seen what he was capable of, I asked him if he'd train to work in stone – well – he'd drink and go after – that sweetest part of a woman's frame – but he was young. Anyway murdered for it, we thought. Then on Fool's Day, over – the – river – I found him. Some slut had taken him in. Well – he was useless – to her. She told me. She'd come on him – crawling in his blood. Oh the Devil burnt up that house, oh – yes. The Artisan Motius – they said the Devil rode over his roof and hauled him up through a window – all alight. Dead, anyhow. So *I* took the imbecile in. How could I leave him – in her hovel? Perhaps – did him – a bad turn. This fell on us.' Then he was feverish and screamed that he also was burning, Fire! Fire! And then he choked and drowned and died.

Jhane went further up the house and came to a small room with a slender bed filling it. On the mattress a young man with wringing-wet yellow hair, writhed and tossed in unemphatic delirium. His skin was blotched by darkness, and beneath one arm nested the black knots of the plague. He was however recognisable. And so Jhane looked into the face of her brother, Pierre.

Inside the walled-up house, it was very quiet. The earth, which had formerly condensed to a City, had now become the house alone.

Shortly before midnight, Jhane had managed to drag the heavy corpse of the mason off the bed, ,and into the chest at the bed's foot. Plague cadavers putrefied rapidly. The chest, of a proper size and air-tight, must serve as coffin and burial together. Having sealed the chest – its linen would be useful elsewhere – with its own iron clasps, Jhane went about the floors, seeing if anything else was to be had there. All access to a well was gone, but previously in the kitchen, perhaps the bounty of the law, she had found a barrel of water. There were also some casks of ale. Jhane now searched and discovered a store of candles, kindling, garlic and withered apples, and some mouldering bread, but if there had been any other provisions, someone had appropriated them.

Above, the young man who was her brother, strove on between sleep and delirium and death. Jhane had sat by him some hours, telling him at intervals that he would live. It was the only panacea she employed, other than to wash his body with the tepid water, and to moisten his lips. She had rolled him aside also, twice, to ease the soiled clothes from under him, replacing them with fresh. When he cried out or shouted, which happened occasionally, she took him in her arms, responding to all he said, replying, whether he spoke with some semblance of logic or only in nonsense, and whether he might hear her or not. (She had been made aware in the strife of the plague that the sufferers suffered far worse when feeling they were ignored, or that the phantom situations of fever went unstraightened. In certain cases she had also pretended to be wives and mothers, daughters and sons, and the victims – crying for these lost kindred – were deceived and calmed.)

It had not surprised her to come on Pierre. She had supposed him dead, but the world had changed. It seemed to her, although she did not dwell on it, that the moment the angel touched her, Pierre had been reborn. Thereafter the mason accidentally located and rescued him inevitably. Ever since then, some invisible cord had been slowly pulling her towards this spot. Reborn, Pierre could not die again so swiftly. And to attend and comfort him as he fought for life was not an expiation. He had been cruel to her, and she had not forgotten it. But what he had done no longer mattered, whereas her own cruel malice had turned her towards kindness and deep pity. Compared to her own wickedness, Pierre's was of a slight order, and probably he had learnt nothing from it.

Because he would survive, too, Jhane did not attempt any of those remedies which the doctors had practiced before her in a number of scenes of the pest-stricken City. Though the black boils were hard and leaking, she did not lance or cauterise them; she did not bleed or radically try to cool or inflame the desperate body on the bed.

For herself, she took no precautions.

She had always been underfed. She ate the apples, and drank a little ale, and slept in separate minutes, sitting on the floor.

A morning came, blooming up through the upper windows. A day passed, declining down through them. These windows had been left alone as they were too small to provide egress. But they did provide some air, for the smoke seemed less. That afternoon, Jhane heard a distant bell give tongue in Paradys. She had almost forgotten the sound. In a while she realised it was not a funeral knell, but the Nonus, from some church away towards the river. Beyond the window, in the vanishing light, roofs and towers stood in islands among the smokes.

When night returned Jhane took off the topaz cross and laid it under the sick man's pillow. The flash of the jewel as she came from the window had reminded her she wore it. If she had recollected earlier, she would have removed it then and placed it ready for Pierre.

Near sunrise of the third day, Pierre screamed, and the evil pebbles of the Death burst open, freeing him of poison.

When she had cleaned him and given him water, he dropped down into an intent oblivion. After the sun had risen, all that day, she sat and watched his skin begin to clear and change colour, the dark patches gradually leaving it. But the ill-treatment, the assault, the rape, the madness – these as much as the pestilence – had aged him and torn his beauty. Through the empty pane of his unconscious face, Jhane could see now a resemblance to his father, Belnard.

He did not know her. This seemed to her a proof that the insanity the mason had spoken of was leaving Pierre. Sane, he would not accept her presence, he would *reject* her presence – once precursor of such horrors.

'You're good to me,' he murmured, and drifted again to sleep. Later he said, 'I'm hungry.' Later again, he said, 'Hunger gnaws at me. There's a snake in my guts. Kind holy lady, please tell them I must have something to eat.'

'Not yet,' she said. She gave him more water.

He trusted her, drank, and fainted again into sleep.

He was very weak and would die without sustenance. What should it be? Milk, with a little bread crumbled in it, a light meaty broth. She mashed apples to a pulp with water heated at the kitchen hearth, and added a sip of the ale. This mush she fed him, but it only made him nauseous, and brought no strength.

'Who else is here?' he said. 'Sister, send some boy to the market. He's sure to go. Give him – 'here he fumbled for coins, and found nothing.'Well, only tell him Pierre asked it.' He smiled charmingly.

'Rest,' she said. 'I'll do what I can.' For he had obviously forgotten a great amount, and it was not the time to tell him they were walled up inside a house.

Almost all the smoke seemed to have cleared from the City, but a heavy rain had begun, and sometimes thunder shook the timbers of the building. The street, peered at through the tiny window-place, looked deserted, though once she saw another cart go past below, lugged by a weary man, mounds in it under a covering, and making east. The mason's house had no upper east window. She could not see if the pall of the crematory fires still flooded upward there.

Jhane set about searching the house again. It was true that she discovered items she had not found on her prior foray. In a pocket of the chimney of the great hooded fireplace in the mason's bedchamber, was a cache of coins. In a cupboard she came on the tools of builders, a saw and tongs, pick-axe and hoe. In a box beneath rested the mason's level, and some wooden shapes whose purpose eluded her. She unearthed some wine also which, as with the cloves of garlic, was a useful disinfectant: the training of the nunnery. She found, too, parchments with architectural drawings, and three books she could not read, ink-horn and quills, a child's cradle with a cloth doll lying in it, at which she recalled the mason's words of the still-births, and the bones of a dead rat. None of these was of any help to her.

Days and nights washed over the house. Each was its own season, a little year.

Pierre, who had begun to seem stronger, now lapsed. He said, 'There's a hard stone under the pillow.'

'Not a stone. It's your own cross.'

'I haven't any,' he said.

'Yes. When you were in the fever, I took it from your neck and placed it there for safe-keeping. Your cross with the topaz.'

He said, 'My father gave it me.' He said, 'It came from the Holy Land. Just the jewel, the crucifix was made for it after. My father was on a great crossade. He killed Saracens. They reject the Christ – as you know, sister. They worship a man. And an angel also – Jabrael, God's Mighty One . . . Yes, the yellow stone, the topaz, he cut it from some breast-plate of a fallen pagan priest, in a shrine there, or so he said . . .' He faded and was senseless for a while. Then he woke and said, 'But the cross was stolen from me. I *remember* that. I was beaten, and the cross – ' Wild with fear he stared at her, struggling not to remember.

'A dream of the fever,' she said. 'It's over.'

Later in the night he said, 'I had a sister. She told me lies about our father. How could she do that?'

He had learnt nothing.

'Sister . . .'

She did, for a moment, start. But all nuns were the sisters of all men.

'Lie quietly,' she said.

'Did I – make confession to you?'

'Never. It was not necessary.'

'But now.'

'Nor necessary now.'

'I can't,' he said. 'I can't.'

'Live? Yes.'

'The little cross – '

'Yes.'

'If I – don't live – take it. No, that's wrong. If I live, take it anyway. For your order, sister.'

Now she did not start at all.

'She said, 'Some gifts can't be given. Your father gave it you. It must stay with you.'

She thought he slept. Then he said, 'Will you put the cross round my neck?'

Jhane did as Pierre asked her. The chain, which had been thieved elsewhere, seemed to puzzle him briefly. Then he lay still, thinking of the feel of the cross, the jewel, on his skin.

'That girl I told you about – did I? My sister, Jehanine. She was a harlot in the City. She came to me to show me her degradation, then she ran and hid herself. I saw what she'd become, just by looking in her eyes. I wish I hadn't seen that.'

Oh, he had learnt nothing. He must live, it was his only hope. Yet he was dying now.

Jhane walked the house, up and down. She opened again the chests and cupboards, held a candle to the mouse holes, but even the mice were gone. She felt no hunger, she felt only beyond herself, a vast space hollow as a bell, in which she was; breathing, moving, alive, slenderly hard and sure as a needle. But Pierre was like the dust, like melting snow, like water. He must be remade. He must have food.

In the watery dawn, some men went by. Jhane called down from a window. They took no notice of her. Perhaps her voice failed to reach them, deaf ears or hearts or minds.

Through the dark, the City bells rang once more every one of the offices. At Laude, Jhane went down through the house, to the kitchen. By the glimmer of the candle, she looked into the empty larder.

As her hands were searching over the bare surfaces, she thought very clearly and suddenly of the Angel Esrafel, companion-captain of the Prince of Light. Standing quite still, arms on the shelf, her head thrown back, she closed her eyes, recapturing as it seemed entirely the ecstasy and healing of his embrace.

Then she opened her eyes and gazing before her, she saw what she had been looking for: food. At the revelation of the sight, she was grasped by utter terror. For an instant she rejected the absolute truth, the miracle, as unthinkable. But in another instant, she felt again the touch of the angel. She accepted that the world was altered. She accepted her own power and strength. Terror left her immediately. There was only the hollow of the night enclosing her hard purity, which could not be shaken.

Then, practical, she turned to seek out the means of preparation, and – the training of the nunnery – such methods as there were of care.

'The boy came back from the market,' said Jhane. She set the bowl on the floor. Propping Pierre half asleep on the pillows, she began to spoon the broth into his mouth. She was very weak. It had taken an endless time. It had taken years even to climb the stair, but maybe not so long, for the broth was still hot, fragrant with the grains of garlic, the dash of wine, the ripe clean smell of the fresh meat.

At first, he was almost unable to take it. But after he had had some, and slept a while, he took more. There was enough of the food for some days.

At the hearth fire, she kept the cauldron heated, and also burned the stained and ruined linen. The wine and apples fortified her now. When she lost consciousness it was never for very long. She had fainted repeatedly in the beginning, kneeling by her cooking.

Some dream told her she had committed a sin, heeding the angel, but she laughed aloud at it. She was full of joy. She would not bother with the rest.

She knew also that miracles attended upon miracles, and that, before Pierre had consumed all the broth, some means of escape would come to them.

One morning, a colossal thunder-clap shook the whole house. It was a group of mailed men banging on the plaster of the lower house with axes and mallets.

Jhane looked down at them dreamily from a window.

'Sister! How are you faring? Are there any more with you? Any still sick with the pest?'

'One man with me. Neither sick now, but starving.'

'You were heard calling, but they said it was a ghost. *I* said, that's the gentle nun went in there, to help the mason. And God will have spared her.'

He was the soldier who had sneered at her when she had done so. Now his face was bright and young with happiness.

'The plague's over. It's gone. Old Death's taken himself off.'

A chunk of plaster gave way and fell with a crash. The men cheered and hullooed, waving their mallets up at her in salute.

'The young man with me is very feeble,' said Jhane. 'Please will some of you come in and carry him down.'

She left the window and went to Pierre to tell him, but he had heard, of course.

He was handsome today, his looks returning like the spring. Under his tunic, hastily pulled on for the outing, the topaz glinted. He did not know her, but he said, 'Sister, my own kindred couldn't have been more tender to me. You saved my life, perhaps my soul. Do you know, I was apprenticed to an artisan. But I heard he died. Well, I'll find one to take me on. God gave me a talent. I must use it, to God's glory.'

Then, when a doorway was smashed, and the men came tramping up the stairs, he said, 'You have a look of my own sisters, isn't that strange?'

But his eyes were still dimmed over.

It was two of the soldiers, not Pierre, who noticed her own plight.

'Ssh,' she cautioned, as another of the men bore Pierre away. 'Tell him nothing. Don't mention it when he's by.'

'But in God's name, how did this happen?'

Used perhaps to the wounds of war, the two soldiers stayed by her, and renewed the wrappings and bindings. As if seeing the rough staunching by fire, however, for the first, and the protruding sawn bone, so very white, Jhane herself turned ill. When she recovered, she was in the street in the arms of the soldier who had sneered, and now held her like his child. A mild rain kissed her face. 'Ssh,' she said again.

'How – ' he said. 'This sacrifice – did you? How – '

'The Lord guided me and gave me strength.'

Of such matters legends were made.

They took her to another house of nuns, much depleted since the Death, whose inhabitants cared for her in costive silence. The surgeon, a man who had fled the City, returned and did not credit the tale. This woman had been attacked by criminals in the hysteria and panic of the pest. Confronting Jhane with his verdict, he was pleased by her acquiescence. He prophesied that the upper portion of the limb might grow infected, in which case the work would be to do again, the cut higher, and she might die. He did not fear this death, nor warning her lavishly of it, for it was not in itself contagious.

She heard no more of Pierre, who had gone away with his golden head lying on the newest rescuer's shoulder. She did not give a thought to paintings and carvings which perhaps, by his skill, might come to adorn the churches of Paradys. Or to the love he would effortlessly win, or the jewel Belnard had given him.

Part of her own self had become a part of him, yet even this reverie did not prevail upon her. Recollecting her act, the use of the tools found in the house, the tight-binding and cauterisation, the subsequent preparation of the meat – into which had intruded a ghostly figment of Osanne, (whose own disintegrated arm had been raised from the well) – then Jhane herself doubted that she could have performed the deed. She did not at all regret it.

A pain-wrought phantom arm and hand, to the very fingers, remained to her below the elbow. Their presence was so decided that often she would reach out with them, finding with surprise she could not then take hold of things in this way. The phantom was, she knew, the incorporeal arm of her spirit. Unlike flesh, it could not be severed from her.

When she left the nun's hospital they were greatly relieved, for the proximity of a martyr and saint had oppressed them.

Jhane herself was unencumbered. She was already putting from her mind the image of her brother. She did not feel holy. No more than she hugged to herself the mad terror of her crimes did she clasp the greater terror and madness of her act in the mason's house. She did not believe she had been valorous, extraordinary, tested, or kind.

The unlocked doors of the nunnery gate had saved them from being forced, for at some time persons had entered. They were gone now, and there had been no desecration, only a certain amount of human dirt left lying. Nor were there any corpses. Jhane set herself, slowly, to clean the yards.

The milk had turned to curds in the refectory-kitchen, and these she ate, along with such fruit and salt fish as the invaders of the nunnery had not devoured. The water in the refectory well was crystalline.

As she ragged and broomed, the flight of a sudden bird among the empty cloisters, or the flutter of stray sunshine, might cause Jhane to glance about her. But the ghosts did not return.

She would have rung the bell in the tower, but, lacking an arm, it was inconceivable she would be able to do it. She regretted this, the gap where its notes should have sounded oddly disturbed her. She missed also the chanting of the nuns, and sometimes thought she did hear it, but the susurrus was in her own head.

At first she went to the church solely to see what had been done there, and if the great window was broken, but only a little debris had been blown in, and rain, which had formed and dried in pools in the uneven floor. The window was intact. So, on days when the sun shone, and at dawn, Jhane would go to look at the picture, at the Angel Lucefiel, Son of Morning and Bringer of Light, sword drawn and still falling eternally through the sky, the solar halo behind his head, on wings of fire, one foot against a gilded orb. Perhaps it was the daylight which blazed through this image that gave it such reason for her. It was the only artistic form she had ever understood, and the only iconic thing, apart from her doll in childhood, she had ever found plausible.

At night, or when exhausted, Jhane went to her former sleeping place in the cell, in the wooden hostel, and lay down there.

Sometimes she dreamed, on the pallet, that new nuns had filled the stone desert and were at the offices, or hoeing the south garden, while the novices learned from painted books in the House of the Novitiate. It seemed to her this might come to be, and that they would accept her, although she had not been made a Bride, and that it would be very simple to live in this way for a life of years, knowing everything by rote, and beyond the rote, wedded to the certainty of the fact.

Then again, she dreamed that the Nunnery of the Angel had been for centuries a ruin, or that it did not exist, that she had imagined or conjured it. Or that, even though the walls and courts were present, the order had not worshipped Lucefiel, the Christ, but some other.

None of this concerned Jhane. Her dreams were not fears or even questionings. Merely rehearsals of different chance.

She did not attempt – she never had attempted – to count the days. Spring came blustering through the nunnery, and lit the columns and the garden with yellow and white flowers.

As she crossed the south cloister, Jhane saw that the stone child by the fountain had become a dwarf, who got to his feet and bowed and capered, revealing the stone child was there after all, behind him.

'Buy a ribbon,' said the dwarf. 'Or have you cut your hair and shaved your quaint skull?'

'I have not,' said Jhane. 'But neither do you have your tray of ribbons.'

'True. When you saw me last I was a king. When I saw *you* last, you were a boy. What are you, female or male? Or both – some abomination.'

But Jhane moved on towards the church. The dwarf went with her, and entered as she did through the side door into the nave.

It was almost the hour of Tiers, and the sun filled the Great Light.

They regarded it, the nun and the dwarf.

When Jhane sank to her knees, the dwarf was taller than she. He seemed to be considering this. Then he walked forward, between Jhane and the window. And he began to stand up in his skin.

He became Belnard her step-father, he became the apothecary of her journey, and then he became – spreading and billowing – the fat woman with the keys – and then stretching thin and bearded, he was Master Motius, and, getting fleshy and smooth again, the mason, and losing the flesh, Conrad the thief, and folding inwards and out, in a quick succession, pious Osanne, the Mother, the young nun Marie-Lis. And then, he was Jhane herself.

There she stood, clad as she had been in the bounty of the nunnery, in that plain gown, but her hair was loose and savage about her, her eyes gleaming.

'It's very clever,' said the real Jhane, still kneeling. 'How do you do it?'

'Ah,' said the dwarf-Jhane. 'That's telling, that is.'

And then he rose up and opened into fire and wings and was an angel, all golden, who extended his hand to her, while through the translucence of his garments she saw his heart burning like a wounded golden rose.

Jhane sighed.

'Was it always you?'

'Perhaps,' he said, 'or not.' But she barely heard his words through the music of his voice. Leave yourself, said the music. You may come back to her.

And Jhane left herself, kneeling there on the floor of the church. She lifted with the angel into the sky. She was an angel herself. She was not indeed, *herself*. There was no gender, neither female nor male. Jhane was a winged creature of the light. Above her the sun, below, the earth, which was a round orb, shining.

They flew freely, the two angels. They embraced and sang and communed without speech and touched all things and glorified all things, and *were*.

Jhane will die?

Yes, although not yet.

And the world? Will the world end?

One day the world will end.

When will it end? Surely sin will not destroy it?

Sin will not destroy the world. While the world has sin it cannot end. Not until the world is perfect may the world end. The world is for a purpose. But when the world is perfect and whole, and all things therein, and all mankind, perfect and whole, then the world will be permitted its finish. There will be a great shining, as in the window you see it, the coming of a great light, like fire. And in that time, the world will end, and all life find its liberty.

Life is the dream, said the angel who had been Jhane.

So be it, said the Angel Esrafel. But let it be a sweet dream, at least.

Then Jhane opened her eyes in the church, cramped and chilled, alone, and night was falling in the window.

She could not read or write, and so she could not set down her vision of the apocalypse. It is often the way. This she understood, and that it did not matter in any case.

Rising, she went quietly to the refectory, lit a candle, and ate curds and drank water behind her wooden screen.

'It is Lucifer, Lord Satan, who rules the world,' said the priest. 'To survive here, we're bound to worship him.'

He showed them a drawing on parchment, a rose transfixed by a dagger.

'Remember this sign. We meet here, under the old church. You will be obliged to render passwords. In time, who knows what riches and power we shall accumulate, through the favour of our Master. I myself,' he said, 'survived the plague. That was his sign to me. God smote me, but Satan raised me to do *his* work and glorify *him*. You're an artist of the City. Who spoke to you of this secret society?'

'Several,' said the young man. 'But Motius the Artisan was once my tutor.'

'The magician? Yes. His house was burned up and flaming fiends carried him to Hell. You understand, there's no escape at last. It ends in fire.'

'Hah. Yes.' the young man smiled.

'But meanwhile, a life of wishes fulfilled. His servants he never cheats. All the joys of the flesh, full dominion over others. The end is horror, but you may have three hundred years of pleasures before that payment comes due.'

Through the heavy frozen passageways they went, into a chamber drawn with symbols, floor and walls and ceiling, where the worshippers waited in silence.

'Should I take off this?' asked the beautiful young artist, indicating a crucifix at his throat.

'No. Why would he fear it? He ousted *that* one long ago. It may amuse him. Leave it on.'

The ceremony began. It had elements of a mass, of a communion, and of a christening, for the new initiates were to be sworn and bound, and marked in blood. Three black cocks were sacrificed, and the sooty tapers set alight. Eastern incense smoked from the censers.

Pierre Belnard had once attended such rites in Motius' studio, but been bored by them. His adventures since had urged him back. There were fever dreams which haunted him still, and memories of the Death, and some story he had heard of a nun who hacked off her hand to feed a starving man walled up in a plague house.

As the rituals went on, however, he grew drowsy.

They had said to him, the other living students with whom he had been reunited, that Prince Lucifer would manifest tonight, to greet his worshippers. Now everyone shouted and howled, and Pierre joined in the tumult, lay on the floor when they did, but felt a sensation of distance, and a wish to go drinking.

Then a film of shadow began to hover in the radius of the inner circle, something not to do with candlelight or gloom.

Pierre came awake. He looked intently.

The shadow had an odd glow, dark on lesser dark, turning first black, then to a muddy hue and texture. A being was after all about to appear.

What would Pierre see! The Fallen One, the Angel who had defied God, envious of the creation of man, seizing the world away to corrupt and ultimately to destroy it?

Out of the mass of shadow something rose. It was the colour of a dead moon, glaring dully with a light that was lightless.

The worshippers screamed, calling a hundred names of the pantheon of Hell – those of Satan himself, and of his demon captains – there was some discord, it seemed, over who the apparition was taken for.

But Pierre knew what he saw. He saw the Devil.

It was the body of a huge man, a giant, and the face of a bestial thing. Its eyes were pits of nothingness. From its lips snaked a serpent's tongue. Horned and clawed and tailed. Deformed, blasted. Ugly, evil and pitiless, and *glad*.

This was the vision of Pierre. He dropped senseless on the floor.

In the years to come, his images of paint and stone would reveal glimpses of an awful revelation. His Hell would leap with rending flame, his cyphers of the Last Judgement of Mankind, and World's End, would display Satan in all his might, eating souls alive, while the earth burned.

EMPIRES OF AZURE

Le Livre Azur

From the hag and hungry goblin
That into rage would rend ye,
And the spirit that stands by the naked man
In the book of moons defend ye!

Anonymous: 17th century

Empires of Azure

In a week, or less, I shall be dead.

Having written this on his card, he handed it to me.

'Why?' I said.

'I'm under sentence of it,' he said.

'Again, why?'

'Ah. There's the story.'

'I'm expected to listen?'

'Perhaps not. I've left an account, a sort of diary, and various papers. My address, you will see, is on the front of that card, with my name. Are you familiar with the Observatory Quarter?'

'Quite. What I would rather discover is your reason for approaching me in this way.'

'Dear mademoiselle, you are a stranger. So far at least, you've heard me out. Those that know me, mademoiselle, won't credit a word.'

'I seem to know you better with every passing second.'

He smiled, and sat down opposite me.

The name on the card was Louis de Jenier, and the address, as he said, on a street among the steep, stepped terraces and balconied apartments that banked the Observatory. He himself was so handsome that he remains difficult to describe. Elegantly dressed, and with a silk neck-tie, his lavish dark hair was parted on the right side, and his hands manicured. His eyes were of an extraordinary unreal saturated blue, impossible to penetrate, like those of a statue, or, more actually, a doll. Since I had never met him before, I could not tell if he were unusually pale, sickening for illness, or had gone mad. He had come directly to my table through the crowded café, most of which had stared, as they do in the north, especially in Paradis, at his novelty of looks and style. Now he said: 'Mademoiselle, let me add that I know you write for the journals, albeit under a male pseudonym. Yes, I've found you out, and tracked you down for a purpose. I gamble on you. I think you begin to be curious.'

'Not very, monsieur. I assume someone has threatened your life,

179

maybe after a love-affair. Why not go to the City police, if you have no influential friends who could help you.'

'No, no one can help,' he said.

When he spoke, a shadow fell, the way it does when a cloud covers the sun. It was not that he sounded fearful or even dismayed. But it was like that moment which comes, for the first time, to each of us. The moment which says ''One day, incredibly, I too will die.''

And in that instant, as I stretched forward mentally towards him, we were interrupted.

Two men were forcing their way through the café. One called excitedly to him, 'Louis! Louis!' But the other, as they reached us, said, 'For God's sake, what are you playing at now?'

He glanced at them, with the cruel contempt of a beloved and misunderstood – and so deeply angry child.

'Well, you were boring me rather.'

'Excuse us, mademoiselle,' the second man said to me, tipping his expensive hat. The other only tipped his eyelids.

'Don't,' said de Jenier to me. 'Don't excuse them.'

'Louis, shut up. Oh this really is too much.'

'Hunted down,' he said to me. 'Well, good-bye. It was a great pleasure to meet you.'

His eyes held mine, but conveyed nothing, only colour. Then he rose, and turning aside with the two men, went away in their company.

My immediate impulse was to follow up his invitation. Not today, for when I emerged on to the street, already the dusk was coming down, the blue hour, and along the boulevards they were lighting the lamps, while on the summits of the Sacrifice and Clock Hill the neons of the theatres and the nightclubs had begun to blaze. Tomorrow then, at midmorning. Not too early, for I sensed he would rise quite late, not too late, for then, I sensed, he would be gone.

I had an article to finish that evening, and went to my apartment on the Street St Jean.

At midnight, when, work completed, I turned down the gas, I had already started to have doubts on the other matter. De Jenier might so easily be a poseur.

Next day, rather than seek his address in the Observatory, I attempted to discover his nature from colleagues and acquaintances. A few thought they had heard his name. My editor at the office of *The Weathervane* believed that there was an actor named Louis de Jenier, a southerner, however, obscure.

Daunted, by my own initial eagerness more than by anything else,

I did nothing more. The day went, and the night, in uneventful pursuits and ordinary sleep. And after that some further days and further nights.

Of course, he was so beautiful, and he was a man and I a woman – worse, he had unmasked me as a woman, casting away my literary shield. It was all very dangerous. I had come to value the calm sky-pool of my life.

And then it struck me, walking out one morning to the bright sunlight of spring, birds twittering on the roofs, and the women everywhere with their baskets of dew-beaded violets – it struck me that this was the last day of the week he had postulated for his life.

I stood amazed, the violets I had just bought glistening like coloured shards of glass in my hand.

Thissot, who was with me, laughed at my aberration. He pinned the flowers to my lapel. 'What have you forgotten?'

'Somebody's death.'

'Dear God. So serious?'

'Perhaps.'

But I breakfasted with him before I set out. It would not do, I felt, to upbraid the liar on a sinking stomach.

Once, the ascent to the Observatory had been wooded parkland. Duels were fought there under the misty trees, and in a number of ruinous little cemeteries all about, lay the unknown bones of the stabbed and shot. But now the cemeteries were wedged between the high walls of tenements. And where the cannon had pounded at the end of the Years of Liberty, neat flats now stood one upon the head of another, with bell-flowers and papery gentians pouring through the loops and slots of iron balconies. De Jenier's street was tucked down between two others. Three or four largish houses dominated it, his being the third. On arrival, seeing its number, I learned the whole building belonged to, or was rented by him. It was a very new house, I thought, not even ten years old. Nothing had been done to it to give it any character. It looked like those villas at the seaside, occupied for only a couple of months a year, kept up by workmen and gardeners, never properly lived in.

I went up the steps and rang the bell. I expected a servant, but when the door was suddenly opened, I saw the face of one I knew. It was the second, talkative man who had come to arrest de Jenier in the café.

It seemed he also remembered me.

'Ah – mademoiselle. Did you – ? That is, I'm afraid I can't let you come in.'

I was not in the least surprised. I felt only dull horror.

'But you must,' I said.

'No, no. Louis – that is – no. It won't do. If you'll leave your card, mademoiselle, a telephone number if possible, where we may reach you – '

I did not want to say, Where is the corpse? Because that would be incriminating, perhaps. I said, 'He told me to come here. Let me in, or shall I call the police at once?'

The man quailed. Oh indeed, so they had not yet resorted to the means of the law.

'All right,' he snapped. 'In, then.'

He hustled me through the narrow opening which was all he would allow.

The hall was clean and empty of anything except for an equally empty umbrella-stand. Two closed doors, a passage leading away below, and an uncarpeted stair leading up.

We stood in this oasis. I said, 'Upstairs?'

'All right.'

He directed me to go ahead of him. The heels of my shoes clacked on the treads, and a strange light began to come down. I hesitated, to look up, but he fussed behind me. I went on without looking and reached the first landing to be told, 'Go on. Go on, then.'

On the top floor under the attics, a double door stood wide, and out of it came the densely-tinted light that had fallen into the stair-well. The room stood at the back of the house, of medium size, a sitting room perhaps, but it was entirely bare. In the polished wood of the floor, the marble fireplace, and on the plaster walls, reflected four cobalt pillars of light from four west windows blind with cobalt glass.

What a fancy. What an artifice. I thought of opium-smoking and other drugs, where the eyes are affected and require deep shade. The window-glass was like a drug in itself. You stifled, grew drunk, stumbled and lost the awareness of balance. It was like being hung up in a thunderous evening sky. No oxygen available. Blue above, beside, below. Nothing substantial anywhere.

I thought we should have to stop there, maybe until I was overcome and fainted or ran away. But now the second man moved before me, also weaving, holding his hands away from his sides slightly, a wire-walker. He took me through another door into a study.

It had a skylight, it was not drowning in blue. I could breathe again, and looked about. Sofas and chairs crouched under dust-sheets. On a sheetless desk lay dramatic impedimenta – polished pens never used, a tidily stacked column of books, scholarly artifacts, such as a skull of quartz, and a leather diary and pencil. One chair stood away from the desk, also unsheeted. Its back had been broken, and some wood splinters scattered along the Persian rug.

On the wall beyond the desk, over the small fireplace, a convex mirror was flanked by two big photographs, both depicting women. One, to the left, wore period costume, perhaps of the Liberty Days, with a corseted, sashed waist and plumed hat, pearl bracelets, long, dark, curling hair. She was beautiful, and had been labelled in copperplate: *Anette*. To the right of the mirror, the other was a contemporary of my own, her figure freer, her face more obviously powdered and mascaraed; she was clad in a sequined evening gown, furs across her breast, her hair, also dark, pinned up with lilies. Her label read: *Lucine*. It was apparent both were the same person in a different role. Across the convex mirror in between them striped a colossal gash. Since glass can only be scratched by diamond, I supposed a ring had been used, but over and over. In fact, the marks were more like those made by a set of claws.

Of the dead body of de Jenier there was not one trace.

'Wait here,' said the man who had brought me. He turned towards the blue room.

I did not want to wait. I did not like the feel of the room with the desk, and the blue chamber outside had unnerved me.

'Where is he?' I said. I reached out and caught the man by the sleeve.

'Let go. This is disgraceful.'

'Yes it is. What's happened?'

He worked his lips. '*Something's* happened,' he said, idiotically.

'I asked you what it was?'

'You're no one he knows. To invite you here was just his joke, Louis told me. You shouldn't have come.'

'Let me see him then,' I said boldly. 'I'll go at once.'

'You can't see him. He – he's not on the premises – '

'You carry on, monsieur, as if he is dead and you have hidden the body.'

I was being rash, but my nerves now drove me. As for this man, he was more nervous than I was. We both trembled. Finally he said, 'You must *wait*. *Please*. I'll return directly.'

He scurried out. I stood a while and looked at the chair and the claw-marks on the mirror. Nothing else seemed to have been disturbed. I picked about, cautiously lifting a corner of a dustsheet, peering down at the splinters on the rug. I was partly afraid of finding something. But what?

That man was taking a devil of a time.

Suddenly I resorted to the desk, and picked up the leather diary. This was, probably, the written account de Jenier had referred to. It was unlocked. I opened it. The inside cover formed a pocket into which a number of documents and papers had been carefully compressed. The fly-leaf had pencilled untidy writing on it, his own. It said, "For you, Mademoiselle St Jean, to do with as you think fit."

St Jean was the literary pseudonym I used, after the wild poet who is said to have lived on my street and for whom my street is named, and who one day mysteriously disappeared for ever. Either Louis de Jenier did not know my true name, or he had kept this as a sort of password between us.

Whatever, he clearly meant the book for me.

I slipped it, with scarcely a qualm, into my purse, and walked quickly out of the study. It was now evident to me that the man who had let me in, having no answers to my annoying questions, did not intend to return. All the doors of the house, but for these two and that of the front entry, were doubtless locked. There were to be no clues. They only wanted me gone. It might anyway be unwise to remain.

As I started across that room dyed cobalt, something peculiar happened to me. I have said I disliked the room, and the study, though for varying reasons, neither quite deciphered. But in the blue room now a wave of dizziness and emotion came over me. I say emotion, but what was it? It was like a sort of smiling fury, a sort of sensuous silent *howling* – it was bestial and beastly. I began to run towards the doorway, and in that instant the double doors, with no one by them, swung in and closed with a bang. The room seemed to rock. The floor tilted, like the floor of a balloon up in the air, caught by lightning.

I was terrified. The hair bristled on my scalp and I moaned aloud. And something insisted to me that I turn, and look at the four windows, the windows of cobalt glass.

So, in the trap, I did turn, and I ran towards them, not knowing why.

I was about three metres away from the two central windows when abruptly one of these displayed a pattern all over itself, an intricate but abstract pattern drawn fine in black ink. I stared at the pattern, stopped in my running. Then I seemed to understand all the glass in that window had fissured. Next second it fell to bits. It exploded – not inward but outward, with a sound as if a huge tap had been turned on.

The glass of the window flared like a bomb of violets, violet and blue confetti, jettisoned into blue space beyond.

After half a minute, I went forward, and looked out of the vertical where the window had been.

The view was perfectly normal. Some house-backs and dormer lights, trees and walls, on the right hand the descent of the City to the river, gracious in the morning. Below, the glass lay glittering all across a small enclosed garden. Between the window and the sky, suspended in air, a rope that seemed to flicker and smoulder, coming down from above. A man's body hung from it, the dark head lying towards one shoulder.

I started to cry, from shock and grief. The blue room had now no feeling in it. Then something made me lean straight out and crane upwards, and I saw two men, the foremost the one who had let me in, and another, vague at his back, both looking down. We stared at each other, they and I, a few seconds.

Then I turned and ran from the room and down the stairs and out of the house. They did not seem to pursue me.

I got as far as the cafés along the embankment, where I had to go in and ask for cognac.

At first I was simply frightened. Pretending to have the spring influenza, I concealed myself in my flat, putting on a hoarse doubtful voice when Thissot called me by means of the telephone in my landlady's parlour.

Gradually I concluded the men at Louis' house could not have known who I was, or my whereabouts. They would not be able to run me to earth. I wondered if they were themselves the agents of his death, but did not really think so. I was haunted by a dull distress and sense of loss. My sleep was peaceful and free of the nightmares that filled my conscious hours. I had locked the diary and documents into a drawer of my bureau.

At last, one afternoon, the city veiled in rain, I lit the gas-lamps and the fire, then went firmly and unlocked the drawer, and extracted the diary.

Even so, I hesitated. I decided I would look at the papers to begin with. They were many. I took them forth and laid them out. Some I saw at a glance had to do with the rental of the house. Others I could make nothing of (or would not), but they were randomly numbered, and since the pages of the diary were also numbered, presumably they were notes or additions to these. Then again there were scribblings in another hand I could not read, except, here and there, for a large black letter T. One sheet in Louis' writing bore what seemed to be a line of poetry, which said only: *Kingdoms of the sky-blue universe.*

In fact, I was daunted, was afraid to delve. My visit to the house, (blue room, breaking window, hanged man), that had been enough.

Then a small notice fell from among the rest. It had a business heading, the name of a shop in one of the by-ways of Sacrifice Hill. I skimmed that, for beneath was a typed message. It seemed the firm were pleased to inform Monsieur de Jenier that a picture was ready for his collection.

I looked at my clock. It was not yet five. If I went out I should be in plenty of time to reach the place before it shut.

Something had galvanised me. Perhaps only the excuse that by doing this, I was investigating the diary – while completely avoiding it.

On the streets the rain attacked a hurrying umbrella world of wet black tortoise-backs. I hailed a taxi-cab, which shortly deposited me high on the south bank, under the shadow of the Temple-Church. The shop lay in a narrow sloping passage leading up towards the Church, roofed by dirty glass on which the rain beat, and with a carpet of peels and papers. The shop itself was a photographic salon. I had not read the bill properly, and had been anticipating art. Art there possibly was, in the dusk portraiture of young women lurking under a shrubbery of ferns within the windows.

The bell jangled as I entered, and from behind a curtain a man glided out to look askance at me. I was not the usual clientele, plainly.

I handed him the chit at once. He gazed on it, on me, and said, reproachfully, 'This has been ready for some while, m'mselle.' I stared him out, but he next said, 'I understood a gentleman was to collect the portrait.'

'Monsieur de Jenier has entrusted that task to me.'

'The work has been paid for,' said the accusatory man. 'The money was sent round.'

Prepared to pay, this alerted me: Louis had bought the photograph but not taken possession of it. What could it be, this mystery? I recalled the phantom women on his study wall, Anette, Lucine.

'Just one moment,' said the man.

He slid behind his curtain, and I heard a faint rumble of conversation, the words: 'Most odd. Something funny here.' And I was, in a manner of speaking, hand on sword-hilt preparing for battle, when back he came beaming, carrying in his arms an oblong item, already scrupulously wrapped. It was quite large, the "portrait".

A chill went over me. The garish electric light, with which the shop was gifted, seemed to darken.

'Will it not,' he probed hopefully, 'be awkward for you to carry, m'mselle?'

A premonition of police – death's revelation – 'I live close,' I lied, and named an area to fool them all.

Then I took the wrapped thing from him. My second of prescience was done and the package felt perfectly mundane, weight, paper, string.

By the time he had cancelled his chit, and bowed to me, and opened the door and let me out in the covered alley, the cab-driver was from his cab, leaning in an arch at the entrance, smoking.

He aided me and my parcel back inside the vehicle.

'That's got a bad name, that has,' he said, 'that place.'

I wondered if he meant the shop only, or the alley entire. But I hardly wanted conversation and did not reply.

Returned home, I went directly upstairs. Again I lit the gas, and the oil-lamp on my desk, and stoked the fire. I propped the covered picture against an armchair.

Then, exactly as I had with his diary, I sat down and looked and looked at the hidden form, with terrific, immobile reluctance.

The clock chimed gently. It was midnight, I had fallen asleep. On my hearth the fire had perished, and the gas was bluely waning.

I got up in a dull trance, and tearing the wrapping off the photograph, revealed it.

She was not Anette, nor Lucine.

Her hair was modishly bleached, platinum blonde, but unfashionably cut in a kind of long, shining hood, that reached her shoulders, but framed forehead and cheeks with a high invert crescent of fringe. Her eyes had been inked in by kohl; that, and the gauffered sleeves of her dress, indicated it was all Garb-Egyptian, which had been something of a rage in Paradis, seven or eight years before. She wore a costume-jewellery collar, too, gilded and set with opaque gems. Strangely, only one earring, pendant from the right ear, a disc, with an odd design on it, perhaps a flower, having eight thin rays . . .

No, she was not Anette, or Lucine. She did not smile or provoke, as they had done, there on Louis de Jenier's study wall. This creature looked filled by *darkness*. Her eyes, though they could have been any

187

rich colour, were miles deep. Through the obligatory minute, as the photograph was taken, she had sat so still her soul might have gone from her body. Look into the eyes, and fall down the miles to nothing. To nothing but – nothing.

But she too had a label, a name. There on the photograph's edge. *Timonie*.

She was portrayed, however, by the same being as had modelled the others. The bone-structure of the face, the set of the eyes and heavy brows; even the figure as far as one saw it, the small shallow breasts and flaunting shoulders – this one too belonged to the group. The three were one. Yet . . . Timonie – was so different.

The silver earring in the right ear had caught a weird high-light. Stared at, the dark flower seemed to wriggle on it, wanting to detach itself. A trick of tired vision. I recalled the large letter T on certain of the papers in the diary. The line of the poem, if it was, returned. *Kingdoms . . . sky-blue universe*. It struck an uncomfortable chord, but nothing more.

'You're full of secrets, Timonie,' I said aloud, but softly. 'I won't like them, I think. I don't care for any of it, this game of yours.'

And I turned her face to the wall before I made ready for bed. I would have to call Thissot, and it would have to wait now until tomorrow.

I did not sleep that night.

'It's curious, I mean that you were asking about him, and then this. I take it you haven't seen any of the journals yet?'

'No,' I said to Thissot, cautiously, as my landlady buzzed about her morning parlour, tweaking at furnishings, ears pricked and elongating visibly to a rabbit's.

'He seems to have fallen down the staircase, and broken his neck. Not found for some days, I gather. This man, his agent, Rudolf Vlok – he discovered the body and ran out in hysterics on the street. Apparently it's not the first death in that house. Some mayfly of a girl was murdered there seven years ago.'

'But the papers quote a profession?' I asked Thissot.

'Our own *Weathervane* does so. An entertainer, your de Jenier, sometime actor, acrobat, mime, mimic. Latterly much in demand in select nightclubs of the south. His speciality had come to be the impersonation of female beauties – ' Thissot's voice assumed a self-protective archness and aversion. 'He dressed as *women*. Starry actresses, singers, and so on. Later quaint ladies of his own quaint invention. *Very* successful. To my way of thinking, that's just – '

I heard what Thissot thought he thought, thanked him, and almost ended the conversation, when I decided to say, 'One other thing – a quotation I came across that's been bothering me. I'm sure I know the source, but can't pin it down.'

'What's that?'

'Kingdoms of the sky-blue universe.'

'Ah – ' he began. Then, 'No, I'm not sure at all. I thought I knew it too, but differently, somehow. Now why am I thinking of alchemy? No, I'm quite eluded, I'm afraid.'

Having placed my telephone coins in the landlady's box, I hurriedly got my coat and hat and rushed out to purchase an armful of journals for myself.

Returned, I spread them everywhere and raked them through. Most carried a mention, and some made much of the sinister aspect, that this was the second violent death in a building barely a decade in age.

Depending on the type of paper, so its bias went. But very swiftly, nevertheless, the facts sprang out.

Here was a smudgy photo-image of Rudolf Vlok, and so I could identify him as the second man in the café, my subsequent guide and deserter at the house. He had been implicit, then, in the fakery of accidental death, along with another, still nameless, and unpictured. And now I could read for myself brief details of a career, and the retreat to this City, of one, Louis de Jenier, the colour of whose eyes they did not even mention. There he was, in that almost new house under the Observatory, among the litter of duellists' cemeteries. And next, I was reading of a wealthy young woman who, years earlier, had conducted orgies of grape and poppy and hemp in that house, until one sunrise found there in a bizarre upper room made blue-windowed for her pleasure. The body was "mutilated". It took another journal, (although I rightly guessed which one it would be), to inform me in what manner. The murderer had cut away ears, eyes, breasts, her hands and her feet, even her teeth and tongue, and capriciously distributed them about house and garden. That time, apart from the blood, the house showed no other signs of savagery, and not a bank-note or a curio had been stolen. While of all her quantity of jewels just one small piece was missed, an antique spider of sapphire, possible to sell anonymously only if broken up into its one large and thirty tiny corundas. There were no other leads, the murderer was never apprehended, and for some months fears of a European "ripper" ran wild. Such a crime was not repeated, however. The fears died. The journal which itemised so much, gave the dead girl her name, but also a second name by which she had come to be known. That was, of course, Timonie. She was what they call a platinum blonde, with very blue eyes. There was no photograph. By then, I had begun to feel I did not need to see one. (But maybe what I know has bled back across my knowledge of that day, time at its eternal trickery.)

In the City, the bells began to ring for noon, the other side of midnight.

There was nothing left now but to put the journals away and take up the diary.

I did so.

I read straight through, referring, where the text so indicated, to the documents that had been in the cover. He had commenced only when events thickened about him. But he was, obviously, used to and adept at writing things down. His script was for the most part legible, and where sometimes it failed to be, the empathic wave of horror which now gripped me, bore me on to perfect understanding.

Outside, brilliant sunlight set Paradis in crystal. But in my rooms, darkness came and blossomed.

To copy out the whole diary would not be wise for me, I believe. Third person then, at a remove, I must present its happenings, propped by all other evidence and occurrence as I knew it, or have come to know it, since. I invent nothing, for even the dialogue is as Louis noted it. No. I invent nothing.

He had escaped Vlok – "the jailor" as he tended to call him – on a train. It had been travelling north to the border, and stopped at a crossing, as a caravan of goats was driven over, to take on mail. De Jenier had happened to be in the corridor, smoking, while Vlok and his assistant sprawled asleep in their compartment. They were en route to another city, another round of private parties and public performances, and on impulse, Louis had suddenly opened the nearest door and jumped down into the plucked fields and vineyards, leaving his luggage and his jailors together for the steam-bannered train to bear away into the evening.

He was about nine and a half miles outside the suburbs of Paradis, through which the train had already passed. He started to walk back to them, got a lift in sombody's young, snorting car, and arrived before the dinner-hour.

It was not the first time Louis had behaved in this way. Life was not serious. The antics of a Vlok, always concerned with profit and decorum, amused and irritated him. Louis rarely obeyed any rules, and routines exasperated him.

Having plenty of money, he checked into a good hotel, then got to work on finding a house to live in. He had not lived in a house for years, not since, that was, his earliest childhood. Both his parents had been beauties, but paid for it. When Louis was five, the handsome actor father had been shot in the back by a jealous rival; the lovely actress mother promptly swallowed rat-poison. The only child of only children, now an orphan of orphans, he was kinless, and placed in an institution. Here he existed in bleak misery and mercurial grace for a further seven years, before a male patron ran off with him, used him, gave up on his uninterest, and left him on the bosom of a world that would be prepared always to rhapsodise and fall abjectly in love with him, but would never attempt to clarify his needs.

If Louis ever properly believed in the reality of others is doubtful. It was not that he was callous, rather he did try to be kind. But so seldom did anyone act in a reasonable fashion when he confronted them. He brought out the simpering fool, the liar, the viper, the cheat. It was the curse of his attractions.

The house had been standing empty a number of years. Though its history had been damped down, it kept an amorphous but nasty reputation. It was boarded up, the attic filled by dead birds.

Open, scoured, and slapped in the face with paint, it was soon ready for its tenant – gaped for him. About its rumours he did not give a damn. He had, in repose, a cheerful disposition, thoughtless and clear.

He furnished the house frugally and carelessly. He had not wanted a home. Meanwhile, Vlok would be naturally in pursuit, and those who noticed Louis' appearance accosted him wherever he went. The hollows of the house were privacy. They gave him what others seek in deserts and on mountain-tops.

He must, too, have made in it journeys and explorations. In the second week of occupancy, he found the silver and sapphire earring.

Of all the rooms he had furnished the room which pretended to be a study the most thoroughly. It may have evoked some memory, even that of a favourite stage-set, the desk with its romantic symbols – books, pens, skull. He had hunted for a realistic astrolabe, not found one that passed the test, for bones and shells, hour-glass, compasses, scales, a pestle and mortar. He did not utilise the desk in the beginning, but he looked at it from the sofas, walked round and round it, rearranging objects. (Contrastingly the bedroom across the way had a bed, with a decanter of mineral water standing on the floor beside it, and a clothes closet.) For the blue-windowed room he had some plans involving musical instruments, a slender violin he had seen, a cittern.

The blue windows were fixed and could not be opened. Through them, the City became an abstract.

He wondered if he might have time, before Vlok caught up with him, to experiment with other shades of blue glass, or with patterns of white glass.

Across from one of the windows, gleaming on the wooden floor in its reflection, lay a disc of ornamented silver.

Louis knelt down. He examined the disc. He thought it had not been there before. It looked as if it had come from the attic, for the dead birds who had nested there had also been something of collectors. The workmen must have missed the silver thing, somehow it had fallen through into the room below. It was an earring, or had been made into one, with a ring and silver hook to pierce the lobe.

Not until he took it through into the study, into ordinary light, did he see the spider, which was sunk into the disc, was composed of one large, and thirty tiny, sapphires.

The piece was fine, not necessarily beautiful. The metal of ring and hook did not match the metal of the disc, which had also been beaten in an odd way, much older. There were two small holes on either side the upper curve of the disc. A wire or ribbon would have passed through them. The earring had been hung on the ear, not from it, once, long ago.

Louis was quite pleased with the find. He left it on the desk beside the scales and skull. He felt no urge to have the jewellery valued or dated. He forgot about it.

During the night, Louis de Jenier woke. Something had woken him: a heavy sound of movement, and repeated soft high little cries, close by in the house.

His first thought was that someone, perhaps even Vlok, had broken in. But the noises were not like those of burglars or even agents.

Louis left the bed, and went out of the bedroom into the passage. The sounds came from the room with the coloured windows. Its doors were shut, although he had left them open. Everything was dark. Louis crossed the angle of the passage, the stairs yawning black to his left, below. It felt very cold there, as if winter waited in the stair-well. He put his hands on both door-knobs and turned them, but the doors to the room would not oblige him.

Inside, the noises went on. Something heavy was being dragged about, something throbbed, like a gramophone which had run down. Then the girl's voice, which had paused, began again to moan and whine, to hiss and cry out.

Then – silence. In the silence, a cold glow seeped out between and under the doors. It was blue, like daylight through the glass.

Louis had a premonition the doors were after all about to open, and stepped back. He had been correct, they did so and forcefully, banging against the wall to either side. A gale went by him. This was not cold, but burning hot.

The scene in the room was done in blues and whites and greys, lit, not by the windows, not by anything visible. There was a sofa, a sort of chaise-longue, not a possession of Louis' own, and on it lay a young woman. She wore only a silk robe, and that barely. From her position and her expression, you saw at once what she had been doing to elicit her outcry – not of pain, presumably, but pleasure. Her face, which was very beautiful, was also slack, and still wanton, the white-blonde hair falling all over it.

She stared directly at Louis, and though she was a psychic recording, what is termed a ghost, she seemed to see him.

And, 'I know you're there,' she said. 'I know you are.'

Louis, cynical enough to accept most things, was not alarmed, merely unnerved. But besides that, the physical aspect of the manifestation, those extremes of heat and cold that were now coming in waves out of the room, were making him ill. Nevertheless he did not retreat, thought he though it useless to go forward, let alone answer.

'I made you come here,' she said. 'I can do that, can't I? Did you like it, seeing me doing that? Better than with any of them, those toads. They can't give me that, not one of them.' Then she moved her body, slim, firm and young, stroking it, its skin and hair. She said, 'Why don't you come close to me? I know you can. I've *got* you.' She shook her head, and through the pale strands, one silver earring flashed.

Then the other noises started up again all round her, the heavy dragging, the dull throb. The girl seemed to hear them for the first. She looked about, and as she did so, a last wave, of utter black, came boiling through the room. It poured over the girl and the light and they went out. The wave poured on, over Louis. It was almost palpable. It was an emotion, incredibly strong. Yet indecipherable. It seemed to go through him as well as over him, and then there was only night in the empty house. He was dizzy and leaned on the wall a moment before going back to bed. There he lay down and heard a distant car-horn in the streets, the bell from the Sacrifice, and later birds singing.

Drained, he slept. When he woke it was midday, the sun standing on the roof.

When he went back to the blue room, it was undisturbed, except that the sapphire spider-earring was lying, not where he had left it, but out again on the floor.

That afternoon Vlok, and his dark, pretty assistant, Curt, arrived at the house.

There was a furious drama, during which Louis remained quiet.

On this occasion, the tracking process had not been easy for the jailor. The jailor was in a rage, which increased on meeting no opposition.

Finally rage resolved into resolve. They would take him, the captive, to their grand hotel. Then, tomorrow, on. Some of the cancelled northern dates might yet be salvaged.

'No,' the captive then said. 'You don't understand. I intend to stay. I meet a girl here.'

Volk volleyed out a string of profanities.

Physically-sexually, de Jenier was dormant, or non-existent. His sexual engagements had been with men, overtures received and complied with indifferently. Emotionally-sexually he responded to women, but as he had no wish to form a union, let alone consummate it, he had learned early on to limit his company, words, glances and caresses. At last, prompted by a promoter more seedy though no less ambitious than Vlok, Louis had discovered how to create all he wanted from himself. His minutes and hours as a woman, women, lightly padded to their shape, wigged and dressed and painted and gemmed for them, afforded him a transcendent excitement, not merely sensual, or if it was, then also a sensuality of the mind. He swam strongly in the sweetness of it. But it did not disturb him. That vital element, a sort of guilt or shame, had passed him by. The dictate of the light says: Know yourself and what you are. The dark replies, By all means, but then become afraid. By-standers, particularly those able to cash in on aberration, tend to encourage and expect the latter state.

'Girl? When did you want girls? My dear Louis. I'll forgive you your antics on the train, my money wasted and my time. Tomorrow, we shall go north together. My God, if you want to, bring the fancy bit with you. A boy, yes? Dressed up as you do it? I thought your taste was otherwise.'

All these entirely inappropriate comments on Louis' sexual life, which he heard without a flicker, were prompted by ignorance, awareness that the guilt-shame should be present, and an undercurrent of resentment that it was not.

'How you bother me, Rudolf,' said Louis. 'I can't invite her with me. She's indigenous, I imagine. A ghost.'

Vlok shrugged. Louis often cried wolf, or inventively lied from boredom.

'I'll send for the luggage from the hotel. If you won't move, we'll stay here with you.'

'Oh please, don't.'

'Introduce me to the ghost.'

'Where shall I sign, Rudolf, and what?'

'What are you talking about?'

'To terminate our agreement.'

An hour later, at the foot of the staircase, Vlok shouted: 'You need me, and you know it quite well. Squander another week, then. But you'll be watched. If you take flight again, my bird, I'll be after you. Depend on it.' The front door slammed.

In another hour, Curt, having received a secret signal, returned to the house. Louis entertained him with white wine in a downstairs room bare of anything but for bottles, a bowl of peeled almonds, and a pot of forced white camelias.

Curt was the slave of both, Vlok's in the matter of finances, and Louis' in the sense of feelings. He betrayed one to the other as need demanded. Now he accepted Louis' errand. It seemed no threat to business enterprise. Curt had also brought, in a small case, the framed photographs of Louis' two most admired animas: Anette, Lucine. Louis permitted Curt to put them up in the "study", either side of the mirror. Across the blue room Curt passed with scarcely a look. He had torn off a camelia for his buttonhole.

'Perhaps you'll let me sleep on a sofa one night. I've never seen a ghost. I'd die of terror.'

'I couldn't allow you to die. No. I won't let you stay here.'

When Louis returned alone from dining, about eleven-thirty, he felt at once, on opening the door, that the house was waiting for him. During the day it seemed to sleep, the way a night-animal must, for it had grown busy after dark.

The moment he closed the door, was shut in with it, its life began, as if, now, mechanical.

He heard from above a violin, that was the first sound.

Not a melody, but three or four quivering wails, then a spasm of tuneless plucked pizzicato. He had not yet bought the violin. He anticipated the unbought cittern next, but instead there came again that deep throbbing, the turntable of the imaginary gramophone let run down. Light started to billow slowly down the stairs, in a plume, like phosphorescent smoke. Nothing was adrift in the light-plume. There was time, if he wanted, to open the front door and get out.

Louis walked into the light, which had now spread all through the channel of the stair, and climbed upwards. He became aware of a faint smell, rather cloying, like a kind of joss-stick.

Nothing else happened, just the light and the throbbing noise, until he got up to the landing of the blue room. The doors were open, and the familiar wave of cold drove out and drank up all his body-warmth. The dead needed that, a live temperature drunk in, to make their show. But before, there had also been heat. And what was that for?

Then the girl was there, in the room.

Her hair was cut in a new way, and the earring glimmered from her right ear. She wore a long skirt of some pleated translucent stuff, held up by a type of silver braces. Her small breasts were bare and her long slender arms and ankles. It was that style known as Garb-Egyptian, taken to extremes, but she looked less oriental and classical than like some artist's model, a bijou waif . . . All but her eyes, of soaking, starving indigo. She stared right at him. It was a terrible stare.

'Are you there?' she said. 'Is anyone out there?' A reverse of what the still-mortal thing is supposed to say when questioning a presence.

Then the wave of heat came. It almost knocked the breath from his body. When it passed, or when he had accommodated it, he began to go forward, slowly, looking at her, wondering all the while, though he knew she could not, if she really did see him, and if it would be possible to touch her.

He had drunk, for him, a lot of wine at dinner, preparing for this. It was what Vlok would call a "loosener".

'Who,' he said to her, 'are you? *Were* you? – Is that more politic? Won't you tell me your name?'

But she was only a recording, a photograph on the room. Time had not somehow slipped. No, he could see it in her starving eyes. She and he were of a height, so the eyes fixed directly into his. They fixed in and on him, and *through* him, still looking for something. He had got very close to her now, wondering what he would feel. There was a slight disturbance in the air about her, even inside the spectral light. And a sort of clammy quality, the aura of fever.

'Why won't you?' she said. 'You tease. You know you meant me
to have the earring.' And coaxingly, 'Are we the same?'

Are we the same? How odd. There *was* a resemblance. Not only the
eyes . . . He put out one hand, letting it alight on her breast,
something he would never dare do with a woman of flesh and blood,
who would then expect more. This one did not seem to register the
caress, and he saw, as in all the supernatural clichés, that his hand,
insisting, presently passed right through her.

For some reason it was that which turned his stomach.

He drew back.

'*Who* are you?' he said.

'Are you *there*?' she said.

And abruptly they both burst out laughing bitterly.

It was nothing shared, only a coincidence, caused by a fluke of
their characters, a similarity of reactions.

'Go away then,' he said.

He did not think such an exorcism could work and was dismayed
when suddenly she disappeared from in front of him.

The light went out also, and the throbbing ceased, came back –
and was only the jumble of his own pulses in his ears.

The violin had been the strangest part. But that did not mean she
had read his mind. He did not know what it meant.

Near morning he wakened, and thought he heard her again, walking about nearby, on bare feet. He thought too he would have to be
careful. There might sometime be a genuine break-in, and he, complacent, would assume it was only his pet ghost-girl. Then he
wondered if, recorded thoughtless phantom or not, she would pursue
him to the bedroom. He experienced then a sort of sexual stirring to
which he was quite unaccustomed. He lay on his belly, floating in the
sensation that was between dreamy anomia and dreamier lust, half
awaiting her fingers on his neck, his spine – passing through *him*,
and how would that feel?

Then he slept until Curt woke him about ten, rapping insistently
on the front door below.

It was a blowing day, a febrile wind tore about the street, coated with
rent blossoms. Wilted, one more broken stem, Curt was propped in
the doorway.

He had brought, as required, scattered and scribbled through a
notebook, 'as much' as he could 'reasonably get' on the previous
tenant of the house. Curt had a knack of worming out information,
of finding what was in hiding.

Curt followed Louis back upstairs.

'Did you see it again?'

'What, Curt?'

'*Her*.'

Louis would not reply, and finally Curt grew tired of watching him returned to and lying in bed, drinking mineral water and reading yesterday's papers. There seemed no chance of communication or breakfast. Even the notebook lay unviewed.

'Were you just telling lies again?' said Curt. 'Rudolf says he's through with you. Every hour brings another tantrum. We're to go south, without you. He has plans to sue.'

'He's actually planning to come over here again. Keep him away, Curt, please. And I'll buy you a present. What about that jacket you said you saw? Yes, *that* jacket. Now go to your hotel and pour laudanum and aspirin into Rudolf's coffee.'

'Well, you'd better buy me the jacket.' Curt smoothed his collar, thinking of collars to come. 'You haven't bothered to read my notes, there. You should be contrite. It's a gruesome tale. I need soothing.'

When Curt was gone, Louis opened the notebook. He kept these notes, in appalling shorthand, making a precis in the diary later.

Female, blonde, rich, she had been noted also for her unusually blue eyes. She had no family, and appeared in the City in the way of such beings, as if from thin air.

For a while she moved from apartment to hotel to apartment, incurring the wrath of each establishment by late and licentious celebrations, drunk guests, lovers of all sexes, drugs and loud music. She was also subject to crazes. A craze to paint the walls and ceiling of one apartment black, a craze of enormous plants. Later came a bicycling craze, during which she might be seen flying up and down the steeps of Paradis, generally attended by bicycling young men. On one occasion, one of these attendants escalated down Clock Hill into a hospital bed. Later yet, there was a monkey craze. That ended in a rescue by a zoological organisation. For, like the paint, plants, bicycles, young men, once a craze ebbed, its constituents were neglected.

At length, she had taken the house in the Observatory Quarter, and put in the cobalt stained glass. She was now in another epoch, where she had begun to call herself *Timonie*.

This ultimate craze, (it was to be her last), seemed to commence with her purchase of an antique earring. A City museum had been forced to offer for auction certain treasures. In with a stash of

Roman marbles and lamp-stands dug from the river mud came one jewel. The catalogue presumed it had been the property of the Egyptian mistress of a Roman commander then in charge of the river fort. She was remarkable for being of the Greek Alexandrian strain, blonde and blue-eyed, but skilled in the old temple arts.

The modern girl in her sleek day-gown, lace gloves, high-heels and flowered hat, bid for and claimed the antique earring of the sorceress-mistress, whose name the catalogue gave as Tiyamonet.

Garb-Egyptian was then coming into vogue, and Timonie entered the vogue by throwing "Egyptian" orgies at her new house. They drank thick beer, and burned fake *kuphi*, the temple incense of the Pharaohs. Timonie often appeared at these gatherings in dresses of transparent gauffered linen that sometimes left bare the breasts.

Then the orgies ended. The doors were closed. After some while, two cleaning women, unable to gain customary entry, called the police.

No one was amazed at Timonie's death, even at the manner of it, (listed by Curt). As moths to candle-flames, so a Timonie to a ritual butchering.

'I performed a test then.' (Louis, writing in the diary.) 'I went into the room, where the earring was still lying under the window. It was easy enough to take it to the small garden at the back of the house. Here I buried it about a quarter of a metre down in the soil, and marked the place with a lump of stone. During that afternoon I wrote this, and I paste it in here:

Timonie. Self-obsessed. But unable to clarify, externalise, and so centre, as someone taught me to do. 'Lovers of all sexes,' says Curt. He even alludes here to the monkeys – and, wilder, the bicycles. Unlikely, not human. As I saw her it was love before a mirror or an invisible audience. Passion so strong it forms the print of an astral photograph on that room. Who is she inviting? She said – Tease. You meant me to have the earring. Are we the same? It must be the other, then, Tiy-Amonet. Waiting and coaxing an Egyptian sorceress. And so the earring becomes all-important and acts like the photographer's silver fixative. Now I've put the fix into the earth. What will happen tonight?

'And that night nothing happened, except a foolish telegram came from Rudolf. And in the restaurant I was taken up by yet another stranger, my bill paid, and I barely got away with a whole skin.

'But in the house complete silence and absence. Unable to sleep. I lay awake all night.

'Then the plan came, to steal her from herself. Timonie. A rape, the usual way. How to dress her, more decorously as I should have to, for the obvious reasons. And how the hair should be done. Planning it, I could see more and more a likeness between us, or how one could be created. I liked the sexlessness of her disembodiment. All look, no substance. I would have to catch that too.'

Coming back from expeditions along Sacrifice Hill, in a booming dusk scraped by the flails of winds, Louis encountered Curt, bent and bowed at the corner of the street.

'Curt. Good news of your coat. Go for a fitting tomorrow.'

But Curt curiously was not cheered.

'Horrible dreams, Louis. That girl. That house must be full of it. Don't stay there.'

'She won't harm me. If it even happens.'

'Perhaps it happens in your head.'

Louis smiled, for he had considered that too, and did not find it threatening.

'Where have you been?' said Curt in a whine.

'You can tell Rudolf,' said Louis, 'that I'm creating a new character, very exotic. That's why I need the privacy.'

'Her.'

'The same.'

'Don't,' said Curt.

'Hush, Curt. You'll adore her. You'll rush me to a photographers', again, to have her immortalised.'

'I kept dreaming,' said Curt, 'pale blue flesh – the way she was – after – '

'She wouldn't like you to conjure her up that way. She seems to want to be seen all in one elegant piece. I don't think she remembers the murder. No, she's stopped her life before that point.'

Curt abruptly extended a page of print. He had torn it from a book in the library of a museum. He explained this with a foolish pride, and how he had felt it needful to undertake this unasked extra of research.

'It tells you about the other one, the Egyptian.'

'That was Timonie's interest. Not mine. My interest is only Timonie.'

Curt stood in the stream of the wind, his eyes watering and teeth clenched. He said, 'I don't like spiders. The jewel in the earring is a spider, and there's a thing about it there. When I was a kid, they used to drop on my face where I slept. I used to wake up screaming and my father beat me with his belt. If you pull off their legs, they grow another one. Eight legs. It's happening in your head, and it

happened in her head. But it can get out of your head, it can get out.'
Curt whimpered. Then he straightened up and turned his back to the
wind. 'Don't tell Vlok what I said.'

But Louis was not affected by any of this, Curt was subject to odd
turns from time to time, and to a superstitious dread of his own
beginnings. Louis did not comment, but he invited Curt kindly to
dine with him, and was delighted when Curt refused.

Tucking the torn page inside the coat, Louis forgot it a while, as
he had previously forgotten the earring.

For some nights, then, nothing took place. No manifestations of any
sort, no manifested glimpses of the girl. It was a playful season with
him, and he began to miss her, and he vowed to dig the earring up
from its grave in the garden. He would soon want it himself in any
case, for her costume. (He had sent Vlok a letter, mentioning this
treat, and so partly appeased him.)

It was at this time that Louis began to keep the diary, putting in
earlier events as a detailed preface. Nothing was now occurring,
everything was dull and normal, and yet he mentions at once an atmosphere in the house, as if the building were a kettle on a low flame.

That week he bought the violin, and placed it in the blue room,
ready to be fiddled at ghostly whim. He began to have the idea, when
next she manifested, of appearing before her as herself, the earring
hung from his ear by silver wire, in the correct way. He would be
mirror to her mirror, if a mirror they were to each other.

'A couple of interesting dreams. I don't often dream, or if I do,
remember. But, saw Timonie on her bicycle, her hair tied up in a
scarf and great rolls and fetters of beads round her neck, looking like
a fourteen-year-old from a convent in her divided skirt and black
stockings. She whirled down Clock Hill, two or three young men in
her wake. It was a dare, all of them hooting with mirth, and carts
of fruit and flowers getting in the way, some swerves and abuse, and
then a clear stretch past the florists and fashionable dress-shops on
the west of the Hill, with just a disapproving face or two at windows.
Last of all rattled along a fourth fellow. I saw at once he was
dismayed, and as he came hurtling off the top of the Hill on his
bicycle, he began to beat at the air, first with one hand, then with
both. He beat, and smacked, and tried to push away something from
behind him. There was nothing there. By now his face was white,
frightened, and – something more. From how his hands went now,
it was becoming obvious the invisible sprite riding pillion was intent
on a seduction. All at once the eyes of the rider blurred. He leaned

201

back, lying on the air, giving in to an irresistible ecstasy or hypnotism. The bicycle, left with no guide but the impetus of the Hill, went careering on and crashed into a pile of wooden crates and a lamp-post.

'The second dream, which came after this one, woke me. It had a quality of the *Arabian Nights*. If I were at all a serious writer, I'd be tempted. There was a vaulted sort of cavern, or hall, classical but obscure to me. The man – he might have been a merchant, some traveller – was well-dressed, in a long robe, but I can particularise nothing of his clothing. He walked up the cavern-hall with an air of unease and determination, for some – what do they call them – some jinn had promised to show him the face of the Devil.

'At the end of the cavern was a kind of curtain. It fell and rippled like water, or perhaps steam. The traveller stood before the curtain, and after a moment or so, it swirled and opened, and in the opening showed a stern pale face in middle life, bearded, with shrewd dark eyes. The traveller started back. He made some sign over himself, and then began to shout. He had some cause, for the face he had been shown in the mist was his own. His language baffled me, yet I know what he said. Then the jinn came. I didn't see it, but the traveller did. He spoke more guardedly, but no less angrily. One of those ethical legendary bargains had been dishonoured, he wanted recompense. And then the jinn – I heard its voice, rough and oddly pitched, like a boy's voice when it's on the point of breaking, the jinn said something to the man, which I understood to mean, Look again, and I will show you instead the face of God.

'At this, a proper altercation. Of course, to see the Devil was one thing, but surely God was not accessible, at the beck and call of lesser spirits. But the jinn persuaded the traveller. So the man looked again at the mist or steam, and it parted. I knew what was coming, and so maybe did he, for now he made no comment. It was the same face, shrewd and bearded, just out of its prime. God's face was the traveller's face, as the Devil's had been.

'I woke up in silence, madly overawed by the depths of my own theosophical sense. I never thought I had that side to me.'

After this entry there is a gap of several lines. At the bottom of the page he wrote:

'In a kind of calm hysteria. Something is going on. I can't hear or see or smell it, it leaves me alone. Forces gathering? What forces could there be. Perhaps poor T is angry, I've stopped her expression by burying the focus. It seems I'm reluctant to go out and take away the stone in proper Christian manner, and dig up the prize. Yes, I am reluctant. I've so seldom been any more than nervous of anything. I don't know. Am I afraid? Is this fear?'

Turning the page, you saw he had written:

'I tried to find the place. Something, perhaps a neighbourhood cat, has moved the stone. I dug about where I thought it must be, found nothing. I'm distrait. I feel as if a cane has come down sharply on my fingers. Bad Louis. Bad negligent child.'

In a dream, the mise-en-scène may simply exist. And so, a hot black night, starred with diamond brooches, moonless. A broad black river, without a bridge, the starlight plinking on it, and frogs faintly chorusing in the reeds. It might have been almost anywhere in a warm climate. On the dim banks shapeless shapes that gave no clue – mounds, huts – beyond, the rising of hills. And here and there, eastwards, a cresset on a wall-tower . . . The fort too lay east, behind now, with the beacon burning in the great iron brazier on the roof-walk. Dis' light.

It was not that he walked inside the skin of the one who walked before. But he walked so close, he was her shadow, and invisible. The intimacy of it seemed normal in the dream. He knew himself separate, a witness. He knew himself involved, and not impartial.

There were trees now, heavy castaneas, a wood beside the water, and there an altar of stone against the post of the ferry . . . He saw these things as she glanced at them, knew them by some trace that came from her. They did not interest her, these known things.

She was alone, not one of her slaves with her, and now there were men standing up in the black of the trees. But they were obeising themselves. They were pulling something forward, showing her – the black and pale flickering among the foliage of the chestnut grove was confusing. Then he saw the face, the lolling tongue and half-moon eyes. It was a corpse they had brought. They laid it on the ground, and she made passes over it. She had put off the cloak. Her arms were smooth and rounded, strong but very female, braceleted wrist to armpit. And her hair was youngly-white.

He did not think, I am dreaming of Timonie by the Nile in Egypt. He knew it was not Egypt. And not Timonie, and not a dream.

Then she made a sign, and all the men slipped away out of the trees, all of course but the naked corpse. Another shape emerged between the castaneas, male and mantled. He spoke to her, and then she said something to him. Her voice was light but throaty. His, harsh, sounding angry, cowardly. They were speaking – not the classical Latin of the modern school-room – but the everyday speech of real life, tailored by a hundred foreign intrusions, and the colloquialisms of a military camp. The City had not been built yet, nor even the Roman town of occupation, just the walls, the towered fort, a storehouse or two. And over there were the bothies of the savages who had been here first. And underneath all, the silvermines for which they had optimistically named the station Par Dis.

He had told her, in a patrician's Roman slang, he did not care for it, now it was to happen. And she said, her accent not the same as his, Too late.

Then she made a kind of channel, in the mud among the tree-roots, all about herself and the corpse. At intervals in this channel she thrust in small sticks that seemed to be lying about on the ground. She lit them, it was not certain quite how. The light was bluish, unclear, like dying gas-glim. Yet as she moved, a single earring flamed and darkened from her right ear, and in the other ear, as it seemed to be, a part of an earring. There was a pectoral, over and between her small breasts bound in byssus. The Egyptian enamel and lapis was of eyes and hieroglyphs, but there hung from it a flat moon-disc spider, in silver, and there another and another was sewn on her skirt. She had placed some little images at points along the channel, the invisible watcher could see them now, though again, not exactly where they had come from. They were very small and appeared to have been formed of simple baked clay, and she was breathing on them, like a god giving life in a myth. Three he saw quite distinctly. A man sitting cross-legged, a great belly and a fat man's bosom on his lap, in either arm an urn, one up-ended to the earth, and one tilted skyward. Near him was a scales, empty and in balance. Now the woman sighed upon two little animals, like lambs or young goats, lying with their forefeet entwined. Having breathed on these, she straightened up. She stood a moment, slender and poised, and unhuman, like some wading bird, attentive to something other than the night.

It was the dark of the moon, and she was making magic, too black for the Roman's fort to hold it. For they were the children of reason. They built roads and armies, forts and baths and laws. Her kind built from shadows, different things.

Somehow the watcher-witness had been excluded from the spell, pushed back on its rim. He was looking at her then, from a slight distance, not seeing her quite clearly. In the peculiar light, her eyes might not have been blue after all, for all of her had a blue cast, jewels and clothing, skin and hair.

Then she turned to the corpse, and spoke to it shrilly, words that made no proper sense – like commands to an idiot or a beast. And the corpse sat up, and answered her in a whistling moan, not even in words.

There came a prolonged sequence after that, during which the dead thing rose and stood, showing that it glowed a little, and that in places it had indecently decomposed. At first it spoke only noises and gibberish, but the sorceress, she, Tiy-Amonet, she shrilled out again and again at it, she threatened it with its unburial, and some loss injurious to its soul-life. And finally it hung its head and began again to whisper, and the whispering formed words. And then she asked questions and the corpse replied. They were to do with a battle, and an enemy. It was for the commander of the fortress, her protector, that she asked. While he stood apart, his mantle held over his face, his eyes rolling with fear and nausea and a wish to be gone.

But it was impossible to tell anything from her eyes. Not even colour.

And as the corpse mumbled on, the watcher heard the frogs, unawed, chorusing, and then a deep explosion shook the world, a pane of light broke into a million pieces of rain.

The rain was not wet. It fell beyond a partition of glass and bricks. Louis de Jenier lay in the bed and watched the lightning of the storm crack again across his walls.

Then he sat up, aware that in just this way the corpse in the dream had got itself upright from the earth.

The night was full of noise, the breakages of heaven. A bolt seemed to pass right through the decanter of water at the bedside, and shatter it. On the pillow a fire-ball flashed and died. The silver earring was lying there, the spider at its centre. Louis put one hand to his face and found that, in sleeping, in the dream, he had lain with his cheek pressed against the earring. He left the bed and opened the wardrobe door and looked into the mirror there. In the next lightning, he saw the impression of the spider stamped into his flesh.

By ten o'clock the next morning, when he went to see about the costume, the spider mark had faded altogether, which was as well. He had arranged a photographic session to follow, to charm and stall Vlok with budding results.

That the earring had been returned was also – not a stroke of luck – but a stroke of some sort, perhaps of lightning.

By the time of the photography at the shop in the covered alley, Louis had recalled, excavated and read the page of print Curt had given him.

'A stranger, reading *this*, will assume I had seen the item previously, and so manufactured the dream on cue. Perhaps I had, because the name Tiy-Amonet seemed always resonant, in the way Timonie had done. The dream was correct in its details, even to the fact of being set on the north bank. Now even I begin to wonder, did I look at Curt's page before I went to sleep? Did I find the earring and put it ready on my pillow – sleep-walking, maybe. No, it isn't any of that. I'm caught in something now, can't stop, must go on. I dreamed *Timonie's* dream, her dream of her own alter-*icon*.

'At the photographer's, in my covert of screens, I donned the costume, exact to my design. Everything was perfect, and such gasps and purrs and *looks* from the camera fellow and his adjuncts, I might have been back in one of Vlok's carefully-chosen nightclubs. Even some muttered asides to me about a client or two of theirs, who would . . . etc., to match the other asides when I entered as a male.

'The mirrors in the screened back "room" were full of the image. I felt drunk, or rather full-flush as you do at the start of drinking, before the weight settles over the eyes and in the brain. A marvellous portrait, they assure me. The earring felt very cold. Then, when I removed it, burning blazing hot in my hand so it was nearly dropped. I keep it in my pocket now. Where might it go if, idly, I put it down. Back to the room with the windows, probably.

'Someone may be playing a joke, or I've gone mad.

'But – I'm addicted. *Too late* as the lady said in her wild Roman I forget but understood. Though we were never taught Latin, but for the religious niceties where I was raised. I can hardly wait for the darkness. My hand's shaking.

'I shan't dine tonight. I only want water from the decanter that lightning speared through. Bathe, put on those garments, the painted mask of cosmetics, the breasts and the hair, the jewel. Then take all of it, and myself, up *there*. Wait.

'If this is fear I'm feeling, it's more potent than a drug. I never felt anything like it before. The difficulty is if I think: what shall I do afterwards? So I don't think it.

'The sky through the windows is lapis-lazuli, and they're lighting the streets. The rain has stopped again. Clear heavens, not a cloud. Every window of the house now like coloured glass. Better start to get ready.'

I looked at this point, in vain, among the documents in the diary pocket, for that torn sheet concerning the sorceress. Eventually I found it pasted in, as with some other of the entries, but at the end of the diary behind many blank pages. It scanned as follows:

Tiyamonet. Reputedly a healer, diviner and necromancer, as many of her race were reckoned automatically to be. Mentioned in several writings of the period, she was the mistress of that previously noted Roman commander, who controlled his part of the Empire's campaign here in the north with two legions, inaugurated the building of walls and fortifications, portions of which remain, and opened the silver-mines. These, actually mined out in fifty years, gave the area its original name, which soon came to be rendered in the records as Par Dis. Dis being Pluto, god of the Underworld, its mineral hoards, and incidentally, its kingdom of the dead. At the wish of her patron, Tiyamonet is supposed to have summoned up spirits and thus re-animated cadavers, then enjoining them to answer questions as to the outcome of impending battles, or the weaknesses of the commander's enemies. An old tavern, the *Imago* – the Apparition – which was destroyed after the Years of Liberty, was built it was said near the site of one such event. It stayed an inn of ill-repute ever after. The personal seal and sigil of Tiyamonet was the spider. The arachnid has always enjoyed connections with witchcraft, mostly due to the insect's abilities as a spinner – see also the Fates – and since it is able to build a trap out of an emanation of its own body – ectoplasm? – the thread and the web. A blue-eyed Alexandrian, Tiyamonet may have been feared in her own land, for in the East blue optics were, and sometimes continue to be taken, for the Evil Eye. When the luck of her patron changed, the commander being killed, as formerly stated, in a revolt of his own garrison, she committed suicide rather than submit to assault and torture. She is said to have employed for this purpose the bite of a poisonous spider, of the species – now extinct – shown in her seal and on the earring. Along with many magicians, Tiyamonet was rumoured to possess a particular secret, in her case to do with the ethereal powers of Air, Pliny the Other's *Regna Caerulea*, Galen's *Caerulei mundi regna*. As with most such secrets, for example, the Book of Gates, the precise formulae of the sorcery are unsure, but seem to have to do with a triumph over time and death. The method of the woman's entombment and rites, if any, go unrecalled. Her possessions were certainly stolen. The spider-earring of Tiyamonet, on view in this museum, came to light in another trove, of far later date, and may indeed be merely a Roman copy; its authenticity has never been verified.

(Nowhere else, in what is left of the diary, does Louis de Jenier make any reference to this information.)

The image into which Louis transformed himself that evening must be the same which is memorised by the photograph. Timonie's image, but modified. He did not, for fairly obvious reasons, bare his torso. He was not a woman in any physical sense. Instead, the pleated linen is very nearly opaque, and folds about him, with cape-winged upper sleeves, the lower sleeves bandaged down to the elbows, where bracelets take over. The ornate collar feminises the shallow breast. The face is exact, might be anything, *is* desperately beautiful. The hair of the wig owes too much to our idiom, Egypt seen through the lens of a vogue, but it will do. The eye-paint cannot be faulted. The earring is probably real.

When he had finished, the house seemed to have become timeless, nearly dimensionless, and he went across to the window-room in the dark, half-thinking the doors might open on a desert, the river of Par Dis, the past, space itself splattered with cracked stars.

But the room was only itself. He sat on the floor quietly, near to one of the central windows. (He had taken the diary in with him, though he could not properly see to write, as the sloping and overlapped letters give evidence.)

After a while the violin, which he had hung from pegs by the study door, began to make a noise. He could not see if anything played it, or even if the strings vibrated. This time there were definite melodics, harmonies and stopping, though all at variance with each other. Then, he heard the cittern, which he had *not* bought and which did not exist in the room save in his plan. After the cittern, there were a number of instruments. All had strings, and some bells. They seemed to be floating about in the air, passing and re-passing over his head, mischievously. The incense smell also came again, more strongly, the joss-stick *kuphi* lit at Timonie's drunken parties. There was a kind of lulling, rock-a-bye quality to all this. And then, something went out of tune. The cloy became a stench, and the combing of the strings began to tear and rip. Then the coldness came. He had been braced for it, but even so it nearly stunned him. It was like falling through ice into some winter glacier. And no sooner had it seemed to cut to his marrow than the awful heat blasted after it.

The room no longer cradle-rocked, it was in quake. The doors, which he had closed, crashed open, then crashed shut again. A high singing buzz sounded from the window-frames. He expected the plaster on the walls to snap off in chunks, and bricks to fly out.

And then the throbbing and heavy lugging noises started, and next the screaming began. They were ghastly screams, not human, like those of an animal in a snare. Agony and primeval terror, mindless, hopeless.

His euphoria had spired into an all-consuming horror. But Louis could not move.

He sat and listened to Timonie's murder, in the eyeless darkness. He vaguely thought, It's this, then. The murder was the fixative. That's usual. Do I somehow have to give her peace from it? And, trying to keep sane among the driving nails of the screaming, he thought of priests, and that some priest must come in to free her screaming soul –

And then the screaming itself ended, not dying out, not in a death-rattle or a groan, but as if the noise had been sliced off by a knife. All the sounds went together.

He thought, Get up, for God's sake. Light the lamps.

And then the lamps were lit. Not from the gas, surely, for he never heard its unmistakable hiss, the *spat* of a match, the ignition. Instead the gas-bulbs were full of some other light, the dying corpse-glow gas-glim of the spell in the riverside dream. Timonie's light, and by it – by it? No, nothing. She was not there, her mutilated body, the several bits of it. Yet on the floor, a pool of viscous liquid ran in a strange way, ran along and along the polished floor, gleaming black under glowing blue.

The black blood was running towards him. He got up. The forward motion ceased. There came a delicate movement at its edge, as if some tiny creature played there in the blood. Then, a gleaming mark appeared on the floor, and another; another and another. They circled away from the pool, returned to and skirted it: paused, resumed. The shape, each time, made in wet black, was of two narrow naked feet.

He stood and watched them. He could not take his eyes off them, these perambulating footprints. The steps of Timonie's dismembered feet. There was a stillness and a silence that enclosed the room. He realised, in these extreme moments, that he could hear nothing from the City. The sealed chamber had dropped through the basement of the universe.

It was searingly hot, even to breathe exhausted him, but he had begun to shift towards the doors. He was not convinced he would be able to open them, but before long he must lose consciousness. Then the footprints began to come towards him, to cut across his exit. Louis drew back to the wall.

Something struck the wall very suddenly, near to his face. Then again and again. He looked, and saw there some smeared, wet handprints.

'*Timonie.*'

209

He had decided he must speak aloud. Must try to reason with the reasonless unreasonable.

'Timonie, what do you want? Shall I take off the costume? Is it an affront? What do you want me to do?'

Then one of the invisible hands struck his face. It was freezing cold, wet with blood – he cried out in revulsion, and pulled the earring from his ear by its loop of silver wire, flinging it away across the room.

It was like throwing a pebble into water. The air of the room seemed to smash into fragments and whirl up at him.

He ran then, for the doors, directly through all of it. They would not move. He shook them, and pieces of wet stinging flesh slapped and clawed at him – he plunged away, and cast himself against the door of the study. To his amazement it gave. He had some notion of hurling something and smashing the skylight, and somehow climbing out on to the roof and so to the drain-pipes. He had a distinct inspiration that he must get into the *air*, off the *earth* or anything that passed for it. Then he stumbled against the chair beside the desk, fell with it and broke its back, and finding himself down, *earthed* on the Persian rug, at once all the strength left him.

In that second, everything stopped.

He felt the house settle, as if dropping back a few inches from the sky. After that, there was nothing to be felt at all.

He wanted frantically to get up and escape the place, but had no energy. He lay on the floor and heard the Sacrifice ringing the four o'clock bell. And next some drunken boys or women singing, fifty streets away, the sound carrying on stillness like a leaf on the wind. And then he thought how cool it was, how warm, and that everything was over and he could sleep now, and so he slept there, lying face down on the carpet among the wood of the broken chair, and clothed rather like the dead girl but for the spider-earring he had thrown away.

Louis entered Vlok's hotel-suite the following afternoon. He was unshaven, his clothes thrown on, and Vlok, taking one look at him, exclaimed: 'You're ill! What's the matter with you?'

'An acute attack of wanting to please you,' said Louis amiably, dropping into a chair. 'I'm finished with that house. Let's go north. Or wherever you like.'

The next thing he was conscious of was of being in bed as it seemed in Vlok's room, but actually in an adjoining suite. A satisfied physician was asking him moustached questions to which he, the physician, already knew every answer, and so was sometimes helpful enough to prompt his patient.

'Nervous exhaustion.'

'Then there's nothing – '

'Monsieur Vlok, the young man needs good food and rest. Get him out of the City as soon as you can. The coast, perhaps, or one of the pastoral areas.'

Louis let go of them both and slept again. The sleep was beauteous, dreamless or amnesiac of dreams. Deep, reviving deaths.

He had brought nothing away from the house but the clothes he put on his body when he took off it the gown and hair and breasts and physical soul of Timonie.

Later, Vlok was murmuring to him nonsensically, anxiously, 'The new costume has been damaged. But Curt will get that seen to. You told me there was a photograph taken?'

'It's been paid for.'

'But the name of the shop.'

'No.'

'Louis, why must you be difficult.'

'I'm ill.' Louis, the sick child, played his part suddenly to its full. 'Don't you want me to get better?'

'Louis.'

'Then let me rest, as the whiskery doctor told you.'

He had brought nothing away. But Curt, dispatched on Rudolf Vlok's orders, had scurried about the house, packed clothes and personal items, and included in his itinerary the Garb-Egyptian dress, wig and jewellery he had found lying on the study floor. Curt also tidily reinstated the broken-backed chair, and next had dust-sheets brought in and laid reverently over all the few furnishings, including the elaborate desk. Off this he had first taken the diary, but it was locked, and rather ingeniously, and in his inquisitive efforts to pry it open unobtrusively – which failed – Curt did not bother to clear any other matter from the desk. Also he forgot the two precious portraits by the mirror. Thus Anette and Lucine were left in residence, while the accoutrements of Timonie, even the violin, were borne away to Louis' rooms at the hotel.

Louis had not asked for this. If he had had a minute or so more to himself before he fainted, he might have thought to tell Vlok to leave everything in the house untouched. Vlok might have obeyed. Or he might not. The violin, for instance, was worth a very great many livres, (it could be sold when Louis' craze for it wore off), and as for Louis' personal accumulation of cuff-links, tie-pins, and so forth, these too were worth a few pennies. Louis constantly abandoned

211

one set of toys for another, and Vlok always sent Curt to pick up after him.

Curt himself had not liked being in the house, especially alone. He would have seen no marks on the walls or floors, or heard anything unusual. He was not psychic or even sensitive in that way, but had a morbid dread of morbidity which occasionally put him right.

'First of all, not a single engagement.' Vlok was idyllic in his selfless devotion. 'You see, someone has painted a watercolour for their brochure. A residence, yes? Comfort *and* finesse. Total quiet and nourishing food. A little Paradise. Cream and cheese and fresh eggs. Fruit straight off the trees and fish from the waters.'

'But the place is in the north. Away from this City?'

'Miles away. No smoke, no noise, no river damps, no neurasthenic fancies. You'll be bored but you must stick to it. A week at least, the doctor says. And you can tell me there, about your new girl.'

'Never, I'm afraid.'

'Oh Louis, so temperamental.'

'Your placatory tone is always your least successful, Rudolf.'

'Now, Louis.'

'And why were there furniture-removers in the other room? Or did I dream that?'

'Furniture-removers? Of course not.'

'Someone bringing something in, dragging it across the floor. It sounded like a trunk.'

'That might have been Curt, fetching up your things.'

'Things.'

'Everything you so carelessly and thoughtlessly discarded at the rented house.'

A long silence. Noticeable pallor. Vlok grew nervous.

'What's wrong? Do you want more of those drops?'

'I want to kill you,' said Louis, with a sweet, dazed smile. 'Never-mind.' Then, after the Vlokian storm had calmed, 'What exactly did he fetch? I seem to remember, you talked about the new costume. You'd seen it, then.'

'And it is being repaired after your maltreatment. Very interesting. I'm not sure this one will work. I'd have to see you, how you manage it. What will you make her do? Monologue? More of that throaty singing, I suppose, but they like it, don't they, your worshippers.'

'What else, Rudolf, did Curt bring?'

212

'He forgot the photographs and won't go back alone. He's avidly been reading all the accounts of that girl's murder. I just hope she has no relatives concentrated somewhere. We don't want any lawsuits over this impersonation.'

'The violin?'

'What about it? Oh yes. Naturally I had him get them to pack that and bring it here. Have you any conception of how much you paid for it – ?'

'And the jewellery.'

'All the jewellery. Including a battered silver earring on a loop of wire. I believe it's an earring?'

'Where is that?'

'You want it? Well, it was on a table in the outer room. Drink your champagne. I'll fetch it.'

Louis did not drink his invalid's champagne. Vlok went into the sitting room of the suite, leaving the door ajar. In the stripe of the opening, as in an ultra-modern painting, Louis beheld the violin out of its case, leaning at a contrived angle, a plash of white muslin that had been part of Timonie's gown and, nearly preposterously, the blonde wig poised on a wig-stand, a faceless wooden head, only waiting for its features to be filled in.

Vlok was a long time.

'You can't find it,' Louis muttered.

Then Vlok returned. 'Here. The chambermaid must have moved it. It looks old so I suppose it is, but isn't it reckoned to be a fake, Curt said . . . Something set in there, once, I'd have said.'

Louis put out his hand and allowed the earring to be laid on the palm. It hardly mattered at last, contact.

'What's wrong now? Louis? *Louis!*'

'Nothing at all. Everything is perfection.'

'No, I don't care for the sound of you now. You're up to something. You were warned, Louis. You must stay in bed for another day at the very least.'

'Yes, Rudolf.'

'And now, I'm going down to dine. Try to have a little more of what's on the tray there.'

'So reminiscent,' said Louis, turning the silver disc, strengthlessly, uninterestedly, in his fingers, 'of the farmer with the pet goose. Eat just a little more corn, my dear. Just a grain. We must get you fit and fine, for on Sunday I shall drive a pin through your brain and kill you for the feast.'

Vlok pranced out. He slammed the intervening door, and presently the outer one.

213

Louis reclined on his halted avalanche of pillows, in the constant light, (the hotel was most contemporary and electric). Beyond the drapes, darkness lay on the City of Paradis like black bloom. There were the sounds of cars and carts and angry taxi-cabs, but the hotel's upper corridors had stilled, for it was both the hour of dining and theatre-going. And in the ballrooms they would be striking up the tango, the dance of sin, which, like so many things, creeds and treasures and marching empires, plagues and mysteries and magics, and even the sun and moon themselves, had originally come out of the East.

Of course, it might have been dislodged, when he cast it away across the blue room in panic. But not every gem, surely, not at once. Unless they were in some way moulded to each other. They had not seemed to be. The one stone, shaped and impressive in size – the body and head; the other smaller stones, thirty of them, the eight legs. All rested individually in the silver disc. Curt had never been shown the earring. He had simply picked it up off the floor. The indentation where the sapphire spider had been had not, it seemed, concerned Curt, though he had read the description of it earlier. Safety in inattention, non-avowal.

Louis seemed to understand it all, and there was undoubtedly nothing he could do. There had been a slight chance, now there was none.

He lay back and closed his eyes in the bright light. He could smell the perfumes of the clean hotel room, hygenic fabrics, soap, and polish, and sometimes, from the partly-opened window, the City's spring, gutters, soot and violets, and from a baker's shop across the street, poppy-seeds and gingerbread.

But the City's sounds seemed to be drawing away. He waited, for the other sounds to begin, that dragging, that leaden revolving *drum-drum*, like a turntable. Perhaps this would not be possible here, away from the house. Then again, it might be, for Timonie had had her say. It was the turn of the other, now, and *she* had travelled wherever her earring travelled.

It had fallen from his hand. He would not open his eyes to see where it was, or anything. He felt drowsy, ill again. The room was growing very warm, and he heard a pale dry little scratching. It was like the noise of a paper settling, stretching itself after it had been screwed up and thrown away.

Louis opened his eyes, Blurred, heavy . . . The room seemed in shadow, the light must be faulty. Something moved on the bed, like a trick of tired vision.

214

Yes, not Timonie, if ever it had been she. She was the recording shown to him, the moving picture. Because, of course, Timonie had summoned it, or attracted it, through the medium of the earring. In the end, it had killed her, and portioned her. There was some Egyptian occult rite, surely, to do with that – some method of revenge – so it had hated Timonie. And it should hate him, too. The sorceress Tiy-Amonet must now be hunting for Louis de Jenier, all out of time, across a landscape twenty centuries too late.

The trick of tired vision was affecting both eyes now. It was moving steadily up across the counterpane, it was on the edge of the sheet. The light smeared and blinked on a hard surface of sapphire blue.

The jewellery spider paused. It raised itself a fraction, the slightly shorter foremost legs, composed each of three gems, exploring the air. Then it lowered itself and walked quietly aside, the individual legs extending, overtaken by others, extending again. It crept quickly on to his right hand. And as it touched his flesh, it hesitated once more.

It felt very cool to him, but the room was boiling, his skin feverish, he thought. The spider was full of poison. There must be a hollow in the larger jewel. She – Tiy-Amonet – had known how to release the poison, in order to facilitate her suicide. Perhaps there was a sort of pincering motion, crab-like, with the front legs, like that which it was making now – He felt the needle-like little nip from far away. He heard himself give a faint gasp, yet he was not startled. The gasp sank in a sigh. He began to sleep. To sleep and wake as if dozing in a drifting boat. The river was black again, and it had a riper scent. It smelled of crocodiles, papyrus and inundation, like the Nile of his imaginings, and of elder ages, of a primal state.

He was lying flat, on a type of stretcher. His eyes were shut, but he saw upward through his lids with unimpeded clarity. Men were rowing the boat, two soldiers with dirty faces. Another, his helmet off and head wrapped in a bandage, crouched nearby. All three looked afraid. They must be the burial detail, or burning or drowning detail. The fighting was over and the witch was dead, so get rid of her, somewhere over there, outside the station and the wall of reason and law.

His – Tiy-Amonet's – hands were folded over her breasts. Yes, the swell of her small breasts was against his arms, which were also hers. There was no breathing, no heart-beat, no ability – or desire – to shift any of the limbs. Yet complete awareness. Was the throat useable? Suddenly he, or she, laughed. He heard and felt the laugh

215

passing through the body, somehow without breath, to be emitted, an eerie warbling note, not laugh-like, but audible.

The three men heard it too. There were some seconds of fear and confusion. Then the bandaged man smote about him. 'Keep rowing. It was over there. Sound carries. Only a fox.' Reluctantly, they rowed on.

Tall reeds rose from the river, and next the boat passed around an islet. It seemed to Louis they were a great distance from the garrison-station of Par Dis.

The body was clothed in its grainy Egyptian linen, and wrapped in a long cloak. All the ornaments were gone, even the metal spiders from the skirt. Someone, less scared than these three, had taken the hoard of the sorceress.

Soon they would reach wherever it was they had been told to reach, and do whatever they had been told to do there, or not do it. It was immaterial. Even burning, in this instance, would not have mattered. The jewel mattered, and the jewel was secure. And the will mattered. But now the will must rest. How long would it continue, the waiting? Be indifferent to that. Sleep now. Rest now.

The river lapped against the boat and the oars spooned it over. There never seemed to be a moon in the past.

They slept together, he and she, a sleep of death.

Curt had brought the leather diary to the hotel and Vlok, in search of business clues, had also attempted to open it, fruitlessly. Louis must have the key concealed somewhere. This was true. Louis had placed the key inside the tube of one of the unused pens on the desk in the study at the house.

'What in God's name are you doing?'

'Getting dressed. As you can see, can't you?'

'Don't be such a fool, Louis.'

But Louis went on tying his tie before the glass. He seemed relaxed and careless. He had breakfasted to a degree, been shaved and manicured.

'Do you want to be ill again?' raged Vlok.

'Hush now,' said Louis, 'sound carries. It was only a fox on the near bank, not anybody laughing.'

'*What*? Oh stop talking in riddles. Where do you propose to go?'

'There's something I want at the house. Curt, naturally, left all the important, useful things behind.'

'Then, if you *must*, I'll come with you.'

Louis only put on his jacket.

On the street, after a sufficient number of blocks, Louis feigned faintness and pleaded for a taxi back to the hotel. Vlok in smug dismay lurched in pursuit of one. Returning with it, he found Louis had given him the slip.

Half an hour later, hammering at the door of the house in the Observatory Quarter, Vlok received no reply. Either Louis was ignoring him, or had postulated the venue of the house to throw Vlok off another, real, scent. Vlok inclined to the latter notion and stormed away.

The house, chandelier-lit by sunshine, was peaceful. Birds skittered over its roofs and sang in nearby trees. A milkcart passed, and from the boulevards below and above wafted the songs of day.

The diary unlocked, Louis wrote it up to date. Then added, 'Timonie was murdered. I am permitted to live. That was Timonie's anger, but it didn't have the power to kill me. The other has no intention of killing me, though Timonie it killed. Indeed, I'm cajoled, invited, made party to private reveries of Tiy in her death hour. And I admit – she's snared me. In the web. Depending and waiting. For this is not a reprieve. Only that I misheard the sentence.'

After that, Louis made a note concerning a journalist who wrote in 'one or two of the better journals. She – I'm sure it is a woman – writes under the male pseudonym *St Jean*. The invaluable Curt is finding out for me where this being dwells, or at least where she frequents.'

He wanted to put his affairs in order. He wanted to leave a legacy of truth with someone he reckoned reputable, honourable. Not he, nor his diary, say why he wanted this.

He was relaxed, as Vlok, (and I myself), beheld him, in the condemned cell. Although he stipulates he has no idea what form the punishment may take, he was as accustomed to being under the sway of another persona, as any actor. The supernatural wooed him; it had got endemically close to him as live human things never did. And in a way, too, he was playing, and I wonder if he even believed it, even at the last second, desperate as it was, entirely.

Louis intended to leave the house and return to the hotel for the night. The sorcery had fragmented and was everywhere – the blue windows, the very source, being in the house, the violin, the disc of earring, the costume, they were at the hotel. The portrait of Timonie was at the photographer's. The spider – that might be anywhere, even travelling in his clothing. Enwebbed, he was not intending to step outside the spell, only to move freely within it.

217

But the desert quality of the house, the privacy, after his fresh term with Vlok, seduced Louis. And then there came a sense of danger, and he could not resist it. He would stay.

He left the diary therefore unlocked on the unsheeted desk, ready to be found. He left Anette and Lucine, too, beside the convex mirror.

There is only one further entry in the diary. It is almost illegible, but by this point, familiarity with the script enables a reader to attempt it. I remember how he was at our first and only meeting. I wonder if I should be appalled at the interrupted abandoned narrative, or only at his lazy perversity. How much choice *was* there?

'Already' (he wrote) 'it had happened. We see with our eyes, but cannot *see* our eyes, except in a mirror. In the mirror, looking, I scored it across with the small diamond in a ring – and was answered. The glass was scored again, back and forth – from *inside*. Magic. Symbol. There will be coherence in patches – A spider: female devouring male – and phases of speech like the moon. I must learn some lines for you, Mademoiselle St Jean. If I find you in time. No elbow-room allowed. To explain. Couldn't anyway. You must guess. Or – but it slips. Slips, down and down.'

Under this was written in a strange spiky jumble, almost like the writing of another: *Caerulei mundi regna.* I had seen it printed previously, and so could decipher it, now.

That vanished poet, St Jean, who some schools of thought tell us died in a duel, mooted for his last words: 'I have no last words.' He also said, Fire is Will, Water is Grief, Earth is Thought, Air a Vision. And though I had never seen Pliny the Other's Latin, or read Galen through, I had once, in translation, come across a non-illuminating reference to *Caerulei mundi regna*, (which Louis had managed to translate literally, as kingdoms of the sky-blue universe) – the Empires of Azure.

Now, shivering all over as if with the influenza I had pretended, I reached the end of Louis de Jenier's diary none the wiser. I was confused and unnerved, (especially at being directly addressed!) and resentful, yes, very resentful. As if I had been reading, on another's recommendation, a rare detective novel, only to find the last pages – those with the solution – deliberately and *neatly* cut out.

He had approached me and coherently informed me of this material. Yet the material itself, implied to be completed before the approach, finished in nonsense. The mirror had been scratched by a diamond in his ring. And then itself had scratched back, unnaturally . . .

These facts I would not dispute. I had been present when doors slammed and windows shattered of themselves. But what *else* had gone on?

It was the awareness of *un*finish that disturbed me more than anything. It made me jittery. As if I was being manipulated. I suppose I knew that a conclusion must be sought, or that it was seeking me.

By now it was early evening. I went downstairs, finding myself very nervous at emerging from my rooms, and assailed the landlady for her telephone. I called Thissot, but he did not answer, and then, in desperation, my editor at *The Weathervane*, but he too was absent. Quite what I wanted to say or ask I am unsure. A contact, a reassurance, is what I truly wanted. Both were unavailable.

So, out I went to my dinner in one of my three usual restaurants, trying to be jaunty and at ease. But I could not eat what I ordered, and the proprietor, who knew me, came over to enquire. 'Oh, it's simply that I've had the influenza.' He commiserated and sent complimentary brandy to my table. I wondered if I should confide in him, but the preamble of explanation daunted me and shut me up.

Nagging always at the back of my mind was the memory that Curt, who had a "knack for worming out . . . what was lost or in hiding" had been put on my trail in the first place by Louis. Would Curt abruptly arrive, and with Vlok? Would they attempt in some way to threaten or blackmail me, or even to silence me? I had seen a man hanging by the neck in an abyss of air, and Vlok at least positively looking down at him – the other in the background had been too vague to see, but must have been Curt himself. Should I go to the police? 'Why, mademoiselle, have you waited so long to come to us with this business?'

I began to have the wish to abandon Paradis altogether. Louis' beauty had enmeshed me, but he was dead, and the rest of it a weird nightmare, lacking even a proper ending. Let me take flight.

I walked home under the watery street-lamps. Rain struck the pavement all about me, dancing. The sky arched over the City and the world. It held so much, that vault, winds, vapours, clouds, distance, and colour. No wonder ancient belief had peopled it with elementals and powers. From there, lightning struck, and the sun blazed, and weather and angels fell. I pictured a teeming universe unseen behind the shields of blue or black. Then the vision left me, I went into the house and my landlady came flouncing out from her parlour. 'Oh mademoiselle, a gentleman has been telephoning you every quarter of an hour.' I thought with enormous relief, Ah, Thissot. I'll have to tell him all of it and risk his scorn. And exactly then the bell whirred and she went to answer, saying to me, 'That may be him again.' Presently she waved me in and gave me the receiver. As usual, she began to busy herself about the room, listening.

Then a voice spoke in my ear, giving me my proper name. It was not the voice of Thissot.

'Who is that?' I demanded, but it was all I could do to stop my own voice from shaking.

'Rudolf Vlok, mademoiselle.'

'I have nothing to say to you.'

'Please, mademoiselle. I must – that is, it is essential that I see you. Tonight if possible.'

'Don't be ridiculous. I have friends with me.'

'Send them away.' he said. 'It must be alone.'

'You must think me a fool,' I said.

'I mean you no harm. But – there are things to be cleared up. You agree, don't you? You've read – that diary.'

'Which diary?'

'Mademoiselle, I shall be at your apartment in ten minutes time.'

'You'll find me gone,' I said wildly.

(My landlady had run down into slow-motion, she was so intrigued.)

'Mademoiselle – it isn't – for myself. I have to say that if you refuse to see me now, there must be a meeting at another time. And that I'll do anything I can, and I have some influence, mademoiselle, to see to it.'

'Why?'

'Only – only in order to settle things.'

'You want the diary returned? I'll mail it to you at any address or office you wish.'

'Mademoiselle – ' his voice had been, all the while, different. It was earnest and determined, and yet placatory. He had said, this call was not for himself. And he did sound to me, now, so much an underling. Someone had primed him. He was anxious not to displease them. It must be some backer I had not been told of, fearful of a mention in the diary, perhaps. Suddenly I thought, Let him come, I want to know. Maybe this can give me the key. It was, after all, still a social hour. The house was full of people who knew me, the rooms and streets well-lit. It would be safer to face it here, whatever it was. I broke in on his rambling insistence. 'Very well. In ten minutes, as you said. If that is all right, madame?' I added loudly to my landlady, making her jump in her lethargic fiddling, letting Vlok know the world anticipated his visit.

When I got up to my rooms, I lit the gas, the oil-lamp on my desk, took off my coat and hat and gloves, and put round my shoulders a shawl of my mother's, which comforts me. I was glad I had had the brandy.

Minutes ticked by on my clock. It struck for nine, and I heard a noise below, and then footsteps ascending.

When the knock came on my door I went slowly to open it, and in one hand I took my lethal little paper-knife.

As I paused, only the door between us, I heard that special thick quiet of presence, of awaiting, and remembered the children's game: *Who's there? Who's there? No one is there. Then ask Monsieur No One in.* At that the hair rose on my scalp and I grasped the door-knob and dashed open my door in a sort of rage.

'*Louis!*'

The lights of my room burned against his face as it poised there above mine. Then I saw the eyes. The circlets of indigo, the centres falling miles deep, filled by *darkness*. I saw the eyes before I saw any of the rest of it, and giving a stupid small cry, I stepped back, and back, until the bookcase stopped me.

It came into my room then, what had been Louis, gliding and silent, with the faint perfume about it of sands and sweet resin, and with the shadow of night.

And after it, Vlok, his polite hat in his hands.

The creature had gone towards the fireplace. It stood there and did not move. It seemed to value the heat. Egypt was a hot country, and here, the north had been far warmer, then.

'Be calm, mademoiselle,' Vlok said. His face had a still, solid look to it. Yes, he had been primed. He was the servant of the fiend. How much had it devoured of him, to make him so obedient? Not so much. He was in all other ways himself. Only, the jailor had become – the slave.

'I'm quite calm,' I said. I added mundanely, 'I saw Monsieur de Jenier hanged on a rope from an attic window. And his death was reported in all the papers. How can it be he's here now, and so convincingly in one of his rôles?'

And I made myself look at the creature. It did not seem to be angered that I did so. But I must be careful of those eyes. They were so horrible, I had nearly died of terror . . . The rest, if one did not know, was only a fashionable woman, tall and slender. She affected a contemporary coat with fur at the collar, a flattering hat. Her hair was blonde as ice. She did not wear earrings.

'No, mademoiselle, I'm here to explain all that, what you – thought that you saw.'

221

I had already noticed that the feet and hands of the woman with Louis' face, feet and hands which give away the man and which Louis would have been careful to camouflage, needed no camouflage. They were not large, not masculine. And the line of the breasts under the coat, a gentle, mellifluous swelling, nothing false to it. Even the bones of the face, very fine, and the brows plucked, and no sheerest shading on the upper lip, the skin nowhere roughened by a razor.

'You say, a hanged man, dangling from a rope, out of the attic window. I'm afraid,' said Vlok, 'it was poor Curt who died. He fell down the stairs in running away – he was so frightened. And his neck was broken. It was a convenience to discover him – later – and to identify and bury him as Louis. Louis was not so well-known here. Not that he couldn't have been – we hadn't come to that. And Curt was nobody. It will save trouble in the future.'

'Who then,' I said, 'who then is this?' And trembled so much I sat down and heard the paper-knife plop on to the rug.

Then, out of the silence, it spoke to me.

'Tuamon,' it said. The voice was like a boy's, high, feminine, yet intently male. 'Tiy-Amonet,' modifyingly amended the voice.

The eyes were turning on me. I looked away. There was no extreme of heat or cold, and despite the pale fragrance of what I must take to be *kuphi*, this was no ghost, it was real. An altered reality.

It said, to Vlok now: 'You tell. Tell.'

'As yet,' Vlok said to me, fussily, with a curious pride, 'she hasn't the grasp of our language. After he lost it – at first – but never mind that. I can see to that.'

I thought, Why not let her talk herself, anyway? Let me hear what it sounded like, the tongue of the Ptolemies, the Greek Pharaohs, the land of Set. Or the Roman's Latin . . . But even from the thought I recoiled.

'I shall be ill if you stay here very long,' I said, not looking at either of them. 'If it's necessary – '

'Yes. I'll be quick then. But you must listen.'

And the other voice repeated, '*Listen*,' as she stood against my fire, all the light and darkness of the room upon her, but vague as something covered by centuries of dust.

Tiy-Amonet, who had *been* dust two thousand years, here in the flesh. Or had it been so long? Might she not have played her trick, whatever it was, before? Timonie had enraged her, for Timonie had not been suitable – since she was herself a female? And Tiy-Amonet rebuked Timonie, and dismembered her body as in the sub-rites of Osirus, depriving the soul of continuity in the after-life, unless all the bits be gathered together. But then there entered Louis.

What had been done to Louis? For Louis was here but Louis was not.

Vlok had seated himself, his hat on one knee. There was something silly about this, and about the way he then began to give me a lecture on the facts. He spoke prosaically, not even making, any more, those apologetic pauses of his over the odder revelations. He looked, and behaved, like a cheap lawyer. How she – it – how the thing called Tiy-Amonet or Tuamon – had informed him, I did not know. Perhaps the residue of Louis had been employed to do it. Before any slightest iota of Louis as we knew him ceased to remain.

It was all quite straightforward. And quite unbelievable. And it happened. Not only was the proof before me, but the air quivered with it – the magic air which the sky let down like a net upon the earth. I never doubted a word. Not even the ultimate ones, demonstrably.

The framework, as I had mentally positioned it, was correct. *Then enter Louis.* And when this occurred, the corner stone was laid.

Timonie had certainly been useless to the essence, the leftover, the spirit and will of the thing once known as Tiy-Amonet. But Louis was nearly perfect. There was a facial resemblance, as with the girl, and the eyes, blue to madness and absurdity – but it was much more than that. It was the mind and the psyche which counted.

The essence, electrified, reached out at once, and began its spinning all about him. Louis thought himself lured by the after-image of Timonie, but it was the spider-witch who worked on him, who showed him pictures of the dead girl, easing him on in stages, until allowing him to feel the recorded horror and fury of her death. By then, and long before the sapphire walked up his bed, its poison had entered him and was infinitesimally active.

The being killed the girl out of pique, but it did not want, primarily, to kill, only to have, itself, life. Louis represented that. And yes, it had had life in this way before Louis, but that was long, long ago. So long, it had been irked at the waiting.

On that last night in the house, it must have shown him the truth. I was not told how, but there would be ways, I imagine. Then he scored the mirror in fear, or anger, or some other emotion. His feelings were in thrall. Yet, he must have been swept by pangs of every kind. Even of excitement. There are plenty of hints of that. Then Tiy-Amonet came down the web to devour him.

When he went back to Vlok the following morning – for he *did* go back – Louis was already losing contact with his previous life, his own personality. He forgot how to dress himself, and how to use utensils of eating. He could not read. The toothbrush and the modern razor baffled him, he achieved their service by other means. Then he would lose speech for hours, then for days. He spoke unintelligibly, gibberish, a compound of his native phonetics and those of some otherwhere, or just of the brain's abstraction. Sometimes he seemed to be blind, dumb and deaf. He lay on the bed in his hotel-suite looking up at the ceiling, unblinking. He did not lack control of any other bodily function, only of the functions of society. He did not demonstrate distress, and only once a torrent of ferocity seemed to take him. During that, he smashed things, and snatching the unused razor appeared to be about to cut someone's throat. But Vlok and Curt overpowered him. Until then, and even then, Vlok half-suspected Louis was playing one of his jokes on them. However, after the razor, the doctor was again summoned. When he arrived, suddenly Louis was better. He talked and acted normally, implying it was Vlok who was inclined to jokes and exaggerations, putting the doctor *en garde*. Louis himself was worn out and charming. The physician, bewildered, fooled, left the hotel, and next Louis left it, by another way. He seemed to have recovered himself, had got hold of Curt, and learned from him where the female journalist frequented.

Louis went across the City, sometimes getting lost – Paradis had not been this way in the times of Tiy-Amonet. When Louis at length found his quarry, he and Tiy-Amonet found it as one. For of course, Tiy-Amonet had no objection to Louis' finding and lucidly conversing with this woman – myself. Indeed, had wanted her found, and conversed with. So I had seen that day before me a creature that was already two creatures, but mostly the creature it had not been and did not appear to be. Soulless also, behind its blind-blue eyes. For what was left of his soul after she had been at it, and what was left of hers? I had seen what he had seen in the dream, the young man swooning back in ecstasy on the runaway bicycle –

Then Vlok pushed in and in a quavering act of normalcy bore *them* away. Which was permitted. I had been made heir to the written diary. It was done.

After that, Louis vanished. Not outwardly that was, but totally within. By the time they reached the hotel, the body was speechless, and almost catatonic. Up in the hotel lift they went, theatricals,

224

covering, and made him a prisoner in his suite. Summoned, but *en garde*, the doctor would not return, and seemed to have alerted besides his colleagues.

There is another meaning for the word *Imago*, this being the thing which emerges from the chrysalis.

When I was told he would last a week, she had apparently judged how long the rest of the transition would take, whatever its outward shows. On the seventh day, Louis' voice had spoken to Vlok one last sentence, over and over. He wanted to go back to the house in the Observatory. He must, he must. Over and over. Until the harassed Vlok agreed and took him there, with Curt at their heels. Presently, I arrived.

During our interchange, Vlok's and mine, Curt had naturally been unable to restrain "Louis", who had gone up to the attic. Here he wandered about, Curt wandering after, all nerves. When Vlok rejoined them, leaving me in the study, "Louis" – or could it have been Louis – had sat down under one of the dirty attic windows, smiling, playing with the silver earring.

Below, I had taken the diary up. And this must have registered throughout the web – which now, it seemed, had meshed all the house, and half the City. A few moments later, Louis rose, opened the attic window, climbed the sill in one step, and tipped himself out.

It may have been, I had begun to think so, the last surge of his persona trying to prevent what was to come, had come, upon it. To baulk and escape, after all.

But, by throwing himself from the attic, he had placed himself for the fall, in the magic condition, the correct one. He was between heaven and earth. *In the air.*

Vlok's face now was like the moon, idiotic, pale, expressionless. He spoke of things that had nothing to do with Vlok the agent, the man of his time. He said flatly, 'You thought you saw him hanging from a rope, mademoiselle, but didn't you see how the rope was, how it vibrated and smoked? Even as he was falling, suddenly one of the windows broke below – the blue windows – and as that happened, a substance started to pour back and upward, out of Louis' neck, about the top of the spine. It was that stuff they called ectoplasm. I admit, I had to look it up to find out. A kind of flesh that isn't flesh. He was Tuamon, by then, you see, and Tuamon can do that, make a fleshly cord out of his own body. And the ectoplasmic rope shot back into the attic, and attached itself everywhere, to the walls, the floor, and it stopped his fall – not dangerously suddenly, but resiliently, like the safety net in the circus. And then I saw you looking out at it too, mademoiselle. At the time, I didn't know any more than you did, what was going on.' (A touch of amusement, at his unenlightenment of then.) 'As for poor Curt, he was gibbering behind me like a monkey. And then you left the house, I believe, so you didn't see what took place. The rope of matter pulled Louis' body gently up, back into the attic, and presently he told me who he, or perhaps I should say, she, was. And at that Curt lost control of himself and ran away, and I've told you the rest of that.'

There was a silence after this. Minutes passed again over the face of my clock, microcosm as it was, as all clocks are, of Time itself, that terrible enormous relentless thing we domesticate with porcelain and ormolu even while it preys upon us.

Eventually I said, with care only to Vlok, not to the other, 'Why did you wait so long to come to me?'

'Till you had read the diary.'

'You knew when I did?'

'Tuamon.'

'Why is the name changed? Why not Tiy-Amonet?'

'Tuamon is the correct name. Tiy-Amonet was the name for the Roman's use. Of course, she'll want to be known by some other name now, of the City, the present day. For convenience.'

'And a further question,' I said. He waited as I swallowed more than once. 'Why do I have to be told all this?'

'*To finish.*'

The voice terrified me. It terrified me every time now. But I had to say: 'Finish – what?'

Another gap. Was it telepathy after all? Vlok said, as if instructed in the actual words, 'He comes from Egypt. He was, and is, a sorcerer. You know about the hieroglyphs in their picture-writing? Well, mademoiselle, to an Egyptian sorcerer, writing is itself a magic, a sort of spell – '

'And old habits die hard,' I said, 'like mutilation for vengeance. Louis began to write about all this, and in all sorcery, every ritual must be completed for the safe-making of spell and mage.'

'Exactly, mademoiselle.'

'And so he – or she, you keep changing the gender now – wants me to complete the account. To write down what you've told me.'

'Just so. Except it would be better if you begin at the beginning, that is, if you will re-write, or copy Louis' account. A broken sequence – it needs to be re-started, and then carried through as one. Also, you see, you are a professional at this – it is, if you will, *your* special branch of magic. You assume therefore the place of the sorcerer himself.' He waited, then said, 'And I am to inform you that it doesn't in the least matter if your view of Tuamon is – unsympathetic. You are naturally afraid and averse to Tuamon, and he expects nothing else. You must write as you feel and see. It will be irrelevant to the ritual, or to the person of the sorcerer Tuamon.'

'Yes. Very well, I do all that. Then what?'

He gazed at me. He put on a look, of an agent whose client may possibly have been exposed to a swindle.

'What could there be, mademoiselle?'

'No, I'm not such a fool as to expect to be paid. I'm inquiring if I'm not to be killed when I've completed the *task*.'

And then it – yes, *it* – it laughed.

This was so awful to me that I found myself on my feet, running towards the door – Vlok caught me. He must have caught Louis this way dozens of times, there was a distinct sense of practice.

'There's nothing to be alarmed at. *She doesn't need your death.*'

'But if I refuse to obey the task, I'll be punished?'

Silence again.

In the end Vlok said, 'There's one more thing that you have to be shown. Then you'll be left to yourself. You'll write everything down. Then publish, if you want to, or not. That isn't of any importance. Just the act of the writing. You can even burn the diary, and your manuscript, providing your own work is finished. Then nobody will trouble you, mademoiselle, ever again.'

I might have asked him if he liked being its slave, or if he grieved over Louis, or Curt. Or a hundred things. But I did not, and did not care. I cared only to have it over with. I said so.

'Then I'll just step down into the street. Tuamon will show you. There's nothing to be *afraid* of. Good night, mademoiselle.' And so saying he nodded and walked out, closing my door behind him. I heard his feet go down the stairs as I stood alone in the room in the gas-light with that thing, and waited for the concluding revelation.

I had wanted the key to the mystery, or it had made me want it.

Before Vlok's footsteps had died away, it moved. The dull fire shone around the edges of the body which had been Louis de Jenier's body. It was taking off the woman's coat, her hat and gloves, her dress –

It was undressing itself in front of me, with no sensitivity.

I said nothing, made no protest. I sank back into my chair, and gripped my hands together. I already knew.

Louis' frankness in his descriptions of the costuming of his rôles

227

had told me anything I needed to know about his quite-ordinarily handsome male body. In these split seconds I became aware that this spider-witch, capable of producing from its own fleshly case a string of ectoplasmic gossamer, could thereby reshape and refashion as it chose. The smallness of the hands and feet, the truthful appearance of the breasts –

A silken camisole, silk stockings, suede shoes. Every stitch.

Yes. Now I understood. Presumably that would please, that I understood, so that I would write it accurately, here.

Physically, Louis was a male. Temperamentally, emotionally, a male. Ethically, a female. He was like one of a pair of twins, boy and girl, torn apart at birth. The female twin had been lost to him. He recaptured her – not through male lovers, who offended the maleness of his body – but by clothing himself to her various possible forms. And in that way he had remade himself into the whole double blossom, both sexes.

But Tuamon had always been that. His presence, now the woman's garments were lying on the ground, was assertively masculine. The pose and the poise of him were masculine. Yet the face under the gleaming hood of hair was a girl's face, with only a boy's arrogance to the brows and lips, and the neck, the boyish shoulders and the arms and the firm apple breasts – a girl's. There was strength in the limbs, in those rounded arms, and the long, muscled legs, the flat belly. And there was strength in the loins, which the room's warmth, or the stillness, or arrogance itself, had caused to flower, so I should have no doubts. And then he – for it was, for all and everything, *a man* – he positioned himself, with no coyness or display, to let me view that the strong loins had also their vulnerability. That this man might be possessed as a woman, too.

Tuamon, taking the feminine name Tiy-Amonet to smooth the sensibilities of a Roman commander attracted to otherness. Tuamon was hermaphrodite. Male and female, in all particulars. The face and breasts of a girl, the essence of a man. The loins of both.

Timonie had been solely and only a woman. Outside and under the skin. She was discarded, and punished. But Louis, under the skin, under the skin of the soul, was potentially dual. He had been worth the centuries.

The gas was turning blue, and that part of the room where Tuamon stood became a vast hollow drum. I thought I glimpsed – lotus pillars, the dune-shaped sarcophagae of Egypt – but then I saw instead an azure sphere, flashing and dazzling with movement and with integral life. In the heart of it, the fabulous monster basked, its eyes like port-holes on a sea of sky, through which passed colossal waves, tidal clouds, while the evening star hung on its forehead, the crescent moon and the full hung one from either ear. And on the disc of the full moon, a blue spider depended from a thread of pulsing ether.

And I did not want the vision to end.

I did not want the safe drab darkness to come back.

And I thought of Louis, closed inside, the food of this power, and I did not feel anything but hunger.

Then it too was done. Over and done.

Reality flooded back to me, and I was ashamed and petrified. And in this state I sat, hugging close my mother's shawl. I sat and the shadow-of-night gathered up itself, and masked itself again, and went by me like a burning whisper, and was gone.

And after it was gone I remade the fire and turned up the lamp, and sitting at my desk, wrote this.

MIRAGE
Louise Cooper

Raised by a sorceress from the depths of Limbo he came into the world without a past or a name.

They called him Kyre – Sun Hound – avatar of an ancient hero; summoned as the last chance to save the dying city of Haven from the ravages of the evil witch-queen Calthar and the sea-dwellers.

But Kyre sensed that he was more than a cipher: he felt a power within him, and a past existence which lurked in his dreams and hazy memories. He had to solve the mystery of his true identity before the hour of the final confrontation.

In the sky, the Hag cast down its baleful light: the Great Conjunction was close at hand. Soon the followers of Calthar would rise from the sea and obliterate the city of Haven and its people, forever.

THE INITIATE
Book 1 of the Time Master Trilogy
Louise Cooper

The Seven Gods of Order had ruled unchallenged for an aeon, served by the Adepts of the Circle in their bleak Northern stronghold. But for Tarod – the most enigmatic and formidable sorcerer in the Circle's ranks – a darker affinity had begun to call. Threatening his beliefs, even his sanity, it rose unbidden from beyond Time; an ancient and deadly adversary that could plunge the world into madness and chaos – and whose power rivalled that even of the Gods themselves. But though Tarod's mind and heart were pledged to Order, his soul was another matter . . .

THE OUTCAST
Book 2 of the Time Master Trilogy
Louise Cooper

Denounced by his fellow Adepts as a demon, betrayed even by those he loved, Tarod had unleashed a power that twisted the fabric of time. It seemed that nothing could break through the barrier he had created until Cyllan and Dracha – victims of the Warp – stumbled unwittingly into his castle. The terrible choice Tarod has to make as a result has far-reaching consequences . . .

THE MASTER
Book 3 of the Time Master Trilogy
Louise Cooper

Tarod had won his freedom – and lost the soul stone, key to his sorcerous power. Cyllan, the woman he loved, had been taken from him in a supernatural storm. With a price on both their heads, Tarod had to find her before the Circle did. Only then could he hope to fulfil his self-imposed pledge to confront the gods themselves – for they alone could destroy the stone and the evil that dwelt in it. If touched by the evil in the stone, Tarod would be forced to face the truth of his own heritage, triggering a titanic conflict of occult forces, and setting him on the ultimate quest for vengeance . . .

From the best-selling author of
THE TIME MASTER TRILOGY
come the first two in the eight book series:

INDIGO

NEMESIS
Book One
Louise Cooper

The Tower of Regrets: Princess Anghara had no business there, no reason for tampering with its secrets.

But she did.

The demons are now loose and her world cursed, prey to the evil wrath of the Earth Goddess. Only Anghara can make amends and save their people, but she too is cursed, with immortality and destined to roam the world known only as Indigo.

Only she can seek out and confront the destructive forces that have been released.

And Nemesis awaits her.

INFERNO
Book Two
Louise Cooper

Cursed and condemned to walk the Earth, Indigo must conquer and destroy all of the seven evils released by her own hand.

Now in a land where volcanic fires simmer deep under the ground Indigo, stripped of her title and family, must face an alien power. A power that warps the minds and bodies of all who fall under its spell.

Only by calling on a fire just as dark, can she hope to rid the land of this corruption. However, fire burns and can she control the flames?

Will the wrath within her prove much more deadly than the fiery demon she has to defeat?